CITY OF BLOWS

A NOVEL

TIM BLAKE NELSON

The Unnamed Press
Los Angeles, CA

CONTENTS

PART THREE

CITY OF BLOWS

PROLOGUE

S olomon Rosenthal arrived in Chicago with two brothers from Latvia just after the turn of the twentieth century. They went to the stock-yards, where trains from the west and south deposited herds of a scale they'd never imagined. The country was slaughtering and butchering the way it would learn to make cars and sewing machines. Solomon took work on the killing floor. Unlike his brothers, however, he didn't drink, and he saved his money. When he found a wife and they had a child, he was always home for dinner. He noticed in his son, Isaac, an incipient intelligence, even a quiet wisdom. A stern sadness emanated from the boy too, but far from troubling Solomon, this reassured him, because in the Fuller Park tenements, and certainly at the slaughterhouse where he was employed, evidence abounded for seeing life as essentially unfair, and those whose outlook tended toward the hopeful, adults and children alike, seemed of lesser mental stuff. Make of it what you would, life was mean.

In time his son's sadness turned hard. The more young Isaac learned, the more he questioned, and the more he questioned, the less it all made sense, and this infuriated him. As he reached his teens, he began to take the frustration out on his father, whom he considered weak and insuffi-cient, but even this Solomon didn't mind. The adolescent's wrath simply continued to expose a wisdom that eventually would serve him. The boy's rages in fact came to delight his father, and this was all the more infuriating to Isaac. By fifteen he would scream what an idiot his father was to have squandered an entire life in service of slaughterhouse owners who paid barely a subsistence wage for work that was likely killing him—that he was like the cattle himself being slaughtered for the consumption of others—and Solomon would laugh with impervious pride.

"You're right, dear Isaac," he would say. "May neither you nor any you make ever be like me. Go out there and run that world that makes you so angry. Right these wrongs. You and your children and your children's children."

Isaac graduated from high school third in his class and then attended college, the first of the family ever to do so in any city or village in any country on any continent. Solomon died during Isaac's second year at the

University of Illinois, prematurely no doubt, as his son had predicted, from decades of toil on the killing floor from which he was never promoted.

As he stepped to shovel dirt on his father's casket, Isaac Rosenthal knew one thing: he would do as his father had wished. Neither he nor his progeny nor their progeny, so long as he had control over it, would ever play the giddy submissive. His home, should he raise children, would be one of exacting discipline, scant frivolity, and some degree of certainty not only about how the world functioned but about how best to avoid becoming the victim of its graceless whims. Such questions that were asked would be answered, and if not, reasons rehearsed to determine why attempting to do so would be folly. He would prepare his children for what he perceived America was becoming. And if one was smart, disciplined, careful, and uncompromising, this would mean being a part of something extraordinary for those at the top, even if quite the opposite for those below.

PART ONE

CHICAGO

Jacob Rosenthal had been to many pools on many Sundays to watch his father's ungainly negotiations with water. In their previous neighborhood the park schedule limited these outings to late spring and summer when weather allowed. But just blocks from their new home on Maxwell Street, Jacob was exposed to the oxymoronic novelty of a vast enclosure that brought indoors what he'd heretofore believed could only occur outside. And with this marvel came smells and sounds he would associate with this day for the remainder of his life.

It was February of 1950. They'd entered through the front door on a street turgid with blackening snow, and moved to the showers and adjacent lockers to prepare for the usual ritual of Jacob watching his father traverse the pool's length ten times—five one way, five back—after which they'd steam, shower, and finally venture out once more, perhaps to the butcher for his mother, or to the cobbler or tailor, and then for lunch, where they'd sit in austere silence. His father was short and slender and, unlike many of the other dads, still had most of his hair, none of it yet gray. Jacob was also small and lean but didn't yet show the tendency toward quiet rage that had transformed his father as a teen. Because of this, Jacob's slightness of frame caused him to be considered frail, a condition manifesting psychologically as well that Isaac Rosenthal had been vowing of late to eradicate in his only son.

The locker room itself, thick with the heat of the oil-fed furnace blasting air throughout, smelled of the chlorine that permeated the place, the eucalyptus of the two steam baths, the sweat of those slumped in those baths, and the stubbornly pervasive waft of excrement—each fragrance unmistakable, the coalescence intimating to Jacob the terrible mysteries of adulthood. As for the men themselves, they were, almost to a person, with the notable exception of Jacob's father, thick, slow moving, beleaguered. Carpeted with hair, they plodded the wood-slatted floor pallets deliberately, their morose cocks drooping from shags of haphazardly powdered curls. If there were other boys, eye contact was glancing. Nor would they exchange words, even in those rare instances when the fathers encouraged it, for here among the men, in the heavy mist of their effusions, something sacred was being exposed, and though it was surely unclear how, matriculation into this grave fraternity was certain, and only then would its secrets be known. The boys sensed that they too, like the naked figures lumbering among them, would one day be responsible for families, businesses, communities of their own.

When Jacob's father reached into his satchel and produced not one pair of bathing trunks but two, Jacob sensed danger.

"Put these on. You're swimming today."

"I don't know how."

"Which is why you'll do it."

The sheer illogic of the interchange, especially to a seven-year-old, epitomized the indecipherable contradictions of adulthood that caused in Jacob the meekness that so frustrated his father. It was provisioned with both ambiguity and clarity, with blatant incoherence and inevitability. He would swim because he couldn't.

Suffused with dread, he found a set of eyes among the penises floating by. They belonged to a blond boy maybe a year younger who'd witnessed the interchange and did the rare favor of allowing Jacob's eyes to find a sympathetic place. Such connections were almost nonexistent for Jacob. He did have a sister, undoubtedly home with his mother gathering clothes for the Sunday wash, but she was three years older. Though much was expected of her, her own experiences were of such a dramatically different sort that while there was plenty of empathy between them, she had no sense what it was like to be Isaac Rosenthal's only son. At school Jacob performed well, but almost invisibly, his frailty so prodigious he wasn't really worth the trouble of those boys just beginning to test the compulsion to hurt and destroy. Most of Jacob's humiliations took place in the home or on excursions with his father where others could not witness them. Jacob had the impulse to go to the fair-haired boy, take him by the hands, and not let go.

Isaac smacked him on the pate.

"What are you doing? Get the other leg in your trunks and let's go."

The pool itself was not particularly big and was perpetually crowded, at least on Sundays, leading Jacob to wonder how his father navigated swimming its length. Two lap lanes had lately been cordoned off, but in these a preponderance of more agile swimmers discouraged entry. As father and son walked the vast atrium, the smell of chlorine overwhelmed all else, as did the din of male voices of every age. Isaac took Jacob by the hand and marched him directly to the pool's edge.

"Now, I want you to listen to me. I'm going to let go of your hand and enter the water. It's shallow enough for me to stand, which is what I'm going to do. You're going to jump into my arms, and then I'm going to teach you to swim. Is that clear?"

Unintended hostilities encroached from all sides: the stiflingly chlorinated air, the damp and gritty cement on which he stood, the abundance of swimmers both in the pool and out oblivious to the dire narrative about to transpire. And then the water itself. Jacob had spent plenty of time in shallow ends, and had even, when younger, been held close by his mother and pulled down the slant of other pools, where she loosened her grip to evince the queer sensation of floating. But the protective warmth of being clutched by her transformed anxiety into what could even have been called delight.

He began to cry.

"Are you fucking kidding me?"

His father knelt before him.

"Look at me. Look."

Jacob did.

"Do you think there's any possibility you'll drown? That any harm will come to you so long as I'm in that pool to catch you?"

"Can't we do this another time?"

"We can't."

"Why?"

"Because we're doing it today."

"But why?"

"Because you're ready."

"I'm not."

"You don't decide that. I do."

"Why?"

"Because I'm your father, and I just know about shit more than you."

Jacob looked at his toes. His father was right: under no circumstance— should the water erupt in flames, should the building collapse, the very concrete beneath them sink into the earth's magma—would Isaac Rosenthal allow actual harm to come to his son.

"Can't I just sit at the edge and you hold me? Carry me in?"

"No."

"Why?"

"If you ask me why one more time, I'm going to drown you myself."

"But what does jumping into the water have to do with swimming?"

"I want you to prove to yourself you can do this."

"But do what? I already know I can't."

"Overcome your fear of the water, because once you've done that, the swimming lesson part will come much easier. You get two for the price of one."

To Jacob's right appeared another father and son. Grinning expansively, the balding man eased himself in. His tremendous girth, shared by his spawn, caused Jacob to suspect the water's surface might rise in increments visible to the eye. The man took a few steps from the edge, then submerged his wide head, rising haughtily. Shaking what remained of his hair, he stepped forward, rowing his arms grandly in stride until he reached the lip of the pool where his son waited. Following Jacob's gaze, Isaac too watched as the man reached with balletic care to pull his boy into the water.

"See? Like they did. Can't you hold me?"

"I can't, Jacob."

"But why?" As soon as his mouth had launched the word, he knew what he'd done. No, he wasn't going to be drowned, just as he'd never had his hands chopped off, his teeth knocked in or his skull smashed, though these and a host of other consequences had been promised for violating past injunctions.

"You want to know why?" His father's wrathful face was now inches from his. "Because those people are fat and stupid. But if you want to be raised by that idiot and eat whatever you want and be coddled like a fucking baby until you're useless and obese, be my guest. Do you want me to ask him, because I'm sure he'd be stupid enough to take you into his home and piss away his time and money rearing you the way he's rearing his little pig of a boy. So, tell me now and save us all the time, Jacob: Do you want out of this arrangement? Answer me."

"No."

"Then you're going to stand up there at the edge of the pool, and you're going to have the guts to jump into my arms."

"All right." He could barely get the words out.

"What's that?"

"*All right.*"

"And stop crying. It's a fucking embarrassment. You're seven, not four."

He met his father for the first time at the age of three, when the man who would raise him returned from the Pacific. A marine, he was fit and sure of himself but moved awkwardly. There was a ruggedness to him that others said preceded his time in combat, and a quickness to anger he himself would describe to Jacob and Jacob's mother and sister as manliness.

His eyes were dark and deep-set, and his ears jutted low and perpendicular from his head like handles there for the lifting of him. His nose was enormous, his cheekbones assertive and high. In the home into which he returned he asserted authority immediately and profanely without hint of reluctance. He beat his son frequently but never, he would aver, capriciously. He didn't speak of the war, ever, even to Jacob's mother, other than to say that he'd wish on no one what he'd been through and seen.

"We did what we did so you'll never have to," he told them, and not with pride but rather as if in reference to an unspeakably costly bill that had needed to be paid the moment it was tallied.

He would say that the marine corps, far more than his parents, made him who he was, though from the beginning it had been a struggle. There was his small size, his lean frame, and of course the fact he was a Jew and, therefore, it was inferred by others, not to be trusted. The last of these concerned him least because he knew he'd refute such nonsense in an environment where actions meant something. Besides, there existed a more immediate concern, one that had special significance to the predicament in which Jacob found himself on this particular Sunday: unlike Jacob, no one had ever taught Isaac Rosenthal to swim. Making matters worse, he couldn't very well confide this uniquely problematic ineptitude in the military's amphibious branch to others who might reveal it at his expense. After all, when applying for the honor of attending boot camp, he'd checked the "yes" box when queried as to all relevant proficiencies.

When the day to demonstrate his abilities came, he was petrified, but he'd taken the measure of those around him and figured the skill they'd devoted months to learn as children he could acquire quickly as an adult, so long as he could study how it was done. Not having the money for lessons, for weeks before reporting he took care to observe how bodies moved in water, and what combination of movement seemed not only most effective but easiest to chance. He'd settled on the breaststroke.

Those present would remember it their entire lives: how the slight, big-eared, humorless Jew propelled himself into the water feet first and simply sank, before thrashing back into view and violently disgorging the water that had filled his lungs. A freckled recruit from Nebraska named Leland McFarland—who would become Isaac's truest friend in the service, and whom he would see pummeled to death with the butt of an Arisaka rifle at Guadalcanal—swore afterward that it had seemed as if Isaac had eight appendages instead of four given the wrath inflicted on the water's surface. Yet no one, not even Leland, entered the pool to save him. Instead, as if

21

studying a drowning wasp, they gawked, paralyzed, as Isaac frantically learned enough of the physics to keep his head, now crimson with struggle, above water, where he began taking raspy, heaving breaths, terrifyingly comical in their volume and pitch.

"Are we done with this charade, Private?" shouted the drill instructor.

"No, sir," Isaac managed in a strained warble that almost killed him, thinking, correctly, that if he could simply get horizontal, where all his observations of the preceding weeks could be aped, he might sort out the challenges besieging him. The question was, how did a human actually do this? It was enough just to stay afloat without sucking in liquid with each paroxysmal gasp. No wonder people drowned with such frequency, even accomplished swimmers. Now he too would succumb, and in a pool into which he'd moronically flung himself while others watched, each too intrigued by the very ridiculousness of it to intervene.

Finally, the likelihood of an embarrassing public death enabled him to maneuver into a position that traced the water's surface. He flailed his hands while leaning forward and kicked back froglike with his legs. To those watching, the majority no doubt wishing him to fail, the ungainliness now exceeded comical to encroach on grotesque. And yet, though strikingly inefficient in terms of energy expended for distance traversed, Isaac Rosenthal was swimming, bobbing his head from the water every few strokes to suck air through an outrageously distended mouth. He managed the two required laps, exceeding the time limit tenfold, after which erupted unanimous applause.

"Private Rosenthal, that was the single-most fucked-up display I hope this pool ever experiences. In fact, I want to drain it for having had that and you in it. But you're going to get a pass for guts, so long as one of these other idiots actually teaches you to swim. I don't expect it to be pretty, but I'm not going to have any marines getting shot because they see you flouncing around in the drink instead of getting to shore. Does everyone understand me?" After a chorus of "Yes, sir," Isaac was pulled from the pool.

"This is going to happen, Jacob. You're going to jump to me, I'm going to catch you, and by the time we get out of this pool, you'll be a swimmer. I don't know what your problem is."

"He's scared is his problem. How old is he?" The voice came from their left, high-pitched for the large neck and body of the heavyset father still holding his son.

"He's seven, and he can swim."

"None of my business, pal, but it doesn't look like it."

"It's okay, sir," offered Jacob, eager to defuse a situation that would soon involve slanders his father's oblivious interlocutor couldn't fathom.

"Shut your mouth, Jacob." Isaac now turned to face the man. "I'm your pal?"

"It's a figure of speech."

"Are you going to tell me how to raise my son?"

"Not how to raise him, no."

"Then what is it you want to say?"

"You wonder why he's upset is all. Like I said, he's scared."

"You know what it's like to be scared, you fat son of a bitch?"

"Pardon?"

Isaac now addressed the man's son. "Have you ever seen your fat father—my good pal there—scared?"

The boy gaped back, stunned.

"He's not answering," said Isaac. "So maybe my kid's scared, and yours is a goddamn moron."

"Come on, Ira," said the man, his large body trembling as he retreated with his cargo of boy, headed, it would seem, for the farthest point from the Rosenthals the pool would allow.

"Now, are you finished, or do you want to call more attention to yourself, because that's why I had to bark at that fat idiot. You know it and I know it."

"Yes."

"Yes what?

"I'm finished."

"Good, because the more time you spend standing up there, the less time you get for learning to swim."

Jacob looked down to gauge whether any room remained between his toes and the pool's edge. Over two inches, he estimated, having just that year begun to use a ruler at school. The class was math, and he was good at it. In fact, he was good at everything in school. The teachers adored him because he was diligent, compliant, quiet, and kind. From what he could tell, his class was about a third Jewish, a third Polish, and a third a fairly even split between Italians and Irish. The fathers mostly labored, meaning Isaac's donning of a shirt and tie every day was something of an anomaly. Jacob's mother lobbied for her son's transfer, to which Isaac responded, "There are enough smart kids in that school, and he'll learn stuff from the ones who aren't smart that he'd never get in someplace where the kids are pampered. He's going to be a lawyer, which means he has to be tough."

"How do you know he's going to be a lawyer?"

"He's quiet, but he won't always be. I was the same way. I can see it in his eyes. He's going to see through people, and that's going to terrify them."

"You say he's like you were," Jacob's mother offered, "and you didn't become a lawyer."

"Because I fought in a damn war. You think I was going to law school after I got back and had him to take care of, in addition to you and Rebecca? Two kids and a wife? He gets to have what I never did—like I never had to work on a killing floor like my poor dad. He's going to law school. Even if he follows me in real estate, he's gonna get a law degree. Listen to me, Jacob. They call this a democracy. And the economic system is capitalism. Fine and good. But both of those depend on the rule of law. You get that training, you'll see shit for what it is, and you'll know not only who's out to get you but what's possible within the rules. Anything. Anything is possible."

"Can I make movies?"

"What?"

"Movies?"

"I don't know why you'd want to. Unless you run a studio, from what I understand it's a dog's breakfast."

"I like them."

"Movies?"

"Yes."

"Well, that doesn't mean you should waste your life making them. But sure, make movies for all I care, so long as you do it better and smarter than everyone else."

Jacob inched forward until the toes of each foot curled over the tiled lip.

"You comfortable now? Feet just right?"

"Yes."

"Now jump."

"If I hurt myself, I won't be able to learn to swim."

"It's water. How are you going to hurt yourself?"

"By breathing it in."

"Jacob, listen to me. All I want is for you to show some bravery. Not only will that make learning to swim easier but you'll have the whole rest of your life—and believe me, you'll remember this the whole rest of your life—to know that when you were scared to jump in the pool, you didn't give in, but you overcame it."

Jacob jumped. How, having leapt into air over water, could he want to giggle uncontrollably and vomit at the same time? There was for starters the exhilaration of flight, his weight somehow refusing to pull him down. He wished others close to him—his mother and sister, his grandparents, a few of his teachers—could witness him soar. Yet his body sensed that the brain and will had put the entire apparatus in terrific danger. He was going to die. At the apex, fear won out, alleviated only by the certainty that his father would catch him. He saw instead Isaac Rosenthal's deliberate retreat. Jacob crashed through the surface and sank, sucking water into his lungs, his eyes burning with chlorine, his chest and brain seeming to explode. His whole being erupted in spasms, jerking desperately as pain ripped through his chest into his arms, legs, fingers, and toes. Instead of struggling to the surface as his father had years before, Jacob remained below it, the sheer physical agony, along with the terror that accompanied it, simply too much to endure.

He blacked out.

He did not therefore see, as others did, Isaac Rosenthal wait calmly until his son was no longer moving before gathering him from the bottom of the pool. Nor did he perceive the expressions on the faces of the astounded witnesses to this manifestly intentional act. He didn't hear his father snarl at them to keep away as he lifted his son poolside and pushed at his chest until Jacob burped water from between blue lips, coughing and retching with a violence that surprised even Isaac.

"He's fine. Keep away. He's fine. Just some water in his lungs. I know what I'm doing."

"I saw the whole thing!" exclaimed a man who quickly emerged as the spokesman for those suddenly arrayed against this callous figure who would so endanger his son. "He jumped, and you backed away, watching him drown!"

"I did nothing of the kind!"

"I saw it! I saw him!" the man declared to an enlarging crowd.

"Will you shut your hole and let me deal with my boy?"

"Someone call the police!"

Isaac turned from his strident accuser, knowing that attention to Jacob was not only essential to reviving the boy but the most effective defense against further allegations.

"Jacob? Jacob? Can you hear me, Jacob?"

Jacob could somewhat, but all he wanted was to breathe, and his head was in more pain than he imagined possible. But was he dead? He coughed percussively, tears spilling from his eyes.

"Jacob. You're fine. You're just fine. That's it. Cough it out."

"Is he all right?" asked a young boy.

"Yes, he's all right!" insisted Isaac.

"Don't speak to my son like that," said the man next to the child.

"Then tell him to butt out of my business. I told everyone he's all right."

"He did it on purpose. I saw it all," repeated the initial appellant.

"Let the man be. Do you need any help, sir?" It was a third father, who seemed instinctively to feel the need to take Isaac's side.

"No, I'm fine."

"Should we call an ambulance?"

"No. Thank you."

"I'm a doctor," offered a kindly older man who stepped forward. Isaac had no choice but to move aside. "Let's have a look at you." The physician cradled Jacob's head in one hand and with practiced fingers used the other to swivel the boy's chin to face him. "Can you see me, child? Do you see me? What's your name?"

"His name's Jacob."

"Pardon me, sir, I need for your son to answer." The doctor turned back to Jacob. "Can you tell me your name?"

The face seemed to float there. Jacob had imagined God this way, as a disembodied head looming in the heavens, and for some reason not the superannuated bearded version consistent with paintings he'd seen but someone shaven, short-haired, square-jawed, and younger. The notion of God showing age always confused him. Why, after all, would God allow himself any deterioration? He'd be a man at his peak, decent, loving, understanding, just, and firm. Was this the divine being, confirming his name, eager to summon him to the beyond? If so, why then could he hear his father? Had his father died too? Was that why his father hadn't caught him? Would he not be free from his father even in death? And why was his father interrupting God? Then again, why wouldn't his father interrupt God? Soon he'd be chastising God, berating him for his deficiencies, insisting he account for all that had gone wrong with the world.

"Son, can you tell me your name?"

"Jacob."

"Jacob what?"

"Jacob Benjamin Rosenthal."

"Is that his name?"

"Yes," Jacob heard his father answer. "It's his full name. I told you he was all right."

"And where are you, Jacob?" asked God.

Obviously, with the concrete under his head, the unmistakable wafts of chlorine, the bare legs and feet all around, the corrugated ceiling above, they were at the pool. So why ask?

"Heaven?"

God laughed gently.

"No, Jacob, you're not in heaven, though surely that's where you'd belong if you'd died."

"I'm not dead?"

"Your father here saved you."

"He saved me?"

"He did."

"I did, Jacob," said his father.

"You're very much alive," said God, who perhaps was not God. "Though I imagine your head doesn't feel so great."

"It hurts."

"You've got water in your sinuses. That's the pressure. It'll go away, but it'll take a while." He turned to Jacob's father. "He's going to be all right."

"Thanks."

"And he shouldn't go back in the pool."

"Of course he shouldn't. You think I'm a goddamn idiot?"

The doctor had encountered every manner of recalcitrance, but never of the severity now before him. Yes, the man wanted to be alone with his son, as would any father should his offspring brush with mortality. Yet there was simply too much about the man that gave him pause, especially in the context of what had happened. The doctor lingered therefore, as if even a moment's further exposure might dispel misgivings. Jacob was used to this sort of caesura between his father and other adults, along with quizzical stares and balking, stuttering responses to whatever vindictiveness Isaac Rosenthal had chosen to voice.

"Okay then, sir," the doctor finally murmured, turning to the group that had gathered. "Let's give them some room so little Jacob can get his senses back."

"I'm telling you, he let his son nearly drown on purpose!"

"Drop it, Abe," said the doctor.

"I saw what I saw!"

"I'm sure you did, but leave it." The physician ushered Abe away as others too receded toward the dressing rooms, showers, steam rooms, or back into the pool.

Jacob attempted to lift his head, which now throbbed violently to the beat of his pulse.

"Easy now. That's going to hurt," his father warned.

It already hurts, thought Jacob. He could see the poolside showers where swimmers were required to bathe before entering the pool, a rule many, including his father, didn't observe. "Give the chlorine something to work with," he would say. Jacob closed his eyes.

"That's it. Rest for a bit, but don't fall asleep," he heard his father say. But darkness only amplified the throbbing. Jacob studied his father's face for any hint of contrition or even concern.

"Just keep breathing," Isaac instructed. Should the doctor have suggested this, Jacob could imagine his father retorting, "What the hell else is he supposed to do?" Maybe, thought Jacob, he actually does regret what happened, and simply doesn't know what to say. But the more pressing question was, had his father actually backed away when Jacob jumped?

"Look at me, Jacob. Look at me."

Jacob did.

"Can you see me?"

"Yes."

"Now listen, because what I'm about to say I rarely say, but I want you to know I mean it. Are you listening?

"Yes."

"Because you might not get this again from me for a very long time: I love you."

Jacob had heard this from his father only once in his life, two years prior, and not in a manner that could be described as volunteered. Before moving to Maxwell Street, they'd lived in a fourth-floor walk-up in Woodlawn, and normally, particularly when descending, Jacob would clasp his mother's hand negotiating the stairs, not yet having mastered the momentum that would gather on the downward journey. From the age of fifteen months, when he'd taken his first steps, the impulse was always reciprocated, giving him stability on both sides, with her on one and the railing on the other.

The entire family was going to visit Jacob's mother's parents, an excursion made once every couple of months and one that always irritated Isaac, who felt, not inaccurately, that his in-laws, who were of Austrian Jewish descent, looked down on his Eastern European lineage.

"You're five years old. Let go of your mother's hand."

"Isaac..." His mother's voice already advertised the reluctance of defeat.

"I'm telling him to let go of your hand."

"I always hold her hand," said Jacob.

"And now you don't anymore. It's a new and glorious day." Jacob's sister had already made it to the bottom, hungry for the plate of smoked sable that always waited at the home of her grandparents, the only two she and Jacob had.

"Are you all coming?" she shouted from below.

"In a moment, sweetie," said Jacob's mother before turning to her son. "Your father's right. You're old enough now to take the stairs on your own. Hold the rail. That's what it's there for." Jacob looked imploringly to his father as a final ploy.

"You think I'm going to change my mind? You're not holding anyone's hand. Those days are finished."

His descent began more easily than he'd imagined, and immediately he recognized advantages. For instance, the rail on its own, by virtue of being fixed, actually provided steadier guidance than his mother, who was often burdened with packages and would occasionally stumble.

"Are you coming?" It was his sister again.

"Damn it, Rebecca, we'll get there when we get there," shouted his father before turning back to Jacob. "Now come on. You've got the hang of it. Let's go."

"Don't hurry him, Isaac."

"Ida, it's walking down goddamn stairs."

Jacob loosened his hand slightly on the milled wood. The building they lived in postdated the great fire by only a decade, and was designed to house as many families in as little space possible. The stairs were narrow and steep, and like the landings and entryway below, they were seldom cleaned beyond the removal of trash once a week. The treads bore gentle valleys formed by a half century of footfalls, just as the banister had been tarnished by the palms of thousands, many long dead. As he rounded the corner, with three flights to go, Jacob increased his speed.

"That's it. You're getting it," his mother encouraged. This new skill, thought Jacob as he rounded the next corner and strode with confidence across the short, narrow landing to the penultimate flight, might even afford the independence he was beginning to crave. He'd be trusted to make excursions on his own, perhaps to borrow a missing ingredient from a neighbor or even make an emergency purchase at the grocery down the block.

Loosening his grip yet more and increasing his pace, he even had the temerity to glance down between the balusters ticking by and catch a glimpse of his sister loitering below. Behind him he heard the footfalls of his parents, distinguishing the heaviness of his father's, now passing on the left, from the lightness of his mother's behind him.

"Keep going," barked his father as he reached the top of the final flight. "We need to be home before two. I have a week's worth of floor plans to look over."

Jacob took the last step from the second flight and followed briskly, even proudly, as his father bounded the final landing. He glanced at his feet to find the first step while reaching for the railing to his right. But with his judgment not yet practiced, his hand gripped nothing at all, and as he stepped forward and down he lurched to his right and his legs gave out beneath him. He tumbled forward, catching his arm between two spindles before flipping headfirst down the entire flight. Ida Rosenthal was convinced her son had perished.

"Oh shit!" Jacob heard his father exclaim before nothing could be heard but his mother's screams. The pain in Jacob's forearm alone was enough to make him lose control, but her hysteria, particularly once she'd gotten a look at his unnaturally crooked appendage, was simply too much for a five-year-old. Jacob began to wail, adding volume and pitch to a commotion the likes of which was rarely heard in the stairwell, even in a building that had sheltered its measure of violence and tragedy.

"Quiet, both of you! He's going to be fine. Jacob, for Christ's sake, you slipped and fell, but you're all right."

"Are you seeing his arm?" shouted his mother. "Are you even looking?"

Jacob did so along with his father, and any hope for calm evaporated when he beheld what seemed like an added joint. His crying turned to screams, further inciting his mother. Doors up and down the building's interior began to open, and to his father's consternation, a small crowd gathered.

"My son slipped, and he's broken his arm. It's under control."

"Jacob, Jacob sweetie, listen to me." His mother had calmed herself, if only coercively. "I'm sorry I screamed and scared you. I was startled is all, but you're going to be all right. You broke your arm, but you're going to be fine."

"It hurts so much!" he shouted.

"I know it does, my angel. It's broken but we're going to get it fixed. I love you, sweetie, and I'm here. I love you. And your father loves you."

"No, he doesn't!"

"Of course your father loves you, Jacob. He just wanted you not to hold my hand anymore. I know it doesn't seem like it, but he did that *because* he loves you."

"He hates me!" As if to confirm this assessment, a spasm of pain shot through his arm, and sobs overtook him. "Make it stop! Make it stop!"

His father knelt over him. "We're going to take you to the hospital, Jacob, and they'll make it stop, but we'll get there faster if you let me carry you."

"I don't want you to carry me!"

"He thinks you don't love him."

"Because I wouldn't let him hold your hand?"

"Because of everything!" shouted Jacob.

"What does that even mean?" retorted his father, unable to resist the urge to contest an inaccuracy. "Is 'everything' the fact that I'm raising you and feeding you and paying for your clothes? Keeping a roof over your head?"

"You just do that because you have to!"

"I'm not fucking listening to this," responded his father. "And trust me, I don't have to raise you. You're my son, but what I do with that is my decision. Now, you're going to let me carry you so we can get your goddamn arm fixed."

He reached for his son.

"Nooooo! Nooooo! Nooooo!" More witnesses crowded the stairwell.

"Jacob, I want you to stop it," intoned his father, lowering his voice with a gravity meant more to warn than to importune. He reached again, taking a leg in one hand, and attempting to shimmy his arm under Jacob's back.

"*Nooooooo!*" It was as if the boy were being sundered.

"Isaac," Ida said quietly, "tell Jacob you love him."

"Are you kidding me?"

"Your son needs to know it."

"He knows I love him."

"He doesn't know unless you tell him."

Isaac paused, his teeth clenched in what looked something akin to rage. "Jacob," he said, "tell your mother that you know I love you."

"You don't! You can't even say it!" shouted Jacob.

Turning to her husband, his mother spoke with the confidence of someone who knew more about what was about to transpire than anyone but perhaps God. "Isaac," she said, "you're going to tell our son that you love him now. Those are the next words that will come out of your mouth." Jacob's father looked back at the woman he had met in 1938 at a high school social and married a year later against the strident objections of her parents, the woman with whom he'd had a daughter ten months later and who would give birth to their second child while he was away at war, and he began to cry. It was the only time Jacob would see his father do so, and it happened quietly: no sobbing, no sudden inhalations of breath, simply tears.

"Go on, Isaac," said Jacob's mother. "You can do it."

"Jacob," he said, turning to his son and making no effort to conceal the vulnerability that had suddenly overcome him, "I love you. I love you. I always have and I always will." Jacob loosed his own new spasm of tears, from emotion, not pain, then reached up with his good arm to embrace his father, who lifted his son carefully for the walk to the hospital.

But over the months that followed, and especially once his cast had been removed, Jacob began first to suspect, and then firmly to believe, that his father had been lying. It was not just that Jacob was still prohibited to hold anyone's hand when negotiating stairs, and that this rule was enforced even while the cast remained on. It was that while his mother afforded him measures of empathy—allowing him more time to dress and bathe, opening doors for him, and even cutting his food—there was absolutely none of this from his father. Remarks like "He's not an invalid, for Christ's sake" and "He's using the arm as an excuse, can't you see that?" proliferated, the burden of the cast now construed as though the entire incident on the stairs and all associated encumbrances had somehow been Jacob's fault, or even willfully intended by the boy.

This inspired a new periphrasis in his father's rhetorical arsenal, as he took to informing his son, who certainly had no need for the fact ever to be voiced, "Get this inside your little skull: I'm not your mother." Such pronouncements would follow any simple request Jacob might have, such as for help getting the temperature of the bathwater right or fetching a plate or glass from a high shelf. Any emotion Jacob dared show following the refusal of such requests would arouse variants along the lines of "Cut that shit out. It might work on your mother, but not on me."

It eventually occurred to Jacob that his father wanted the three words his mother had coerced in the stairwell, and the tears that accompanied them, back. Though nothing was ever spoken, nor was there any memorializing moment, Jacob had had no choice but to yield them and more.

For in their reclaiming, not only did his father's chilly aloofness again predominate, but it did so now with vindictive purpose. Interactions became quietly aggressive, laced with suspicion, his father's tone seeming always to imply that Jacob was up to something, endeavoring to subvert the way his father meant to raise him. What made this especially painful was that through it all Jacob remained desperate for the love he'd possessed so briefly.

What, then, to make of nearly drowning in his care, and the lingering ambiguity as to whether this had been intended? What to make of, in the aftermath, for the second time in his life, his father insisting he loved his son?

"I need to know you hear me, Jacob."

"I hear you."

"Just in case, I'm going to say it again. I love you. But before we go any further, I need to know also that you believe it. Do you believe I love you?"

It became clear to Jacob that one of two explanations for what had happened was about to be revealed. Either the near drowning was an accident, for which stating paternal love was meant by way of exculpation and even apology. Or, and the tone of his father's voice made this the more likely option, Isaac Rosenthal had actually meant for his son nearly to drown, and there was a deeper lesson involved, probably involving not allowing oneself to be duped, even by a parent.

Neither option inspired Jacob to give his father the affirmation he wanted. There even loomed tantalizing rewards associated with withholding it. First, at certain rare moments (such as the breaking of an arm or near drowning), the imputation of emotional dereliction could be weaponized to great effect. His father being forced to say "I love you" only proved this. The problem, however, was that it wasn't a strategy he could deploy on his own; he had the torpedo but needed his mother's help to fire it. Without her there, who knew how his father would respond should he push any further?

And yet a dread lurked that made her absence irrelevant. Like all other boys, Jacob had stood at shul and heard tell of Abraham and Isaac and their trek up Mount Moriah, where God intervened only with Abraham's knife at its apex. But unlike the rabbi, who seemed fixated on the faith of the father (who would kill a child sharing Jacob's own father's name no less), Jacob thought only of the boy, and by way not of empathy or sorrow but of inculpation. What must the biblical Isaac have done in secret away from

33

his parents to anger the Lord to the extent that He wanted him killed? Not even the intervention of the angel arrested this line of thinking. After all, had Isaac not been ushered gravely up the mountain? Had he not experienced the castigating terror of seeing his own father crouched over him, ready to plunge the knife? Why would God perpetrate this against an innocent? The Isaac who was the son of Abraham must therefore have deserved it.

What was Jacob's father about to reveal had been his near-capital crime? And were he not to provide such evidence, what had Jacob done that had compelled God to engage his father as an agent in the manner of Abraham? He wished to learn none of this, and that became his urgent challenge. Were he to say, as he had on the stairwell, "No, I don't believe you love me," and then add "and you never have," he would be contradicting his father, and Isaac Rosenthal needed always to be right. This was no pro forma rule sufficiently followed with words alone. Adherence couldn't be faked. Should his father detect even a fleck of doubt in his capitulation, he would pursue a more believable delivery until it was provided or the actual sentiments behind the dissembling revealed. Since a perjured concession would result in painful interrogation anyway, Jacob told the truth.

"No, I don't believe you."

"And why is that?"

"Because you never act like it, and you never say it."

"Now, that's not true. I've told you I love you. You know this, I know this, your sister knows this, your mother knows this, the entire building back in godforsaken Woodlawn knows it."

"Once."

"More than once."

"Only when I broke my arm."

"What about just now?"

"That doesn't count."

"You said I've only said it once. Did I not just say it?"

"You did."

"So already that's twice, and we haven't even spent any effort summoning other instances, such as before you have the capacity to remember. So, I think we can agree that your claim I've only said it once is a little suspect, not to mention unreliable. In addition, I've made it clear to you I'm not one for saying that all the time. That's your mother's way, and believe me, you don't want how you're raised to be up to her. It would be nice for a couple of days, but by the time you became an adult it would be a fucking disaster for you, so be grateful you have to deal with mean old Dad not gooing all over you with 'I love you' every ten seconds. Now what was the other ridiculousness you said?"

"I don't remember."

"You're lying to me now. Don't be a chickenshit. Of course you remember."

"That you don't act like it."

"Ah, right. That I don't act like it. Like who, that obese idiot over there who cradled his son like a fat baby instead of having him jump into the pool like I did with you? That's love? Trust me, it's not. That's a perfect example of what I was just talking about: a father taking the easy way out, like he does at the lunch counter every day when instead of having the discipline to skip the third piece of pie, he stuffs it into his *punum* and then waddles off to work God knows where. But this to you is love."

"I wasn't even thinking about them."

"So just what were you thinking about? How I keep you clothed and fed?"

"You have to do that."

"This again. Let me tell you something. I could easily run off and leave all of you, which believe me, some men do. When I left for the Pacific, I didn't even know your mother was pregnant, so you were not what I signed on for. We were going to have one child, that's it. I choose to give a shit about you and your sister both instead of going to the track or the neighborhood bar every night or buying whores like a lot of the assholes in our old neighborhood, which by the way, I worked my ass off to get us out of, so let's not forget that while we're inventorying all the reasons I don't love you. My own father was a goddamn sap at the slaughterhouse, but he taught me one thing: loyalty to his family. So other than being completely responsible to you and your sister and your mother, what else? What's your other proof?"

"I don't know."

"You're lying. I want you to be a man and tell me what your other proof is."

"That you're always so mean." And with this Jacob let himself cry once more. His father ignored the tears. Perhaps he recognized his son simply wasn't going to be able to bear a growing number of infractions. Already wrong, a liar, and gutless, if being a crybaby were added, the boy might ask to be tossed back into the pool rather than endure further rebuke.

"Let me tell you something, Jacob," his father said in a voice suddenly inflected with warmth. "I don't like talking about the war. In fact, I never do, not even to your mother. I hate these jackasses who go on about it. My feeling is that the ones who do probably weren't actually there, or at least in any real danger or around any of the real misery of it. But I'm going to tell you a story, which isn't about the war proper, which you're really not old enough to hear about. This was when I was training, and it's not the swimming story so don't worry. This is about the rifle I carried as a mortarman. An M1 carbine. Smaller and lighter than the M1. Same as in the army, because we had to buck the stand and tubes. Anyway, as part of our training we had to learn to take our guns apart and put them back together, and of course to keep them clean in the process. Like with anything, some guys were better at this than others, and I guess I was pretty average. But for whatever reason—I don't know if it was how the stock was milled or the bolt and receiver were fitted, but my rifle was a stubborn one to take apart and clean, and when we were timed on it, I usually failed to do it properly.

"Our drill instructor was a real son of a bitch. One of his favorite 'techniques' I'll call it, was to pop you in the forehead with the brim of his hat when he was berating you. And he would do it repeatedly, really pop you, until he drew blood, so in addition to being screamed at, you had blood running down into your eyes. You also then had this mark of shame on your forehead for a week while the scar healed. A few guys even had to get stitched up. But the second time I didn't reassemble my rifle properly—and trust me, complaining about the fittings was not an option—after giving me this scar on my head you can still see, he took my gun from me, pulled it to pieces because I hadn't put it all together yet, and threw them all around our hut. Then he put us on fifty percent alert for five nights straight, which essentially meant the platoon got no sleep after days of drilling and on the hump, and he blamed it on me for not being a marine who knew how to take care of his weapon.

"So now, in addition to being the little Jew fuckup who lied about swimming, I was the little Jew fuckup with stitches in his head bringing them all down. I'm not going to go into what happened to me as a result, but it was very ugly on every level. Physically painful in terms of the beatings I took, and just terrible in every other way. I hated that instructor more than I've ever hated anybody. But I filed down the fittings on my rifle and I learned that goddamn weapon, let me tell you, and I became one of the best marksmen in my platoon because it was so clean and true. And this was against guys with real M1s.

"But that's not the end of it, because on Guadalcanal, which is a miserable filthy place with more mosquitoes and disease than anywhere on earth that we had to take from thousands of crazy, suicidal, starving, extremely brave

Japanese, that faulty not-so-well-made gun that had been with me since boot camp was like an added appendage. It was there when we made a beach landing and it was full of sand and I disassembled it and cleaned it behind the second berm we hit, there every day slogging under the canopy in jungle so thick it took an hour to go fifty yards, when we were fighting uphill against where the Japanese were dug in their emplacements for dear life. And, again without going into detail, trust me when I say it fucking saved my life on more than one occasion, and therefore so did that bastard drill instructor. In fact, Jacob, I grew to believe, no, to know, that he loved me like he loved every marine who came under his care. I have no idea where he is right now, if he's still in California where I trained with him, or selling cars or insurance somewhere, but I can tell you this, I owe him my fucking life. Am I making sense?"

His father had never spoken so many words meant only for Jacob. This bespoke narrative, along with the quietly sensitive tone contrapuntal to its subject matter, carried all the accompanying power of his paternal tears in the stairwell.

"Jacob," his father repeated, "am I making sense?"

"Yes."

"Tell me how I'm making sense."

"I don't understand."

"What's the point of the story?"

"That just because the man was mean didn't mean he didn't love you."

"And I'll go a step further. As much of a son of a bitch as he was, what he most wanted was for me to be a great marine. He didn't want to yell and scream and humiliate me and make my forehead bleed into my eyes for his own enjoyment—though if I'm to be completely honest, maybe a part of him did enjoy it, what the fuck do I know?—but mostly he wanted me to be great with my rifle, because he knew it was a matter of life and death. And God bless him, he didn't give a shit what I thought of him. He gave a shit about the marine corps, his country, and me. In that order. I earned his respect along with every other recruit and volunteer who made it through, and he loved every single one of us. Did he ever say it? Hell no. He did much better than that. He *lived* it by making sure I was the best soldier I could possibly be. That makes sense to you, right?"

"Yes."

"Now, I know this is difficult for a little boy to hear, but you're old enough now to understand it. And it's this: I don't frankly care if you like me, let alone love me. I really don't. It's my job to raise you right. And when

I say jump in the pool and I don't hold you while you climb in, there's a reason behind it. It may seem to you like I'm being mean, but it's a goddamn act of love, particularly when I've got to put up with Fatso over there telling me how to raise you. My son is going to be able to get up on his hind legs and jump into a pool by the age of seven. That's just the way it's going to be. And my son may not realize it now, but he's going to thank me someday—maybe not to my face, but inside his adult head, for rearing him to be brave and capable and to take care of himself. Am I still making sense?"

"Yes."

"Okay. So far so good. But obviously that's not the end of the story, is it?"

"It's not."

"Because you did jump into the pool, didn't you?"

"Yes."

"And then what happened?"

"I couldn't swim."

"Come on, Jacob. You couldn't swim, we all know that, but what happened as a result of that?"

"I almost drowned."

"Because?"

"I don't know what you mean."

"What was supposed to happen so that you wouldn't drown?"

"I was supposed to jump into your arms."

"That was the agreement. That you would jump, and that because you can't swim, I would catch you. And that didn't happen, did it?"

"No."

"Tell me why you're crying, Jacob?"

"Because you lied to me. Because you let me drown."

"No, I saved you from drowning," responded Isaac, still not deviating from his quiet, sympathetic tone. Jacob wished he could hear it for the rest of his life. He wanted to bathe in it.

"Only because there were people around."

"You're saying I wanted you to die?"

"Why else would you do what you did?"

"Listen to me. Jacob, stop crying and listen." But Jacob couldn't. The confirmed betrayal, the brush with death, the lesson about love and hard schooling from his father's time in boot camp, not to mention its tangent about men in war and the implication that his father had shot his rifle and perhaps even killed people, and finally hearing his father loved him for only the second time in his life, allowed for no other response.

Isaac waited a good half minute before he spoke once more. "It wasn't to see you drown, and it wasn't to play a trick on you either, although I can see why you'd think that. First of all, I wanted you to jump into the pool, and I knew you wouldn't do it unless you believed I was going to catch you. You're going to have a lot of instances like that in your life. They're not usually going to be physical or with your body. Other kinds of risks, like doing something for someone because they promise they're going to do something for you. We rely on each other and the things we do and say. Do you understand what I'm saying?"

Jacob nodded.

"Now, what did I ask when I asked you to jump into my arms? What did I ask you to do?"

"To trust you."

Jacob gazed up in into the face of his father and saw wrinkles, blemishes, crags, and the scar he'd never understood to be a scar. He saw heartbreak and failure, the hardness of war and the ravages of countless disappointments and tragedies he'd never know. He saw tenderness and pity, regret and no small measure of angry pride.

"But ..."

"But what, dear Jacob?"

"But if ..."

"If I wanted to teach you about trust, why didn't I catch you?"

Jacob nodded.

"It's not what you think. That you should never trust anyone. Every idiot says that. I've told it to you myself."

"So then why did—"

"Other people—and not me. You have no idea how painful it was for me to teach you this in the way I did—but other people don't want to see you swim. They want to be doing the swimming. They'll tell you to jump saying they'll be there, but when it comes down to it, they won't be. They'll be halfway across the pool. Mostly they'd sooner see you drown."

NEW YORK CITY

D avid Levit relished trips to Los Angeles, especially when others paid. He belonged to three film industry unions, each requiring producers to fly members business class. He'd made the journey frequently enough by the age of forty to have established a ritual. Heading west he would request a midmorning flight. On the way to the JFK executive lounge affiliated with the given carrier he would organize a four-shot espresso and a muffin. He took his espresso straight, with neither milk nor sweetener, then nursed it over several hours, meaning its addictive bitterness could be savored while he read the news and opinion pages of several papers. He was tall, just the other side of six feet, but slender, and could sit comfortably in any seat. But business class made the inconvenience of six hours on an aircraft nearly irrelevant. Inevitably he would run into colleagues either in the lounge or while boarding, and of course, while never spoken, it went observed whether one was seated up front or in coach. The former meant others were paying, and work was involved, the latter that work was being sought. One never wanted to be in the second category, while the first connoted professional vitality. Why else would a studio or production company spend thousands to ferry you across the nation?

I'm not looking forward to this, he texted his wife, Charlotte.

Then why are you going? she replied immediately.

If I don't, I'm not doing the film.

Imagine that. He could hear the tartness.

Are you at rehearsal?

About to get on the train. Call when you land.

In principle he would direct a movie based on the 2008 novel *Coal,* by an African American writer named Rex Patterson who was known for his brittle prose, aggressive and unpredictable political leanings, and violent plotlines. Though the book was wildly popular when it was published twelve years earlier, Patterson's predilection for the sensational had most likely prevented him from taking what otherwise might have been his rightful place as a leading writer of his generation rather than that of provocateur. His one previous success, a book called *Servitude,* had not only been a bestseller but had earned him a Pulitzer Prize nomination and a National

Book Award. In it he had applied his taste for carnage to a Southern Gothic plotline that involved inveterate racism, giving the mayhem just the right political inflection for mass consumption, particularly coming from a Black man in America. There had been a film version, but this was the only of his ten or so novels ever to have been adapted for screen, and not successfully.

As for *Coal*, David and the film's producer believed this far more provocative work had the potential to make a great motion picture. And that qualifying clause had David on the plane, for activity around a novel—even when hundreds of thousands or even millions of dollars were spent developing it—didn't guarantee that a frame would ever be shot. This book, like its predecessor, dealt very much with race, but the milieu was impactfully different, and the risks it took far greater, especially given the increasingly restive cultural fault line of race in America. Titled after the first name of its young Black protagonist, *Coal* took place in Jim Crow Los Angeles and explored in sanguinary detail the stubborn venality of pretty much every character—Black and white, male and female—save its titular one. Because of this, along with the disputes it inspired both within the African American community and without, it had been optioned within days of its publication. Since then, however, accruing money against it with a timorous studio and a succession of inept screenwriters, it had failed to get made for fear of mass opprobrium. Its current producer, who had hired David, had spent handsomely to wrench it from turnaround, and vowed to get it finally to the screen. How this man would make his money back, and why he'd chosen David as the project's steward, made less and less sense, as did David's own motivations for enduring the abuse he'd taken simply to remain associated with it. Yet directing the film, especially once Charlotte had encouraged it—and she unambiguously had—had become unreasonably imperative in ways he still could not entirely define.

David left the lounge after finishing the whole-grain muffin he'd chosen over its gluten-free counterpart when he ran into two actors roughly his age also headed for the LA flight.

"Hey, David," said the slightly older one, with whom David had worked off-Broadway in 2011. They had not seen each other for over a year, and his friend's tone had an inappropriately terse gloom. These two saw me in the lounge, David guessed, negative sentiments were shared, and the laconic greeting was theatrical in its way. When the other actor tossed out his own underwhelming salutation, accompanying it with a furtive glance to his partner, it confirmed David's suspicions. He was used to this at some level, and a part of him empathized, because there was little reason on the surface of it for David to have an acting or directing career at all, though he'd spent four years at drama school after four years in college in pursuit of one.

While at Juilliard nearly two decades before, classmates had perceived David with equal measures of pity and curiosity, wondering how he'd gotten into such a selective program. His success after graduating had been even more galling, perpetrated by sheer chance—the right part at the right time—in a film that shouldn't have succeeded but somehow did.

Written and directed by a first-timer who now made movies to which websites were devoted, the film, called *Hillbilly Wedding*, featured David in the second male lead as the dim-witted sidekick of the groom. It took place in West Virginia, where David had grown up, and he played the barely literate naïf with enough veracity that overnight his fortunes as a film actor were secured. What made the opportunity most appalling to peers was that he hadn't even had to audition, as the filmmaker, a college housemate, had conceived the role with David in mind. The director's name was Noah Mendelson, and for their junior and senior years they'd lived with three others in a house off campus where David would regale the group with impersonations from back home.

Their relationship had been far from easy on David. Noah had grown up in the Washington suburbs, the son of an Oscar-winning documentarian, and possessed an ineffable ease with women to go along with very good looks, ensuring a steady stream of coeds in and out of his room in their rickety nineteenth-century colonial. David, long and reedy, with a visage more suited for rendering in stone atop cathedrals, spent many nights on the other side of Noah's wall enduring evidence of raucous pleasure, both vocal and percussive. White, Asian, African American, Hispanic, Jewish, gentile, atheist, agnostic, pagan for all David knew, women showed up at all hours as if participants in some kind of seedy pageant interview process. So manifest was Noah's prowess both as a recruiter and performer that David took to seeking his advice, though not having the looks, the ease, the confidence, or, David suspected, the equipment, it was to little avail. When, at the age of thirty-two Noah offered him the role in *Hillbilly Wedding*, David couldn't help but consider it recompense for making his nights of solitude parsing Juvenal and Cicero all the lonelier.

After Juilliard, David liked to describe his four years acting off-Broadway as being that of a trench warfare actor, auditioning once or twice a week to play roles in smart, wordy plays to audiences comprising mostly other theater makers. But one kept at it, counting on commercials, voiceovers, and the odd movie or TV episode to get by. He'd lie awake nights tallying accumulated wages: five thousand for ten weeks (including rehearsals) in the play at Manhattan Theatre Club, thirty-five hundred for the week on the film, twenty thousand for the Sony commercial ... another couple of plays or a guest spot, and I should be all right.

Because *Hillbilly Wedding* was a low-budget indie, the distribution of which was far from assured, the best he could expect from it was some footage for his reel should casting directors deign to watch it. He'd spent four weeks in North Carolina filming and had earned just under eight thousand dollars. This would trigger his Screen Actors Guild insurance for another twelve months but still had him behind for the year.

He returned to New York scrambling and scared. He booked a commercial six weeks in, but it was for British television, meaning no residuals when it played, which was what made American spots, particularly the national ones, especially lucrative. A friend from college who'd elected to forgo graduate school was making six figures a year doing these. He understood the aesthetic principles and could saunter into an audition waiting area, have a cursory look at the storyboards and copy, and leave after taping with the offer all but booked. David, with his fancy training, struggled. He soon discovered, however, that outrageous choices of the type that would have had him defenestrated from the third floor of Juilliard were his best option for standing out. If the part was weird enough, and he could dispense with all dignity, he had a shot.

Mostly these involved characters who exposed the perils of choosing a brand inferior to what was being flogged. He aped an English knight pursuing the hand of a princess, his offer to slay a dragon bested by a T-shirted hunk with a six-pack of the advertised lager; he played an inept office manager negotiating a down-market color printer that splattered him with ink; he did a dimwit whose inadequacies couldn't prevent him from mastering a brand of riding mower. He specialized in "test subjects." These were electrocuted, drowned, punched, trampled, hung from buildings, dragged from cars, and even dropped from a plane (achieved in a studio with wires against a green screen). If he had words, they were never spoken in his own voice, and his appearance rarely lacked augmentation, whether a wig, facial hair, prosthetics, or some transmogrifying mask or suit.

The booking of these lucrative jobs—even more than those in theater— gave him hope early on without which he might have quit acting altogether. His parents and siblings could only marvel. "I saw the latest evidence of your Juilliard training today," his mother told his answering machine after she'd seen him play another hapless Brand-X loyalist. "I preferred you in *Arms and the Man.*"

At Juilliard he started to write and direct short plays. He'd experimented with this unsuccessfully in college, but proximity to so many actors willing to say his words inspired a redoubling. Moreover, his best friend, Adam, a writer himself, insisted he not limit himself solely to actor training. It helped that David was reading some of the best scripted material ever written, given Juilliard's obsession with Shakespeare, Chekhov, and Shaw.

Weeknights after rehearsals he'd leave school at ten o'clock with a book and his notebook and occupy the same stool at a bar he'd found within walking distance of Lincoln Center. Called *The J&G*, it advertised STEAKS AND CHOPS in green and orange neon, though neither ever appeared. David was partial to the chili, overturned straight from a Hormel can into a ceramic mug that spent two minutes in the microwave before being deposited between the beer and the scotch in front of him. For the first few weeks he'd read and write, talking only occasionally with the two alternating bartenders, brothers whose father owned the place in spite of a wrathful landlord who wanted them out. The sons' names were Jimmy and George, thus the bar's name. Their progenitor, always occupying a stool near the register, answered only to the name of Woozy.

David's girlfriend at the time was a senior at Brown, a classics concentrator spending the year in Pompeii, so his social life languished while he resisted the need to break up with her. It didn't help that to reach their dressing area, drama students walked a gauntlet of floor-to-ceiling lockers occupied by members of the dance division. Leaving aside why the dancers didn't have a changing area of their own, the whole arrangement seemed luridly unfair. Like creatures of some higher order, they inspired in David an impossible tangle of confusion, self-doubt, and yearning. While none would likely show interest in him given the abundance of leading men on the floor, the simple ostentation of removing all but their leotards to stretch in ways that to David always felt suggestive made avoiding eye contact impossible. He'd skulk past daily like Raskolnikov headed to his closet, willing himself not to stare.

The bar offered refuge. He learned he had discovered not only one of the few remaining dives on the Upper West Side but also a hub for the numbers racket and sports betting. All of it ran through a Dominican in a straw hat named Freddie, who wore a trio of alternating three-piece pinstriped suits, one navy, one gray, one black. The bookie would arrive at around ten thirty just as the Mets game was ending and take his place with a Mount Gay on the rocks against one of four fluted Ionic pillars of milled wood that bisected the establishment. At his back lay a narrow seating area beneath a stained, earth-toned mural of a Tuscan hillside featuring ancient ruins. As other East Coast games concluded at around eleven, a steady trickle of clients would wander in to settle transactions, after which they'd remain, and the J&G would quite suddenly be packed.

One night a man next to David introduced himself when David looked up from his copy of *Death on the Installment Plan*. Feeling more than a little ridiculous, he nudged the paperback from view.

"Why go to a bar to read?"

"I'm drinking," David said, pointing to his third boilermaker.

Clean shaven and not yet fifty, the man wore a beading white button-down and sipped a double Ballantine's George had just set before him. He had the tic of puckering his mouth involuntarily every twenty seconds or so as if needing to reassure himself he still had lips.

"But why not read in your apartment?"

"I guess I just don't want to go home yet."

"I don't see a ring," the man announced without looking at David's left hand.

"Oh," said David with a laugh. "Yeah, I meant because there's nobody there. My girlfriend is not only out of town, but out of the country."

"If there was nobody at my apartment, I'd be there getting drunk by myself instead of here with you. I seem to have a knack for inviting women into my life and then giving them every cent I have to book after two years. Well, the first one after five. I must like it on some level. You think?"

"I wouldn't know," replied David.

"Well, give me an opinion. I mean it," said the man. "You look like you've been kicked around a bit yourself." David took this as a compliment, as he'd been fetishizing the lives of the twentieth-century malcontents he'd been reading as counterpoint to a syllabus at Juilliard that had yet to venture past Turgenev. Yet it confirmed certain fears having to do with his future in a profession so dependent on appearance.

Returning that night to his apartment, he spent an embarrassing span in front of the mirror. He was weak of chin and heavy of brow in proportions that could be called vaguely simian. His right front upper incisor was chipped and gray from a jungle gym accident when he was twelve and the shoddily performed root canal that followed. His face was thin and bony, though with more jutting incoherence than could be called handsome. Front and profile his nose was big for his face. He was also what was referred to back home as walleyed, meaning his right and weaker eye would stray while the left remained focused on its target, from a condition known as amblyopia, or lazy eye. Finally, there was his Adam's apple, of great embarrassment since adolescence as it jutted from his slender neck in a manner that rendered him somewhat gruesome in profile. Yet were he to suppress the intoxicating comfort of self-pity, it might not be accurate to call himself ugly. His girlfriend even ventured the word *interesting*, and he could adduce this, along with her comeliness, to prove that the situation with women not altogether hopeless.

Her name was Olivia, and they'd gotten to know each other in his Plautus class second semester junior year, though he had, along with every other classics concentrator, been eyeing her for years. He'd done his best to get introduced during his junior year at a department function. He attended as many of these as his theater schedule would allow, sipping cheap Chianti and devouring cubes of pepper-jack cheese impaled on toothpick sabers, relishing how not only the professors but the students too communicated without embarrassment in the syntax and vernacular of centuries past.

"Where did you prepare?" a junior concentrator inquired during orientation.

"What?" David answered.

"Where did you attend high school?"

"You're never going to have heard of it. It was in Charleston."

"South Carolina?"

"West Virginia."

"The Mountain State," the elder intoned, savoring the sensation of using an appellation he'd read but probably never spoken. "And why are you concentrating in classics?"

"I liked Latin in high school. What about you?"

"I will be following the *cursus honorem*," came the response, accompanied by a knowing grin. *The course of the honored?* What the fuck is that? wondered David, not yet having taken Roman history. "I'm going to study the law," came the follow-up.

"Go to law school?"

"What a knack you have for parsing the language. I'll try and put nothing past such a keen mind. Will you do Greek too?"

"Just Latin."

"You seem quite certain."

"Latin rescued me."

"I'll wager, without offense I hope, that you're the first Mountaineer ever to have uttered that statement."

Until the eighth grade David had been so wretched academically that the private school he and his siblings attended tried to remove him twice. Only sheer mendicancy on his father's part in an hours-long meeting with school administrators enabled him to remain. David's parents placed academics over all else—certainly happiness—so the thought of expulsion for laxity felt dire, especially to his mother. His father's success in retaining David's place probably caused her to rejoice with more ebullience than she'd mustered at his birth.

In the seventh grade he'd managed a respectable B in English, a C– in science, a D in math, a D– in history, and he failed French. He knew he deserved each, but not passing French was especially irksome. The teacher had excoriated one of his friends, a gentile, for referring jokingly to Germans as Nazis. The passion of her rebuke left little doubt that this woman, whose last name was Becker and who was careful to point out that her parents came from the disputed region of Alsace, would have been something of a sympathizer back in the early forties. "That you would think that's funny just shows how ignorant you are," she had shouted at the young quipster. "Imagine if you were German. How would that make you feel? It wasn't *just* Jews who were killed, though you wouldn't know it for how they've cornered the market on the Holocaust. So, if I ever hear anything like that in my class again, you'll be kicked out and lose five points on your grade."

Cornered the market? The woman seemed to be deploying an idiom for economic rapacity in association with those whose religion he shared, even as it related to their mass murder. Jews weren't normally derogated in West Virginia, where David felt more exotic than despised. He got a superfluity of questions, particularly from friends' parents, the answers to which produced histrionically supportive nods and occasionally fits of curious, admiring wonder. David's father, who grew up on the East Coast and moved to Appalachia for David's mother, would often say that in West Virginia it was far worse being an atheist than a Jew. "Here we're like original Christians. Sure, they won't let us in the country club, but they won't let the Catholics in either. Hell, being on a par with the Catholics? I've never felt so loved!"

David decided not to continue with French.

"I'm speaking with Dean Warren about this," Ms. Becker warned when he told her. "I'm not letting you weasel out of my class just because you flunked." *Weasel out?* Would she have said that to a gentile? In the dean's office he held firm and was allowed to switch over to Latin 1 for eighth grade.

He adored the teacher, Mr. Lowry, and was hooked from the very first class when he and a half dozen seventh graders learned the first declension. A peculiar sort of kid took Latin because it required an extra step for parents and a twelve-year-old to recognize the value of learning a dead language. For the first time in his life, though the sole eighth grader, he was grouped with some of the school's most diligent students.

Then there was the language itself. A succession of English teachers had tried to impart to him an understanding of the parts of speech, using every strategy from merciless inculcation to old-school diagrams, but David entered eighth grade with as little grasp of the difference between a direct object and an indirect object, an object of the preposition and a possessive, as he did of any of the other thousand and one concepts, regardless of subject, he'd failed to learn since kindergarten. But with Mr. Lowry teaching a dead language with rules forever fixed, the duties of words began suddenly to reveal themselves, the exquisitely clean logic, at once closed and infinite, comprising one of the most beautiful systems of any sort he would ever encounter.

At thirty-five, Mr. Lowry was relatively young for a teacher in Charleston. He exuded unrestrained flamboyance that only later would convince David he'd been gay, inspiring further admiration given how dicey that must have been in West Virginia even in the mid-nineties. He had majored in classics at Connecticut College and then studied for the priesthood in Chicago before realizing that the cloth was not for him. He came to Charleston when David's school advertised a vacancy after the post's septuagenarian knuckle-rapper had finally retired. Competition for the position would not have been much of a challenge, for the types who devoted the years it took to learn Latin well enough to teach it weren't pining for scant pay and rooms full of obstreperous middle schoolers in coal country. But this preternaturally elegant man with his waxed moustache, lean, erect posture, and dialect that blended Cambridge, England, and Cambridge, Massachusetts, reached into David's brain with delicate manicured fingers and began to fix all the ways it wasn't working.

"Throw me the damn ball!" his friend Jack said on the Friday of the first week of eighth grade, and as David complied, he said to himself, *ball* is the direct object, *me*—a pronoun—is the indirect object, *throw* is the verb. But it got better, because in Latin all this was determined by word endings, not, as in English, by word order, meaning one could rearrange a sentence's parts to transform its rhetorical intent.

At that time the textbook in use was called simply "Jenney." Put out by Prentice Hall and compiled by the eponymous Charles Jenney Jr., it prepared students for reading the beginner texts of Livy, Suetonius, and Julius Caesar—two historians and the general-turned-emperor, who wrote mainly of military exploits. The vocabulary therefore involved battles, politics, and basic civic and rural life, the rudimentary sentences hilariously dry, utterly devoid of elegance and beauty. A favorite of David's read: *Legatus equum agricolae laudat*, or *The lieutenant praises the farmer's horse.*

"But just suppose," enthused Mr. Lowry, "you want to focus your reader's attention on the horse instead of the lieutenant. What could you do with this sentence? Mr. Levit?"

"Put the word *horse* first."

"Come immediately to the board and do so. This unlikely trio is desperate for its brief drama to be shared with the middle schoolers of quaint but mighty Charleston."

David wrote *Equum*, with its accusative ending making it the direct object first, followed by *agricolae*, with its genitive or possessive ending second, and finally *legatus*, with its nominative ending making it the subject third, before the verb *laudat*, the third-person present indicative singular form of *laudare*, "to praise," occupying the final spot. In English, the new sentence could be read: *The horse of the farmer the lieutenant praises.*

"That's it!" exclaimed Mr. Lowry, "Young Mr. Levit has bestowed primacy on the dear horse, relegating the scoundrel of a lieutenant way back by the verb where he belongs!"

He studied for each test avidly, accomplishing an uninterrupted string of As for the first time in his young life. He sat in the front row to avoid distraction, and when he'd dare an imitation or joke (as had been his disruptive tendency in years past), it had to do with the subject at hand, provoking little if any reprimand. He continued with the language through high school, and by the time he'd completed the AP course as a senior, having studied Horace, Virgil, and Catullus with a teacher he revered as much as he had Mr. Lowry, he decided he'd continue doing so in college. His success had migrated to other subjects as well. With the added advantage of hailing from West Virginia, giving the university the geographic diversity to which it aspired, he gained admittance to Brown.

"What are you planning for the summer?" his mother asked in the spring of his freshman year.

"I'll come home and get a job someplace."

"David, this is a moment when you can do anything, try anything."

"What are you saying?" His father had left her the year before, so he knew that discouraging his company for the summer was costing her.

"Go somewhere and do something risky. You liked acting in high school. Aren't there summer theaters all over looking for apprentices?"

"Mom, it's already April. I'm sure those types of jobs are all taken."

She had studied philosophy in the sixties at Mount Holyoke and through the alumnae network discovered a recent graduate running a small theater in Maine. He auditioned and was admitted to the junior company, with whom he spent the summer performing Lanford Wilson, Tom Stoppard, and Noël Coward outdoors nightly for tipsy vacationers. He also found himself sharing a bed with the company ingénue, a petite Bowdoin sophomore from Rye, New York, who had no options other than David, as the other three male company members were gay. He'd gone to college intending to be a professor or teacher. Now he would continue in classics, but not as a career.

The first and most essential order of business was to enroll in a beginning acting class, which he did immediately on his return to campus at summer's end. Nine of the dozen available slots went to freshmen, nearly all of them from New York City, Chicago, and Los Angeles. The women were confident, free-spirited, and self-consciously chic. They wore dark clothing, loose-fitting but curated to flatter, and David fantasized about each relentlessly. Already like women in their late twenties, they leaned in when talking, gesticulated seductively, and moved with sensual ease. They spoke through full, confident lips that David would watch instead of their eyes. Within the month, three were on the arms of upperclassmen, while two seemed to be dating each other.

The professor normally responsible for beginning acting was on sabbatical, so an adjunct was brought in. Logan Charles had been a stage actor in the early seventies, appearing twice on Broadway but mostly regionally. He spoke with impossible resonance from the bottom of a massive gut recounting experiences opposite names of apparent significance, though David had heard of none of them: Elaine Stritch, Estelle Parsons, Marian Seldes, Hume Cronyn, Jessica Tandy, Lee J. Cobb. Some collaborations had to have been imagined because if one tallied their number, there wouldn't have been room in a single career.

On a cigarette break during the second class—many of them smoked—he queried one of the New York actresses as to whether "the studio" to which Logan kept referring was somewhere on campus. Her name was Julia Greenberg, and she'd grown up in a townhouse two doors west of Madison Avenue on Seventy-Seventh Street in New York City. She stood just under five foot three with curly brown hair that frothed onto tiny shoulders. A sweater three sizes too big crowded her neck on one side and exposed an upper breast on the other. She had olive skin and big green eyes and blew smoke expertly from the corner of her mouth.

"He's talking about the fucking Actors Studio, which is a bad sign. It's in New York. This guy's an idiot. I can't believe we're going to spend a semester listening to him. What's your name?"

"David."

"Hi, David. Where are you from?"

"West Virginia."

"That's so fucking cool."

"Do you maybe want to do our first scene together?" He fought the urge to upchuck. She offered a throaty giggle.

"Are you gonna be all right, David?" It was as if she were speaking to a child. "Don't worry, I don't bite."

"Sorry."

"The thing is, I'm doing a scene already with Lynne. But maybe later in the semester. If we can make it that long."

Lynne, also from Manhattan's Upper East Side, was the daughter of one of the most powerful producers on Broadway. Taller than Julia, with firm, matronly curves, she had a voice in which one could curl up for a lifetime. And what was it with these lips? Those on the girls at his Charleston high school were thin and prim, always on the verge of a presentational smile. These ethnic city mouths, made for irony and argument, were of another sort, and it struck him that should he ever matriculate socially into this group, his greatest challenge would be to manage his unrequited lust.

The scene Julia and Lynne put up the following week was from a David Rabe play called *In the Boom Boom Room*. Until his summer in Maine the most modern playwright to whom he'd been exposed was Arthur Miller, from playing Willy Loman his senior year in high school. Nothing had prepared him for the pique between the two actresses in front of him. They didn't seem to be performing at all. He could sense every turn as they spoke words that sounded thought up on the spot, and with such unencumbered intimacy and sharp give-and-take. Most important, they demonstrated no awareness of being watched, yet a keen understanding all the same. The writing and performing was real life, but better. I'll never be able to do that, he said to himself. I could spend a lifetime.

"You know I met Rabe," Logan Charles announced afterward. "In '71, backstage at the Longacre where I was seeing Pacino do *Pavlo Hummel*. I think you ladies captured the spirit, but I didn't find it personal. I did a gay two-hander back at the studio. I won't name the actor, but we spent a night in bed together before we put the scene up."

"Are you saying Julia and I should fuck tonight and bring the scene back in?" Lynne asked. I could honestly marry her tomorrow and be happy for the rest of my life, David thought. She could teach me how to live, how to think, how to be.

"You can't pretend feelings. I think about that line from *Long Day's Journey* where Jamie says"—already he was choking up—"he says, 'I thought only whores took dope.'" A single tear wended down his robust and reddening cheek. He pointed. "You see? There it is."

In spite of a succession of such dubiously instructional anecdotes, David put up scenes for critique weekly. Logan was also to be directing that year's first production on the university's main stage, Maxim Gorky's *The Lower Depths*, and David determined to secure even the smallest role, which he did, playing Alyosha, who had just three scenes. The cast included four of the women in his acting class, among them Lynne and Julia, given plum roles in spite of their chaste preparation as Rabe's bisexual strippers.

Every day brought a new amorous fixation, not only on actresses in the play but in the entire theater department, regardless of ethnicity, shape, essence. He wanted to be like all of them, male and female: infectiously free of inhibition, easy with others, erudite. Many took courses in semiotics, part of a department called Modern Culture and Media. They discussed "signifiers" and "narrative fracturing." They read Marx and Hegel, and someone named Derrida. David wasn't so naïve as not to consider it monumentally pretentious—arguably the very definition—that twenty-year-olds were "deconstructing texts" penned by literary giants, nor was he convinced these young acolytes understood the words they were using, but he was infatuated by their audacity all the same. He'd been let inside a room he simply didn't want to leave. Even the pretention had its own strange allure.

Late that same year he began to meet some of the undergraduate playwrights. One, named Arthur Berger, had written two full-lengths by the age of twenty, which astonished David, who could barely eke out a ten-page paper. They would walk from rehearsals of Arthur's play to a bar on Wickenden Street east of campus, huddling along the back wall where they wouldn't stick out.

"I don't know why you're so scared of these New York City kids," Arthur said one night. "Don't you see how lucky you are to have grown up in the South?"

"Everyone treats me like a rube."

"They treat everyone not from the city like a rube. Julia grew up on the Upper East Side and went to Brearley, and now she's walking around like she's some kind of badass."

"What's Brearley?"

"An all-girls private school. As high status as it gets. I've been in their apartment. It's insane. Fourteen rooms, and a Chagall in the guest bathroom. The entry foyer has a Manet. A Manet *oil* by the way. Her dad's a senior partner at Goldman Sachs, and her mom is a socialite who's always getting her picture in the style section."

"What style section?"

"It's a *New York Times* thing. You really are a rube."

"I like her."

"You want to fuck her."

"You don't?"

"Of course I do, but I'm not gonna get all depressed because she's not interested. This is just college. Wait till we get out into the real world, when people are really out to get you."

"The thing is, Arthur, not that anyone, including you, should give a shit, but I want to do this."

"Do what?"

"Be an actor," answered David, the first time he'd revealed it to anyone.

His favorite class that semester was Plato. The professor, a woman poached from Harvard named Mildred Craven, could parse the language methodically while rendering the dialogues as contemporary as if they'd been written weeks before.

"It's like we're being taught by Athena," David told his friend Daniel. "I feel like I should avert my eyes. She's like this empirical inclusion of Platonic beauty."

"If you really want to challenge yourself," said Daniel, "and maybe get over your weird infatuation with Professor Craven, take semiotics. Learn the enemy. That's why I'm here."

"What do you mean?"

"I don't feel I can read the people who are trying to dismantle the old ways of thinking without reading the original ideas they're challenging."

"Oh my God. You're just like all these other pretentious idiots. You think Plato and Aristotle need to be dismantled?"

"Of course they do. Trust me, this shit is revolutionary, and it's already having serious impact on the way we think—and not just about art."

"Oh God."

"Wait and see."

David took Introductory Semiotics, taught by a bespectacled leather-jacketed man in his seventies named William Silverberg, who sipped coffee from a metal thermos while expounding without notes on some of the most abstruse texts David had ever tried to read. Confirming earlier suspicions, he found it ridiculous that undergraduates, many of them freshmen, were assigned writers like Derrida, Lacan, Marcuse, and Husserl in such staggering page counts every week with the expectation they'd get anything out of them. He had to force himself through each paragraph half a dozen times, the material was so impenetrable. He also became convinced that the irritating game of these writers was to achieve an opacity so willfully dense as to render the rhetoric itself a kind of proof for what was being mooted: that the distance language must go in pursuit of actual truth will also always obscure truth.

Most infuriating was the practice of dismantling texts in ways overtly demeaning to authorship. Why deny writers their due for having sat with a blank page and come up with the narrative or ideological goods?

"The seduction of an author's biography constitutes yet further distancing from our understanding of the work itself," offered Professor Silverberg. The tendentious verbiage aside, David disagreed so vehemently that he would sit shaking in his seat. In support of their arguments, the professor and his graduate assistants referenced Marx mercilessly, explaining "the means of production" as being concealed by storytellers with stylistic constructs meant to draw the reader in, and how through deconstruction one could expose these workings, just as in *Das Kapital* Marx proved how capitalism hid the true costs of the products it manufactured and sold.

"What the fuck else is a storyteller supposed to do?" David asked his section leader.

"Actually make the political statement of reminding us we're reading a novel," came the response, "thus foregrounding the labor that goes into it. Strip away the lies by making the novel as much about the writing of the novel as the story itself. The author exposes the artifice of his power in other words. Art as political statement, which it is anyway."

"What you're advocating is going to lead to some incredibly tedious fiction, the same way communism led to the manufacture of some pretty shitty products."

"Let me introduce you to twentieth-century literature, David. Perhaps you haven't met." The class giggled. "Which is to say, these ideas aren't new. And they don't just apply to art, but all of language and culture."

"I don't think Faulkner and Joyce and whoever else you're going to bring up were thinking about the means of production or foregrounding their power as storytellers when they wrote their masterworks. Faulkner was a night watchman at the time."

"Once again, you're getting caught up in biography."

Even the way they were to write papers was brutalized.

"You will compose one essay per week for the entire semester," announced Professor Silverberg. "These are never to exceed one page. They are to be laid out in standard twelve-point font, with single spacing, and no margins." He presented an example: a lone sheet packed with text. "You use only the paper you need, presented in a visual form that represents the density of your ideas. Form is content." David wondered if the professor would have assigned this formatting were he to be doing the grading rather than the poor teaching assistants who'd have to slog through dozens of undergraduate odysseys into Marxist literary theory without benefit of spacing and margins.

"The unfortunate souls who have to read these," he said to a dark-eyed sophomore in olive work pants, Doc Martens, and a torn white T-shirt. He prayed her black lipstick was meant to contrast the proletarian garb. Already he fantasized taking her for coffee at the Blue Room—a campus redoubt for Modern Culture and Media concentrators—for an interview.

"What's that supposed to mean?" she asked.

"Just that I think there's a point to margins and spacing other than conspicuous consumption."

"I think it's fucking brilliant."

He had no idea that the university's film studies program had been subsumed by Media Studies. The thinking was that since the larger discipline centered on the analysis of communication, scrutinizing the ever-evolving strategies in the field of filmed narrative offered fertile ground for exploration.

Professor Silverberg taught an intermediate course that screened a new film each week. To David's surprise, not once did he denounce the concept of authorship. In fact, a plurality of the movies were directed by a single filmmaker, Alfred Hitchcock, because his use of camera angles, editing, framing, sound, and casting had a formal clarity that rendered deconstruction easy and clear. They studied *Rear Window, Marnie, North by Northwest,* and David's favorite, *Vertigo.* Some of the so-called theory David could do without, such as constant references to "the male gaze," and "fetishizing," and how the camera presented as a "hegemonic apparatus," but the breaking down of movies into a system all its own got David thinking in new ways about how stories were told. Just as in Latin one could rearrange word order to suit rhetorical intent, one could do the same with image and sound. When a filmmaker chose to go to a close-up, use music, or move the camera was not so different from when Mr. Lowry had him rearrange what word would come first: *farmer, horse,* or *lieutenant.*

He'd always embraced his father's adage "If you find you're the smartest person in the room, leave that room," and though he could inevitably discover ways in which any one person was more clever than another, he took to applying this broadly when choosing how and with whom to spend his time.

This led him, late sophomore year, to befriend an unruly Byronic figure a year older named Adam Borstein, who had a mind so restless that spending time with him caused a kind of exasperated fatigue, even while David could scarcely tear himself away. In a word, he was smitten. They would meet in the late afternoon and often not separate until two or three in the morning with Adam still ranting, always demanding more, and David desperate for space but always regretting they'd parted. Adam had a reputation on campus as being unstable, but none of that obscured his extravagant mind, limitlessly inventive vocabulary, and abiding loyalty as a friend.

He was, for starters, beautiful. From the Philadelphia suburbs, he'd played tennis competitively in high school and was recruited for the university's team, on which he lasted a year before choosing to concentrate on academics and his hope someday to write fiction. He stood six feet two inches, with wide shoulders, long, thick legs, and a slender waist. Stripped naked— David had seen him so through his first-floor window one night, pacing his room, pen and notebook in hand—he was the stuff of ancient statuary. A cleft chin dominated a face of hard angles that suggested a barely restrained ferocity. His eyebrows were dense and almost feminine over deep-set eyes of an iridescent blue with long, dark lashes both above and below. His mother, not surprisingly, had been a model before succumbing to mental illness. "I have her eyes, but a lot of the other afflictions too," Adam would often share. His mouth rested mostly on the edge of a smile poised for laughter or a sharp comeback, and into it he would shove cheap candies—everything from Three Musketeers bars to his ever-present Twizzlers—tearing off the wrappers and masticating with the hyped enthusiasm of a child in the backseat of the car at the start of a family trip. A heavily sweetened coffee accompanied him day and night. He rarely slept.

Women adored him, but intimacy meant extended time together, which was effectively impossible. One needed after all to rest, enjoy the occasional silence, some time away, none of which he'd allow willingly. In this way, he was too much known, and not known at all by those close, his intensity, along with the crushing overabundance of thoughts and words, at once seductive and impenetrable.

"I'm trapped," one of many successive lovers complained to David. "I'm obsessed with a guy I can't fucking stand to be with for more than an hour. He's ruining my life."

Regarding David and Adam, rumors proliferated.

"I was up all night with Barbara," Adam said, his voice breaking with glee.

"Yeah, spare me the details," David responded.

"No, it's not like that. She was talking about us."

"Who 'us'?"

"Me 'n' you 'us.'"

"In what respect?"

Adam clutched David's ass. "She'd have it we're amorous."

Not a day passed without some contact, either in person or by phone, and for his graduation David gave Adam *The Collected Dialogues of Plato* in a hardbound copy edited by Edith Hamilton—the same textbook assigned by Professor Craven.

"A little over a year from now we'll be up late reading these together in New York City."

"Only if I can be Socrates. And who says I'm going to New York City?" asked David.

"What, you're going to go to Los Angeles? You're a theater actor, David. And not so easy on the eyes, as you're never shy of pointing out. You'll get better with age, so go to grad school. Anyway, I'm gonna need you in New York. We're going to need each other. Trust me on this."

He was admitted to Juilliard the following spring.

Upon David's arrival in New York his class began its training with a diagnostic performance of Shakespeare's *Antony and Cleopatra*. Called "the Discovery Play," the slot's unvarnished results would expose each student's deficiencies without benefit of ad hoc instruction, as rehearsals involved blocking and nothing more. In David's evaluation the first-year acting instructor, an octogenarian just under five feet tall who'd been at the school since its inception, announced that David probably hadn't ever acted in his life. That's a bit strong, David thought as he caught his breath. But the old sage wasn't finished: "I'd like to say there's a technique there we need to tear down, but you don't even have that. Of course, we admitted you for a reason, so don't lose hope!"

David saw Adam constantly. In spite of a year in separate cities while David finished in Providence, they'd remained close through letters. "Not phone calls," Adam demanded in words gouged into the paper. "And we need to write each other back reflexively. Like Ping-Pong, otherwise it's not a conversation."

Over the year apart Adam had fallen in with another former Brown student who'd graduated the year before Adam and two years before David named Sammy Cohen, who was pursuing a master's in history at Columbia. Adam introduced him to David one night at the J&G, and David understood immediately what so captivated his friend. Ascetic and fierce, Sammy communicated in aggressive bursts that demanded a person dash to keep up, as if chasing fireflies. He listened avidly, always evincing a keen sense not only of what you'd just said but of where your contentions might lead, even if you didn't quite know yourself.

"I swear to you, you've never met anyone like this guy. Just breathing the same air with him makes you smarter," Adam insisted.

"That's what I've always said about you," responded David. Quickly they became a trio, mostly on weekends when David's Juilliard schedule would allow. It felt like they were building a connection that would last their lifetimes.

Adam wrote feverishly but seemed in no hurry to be published or even start a first novel. He would read to David and Sammy from his notebooks, which were of the cheap three-holed spiral variety with bright covers a grade schooler might choose. He crammed these top to bottom and side to side with words and drawings that chronicled his life, with quasi fictional stories interspersed. The never-revised prose was aggressive and unafraid, suffused with sadness, wit, and empathy. David urged him to share it with more than friends, but Adam balked, insisting he wasn't ready for journals, agents, or publishers; that as soon as he'd done so, a part of him would perish. "It's like childhood," he said. "Once it's gone, it's gone. I've got my whole life. As soon as I have success, that becomes a kind of defining feedback. In a sense the style becomes ossified. This dross," he continued with a grin, waving a garish spiral, "is for the biographers."

"That assumes a lot."

"You could learn a bit from my confidence, David."

"Meaning?"

"It's pathetic how you obsess over hierarchies in your training program. Hierarchies that are temporary and misleading."

"They don't even consider me an actor. The students see that and treat me the same way."

"That nonsense has nothing to do with your life subsequent to graduating, and it's inhibiting you. Don't let any of them define you. Learn from them, but tailor the program to what you project is going to be your future— which, trust me, isn't just going to involve performing."

"You think I won't have a career?"

"I think you're not going to be comfortable subordinating yourself to the decisions of others, which is what actors have to do. Some people can do that and wait their turn, and good for them, but that's not you. What are you reading right now?"

"*Notes of a Dirty Old Man.*"

"After that read something completely different. Jane Austen or Thackeray. What about the paper? Every day? The whole A section?"

"What's this all about?"

"That school is getting inside your head. You're becoming underwhelming. Sammy and I were talking about it."

"That's good to know."

"That we fucking love you? We have to be able to talk about shit with you, lean on you. Stop it with the self-doubt. Read every book of interest you can get your hands on. And you need to be writing."

"Writing?"

"You did it in college."

"Tiny little dialogues no one ever saw but you."

"Well, you need to do it again so you're more than just a mopey guy depending on the approval of others. Plus, Jesus, you have free actors!"

He began with short interactions based on people he was meeting at the bar. The only one he dared show Adam—taken almost verbatim from the source—came from a Vietnam vet who'd told him of returning from Southeast Asia to San Diego.

"Three of us went from the ship to the first bar we found and didn't leave for hours. I say good-bye finally and start walking. No idea where I'm going. Discharged. Not going back. No chance of it. Completely fucked by what I saw and if I'm gonna be honest did, but alive. And this girl comes toward me, still near the navy yard. It's clear why she's there, and I start talking with her. Blonde, but not a natural blonde. And tough in a crude sort of way. Also part Asian, or at least she looks it or I put that on her, I don't know, but it's this weird combination, which is, obviously the blond hair is a wig. And she says pay up front, which I do, and bam. Two guys, and the cuffs. I begged them. Begged. Said it was my first night back, I'd done three tours. Nothing. Hauled in and booked. No one to post bail. I actually say to the judge, 'Your Honor, I killed people over there, which this country drafted me and trained me, and paid me to do. For going with a prostitute, which was basically entrapment because she wasn't one, I get put in jail? Fucking solicitation?'"

"So what happened?" asked David the night he heard the story.

"I didn't have money to pay the fine, so I got jail time, but he said the few days I'd spent already counted. 'Then why were you going to make me pay the fine?' I asked. He said he hadn't thought about it. A fucking judge, and he hadn't thought about it. Anyway, I was out."

"Well, I guess at least there was that."

"Oh yeah, asshole? Except now I had a record. Have a record to this fucking day. You think that hasn't had an impact on my life? Fuck this country."

"It's good," said Adam. "You've got a better ear for dialogue than I do." It was perhaps the most important confirmation David had received in his life, if only because of its source.

That winter he traveled to Europe to visit Olivia as planned, and they broke up. It was painful and morbid, and an enormous part of him was convinced he'd made a terrific mistake. He was in awe of her prowess in a field he could appreciate, and he admired even more her ambition outside of it. Her transcript a carpet of As, she took computer coding, applied math, and molecular biology, along with both Latin and Greek, and was a lock for Phi Beta Kappa. Sexually she'd do whatever they wanted, wherever they wanted, but it was clear that no such exploits, at least with him, would ever intrigue her as much as analyzing the text from a tombstone at Praeneste, or poring over ground plans from Cicero's villa on the Bay of Naples. Her restraint was such that early on he became unsure of himself as a partner.

"Have you talked to her about it?" asked Adam.

"What would that even sound like?"

"'Hey, Olivia, just asking, have you had an orgasm yet?' And if she has, tell her she could let a fellow know with some full-throated encouragement."

She claimed to be as happy as she'd ever been—not because David was some sort of dynamo, she was quick to point out, but because a deep emotional attachment accompanied their physical life.

"I'm falling in love with you."

"Okay then ... how do I put this ..."

"What, you'd like me to scream and moan?"

"A little bit of in-game feedback would be helpful."

That evening she gave it a try, even moving with him more than usual to accompany the vocal display.

"What?"

"This just isn't me," she answered, looking down at him. "Instead of enjoying myself, and say, making out with you while we're intimate, I feel like I'm performing. I want to enjoy you and enjoy myself, not demonstrate that that's what I'm doing. I feel like an actress." The slight against thespians aside, even saying "when we're intimate" instead of "when we're fucking," or even "having sex" indicated remove from the carnality he wanted. It further distressed him to know he was being completely unfair, wanting from her a combination somewhat mutually exclusive in both men and women. For the most part—and there were certainly exceptions—the brainiest people he knew weren't so great with their bodies, and vice versa.

Early in his junior year, well before Olivia, he spent three consecutive nights having experiences he'd never considered possible with a woman from his film theory class named Mandy. Her body was big and curvy, and her libido liminal to terrifying. They explored positions so strange, and frankly demented, that he had more interest in talking about them with friends than in ever repeating them. She was athletic and demonstrably generous, loudly appreciative with orgasms that rippled through her body in waves.

"That was almost postmodern," she announced after their second go on the first night. The words hovered.

"Wait, what?" he finally asked.

"It was just so complete."

"Look, I don't want to spoil a compliment, one you probably deserve more than I, but how exactly is that postmodern?"

"We were fucking and nothing else mattered. Like when you just let go all sense of self. Hegemonic." One couldn't spend fifteen minutes with a certain type without being whacked across the face with this word. Coming from the Greek root *hegemon*, meaning "ruler," it had spawned an entire subdiscipline that examined how certain sociological and/or cultural forces dominated others.

"You mean a power struggle?"

"No, like neither of us had *any* power, but together *all* the power."

He wanted to leave as quickly as possible but was restrained by the slavish need for more of what had happened physically. He returned for the next two nights, arriving late after rehearsals rather than using his key to the classics library. He arranged for Adam to meet the two of them at the Blue Room right before she had to get to a seminar.

The conversation afterward was succinct.

"David, what are you doing?"

"The sex is insane."

"Good, and now you've had it."

"That's easy for you to say. Women chase you down the street."

"She's not for you. End it."

Soon enough she was on to a sophomore named Duncan, said suddenly to be missing morning classes and asking for extensions on papers, though he'd never looked happier.

Other factors motivated Adam's advice regarding Olivia. During his first semester at Juilliard David did not remain faithful to her, sleeping with two actresses, one in his class, another in the class above. He had also taken a woman home from the bar one evening.

"Look, David, late at night," Adam asked, "when you're alone and the urge takes you, do you ever think of Olivia?"

"No."

"I don't mean always. I mean ever."

"Never."

"And I don't need details, but in terms of pure desire, with one being indifference and ten raging lust, where was it over the summer when you guys were on the verge in a sexual sense?"

"Maybe a four. Routine."

"Let her go."

"But I'm going to Italy in three weeks."

"So do it in person. It gives you the option of changing your mind, but you won't, and you shouldn't. Down that road lies only unhappiness for you and her. Let her be with a guy who deserves her and will treat her right. Sorry, but that's not you. She's eventually going to find you infuriating, unreliable, and very hurtful. You're the kind of guy who could ruin her life."

"Jesus, Adam."

"And she could ruin yours."

"How do I keep letting you tell me to break it off with women?"

"I'd expect you to do the same for me. We get these prescriptive ideas about the sorts of people we should be with—smart, from a wealthy family, Jewish, not Jewish, middle-class, a lawyer, a yoga instructor, a philatelist, a phrenologist—but ultimately attraction deals with stuff that's ineffable. She's away for one semester and you're taking women home from your bar."

"One woman."

"One woman who went with you, but it could easily have been a dozen if you'd had your way."

"Adam, there haven't been a dozen unaccompanied women at the J&G all year."

"You and Olivia have discussed marriage, and more than once. That's a threshold." He jammed a Twizzler into his mouth. "Your life has gone from the possible and undefined to the binary and defined. Every interaction, from getting a slice to sleeping together, is imbricated with the new terms. It's not, in other words, is he or she the marrying sort? Those are tacit questions that color a serious monogamous relationship pretty much from the outset. But now everything you do and say is some semantic version of 'either we're moving forward toward marriage, or we break up.' You've been cheating on her, and you need to set her free from that, or she needs to figure it out and dump you. It's finished."

The night before he was to leave for Europe there was an all-Juilliard party, and he ended up spending much of it with one of his classmates, an offbeat woman from Louisiana named Charlotte, whom he knew to be dating a graduate student at the New School.

"So, Italy tomorrow?" she asked.

"Yeah."

"Not looking forward, David?" She tended to intersperse his name in conversation with a wry formality that was unambiguously flirtatious. "You'd rather be going to France? Yugoslavia? Monaco?"

"Italy suits me fine. I'm just not sure what's going to happen there."

"As in the future of your relationship?"

"Yes."

"You and I are in the same boat, which explains my ambivalence toward going to Maryland to be with my boyfriend's family."

"You want to come to my apartment tonight?" The question had escaped his mouth almost before he'd formulated it.

"Yeah, David, I think so."

Once there, they didn't set right to it. While he poured two scotches, she perused the hundreds of books lining the shelves he and Adam had built to cover one wall of his cramped living room.

"Don't be impressed," David said. "I had help putting up the shelves, and those are all the books I've ever owned. I don't throw any away or leave any behind."

"You sound like you're apologizing. What's that about?"

"I guess I feel a bit anxious what you'll think."

"Is that specific to me, or do all the girls make you anxious?"

"Specific to you."

"Good."

"Why's that?"

"Just a feeling, David."

She took down his *Norton Anthology of Poetry*. She had studied American literature and, like David from West Virginia at Brown, was one of few representatives of her home state in her class at Sarah Lawrence. Her voice came from deep down and suggested generations of ethnicities he couldn't place.

"What's your background?"

"Please don't say I'm exotic."

"I guess I won't."

"My mom is Jewish and Catholic, and my dad's Black. Haitian."

This isn't happening, he thought as she lay on the tattered rug reading Shelley and Keats. Her indolent pronunciation made the words more seductive than their nineteenth-century British writers could ever have intended. By this time he'd had plenty of time with her in speech classes, during which, as with him, instructors would beat back the sounds that seemed most to distinguish her. While this made sense—one didn't want to sound regionally specific to parts of America when doing Shakespeare and Chekhov—David found its threat to Charlotte hard to abide.

"Don't let them!"

"What, David? You think there's gonna be nothing left of little old me? Trust me, that's not gonna happen. I am gonna let them turn me into an actress, though, and I suggest you do the same."

"What's that supposed to mean?"

"Let them help you."

"I'm trying."

"It seems like you're hedging your bets."

"How's that?"

"Carrying the Céline and Musil around? It's kind of insufferable. And always with your nose in the *New York Times* until right when class starts? Like you're announcing to everyone that you're above it all. You're interesting. You don't have to try so hard."

"Wow, Charlotte."

"Make sure you heard everything I said, David, because I'm not going to repeat it. I said you're interesting."

Dance, movement, and voice classes filled the first half of each day, meaning everyone compulsorily in tights until lunch. He developed a good sense of her muscular body and wide shoulders as their flirtation evolved.

"We're not gonna have sex tonight, David," she said, closing the anthology. "We might do other things, but if there's more down the road for us, I don't want it to start off with full-blown cheating. One day we might really need to trust each other."

In his bed they remained clothed. When hands roved, she inhibited it. They kissed, talked, and occasionally dozed until just after six, when she had to leave to pack for a nine-thirty train. His flight wasn't until evening, so he slept until two.

By noon the next day he was with Olivia at the foot of Vesuvius.

"Why come all the way to Italy to ruin this, David?" He met her colleagues, she never letting on that there was trouble between them. They went to Rome and stayed, as planned, at a pension near the Palatine Hill. They walked endlessly, they talked, they wept mawkishly, they kept ending up in bed, but when he left as scheduled on the second of January, it was over.

In a bar at Da Vinci Airport he dispatched two double scotches to stifle the conviction that he'd never succeed at being faithful to anyone if he'd failed with Olivia, let alone love anyone if he couldn't do so lastingly with her. Yet he kept thinking about Charlotte.

On the plane home he did his best in a center seat between a billowy American in his fifties and an even heavier Italian in his seventies, both of them angrily restless. He had another double scotch and within minutes of the final sip was in the bathroom at the back of coach throwing up. He rinsed his mouth and face, but when he returned to his seat the American turned to him, histrionically waving his hand in front of his wide nose so David dare not misconstrue.

"Oh, this is just great."

"Yeah, isn't it?" David said back.

It took two hours to get to Manhattan, between the tram to the train, then the subway from the LIRR at Jamaica Station to the Upper West Side. When he reached his apartment, he was asleep within minutes and didn't wake for thirteen hours.

On his machine were messages from Adam, Olivia, and Charlotte.

He called Adam first.

"You did the right thing," he said, not giving David the chance to rehearse misgivings or speak his burgeoning feelings for Charlotte. "Now listen. I'm going to Israel."

"When?"

"In three weeks."

"For how long?"

"At least six months, maybe a year."

"Why, Adam?"

"I'm lonely. Restless."

"How can you be lonely? I'd spend every night hanging out with you if I could. So would Sammy."

"I exhaust you guys like I exhaust everyone. In another country I'll have half a year at least before they get tired of me. Besides, David. I'm not moving there for good."

"What did Sammy say?"

"Doesn't care. He's going to Paris for the semester."

"What!" No Olivia, and now no Adam or Sammy.

"A lot went on while you were away. He quit his job and got a last-minute spot at the Sorbonne."

"How does that even happen?"

"He had applied, turned them down, then changed his mind."

The three saw one another once the following week, then both friends were gone. With Adam especially, he couldn't escape a feeling of abandonment.

"I'll see you in a year, David. I promise. And you can always visit."

Charlotte only added to his disappointment.

"I got to Maryland and felt terrible about our night in your apartment. The upshot is you're going to have to find some other girl if you were counting on me for the rebound."

"I was hoping for a lot more than that actually. Break up with this guy."

"I wouldn't be ready for you now, David. You and I are a whole other thing."

"What the fuck do I do in the meantime?"

"Do what you're here for. Work."

He hadn't entirely understood what differentiated Juilliard from the other schools that had interested him, but as he immersed himself in the training, he quickly learned that he had chosen the most conservative among them. The drama division was run by an ex-RAF pilot named Edmond Wood, who'd directed plays while a prisoner of war in Germany.

"Obviously he wasn't in Auschwitz," David remarked to more than one classmate.

Edmond also taught Shakespeare. His bedrock thesis, adhered to dogmatically, was that the playwright's words represented spoken or "living" thought, meaning an immediacy of experience and an absence of subtext. To that end, because much of the writing was metered, the author furnished unambiguous clues as to how any given soliloquy, speech, line, or even word was to be performed. Any deviations in the iambic pentameter indicated changes in thought, emotion, or action. In service to this approach, certain precepts needed to be observed, mostly by way of prohibitions: never stress a pronoun, never stress a negative, such as "no" or "not." And David's peculiar favorite: if a word began with the same consonant with which the preceding one ended, Shakespeare was insisting the actor pause to find the second of the two words.

Text work in Edmond's fourth-floor office, with the entire class seated variously on chairs, a low sectional sofa of fading malarial yellow, and finally the floor, initially struck David as one of the most counter-creative enterprises he'd ever experienced. They began with the opening speech by Rumor, from *Henry IV, Part 2*: "Open your ears, for which of you will stop / The vent of hearing when loud Rumor speaks?" Edmond chose a tough blond actress from Houston.

"Go ahead and read, Melinda."

"You mean just start?"

"What else? That we sit gazing at each other?"

Forewarned for obliteration, she readied herself, then commenced. "Open—"

"Stop. What are you doing?"

"I was reading."

"Is this character meant to be from—where are you from?"

"Texas."

"Are we learning speech at this school?"

"Sorry."

"Start again."

"Open—"

"Stop. You're attacking us. Why would you do that?"

"I don't—"

"You said the word like some sort of assault. The audience will flee. Two syllables in. It's a trochee, so you've got to be careful, not use it like a cudgel."

"Okay."

"And look above the speech. We're beginning the play. This writer is absolutely specific with every word. We need to be relentless in our pursuit of that, and you're not being specific at all. Read the first word at the top of the page."

"Induction."

"Exactly, this is an induction. Not an introduction. An induction. Meaning what?"

No one dared answer.

"To induce. You must induce."

David raised his hand, eager to apply the rigor just encouraged.

"David?"

"Just in terms of being specific in the way you're asking, I think the verb associated with the noun *induction* would be 'to induct,' whereas if Rumor were meant 'to induce,' the noun would be *inducement*." The ensuing silence in a room of twenty actors caused David to marvel, and not in a good way.

"Yes. I see," said Edmond eventually. "Let's call it induct then." He turned back to the actress from Texas. "Go on then, have another go now that David has deigned to enlighten us."

"Open your ears, for which of you—"

"Now you're just murdering it."

The class lasted an hour and a half and met twice a week. It took two sessions to cover the initial speech of forty-one lines. Not once did Edmond ask David to read.

"What in college might have felt like spirited intellectual exchange, Edmond considers an attack," warned the first-year speech teacher.

"What?"

"Apparently you made it a point to show him up."

"I wasn't doing that at all."

"I'm just telling you to watch out."

The training applied the technique, or at least the spirit of it, to all material, including contemporary plays and, by extension, film and television. On the surface, there would seem to have been scant overlap, since virtually no writers after the end of the nineteenth century wrote in verse. But two extrapolations held sway. First, the demands of Shakespeare were such that playing him well meant likely success with any other text. This felt true the more of Shakespeare's plays David read because of the technical and emotional skill required to navigate not only the language but the extraordinary situations in which the characters found themselves. More important, however, was the insistence that thought and emotion were most compelling when transpiring as the words were spoken. Shakespeare, an actor himself, used deviations within the verse to demand that actors live inside predicaments as they occurred, and this, ultimately, was a bedrock of acting: to have compellingly real experiences while moving a narrative forward. Rather than inhibit this, technique made it possible.

"You're getting better at this, David," Charlotte informed him after he and a classmate had put up a scene from *Julius Caesar*.

"I'm doing what you said."

"What's that?"

"Taking the training seriously while I wait for you to go out with me."

"It's paying off, and in more ways than you know."

Late that spring after he'd just put up a one-act he'd written about unrequited attraction that Adam helped him revise in back-and-forth missives to Israel, he made his way through the gauntlet of dancers toward the actor dressing rooms when he sensed eyes on him. He knew her to be the best friend of a woman dating one of his classmates. She was of Turkish descent but grew up in Philadelphia. Named Miray, she was big boned and strong, a good two inches taller than David, and he couldn't believe but that he was misinterpreting her unwavering gaze. That afternoon a note awaited him on the communal board. "It's clear from our morning eye contact that we should meet and see if the rest of us have the same curiosity our eyes do."

Over dinner that Friday, they found immediate rapport, though she advertised a healthy suspicion toward book learning, having broken up with what sounded like a truly repugnant Yalie several months prior.

"When he started sending my letters back with corrections, I'd had enough."

"Are you serious?"

"He called my prose 'atrocious.'"

"No."

"He actually said that on the phone. I can't spell for shit, and I write the way I speak. So what? I can look at women picking through the pears at Food Emporium and choreograph a dance from it. I can also bend over backwards and grab my ankles."

He had her clothes off before they'd made it halfway into his living room. She seemed to be enjoying it, though he remained fully dressed.

"This is like that Manet painting," he said.

"What?"

"*Luncheon in the Grass* it's called, or something like that."

"I don't know it."

"Two men fully clothed at a picnic by a stream with a naked woman."

"Got it."

"So, what's wrong?"

"I just feel like a body."

"You do?"

"Don't take this the wrong way, but it's pretty easy for me to have this. I can find any guy on any street corner."

"I don't doubt it."

"That dinner conversation, or what you wrote, that's what I'm interested in."

"Who's to say you can't have both?"

"You can ... ," she said, with little conviction. How was this even happening? Here he was, not a scrap of clothing removed, with an almost perfect specimen of a female body before him discussing what he was beginning to suspect underpinned every meaningful intimacy he had with women: the terms of how to relate.

"I liked our conversation too," he said, pleading. "How you see the world in terms of movement and not sound. How you perceive the air as something with density."

"Oh God, David, stop."

"What?"

"It's like you're arguing in front of some jury in my head to prove you listened to what I said at dinner so I'll go to bed with you."

"But I was interested in what you had to say at dinner."

"I actually believe that," she said, studying his face.

"So?"

"You didn't even bother to show me around, offer me a drink, even something cheesy like a fucking back rub."

"Back rubs aren't really my thing."

"Clearly."

"I find you attractive. Is that a problem?"

"When a man meets a woman, that's the first gauge. Is she attractive. Body, hair, skin, lips, ass, what would she be like fucking me. True or not true?"

"And women?"

"Men look. Women do too, but women listen."

"Do you find me attractive?"

"I do, David. I didn't, but I do."

"What do you mean, you didn't?"

"I'd watch you walk down the hall toward the drama division, always looking at the floor in front of you, as opposed to the guys who make eye contact and see if we'll look back, or even smile at us and talk to us, and I found you curious. Then I saw your play, heard it, and the next day when you walked down the hall, I had a different sense of you. You were looking at the floor not for you, or any shame you had, but for your sense of us and what we'd think of you if we caught you staring. It was this total retreat into yourself, and I found that decision, inside of the mind that wrote that play, kind of sexy."

"Jesus."

"Do you have that painting? I mean an image of that painting? *Picnic in the Grass*, or whatever you called it?"

"*Luncheon on the Grass*." He was already rising for his *Janson and Rosenblum's Nineteenth Century Art* from the same bookshelves that held the *Norton's Anthology* Charlotte had chosen—the shelves he and Adam had installed before he'd even bought a bed.

"Well, this is interesting," she said, staring at the color plate. "You didn't remember there are two women. There's one back there bathing, also naked, so there's more going on here than you described."

"I'm sure there is."

"And the one in the front is looking right at us. I wouldn't call her angry; it just seems like she knows something, maybe about us, that we don't. But what most distinguishes the two women?"

"You're going to say that they're naked."

"I am."

"I don't think Manet would agree with you."

"Then why are they naked? It's actually the fucking point! And these men aren't even paying attention to them; the one is just talking to his friend, which is probably the reason the woman is staring at the viewer. As if to say physical beauty aside, we're invisible. It's what we deal with every day of our lives. And her look is kind of asking if we realize that. When was this painted?"

"It should say there. Around 1860 I think."

She looked.

"1863. And what did people say about it?"

"It was very controversial."

"I bet it was. *Luncheon on the Grass*? It should be called 'Being a Woman.'"

She dropped the book between them and sat knees up, as if fully clothed, hiding neither her round, gorgeously proportioned breasts nor her vagina, turned up at him under its trimmed patch of hair. The entire episode, along with his instinctive response to it and her, seemed to be making her point.

"So, what now?"

"I think I go." She rose to gather her clothes, not rushing the process. This wasn't, it was clear, to punish him, but because the dignity she had claimed applied to her physical beauty as well. He wondered if he'd ever felt so humiliated.

"Are we going to try again?" he asked.

"I don't think so. But as weird as this sounds, I'm glad it happened."

"I'm going to put you in a cab."

"I'll take the subway."

"At least let me walk you down."

They waited in front of the turnstile until they could hear the 1 train arriving below. She leaned in to kiss him.

"That's more what I was after."

Back in his apartment he poured a vodka and sat staring at the Manet painting. At dinner she had described liking his play more for the *why* than the *what* of its characters, but he suspected she had read into the work qualities he'd never intended. Obviously, it was about his frustrations with Charlotte, something both women understood at some level.

"I'd love to know which of the actresses on the floor is the source of all that feeling," Miray had wondered aloud on their way from dinner to his apartment an hour before.

Charlotte had exposed no such curiosity.

"I'm glad you keep putting our situation to good use," she said, jabbing her chopsticks into his seven-dollar lunch special at a Chinese restaurant on Ninth Avenue.

"It wasn't just about you, Charlotte," he lied.

"At least let me think it was. Jesus, David!"

Though he forgave himself for the zeal with which he'd pursued something physical with Miray—he'd been thinking of it from the moment she initiated eye contact in the hall—he was overcome with regret. The world raced forward while he puttered in acting school writing slight little works that, to make matters worse, he himself didn't entirely understand. But mostly he thought of Charlotte. His pursuit of every woman, from Olivia to Miray and every misadventure in between, constituted a haphazard lunge toward what he wanted with that inexplicably remote woman from Louisiana who found him so easy to resist.

That summer he remained in the city and frequented the bar more and more, drinking too much and writing little. Letters from Adam berated him for the drop-off. By September he had nothing other than a one-act play—a sketch really—about what came most easily to him: hayseeds from West Virginia. It was as if his writing had regressed. He gathered most of the men in his class and handed out roles with apologetic reticence. Eager for second year to commence, and grateful for the opportunity to say words by a living writer, even if he was just a classmate, they projected enough enthusiasm to get the work on its feet, but little more. The skit lasted twenty minutes and was scheduled during lunch when anyone could attend. Miray appeared, along with a few other dancers, some musicians, and most of the drama division, including faculty, though Edmond predictably abstained. Afterward David caught Charlotte looking his way. She broke eye contact, but a half hour later he found a note from her requesting they meet.

"How was your summer?" she began. "You were here?"

"I was."

"What did you do? I hope more than write what we just saw."

"You didn't like it?"

"It was funny."

"Okay."

"You think it was more than that?"

They sat before the reflecting pool in the plaza that contained the Metropolitan Opera House, Avery Fisher Hall, and Lincoln Center Theater which stood low along the western edge. Beyond the Henry Moore sculpture in front of them loomed the school where they'd spend the next three years.

"I broke up with Alec over the summer."

"Wow."

"At the beginning of June actually, right before I left for New Orleans. I just didn't tell you."

"What does this have to do with me?" he asked tentatively.

"What do you think it has to do with you?"

"How do you know I'm not seeing someone?"

"If you were, you'd have written something more interesting than a skit that was more about what folks think people from West Virginia are like than what people from West Virginia are actually like."

"That was a complicated swipe."

"I want to go out with you, David. But I don't mess around."

"I'm aware of that."

"Are you willing to give it a try?"

"What, you think I'm out of my mind?"

It was as if every strand of his life, going back to eighth grade when he'd transformed as a student, through the welter of contradictions studying both classics and critical theory in college, to his friendship with Adam, who had demanded he take himself more seriously in every aspect of life from what he read to the women he dated, had led to her decision finally to be with him. Whereas over the summer he couldn't write, now he couldn't not write, and he did it for her. Not to please her, but to be worthy.

He also re-intensified correspondence with Adam, who in late September informed him he'd be returning from Israel just before Christmas. "You're not only writing again, but it's getting better, and it annoys me I can't take credit. Is it this woman? And without too much jinxing fanfare, I'm also working on something bigger finally, which I reveal not because I think the earth is going to shift in its axis, but because you and Sammy are constantly hectoring me about it. It's too big, as in voluminous, to ship off by mail, and I don't want to send a digital file—I still only trust paper and ink—but … in person before the year is out. I expect the next year to be great, so if you aren't nauseated by my uncharacteristic and sentimental optimism, get ready. I miss the hell out of you, David."

"I'm actually afraid you're going to fall in love with him," he told Charlotte.

"Why's that?"

"Looks. Talent."

"I look forward."

Most nights they slept at David's apartment, though hers was closer to school. He'd write late while she slept, printing after midnight on a temperamental machine that spat in piercing jolts as if shredding the paper. By Thanksgiving they'd christened every room in the drama division—classrooms, both dressing rooms, even Edmond's office one night during a fourth-year production of *Major Barbara* just down the hall. In spite of the intensity, or perhaps because of it, he also feared her: easily as smart as he, she was twice as shrewd, and as an actress none was more captivating. In the mornings he would wake and simply stare, thinking to himself, this has to end, I can't be so blessed.

They met Sammy, back from Paris, one night at the J&G after rehearsals for their second-year Shakespeare.

"You're dating a Black woman, David," he said with equal curiosity and respect when Charlotte stepped away to make a call. The comment surprised David, not because he found it inappropriate—after all, it was true—but because somehow he'd not considered it to be of enormous significance. Charlotte was simply the person with whom he needed to be. He realized suddenly he hadn't even informed his mother of the fact, though she'd be more relieved that Charlotte was part Jewish matrilineally than troubled by the ethnicity of the father.

He did remember a discussion with Charlotte early on.

"Would you rather be involved with a Black guy?"

"Well, obviously I have been. Alec was Black, and most others before him."

"So?"

"I guess aspects of my life would be simpler."

"How, specifically? I mean, I can guess, but …"

"The thing is, after Jim Crow it's not like the country got less racialized. It's just that the terms changed. You talk to my mom and dad, and they'll say a lot of whites in Louisiana, it just made them more pissed off. And with certain Blacks it was seen as barely a start—perfectly understandable when everything still felt rigged against them, but it just made them more militant because they wanted something more complete. To be frank, right now, I just want done with it all so I can get on with my life. Am I a proud Black woman? Of course. Is racism everywhere? Yes, and I hate it. I just don't want to make my blackness the whole of my life. There's a lot more to brothers and sisters than just being Black. The problem is, a lot of folks, Black and white, don't want that to be true."

The first semester ended on December twentieth, with students called into Edmond's office one by one to learn whether or not they were "warned," meaning possible dismissal at the end of the following semester. The school depended on this culling to make a class manageable for casting the fourth-year repertory. At least a third of their number would suffer this probation—meaning between seven and nine from their class of twenty— and then three to five asked not to return come May. Appointments were arranged by the four groups of five into which the year was divided, and as David was in group C, his meeting occurred after lunch. Charlotte, in group A, learned her fate, never in doubt, just before ten.

"He said my work has been 'perfectly lovely,' and that they couldn't ask for more."

"Of course he did. What else?"

"Allegedly I'm also pretty enough to play leading roles."

"Unbelievable they can say shit like that to us."

An epidemic of warnings began the afternoon session—three one after another before David finally entered Edmond's office at 3:10.

"Sit down, please."

"Hi, Edmond."

"These meetings are never easy, but we're not interested in lying to any of you."

"Okay."

"The faculty say you do what they ask and that you're improving. I find you difficult, frankly intolerable at times, always flaunting your education, but that's your business. I certainly wouldn't ever want to work with you."

"I have nothing but respect for you and this program."

"You're not going to have an easy time of it is my point, and you could do more to lessen the challenges you're going to face."

"What challenges are those?"

"For starters, with your looks you need a level of ability you're not showing us." What is it with this place and people's appearance? he asked himself for the second time that day.

"Am I warned?"

"Certain faculty members believe it'll be useful for someone like you to be out in the world with the training." David had little interest in mining the phrase "someone like you," though he did fight memories of his middle school French teacher. "We're going to keep you. But you're not going to get sizeable parts."

"So ... not wanting to be difficult here—"

"Is that meant as an attack?"

"I'm gathering information. When you say no sizeable parts ...?"

"You'll be in plays, and you'll have words to speak, but not of a plenitude where memorizing them will be difficult."

"It's almost worse," he told Charlotte as they packed for New Orleans, where he would meet her family. "As if they want me to choose to leave, rather than having to boot me out."

"Look, David, fuck them and what they say. Just learn all you can. It's like your friend Adam told you, get the education on your terms, not theirs."

"Do you think I deserve this?"

"Don't make me answer that."

"I guess you just did."

"I don't think you're an actor yet. No one does."

"You too?"

"I think you will be. And a writer and maybe even a director."

"When?"

"Obviously that's up to you. Edmond's doing you a favor. The guy loathes you, but he's keeping you around. They think you might actually go out and do something interesting. Prove them right about that and wrong about everything else."

He woke to the announcement of their descent over Lake Pontchartrain from a dream in which he'd taken Adam and Sammy to Charleston. They would live together in a house not dissimilar to the one in which he'd been raised. He considered its significance as he and Charlotte traversed the jetway.

Her father met them at baggage claim. The two had a guarded relationship, compelled by her having discovered him with another woman—the mother of a grade school friend—at the friend's house when Charlotte was twelve. What most startled her was that her mother showed little surprise when Charlotte ran the quarter mile home to inform her. It would take three years for her parents to divorce, by which time she came to understand that her dad, one of the most successful black attorneys in the city and a staunch Republican, had appetites he couldn't control, only one of which was for other women. Charlotte was convinced her mother still loved him, even though he was now remarried, this time to an African American woman ten years his junior and an attorney herself. So far as Charlotte knew, he'd given up philandering, along with alcohol, and was home for dinner by six thirty every night in Metairie with his new family. He was accountable to them in ways he hadn't been to Charlotte and her mother, but he'd never lost contact with his first daughter, never missed a child support payment in the wake of the divorce, and was covering her entire Juilliard tuition. Like David, she would be one of few students in the program to graduate without debt.

It struck David immediately how captivatingly handsome the man was. He stood straight and sturdy, just shy of six feet, with a wide jaw and Charlotte's strongly featured face. At his side stood one of the two children from his second marriage, the son, whose name was Matthias.

"The other's at home doing schoolwork," he explained, "under her mother's watchful eye. Tessa doesn't work as hard as you did, Charlotte, so we have to keep on her."

"You never had to ask Charlotte to do her homework?" David asked.

"We had to ask Charlotte to *stop* doing her homework," he responded, and David quickly understood that this man, whose name was Carlton, was as eager to make a good impression on David as David was on him, such was Charlotte's tacit power.

They ate at Jacques-Imo's, where Carlton insisted David try the shrimp and alligator sausage cheesecake and the Cajun bouillabaisse. David was desperate for a drink, and thankfully Charlotte ordered one for herself without her father showing offense. After she'd had a straight bourbon and he two NOLA blond ales, the conversation flowed more easily. An abundance of supplicants visited the table, evidencing Carlton's power and charm as well as a temptation he was entertaining to run for parish office and eventually mayor.

"Do you really want all that hassle, Daddy? And besides, wouldn't it be a pay cut?"

"Daughter of mine, you don't understand a thing, do you? A pay cut? Sure, for a few years. But politicians retire, go back to private practice. Besides, I love this city and think I could do it some good. The problems are fiscal."

"Please, no," said Charlotte, who was a Democrat and decidedly left of center.

"You can't offer services without a tax base, and you can't have a tax base without businesses hiring people. Business better than the government. Read Hayek's letters to Keynes."

"I'd rather not."

David had four beers at dinner, and by the time they reached Metairie he was in a torpid fog. They were given separate rooms. "Maddy doesn't want to answer questions about why you're sharing a bed without being married," Carlton explained.

David didn't wake until after ten, when Charlotte appeared at his bedside.

"Your mother is on the phone."

"How'd she get this number?"

In the kitchen he met Charlotte's stepmom, a petite, pretty woman in her late thirties who presented a cordless receiver.

"Thanks," he said, taking it. "Mom?"

"David, I don't know how else to tell you this, but your friend Sammy called ..."

"Yeah?"

"Adam Borstein was killed."

"What?"

"He was in Israel."

"Mom, I know where he was. What happened?"

"A bombing on a bus in Tel Aviv."

He reached for a chair and sat.

"Sammy wants you to call him as quickly as possible."

On their way to the airport Charlotte, who would remain in Louisiana, arranged that they meet her mother. In spite of her Boston roots she seemed as resolutely New Orleans as Charlotte's father.

"I wish I could tell you you'll move past this," she offered, taking his hand with disarming confidence at a coffee shop near her apartment in Mid-City. "But you won't. You're going to think about your friend at the most unexpected times for your whole life. And that's a good thing, if you'll let it be." He looked in her knowing eyes and, fully aware how the sudden loss of Adam informed the conviction, knew she would become his mother-in-law should Charlotte continue to find him worthy.

His cab crossed Manhattan through East Harlem, where Adam had once lived. Any prospect of a meaningful future felt hollow, even specious. He met Sammy for dinner at Hunan Balcony on Broadway, one of their old haunts as a trio. David's feelings of inadequacy, inspired by always having felt the least accomplished of the three, returned, and he could only conclude from the bitter, taciturn face opposite that it would have made more sense meritocratically for David to have perished. Thousands of Adam's journal entries, dozens of stories, and the beginnings of a novel proved it. Adam had curated who and what David was. And as it had transpired with David, so it had with countless others, because to have known Adam was in many ways to want to have *been* Adam.

A memorial service was held at the synagogue in which Adam had been bar mitzvahed in Cheltenham, just outside Philadelphia. David and Sammy stayed with Sammy's parents in the Center City apartment where Sammy had been raised. Along with Adam's brother and father, both Sammy and David delivered eulogies they'd sat writing the night before at the kitchen table where Sammy'd learned to use a knife and fork.

Several dozen contemporaries from Brown made the trip, from Boston, New York, Washington, and in many cases much farther, for the hastily organized event. It had been but four days since the bombing, and here they all were, without a body to inter, but mourning their friend nevertheless. At the reception David found himself in conversation with the same woman who'd once suspected Adam and David were lovers. They stood awkwardly over plates of smoked salmon.

"How could I not have thought it? You guys were together day and night. You carried the same books, used the same words. If I didn't find you both attractive, I wouldn't have been so freaked out."

"Wait. Because we might have been gay?"

"Because I wanted in on the action."

"You've got to pursue that, David," Sammy urged. "If Adam knew that you had the opportunity to get some nookie over his funeral meats, he'd want that to happen. That smoked salmon could ... what is it? You're the Shakespeare guy ..."

"'Coldly furnish forth the marriage tables.'"

"Exactly!"

"Maybe a while back, Sammy."

On the train back to New York alone that evening, having shunned an opportunity he once would have craved, David understood that the near simultaneity of Adam's passing and a future with Charlotte defined the inescapable: his adult life had begun.

LONG ISLAND

B rad Shlansky received the rare incoming call from someone other than one of his sisters during his morning workout in the basement of his home in the Los Feliz section of Los Angeles where he lived with his wife and their twin boys, who'd just turned two.

"Did you hear about David Levit?"

"What about him?"

"He's casting a new movie."

"How do you know that?"

"We discussed it in our staff meeting. Plus, the producer slipped it to me for Claire Fisher a few weeks back, which I didn't tell you because you've been so fucking moody lately."

"Who's the producer?"

"Jacob Rosenthal."

"Don't know him."

"One of the biggest pricks in LA. But he gets his movies made. Directors rarely work for him twice. David Levit is in for a rude awakening, but people are high on the script. Jacob Rosenthal swings for Oscars, and this wouldn't be his first."

Brad did his best to ignore the titillated mockery.

"What's the film?"

"It's based on a novel even you've heard of."

"What the fuck is that supposed to mean?"

"Let's just say you're not exactly the literary type."

"And what, suddenly you graduated from Princeton?"

"Ever hear of a novel called *Coal*?"

"Yeah, I've heard of it."

"People have been trying to make it forever."

"Then why haven't they?"

"I have to tell you it's hard to get a movie made?"

"What's it about?"

"Kind of deals with the Black Lives Matter business."

"Wasn't it written a dozen years ago?"

"So, it was ahead of its time. When Jacob Rosenthal bought it last year, it was all over the trades. It looks like David Levit can get a movie made so long as you're not producing it!"

Undisguised cackling ensued, then a pause during which Paul Aiello, the sole Italian American partner at United Creative Management, where Brad was represented as a producer, was taking a victorious sip of the black coffee from the mug refilled by his assistant all morning.

"You done?" Brad asked.

"I can hear you seething through the phone. I told you not to try and make *Appalachian Winter* with that stuck-up Ivy League dickhead. And now here he is moving on with another movie already set up while you and Sarah and Emily are sitting there with your thumbs up your asses."

"And whose fault is that?"

"I've given you every opportunity."

"Talk to my pals at Lone Star Pulp lately?"

"This morning in fact."

"Well, good for you."

"Seriously though. How long has it been since *Revenge*?"

"I'm not counting. But clearly you are."

"Me? I was busy all night."

"Where'd you meet this one? A casting session at Beverly Hills High?"

"Capo in Santa Monica actually."

"When is David supposed to be making this film?"

"If it's being talked about in our staff meeting, it's already in the works. You complain about me? And the Lone Star guys? He's making you look like a fucking dope, Brad. He's leaving you in the dust!"

Brad both admired and reviled Paul, but this was true of many with whom he had significant interactions in Los Angeles. They'd bonded long ago as young coin collectors on Long Island, where Brad's collection had begun the day he wandered into Bill's Coins and Stamps in the same shopping strip in the town of Woodmere where his parents presided over one of a half dozen check-cashing establishments that catered mostly to an African American, Hispanic, and immigrant clientele.

"Without us these people would have no place to go," Brad's father, Carl, told Brad and his sisters, Sarah and Emily. "No way of converting a piece of paper with typing and scribbles into cash they can use. Do we charge for it? I have a family to raise and feed, rent to pay at the stores, and extra insurance and security in case some animal who knows we're a cash business comes in waving a pistol like a maniac. These drugs—cocaine, crack cocaine, heroin. I almost don't want to go to work, it makes me so sad. And by the way, does the clothes store charge for pants and shirts? The barber to cut your hair? Does my uncle charge for the groceries he sells? Without me and your mother, what would these people, and most of them are good people, what would they do? Tell that to anyone who judges."

His father had been meticulous choosing locations, the most profitable being near discount groceries and liquor stores. Ideally, one found an interior of the right size at the right price near both. Customers paid, depending on the year's law, between 2 and 2.2 percent of the face value of any check, or one dollar, whichever was higher, rendering it a high-volume, work-intensive but remunerative business.

Carl Shlansky liked to say he had no monopoly on imagination. It didn't take a genius to understand, as he had when he worked stocking shelves at his uncle Julian's discount grocery in Inwood during his teens, that for the ten or so Blacks or Hispanics and sometimes Italians who came in daily with checks his uncle refused to cash, there were probably a hundred more asking elsewhere. When at the age of twenty he suggested his employer add the manifestly underrepresented service, his father's brother demurred.

"I sell people Pop-Tarts and beer day and night. I don't need to cash their goddamn checks. That's what banks are for. Besides, you know what sort of interest I'd have to charge? It would be immoral."

"It's probably regulated like everything."

"How do you know from 'regulated'?"

"I've started to look into it."

"So if it is regulated, all the more reason to stay the hell out of it. I've got enough of that with the government and the goddamn inspectors."

"The point is, the bank won't give them accounts without minimum balances, and these people live hand to mouth. It's terrible the way they're treated."

"Why is that my problem?"

"You're a part of their community. Not to mention that making it your problem could be profitable."

"One thing I'm not is part of their community. And they'll tell you that faster than I will."

"Without them you wouldn't have a business."

"And without me they wouldn't put an affordable dinner on the table. Everyone wins."

"You could provide something they need. I've looked at it in the Rock-aways, and these places do very well."

"Please. The Rockaways. And again, we get to the question of morality. Making people pay for their cash."

"Uncle Julian, the banks do that. It's a service. And you sell, let's just say, less-than-healthy food to them!"

"'Them'? What a Freedom Rider you are."

"My point is, why don't you diversify?"

"Listen to the vocabulary. Do me a favor. Go take a basic course in eco-nomics and then come back to me. How is it diversifying to offer a service to the same clientele I'm already depending on? Diversifying would be to open a clothes shop in Roslyn. Different product, different clientele. You like that word? Clientele? That's what they call customers on the North Shore where I would 'diversify.'"

When at twenty-three Carl solicited banks to try the idea on his own, he had neither the collateral nor the credit history, fueling his desire even more to serve those deemed insufficiently solvent by the same institutions now rejecting him. His uncle fronted the money, and at a low rate. Carl had been his hardest worker for three years, and not once had he snuck his hand into the till. Moreover, he was family, and to Shlanskys, family was everything.

Carl rented space a block away from his uncle, and in addition to check cashing, he offered bill-payment services, money orders, money transfers, and simple concessions for the peckish. A synergy evolved. Proximity to his uncle's grocery meant more business, and his uncle's location now be-ing within walking distance of a check-cashing establishment furnished an edge over his own competitors in the area. After a year, uninterested in pride inhibiting growth, Carl collateralized his single store at one of the same banks that had originally denied him and opened another in North Valley Stream. By the time he'd met his future wife, a blond beauty from Merrick named Miriam, he'd established a third in Far Rockaway, with three more to come.

When he was six his parents moved Brad and his two sisters to the south of his father's new flagship Woodmere location into a home Brad could proudly observe to be bigger than those of all but a few of his friends. Each child had a capacious second-floor room, and a den off the living room downstairs was large enough to host movie nights every Sunday. The house became a sort of hub, in part because of its address on the leafy and centrally located Longacre Avenue in Woodmere Park but also because

Brad's mother, who left work reliably by 2 p.m. each day, made it such a place—the door always open, the refrigerator reliably stocked, table leaves at the ready for as many settings as might be required come dinner.

By the time Brad reached fifteen, his coins and the equipment essential for their storage and display had colonized the Shlansky basement. Brad had become expert not only at the most up-to-date market fluctuations of every year and place of origin of every type of American minted tender but on how to treat and care for their example. He had also cultivated an authority and vocabulary that made him one of the sharpest traders in not just the five adjoining towns of Woodmere, Cedarhurst, Lawrence, Inwood, and Hewlett but all of Nassau County.

He often looked back in wonder at those years. The animating discovery occurred by chance just after his tenth birthday. His mother had hosted a United Jewish Appeal fundraiser, very much against Carl Shlansky's wishes, particularly in the context of his work.

"Go ahead, just put a big menorah in the yard, Miriam. Or maybe we put yellow stars right there on the door of every store, just so there's no doubt the check cashers are Hymies."

"Bite your tongue. And our name is Shlansky. Our stores are called Shlansky's Same Day."

"Not everyone knows that's a Jewish name."

Brad's older sister, Emily, then thirteen, laughed. "I think you'd lose that one, Dad. And doesn't Marvin wear a kippah in the store?"

"In the Woodmere location, which he never leaves, smart aleck," his father shot back. "We don't need to announce the fact is the point."

"We're having the fundraiser precisely to fight the kind of prejudice you're scared of," said Brad's mother.

"Don't talk to me about prejudice with what the poor people we serve go through."

"Say that when they're burning our stores down. Because let me tell you something, buster, they would much rather deal with the banks than the Jew check cashers."

"All the more reason not to draw the attention!"

But the event had gone on, and to express her zeal, Miriam had brought out her wedding silver for food she spent days preparing. The rabbi spoke at length, along with the vice chair for the eastern seaboard who traveled in from Washington.

"Do the attendees understand," he asked the spellbound gathering, "that there are more Jews in New York than in all of Israel? And this tiny country, not half a century old, has already fought three wars against an array of more than formidable neighbors on all sides. Imagine, and I know it's difficult, because here we are after all, in the greatest, richest country in the world, among three hundred million—not to mention America has treaties with England, France, Japan, Australia, even a now reunified Germany if you can believe that one—but forget all that and imagine we're a tiny country. Not big America, sea to shining sea, but a little nation barely the size of Rhode Island. And we're attacked not just by Canada but by Mexico, and all of South America and the Caribbean. Even Bermuda joins in the fun. And no one there to defend us. In fact, most of the world wishes we'd lose! That's Israel without help from people like you. And for those who would say it's all about land and settlements, I say, then why did Israel sign Oslo last year? And now, just a few weeks, ago a second accord in Egypt? And President Rabin offering the open hand and not the fist! President Clinton doing the same!"

"Miriam, this was the greatest event of its kind I've ever attended," volunteered a fawning Rabbi Simkin at evening's end. "I'll get you the totals tomorrow, but this was big."

When Brad returned from school the following afternoon, Jacintha, their housekeeper from before Brad's birth—"truly a second, third, and fourth mother to you and the girls," as Miriam Shlansky took pains to describe—was still cleaning the silver. He'd been told by every serious collector and seller he'd met that under no circumstances was he ever to polish his coins, as doing so would not only abrade them but initiate chemical reactions that could never be undone, such damage always detectible to the most cursory glance of the experienced numismatist. He could not believe, however, the sudden luster of the spoons, forks, knives, and serving utensils moribund with tarnish just the day before.

Snatching a cookie still warm from the baking sheet, he scurried downstairs to his Mercury dimes, by then already numbering in the dozens, and found the 1945D "fair" that had been thrown in as a lagniappe with the "mint" 1904S Morgan dollar he'd purchased recently with two months of chore money. After a brief tutorial, he set to work with Jacintha's polishing rag. In fewer than twenty seconds and with minimal effort, he'd improved, at least to the unpracticed eye, a coin dulled by decades of indifferent circulation to one that might have been delivered to his kitchen from the mint in Denver the week of its striking were it not for some barely discernible wear.

Holding the specimen by its edges, he began to devise a plan that began with separating every silver coin of little to moderate worth from his collection. By the end of the evening, with the aid of the polish and a fresh rag, he'd transformed each of these, most into representations of "fine," and some into "very fine," careful to vary his work to avoid suspicious uniformity. He also reorganized his examination area into something that approximated public display, doing the same with the basement itself. What had been off-limits to others since his parents permitted its colonization would now become something of an emporium.

In the sixth grade at Woodmere Academy Brad, who had an enviable head of thick curls, blond like his mother's, struggled with acne and was by no means sought out socially, nor did he feel particularly liked by the more popular kids with their clear skin, slender bodies, and burgeoning good looks. Yet with his nimble mind and keen taste for what interested other boys ostracized like him, he'd become a leader of sorts. When he'd begun collecting coins in the summer of his ninth year those among this cadre of misfits took an interest. By the time they were ten, the pursuit was all the rage.

Simon Zeligson's size alone could easily have earned him the distinction of the runt of this group. But his low status still puzzled Brad because he also knew Simon to be the smartest, particularly at math, in the entire grade at a school that prized academics. With his dark hair, pale skin, and almost impossibly anemic frame, he sat at the front of each class and demonstrated his acuities with such passion that even some of the instructors were put off. He dined at the Shlanskys' often and in political discussions with Brad's father flashed a fluency with the day's events rare among adults, let alone eleven-year-olds. How, Brad would often wonder, can this star in the classroom and marvel to parents be such a loser in our cohort? Perhaps, Brad suspected, everyone understood, including the teachers, that pipsqueak Simon had more assurance of success later in life than any of them, and each felt entitled to get their licks in while they could.

It therefore didn't bother Brad in the least to test his business plan on Simon before anyone else. Nor did it dissuade that the pipsqueak possessed a 1950D Jefferson nickel in "very fine" condition, a coin Brad had been coveting since Simon had received it for Chanukah months before. He called and instructed its owner to bring it to school the next day, and together they would come directly to the Shlanskys' once last bell had rung. After a couple of cookies and hot chocolates, they descended to the basement where Brad had laid out three newly gleaming Mercury dimes on a patch of blue felt promoted from his sister Emily's bin in the craft room on the second floor. These consisted of the 1945D that had been the result of his initial experiment, a 1938S, and a 1929P. They shined brilliantly on their azure carpet, heads up, perfectly parallel in profile, wings snug to helmets, chins jutting forward, as if waiting for Jupiter to dispatch them on errands.

"Whoa," said Simon.

"Can you believe it?"

"Where did you get these?'

"My dad took me to a guy in the city."

"Whoa," he said again. "A dealer in the city?"

"You know it, man."

"Jesus ..." Simon reached.

"Don't even think about it." Brad produced a disposable plastic glove of the sort Jacintha had worn when cleaning his mother's service. "Put this on. All three of them are practically mint. They shouldn't even be out in the air, but I wanted you to get a good look."

Simon sheathed his hand eagerly.

"Slow down, dude. We've got all afternoon."

"This is insane. It's like being in the coin shop."

"Bill would shit his pants if he saw these."

"But a '45D isn't exactly rare."

"Listen to this guy. In near mint it's still pretty insane."

The glove on, Simon inclined a supplicating glance.

"Go crazy, man," Brad encouraged. "I just didn't want your fingers. One print and the thing loses half its value under the loop. Or," Brad threw in perilously, "I'd have to polish it, which even a naked eye would detect, and then all the money I saved up to buy it would be down the drain."

Simon lifted the coin with comical reverence.

"At Bill's this would be in hard plastic," he whined.

"Exactly," agreed Brad, "which is where these are gonna go back once you're through looking at them. Here." He handed Simon his loop, swinging the device open on the hinge from inside its tear-shaped covering. As Simon pulled the magnifier to his eye, Brad continued his soothingly enthusiastic patter. "The gleam is fucking insane. There's not a blemish. It's what silver is supposed to look like. And you get every detail on the pileus."

"The what?"

"The liberty cap. The helmet. Every bit of the feathering too. And do you see the details on the nose? You can practically smell with it. You can smell him smelling! Check out the back." Simon turned the coin over. "Is the olive branch insane, or what?"

"It's amazing."

"And the fasces?"

"Is that what that column is?"

"The staff of justice. Can you believe the definition? You can count the fluting. And look at the horizontals."

"How do you always know so much more than the rest of us?"

"What are you talking about? I'm obsessed with this shit, the way you are about politics."

"And what are these?" Simon pointed at the two coins below.

"Well, you've got a 38S and a 29P. Check 'em out."

"From the same place?"

"Exactly."

Simon replaced the coin he held and took up the one just behind it.

"The 29P is 'very fine.' A tad less definition."

Simon was already examining it, the loop snug to his glasses over his left eye.

"How can you tell?"

"For starters, if you look really close at the wings on the helmet, the feathering isn't as detailed as the '45. Then the 'e pluribus.' It's very faint, but you can see some smudging. Also, it's just not as pristine all around. It was in circulation. Barely, and I mean barely, but it was. Probably mostly sat in a roll in a bank somewhere."

"Wow." Simon turned the coin over.

"Now, on the fasces you can also see a tiny bit of wear, and a nick just below the middle horizontal." Brad had despaired over this the previous night, mostly for just having noticed it. Had it been adduced in the negotiation, the imperfection would have saved him at least thirty cents.

"Yeah, I see it."

"Now, you go to Bill's, they're not gonna point that out, but I'm actually as interested in the flaws as I am in perfection. Like, where did that nick come from? Some woman's fingernail? If so, where's the woman? Is she still alive? But that coin was barely in circulation. So this is where it gets really interesting. Was it something in the reducing machine or the hub or the die when the coin was struck? Where's the die, even? Still in Philadelphia? In a museum somewhere?"

"That's so cool."

"But regardless, there's an imperfection, and if it's from the striking process, it could make the coin more valuable, not less. Suddenly a coin that's worth seven bucks is worth five hundred, maybe five thousand, which is what's amazing about collecting."

"You think that's possible with this?"

"Of course it's possible. Is it likely? Who the fuck knows? There's a flaw there, though, on a coin that sat in a roll in a bank vault. Very few collectible imperfections are as obvious as a 1955 double die or some penny with a quarter stamp, where there's just no other way the coin would look like that even though they got into circulation before the mint figured out they'd screwed up. It's like I said, the shit that doesn't get noticed at the time, but because it gets noticed later, it can be totally crazy. That's why you collect. It's like finding treasure in your backyard. But you gotta live and breathe it, which is what I do."

Little Brad had said could be described as false, other than every word concerning the provenance of the coin Simon held and that of those below. His description of the collector's pursuit, always in search of the undiscovered and overlooked, reflected, for all the irony of it, unvarnished truth.

"Look at it this way," he continued. "There are two kinds of collectors: the ones who do it almost like robots, filling their books until the last slot is filled, which if you have the money, since we're so close to New York and Philadelphia, you can do. You see these guys at the shows with their stacks of blue books and binders. They finish wheat pennies, they move onto Indian heads. They do that, then it's buffalo nickels. I'm after the shit no one even knows is there until it is, and then everyone kicks themselves because they never realized it. Of course, no two coins look alike, so you can go nuts, but to me 'error collecting' is what it's all about. That nick right there could be from a fingernail, but it could be a die crack, which is fucking insane. Who the fuck knows?"

"It's so cool."

"Get a look at the '38S." Simon lifted the final coin. "That's what I love about you, Simon. You get it."

"What do you mean?" Simon asked, his cheeks reddening, tragically unused to compliments from any of the boys in his class.

"Jonathan and Greg, or Nathan, even with the glove on would be pawing these like they were about to stick 'em in a vending machine."

Simon once more applied the loop. "So is this one mint?"

"Absolutely, unless the seller ripped me off, which he didn't, I can assure you. The shop's in Midtown. You should have seen the money changing hands and the trades that were going on. Way over my head. It was fucking big league. All right. I'm gonna put these up so we can play Ping-Pong."

"But wait, I thought ..."

"What?"

"That we were gonna … maybe trade."

"For what?"

"My '50D. I brought it."

"Oh shit, man, I completely forgot. Here's the thing. When I called you about that I had misread the Yeoman," he said, referring to the coin collector's bible.

"What do you mean?"

"I thought I could do a fair trade with these three straight up for your nickel, but I'd be ripping you off."

"By how much?"

"Gimme a sec." He took up his Yeoman 1995 and thumbed through. "I looked it up last night after we talked, but I want to make sure. Yeah …" He paused, seeming to tote in his head. "A little over five-fifty."

"Shit."

"Plus, Simon, I thought about it, and your parents gave you that coin."

"I know, but these dimes are insane. And three of them."

"I'm just not gonna rip you off, dude. I mean …" He paused once more, aping further rumination.

"What, Brad?"

"Hang on a sec." He crossed the room to the desk where just the evening before he had organized his books and cases, along with his second viewing lamp and collector-approved cleaning fluids for more immaculate display. He seized a book of Indian head pennies.

"Let me just make sure …" He took up the Yeoman once more, finding the appropriate listings as if to confirm what he suspected. "Yeah…all right, to make this work, I'll throw in an 1892S Indian head 'very fine' and it's a fair deal."

"But are you sure you want to trade the dimes?"

"First off, I can see how much you want them. And secondly, I'm going back next weekend, and practically every coin in the store is 'uncirculated' or 'extremely fine.'"

"Can I come with you?"

"I actually tried to invite you this past weekend, and my dad said this was supposed to be just him-and-me time. Not even Emily and Sarah were allowed."

"Are you serious?"

"He's on a fuckin' kick."

Simon's '50D nickel was worth twenty-three dollars, due to its low mint-age of 1.63 million immediately recognized by speculators, taking many of the coins out of circulation within a year of their striking. The 1892 Indian head, in "very fine," the feathered headdress resplendent with detail, and every letter of LIBERTY practically jumping into the loop from inside the headband, had a book value of six dollars, which Brad had represented accurately. The three dimes, though now virtually worthless from their encounter with the offending polish, had cost Brad two dollars between them. Brad had added thirteen dollars of value to his collection.

When they emerged from the basement he wanted Simon gone. He needed space to contextualize the transaction in a way that allowed it to sit comfortably because he had no intention to desist. The gains he imagined were simply too great. One problem presented itself, however, and it had to be solved before Simon's restlessly protective mother arrived to drive him the four blocks to his home two streets over: how to keep the coins he'd just traded from presentation at Bill's Coins, where Simon might be divested of his pride in such tainted merchandise.

"Look," Brad said, "you're going to bring those to school; I know I can't stop you from that." Brad even wanted this, since it would advertise to others the opportunity to have their collections hollowed of their value. "But don't, ever, under any circumstance, take them into Bill's."

"Why not?"

"Are you kidding me?"

"What?"

"If he finds out I'm going into the city and buying coins there to trade— coins he can't get his hands on out here—he won't let me in his store. He'll go nuts. He'd probably call the police."

"The police?"

"I'm practically acting like a store here. I mean not really, because unlike him I'm not making a profit. And of course I'm allowed to trade like any other schmuck, but this is high, high level. I'm taking business from him, and not paying rent or taxes."

"I never even thought of it that way."

"Why would you? You're too busy being the smartest kid in our whole class. But we're all going to benefit from this, because if I can keep getting my dad to take me into the city for our 'Brad and Dad time,' I'm gonna be bringing back some crazy shit, and, trust me, sharing the wealth."

Back in his basement, Brad reasoned it out. Simon's nickel was better off with him. It was Carl Shlansky, not Simon's father, who toiled seven days a week and took to bringing Brad along weekends to a shopping strip next to Bill's. It was Brad, not Simon or any of his friends, who bought a first, then a second, and then a dozen wheat pennies, half filling a book methodically over three months before bringing it triumphantly to school. It was Brad uniquely among the group who had paid for or traded for nearly every coin he had. As for Simon and his Jefferson '50D, until he'd been given it on the third night of Chanukah—not even his biggest present!—Simon had had no interest whatsoever in the coin. Instead, his reedy-voiced father had skulked into Bill's on his way home from a day filling molars in Cedarhurst and asked in his pathetically meek way what could be had for under thirty bucks. He'd probably even been overcharged. Brad collected the way he saw adults do it, as a long-term obsessive who understood the valuation of every piece. If a boy such as Simon really appreciated the pursuit, would he have been snookered so easily? Any numismatist with serious interest could discern when a coin had been buffed with an offending polish; for this very reason was the practice so vehemently discouraged. And with a superfluity of such dilettantes in the grade, Brad felt justified arrogating to himself not only the right but the obligation to gather as many under-appreciated specimens as he could from whoever might succumb to his methods. He'd show no mercy.

Over the next three years he was relentless, and miraculously, not once did any of his friends ever expose a corrupted example at Bill's. More aston-ishing, he successfully inhibited their presentation in any venue at all—whether store, convention, or swap meet—by continuing to promulgate the threat of constables showing up at his door. It also helped that gradu-ally his peers began to migrate to other pursuits: sports, Model UN, jazz band, D&D, and eventually girls, leaving choice coins neglected in closets and drawers. And while his friends' interest waned, their need for dispos-able income increased. One by one rump collections went to Brad, willing but never desperate to buy at a discount, excluding of course any of the coins that had originated with him, which he explained were beyond his ability to afford. Occasionally he was accused of being an erstwhile swindler, accusations he denied aggressively, protesting that he too had been hood-winked when a credulous novice.

In time he could operate in circles well beyond his school and Bill's Coins. While he did still frequent the shop, usually to meet other traders, given its proximity to the flagship Shlansky's Same Day, he no longer pur-chased from Bill himself, who he'd long understood applied a considerable markup. Besides, having developed the ability from so many years with his

Five Towns peers, he found it easy to identify the weakest among traders he encountered elsewhere and swiftly relieve them of coins they too were ill equipped to appreciate.

Halfway through his eighteenth year his parents announced that insurance appraisers would visit the house within the week. After questions as to why were deflected, Brad asked that his collection be included in the remit. The cheery duo, a man and woman in their fifties who'd spent the day itemizing every piece of jewelry, furniture, art, and silver, entered the basement expecting an adolescent's hobby, the valuation of which could be swiftly generalized for a nominal fee. They refused even to begin when they saw the extent of what the curly blond teen revealed.

"Even if we had the expertise, which we don't, it would take a full day," said the gentleman, turning from Miriam to Brad. "You've got an entire store down there, young man. On first glance I'd wager it's worth more than your mother's jewelry. A lot more."

"Well," said Miriam Shlansky, more impressed than offended, "it looks like we're going to need to bring in an expert."

"There's no hurry, Mom. I was just curious."

"Well, now so am I!"

Three months later, with Brad's older sister, Emily, away at college, Brad and his younger sister, Sarah, returned home from school for a quick dinner before rehearsals for a high school production of *Twelfth Night* to find neither of their parents home. Jacintha knew only that their mother had called, frantic with instructions and stingy with explanation, insisting that dinner be served to her children, and that she would be home as soon as she could. Never in his seventeen years could Brad remember his mother missing a family meal. His father had been absent perhaps a dozen times in that stretch, and exclusively because of problems at one of the stores. Throughout dinner neither sibling spoke. Sarah, fair-haired like Brad and her mother and, also like Brad, of sturdy build like their father, stared into her plate, not taking a bite, each of them overcome by the grave certainty their lives were about to change. Still, they went to rehearsals afterward, where she was stage-managing and he playing Toby Belch. When they got back, their mother still had not returned.

Just after eleven thirty she burst through the kitchen door, a riot of hysteria and tears. Their father was in intensive care. He had collapsed in the process of cashing a pension check. His heart had failed. The doctors warned of little hope—why had he never seen a cardiologist sooner? they kept asking, particularly given his past as a smoker—but she didn't believe them. Carl Shlansky was going to pull through. Their mother would return to the hospital with her toothbrush and a change of clothes and remain there until he could leave with her.

"Was there any warning of this?" Brad was able to ask.

"No!"

"Mom, I can tell you're lying."

"There's been a lot of stress, Brad. Three weeks ago he had pains, which he always does from the Szechuan, but he was having trouble breathing and had to lie down for an hour. Then it passed. The same thing four months ago."

"Is that why the appraisal?"

"What?"

"Remember, when I tried to get them to do my coins?"

"No! Everything's a mess! I'm so scared!"

"What do you mean, everything's a mess?"

"I don't want to go into it! And now this!"

Miriam and Carl Shlansky, adored by so many, especially their children, lived exclusively within the confines of work and home. No activities taxed them in any way other than maintaining their six stores, the occasional fundraiser, and providing for Brad and his sisters. Neither was particularly heavy, but nor were they what one would call slender. While earlier in his life Brad had heard them discuss the health concerns associated with aging, their eventual solution had been not to change their behavior or routines in any way other than to stop seeing doctors.

"Look at me," his father once said, raising the first of the two to three beers he would drink each night with dinner. "I'm healthy the way a modern man should be healthy. I work my ass off, and I'm comfortable because of it. I have three beautiful children and a wife I completely adore. I eat what I want when I want, and I enjoy it. What, I'm supposed to do sit-ups at a gym or run around the block? Take a goddamn aerobics class? I'm on my feet all day, which trust me, if I weren't, I'd have a belly like you wouldn't believe. I want to enjoy my family when I'm not working. Otherwise, what's civilization for?" Brad thought of this watching his mother ululate in the kitchen, violent dread passing through her in waves as she struggled with the fear her husband wouldn't last the night. Carl Shlansky made it to morning, but barely, expiring just after dawn while Miriam held his hand. She remained in the hospital, to which Brad and Sarah were summoned, and by the time they arrived she was in a room of her own, heavily sedated.

"Your mother is in very poor shape," the doctor informed him out of earshot from a hysterical Sarah.

"When you say poor ..."

"Her heart shows stress like your father's, and her kidneys are a wreck, but there's the emotional component as well. I gather your parents were very close."

"Yes. Sort of obsessed with each other."

"She's going to wake up in about seven hours, but judging from how she was this morning, I doubt she'll be ready to leave. I can send her to the psychiatric wing, but I'd rather not do that if we can monitor and stabilize her here and continue running tests."

"Of course."

"Are you aware of any medical power of attorney your mother has?"

"My father."

"Anyone else?"

"Not that I know of."

"How old are you?"

"Almost eighteen. We have a sister who's twenty-one."

"Where is she?"

"On her way from Ithaca."

"Cornell? My niece is there."

"Ithaca College."

"Ah." He nodded. "Well, your sister's going to need to sign forms."

Emily's assent unleashed the hospital's full powers not only for his mother's recovery but for a battery of diagnostics prescribed for her future welfare. When the new widow awoke, she cleared the room of everyone but Brad.

"Mom, Emily and Sarah want to be with you."

"Shush, Brad. You have to go to the flagship. You need to let them know what happened, and you have to assure them I'm coming back. Make sure they understand, Brad. But I also need you there while I'm not."

"That's fine. Whatever you want. I love you, Mom, but I have school. And rehearsals. Besides, I should be here with you."

"I have Emily and Sarah, darling. You can go to rehearsals after the store closes every day, and you can visit me when you can, but if you're not here, I'll know you want to be, which is what's important. As for school, you could pass your courses at that ridiculous place without going to a single class for the rest of the year, and you know it. The only reason you don't get better grades is because you're more interested in your coins than schoolwork. Besides, this is temporary what I'm asking. I just need one of us at the store."

"Why not Emily? She's older."

"I adore Emily. She's plenty smart, but she's soft." It was true. Darker-haired and the heaviest in the family, Emily seemed to have as her chief goal in life to do no harm. "You go in, talk to Marvin and the others. Let them know firmly that you've got your eye on all of them. And keep everyone but Marvin out of the safes, do you hear me? Out of the safes."

"I'm a seventeen-year-old kid, Mom!"

"And smarter than anyone I know, with a coin collection worth more than my jewelry. We run a cash enterprise, and they need to know they're all being minded. This is a family business, Brad, and that's how family businesses work. You step up and you take care of your own. It's a few goddamn days."

She remained in the hospital for four, in each more lucid than the one previous, and on fewer drugs, though the tears wouldn't relent. The doctors prescribed a Mishna of dietary restrictions, along with an antide-pressant. Brad presided dutifully at the store, each teacher keeping him apprised of required classwork so he wouldn't fall behind. Without his coins for distraction, he had hours each day to get a sense of how the operation worked.

For starters, when his mother had referred to it as a cash business, she hadn't simply been describing the trade of legal tender minus fees for each check presented. As if ignoring all modern convention, Shlansky's Same Day relied on as little electronic bookkeeping as possible. Bank accounts existed for each location to be sure, along with a central ledger to which the others were tied, but a quick examination exposed even to seventeen-year-old Brad what could not possibly be a comprehensive rendering of his parents' small empire.

"Sure, those are the books," confirmed Marvin Liebner, the Shlanskys' most trusted adjutant, "but your parents have always preferred to keep some money aside not reflected on paper."

"How much money?"

"Only your father, *alav hashalom*, knew that," Marvin responded. He walked Brad to the safe in the back. "And only he knew the combination. And of course your mother."

"So basically they're—"

"Stop right there," Marvin interrupted firmly from beneath his kippah.

"What do you mean?"

"I mean I don't know from 'basically' or anything else, and I don't want to know. So tell your mother not to worry."

"Okay... ," said Brad uncertainly. "I'm still not sure I ..."

"Let's just say that your father has always felt that the government is owed its due, but not *more* than its due, which goes for federal and the State of New York. Especially the State of New York for telling him what he could and couldn't charge on a percentage per check, knocking off basis points year after year instead of letting the market dictate."

"How much do you *think* is in that safe?"

"This or any of the other safes? My guess, a lot. You ever see either of your parents use a credit card?"

Carl Shlansky loathed debt, spiritual or tangible, and other than borrowing against his stores for early expansion, he conducted his life in avoidance of it. He'd purchased the house on Longacre Avenue with a small mortgage, and only then because Miriam, desperate to live in Woodmere Park, had fixated on the place and they feared amassing the cash would outlast its time on the market. At fifty thousand dollars on a fifteen-year fixed, it was the greatest amount he'd owed since his first expansion and he'd paid it off in six years, much to the bank's surprise given the low rate. As for credit cards, he and his wife each had one, but "only for absolute emergencies," meaning month after month of negligible bills. Interrogations from Carl would persist nevertheless, the inquests so demeaning to their mother that Brad and his siblings would absent themselves out of embarrassment for her.

"I don't understand, Dad."

"The credit card companies want you to spend, and they want you not to pay."

"But if you pay on time, there's no charge."

"You're not listening, you're speaking."

"Go on."

"First off, you're wrong because there's a yearly fee, and if not, other hidden charges as well. And the more you spend, the more addicted you become. It's like with anything. Once you're hooked, you start thinking about money in a different way, and inevitably you can't control yourself and you lay out more than you have, meaning you no longer pay on time because you can't, and they've got you. This is why I hound your mother the way I do. Let her start spending on that piece of plastic now, and in a year the bills will be in five figures, and I'm paying their eighteen percent."

"I don't see Mom like that."

"Who's in the check-cashing business handling people and their money every day, you or me?"

"You."

"You have no idea. You may be right about your mother, but I'll be damned if I'll take the chance, especially as much as she loves all of you and wants you to have whatever she thinks will bring a smile to your faces. Jesus Christ, we already feed half that goddamn school as it is. Emily and Sarah have girls over every night, which isn't even to mention the six pizzas every weekend for movies in the den. But that's not even the half of it."

"Okay."

"Those bills they send every month?"

"Yes."

"It's a record the credit card company has of what I spend and where I spend it, and forgive me, but I'm not interested in these *shmegegges* knowing what I lay out for, and especially how much."

"I understand."

"No, you don't." A ferocity overtook his father's face, eyes narrowed near to closing, mouth tightened in a snarl. "You don't even close to understand. Because listen to me: if it's on paper, someone, someday is going to use it against you. And that's what they want, Brad." He raised a cocked finger to jab the air between them. "They want to get an advantage. Which is why I have three things." The pointer finger straightened upward, followed by the middle and ring as the list accumulated. "I have your mother as a partner, and no one else. I have Marvin under me in charge of all the stores. And most importantly, I have a great family. As happy as I am, I swear to you, without all that, this world would eat me alive."

"Your father," continued Marvin, patting the safe as if a child stood between them, "only wanted people to know so much, and that included me."

"How do you keep the books?"

"I wrote in them what he told me to write."

"And they balance?"

"They balance."

Seated at his father's desk, Brad examined how. With poetic economy, Marvin's tabulations, all handwritten and never copied elsewhere, listed a plethora of expenses for upkeep in each Same Day location that kept profits manageable in terms of what the state and federal governments might demand as their percentage. There were ceiling repairs, plumbing leaks, electrical malfunctions, broken windows, paint jobs, weekly cleanings, exterminations—a veritable torrent of outlays typical to brick and mortar that could sufficiently burden the negative cost column year after year. All remuneration to listed contractors happened in cash, with a signed receipt presentable to anyone who asked.

"And if an interested party wants, let's say, to square these with the invoicer?" Marvin asked with a beatific grin. "Your father, he was a generous man. He liked to hire the little guy. A lot of these crazy fellows who did repairs, who knew where they came from? Let the government find them if they're so interested."

"So then half of these … ?"

"I put in what I was told to put in. I don't know from half of anything."

Far from alarming him, the discovery was an exculpation of sorts for Brad given the seamy doings associated with his own assets. In fact, he felt relieved, as if his father was furnishing posthumous approval for his son's misdeeds. Only Sarah had ever confronted him, after venturing into the basement one morning when he was at it with the polish.

"Aren't you not supposed to do that with coins?"

"What are you doing down here?" He rose threateningly. "Get the fuck out!"

"You're cheating your friends!" she sang, retreating up the stairs.

Within minutes he was in her room proposing a deal: 2 percent of his profits for her silence.

"How will I know what the profits are? You never sell any coins." She was nine but possessed already an understanding of human nature as keen as Brad's.

"Because when I do sell anything, you'll get your two percent."

"In other words, I get nothing now."

"It's like owning stock."

"Stock I could sell, couldn't I?"

"Yeah, well, not this stock."

"How do I know you won't sell coins and not tell me?"

"The whole collection is itemized in a notebook down there. You can look anytime. And Jesus, you don't trust your own brother?" She didn't answer but became his silent partner all the same.

On his visit to the hospital each day Brad chose not to mention his discoveries to his mother, instead assuring her all was. well at the flagship, and that he'd dispatched Marvin to the other five locations to do his usual check-ins.

"Marvin's not good enough. You show your face in the other stores too, Brad. I told you." She took time to list them. "Inwood, Far Rockaway, North Valley Stream, Rosedale. And especially Lynbrook. The employees need to see you. And be friendly. We don't need enemies."

Fully enlightened now as to why, not to mention what might have been stressing the heart of his father, he obliged without asking what qualified him as a seventeen-year-old ombudsman in some of the rougher environs of Nassau County. Besides, what might lie stacked inside the safes now interested him far more, even as his mother also tasked him with burying her husband.

"Make it a funeral befitting the man," she insisted.

"Meaning what exactly?"

"I want a lot of people there. Not an empty seat, which shouldn't be hard. And I want the rabbi to speak. Not the assistant rabbi. The rabbi. And the cantor should sing. The president of the temple should also speak. And Marvin. It should be in the main sanctuary with the false wall open. I want announcements in *Newsday* and the *Nassau Herald*. I want Emily to talk last, but you to write it."

"Mom—"

"Do as I ask. She's the oldest, God bless her sweet soul, so she should speak, but you'll make sure she gets it right."

Five days after his death, on the day his mother returned home, they buried Carl Shlansky, the funeral meeting each of her demands.

"Put simply, Carl Shlansky was one of the greatest men any of us knew," Emily began, having accepted, too easily for Brad's taste, the humiliation of her younger brother writing every word. "Imagine having that as your father. Does it sound intimidating? Like too long a shadow to emerge from under? Not with him. He never spoke in a conceited way about himself, never bragged, never lorded over a soul. He went to work every day with a smile, and was there with us for dinner each night, welcoming, with my mother, anyone who wished to sup at our table." Brad smiled as she spoke the word *sup*, which he'd substituted for the more colloquial *ate* that morning.

"Outside our walls, for the poor of Nassau County, he was a kind of savior, cashing any check brought into one of his six locations with nothing more than an ID. Were some of these fakes? Overdrawn? Hot? Yes. Sometimes the bearer of the check didn't even know. Would my father ever ask for the money back? Rarely. 'Emily,' he would say, 'what do I need with the fifty or seventy-five bucks? What, I'm gonna go chase down some poor woman who doesn't have the money anymore anyway, and probably never did, the poor soul, adding insult to her injury?' And when one of those people came back with another check, he would cash it if he had the impulse to give them a second chance. A third chance? Not likely!" The mourners laughed knowingly. "That was our father."

Though reading words that weren't her own, Emily broke down, scarcely able to continue. "Yes, when he needed to be, he could be as tough as anyone. And we ... we ... we loved him for that too." The rabbi brought her a tissue. "He gave freely to Israel, he gave freely to the temple and JASA. But our father also gave to the communities he served: homeless shelters in Inwood, the Rockaways, and North Valley Stream. Soup kitchens, homes for the disabled throughout the county. Just look around in this room for evidence. You'll see people of every color, religion, age, and economic level." Brad craned his neck for confirmation, finding it mostly in the back. "Our father was kind. Our father was loved. I believe, though he was taken by God far sooner than he or any of us wanted, that he died ... he died ..."

Again Emily began to sob, this time to the extent that Brad feared she might not be able to continue, but once more she rallied. "That he died without regrets, without guilt, shame, or even sadness of any kind. He, along with our mother, who sits there in the front row and was married to my father for twenty-four years, raised my sister and brother and me to be citizens of the community like him. And I say to you today we will carry on his memory through our actions, our love, our loyalty, our friendships, our children, God willing ... and our own lives and how we live them. We'll always love you, Dad, we'll always miss you, we'll never forget you."

Now a blubbering wreck, she had to be ushered from the stage not just by the rabbi but by the president of the temple. Jesus, Brad thought to himself, I'm the one who wrote the damned eulogy, and I didn't shed a tear. His mother reached across the weeping Sarah to grasp his hand.

That night, his sisters asleep upstairs, Brad and his mother split a bottle of Fetzer zinfandel, her favorite.

"Brad, you're the most wonderful son a mother could have."

"Thanks, Mom. I'm glad you feel that way. You're a wonderful mother. I just..."

"What is it?"

"Why didn't I cry? Does that make me worse than everyone else?"

"It makes you, if you want to know the truth of it, the most like your father of any of you, even though you look more like me with your beautiful hair. You got the best of us both, and that's why you're going to be the one who carries on what we started, your father and I, and it's why you're now going to have to step up and be the leader of this family."

"What are you talking about, Mom? I'm going to college next year. Anyway, you're the leader of this family. You always have been. You've been in charge as much as Dad has."

"In certain respects, yes, in certain respects no."

"In all respects."

"Inside the walls of this house I'll grant you. Your father was like a lamb at home. Except for when it came to credit card bills." They shared a smile as she poured them each another glass. "But as you know, in spite of all that malarkey in the eulogy today—which was excellent by the way—"

"You don't have to keep saying that."

"It bears repeating. But you know as well as I do that your father met everyone with his *haimish* smile; everyone loved him, but if you crossed him or were disloyal, there was no greater son of a bitch. He also played by his own rules, and there was no one more clever at that. He did what he wanted, and others be damned. There was no other way to accomplish what he did. You're no different."

"I'm not sure what you're getting at."

"You think we didn't know what you were up to with that coin collection of yours?" Brad waited. "We watched you clap all of those friends of yours on the back, with their fancy parents who looked down on me and your father because we cashed checks in neighborhoods they'd never go. We watched you swindle those kids out of every nickel, literally, that they had, all the time with a friendly embrace like you were doing them a favor letting them get the better of you. And we saw the look on your face when you couldn't make a deal."

"When was that?" There'd been occasions, but mostly outside the house with older collectors who would do no more than chortle dismissively, sending him on his way. That his parents ever perceived disappointment surprised him more than any awareness of his racket.

"A time or two." She took his hand. "You don't cry so much, my darling Brad, because you're already a step ahead of the rest of us. While we're all crying, you're figuring out what's next. How to get and keep what's yours."

She returned to the flagship in Woodmere the following Monday, with only Marvin to help her run it. In addition to being the sole manager Brad's parents trusted, he was the only among the cohort they truly liked. "Marvin and his yarmulke will be there with us when we're cashing pension checks in the retirement home," Carl Shlansky once said to his son.

"Even I know this isn't good," Marvin whispered to Brad when he'd stopped by the location one Sunday after a visit to Bill's. "She doesn't eat. She cries and doesn't eat. She's lost ten pounds at least. Is she taking the pills they gave her?"

"I ask and she says it's none of my business. What am I supposed to do?" asked Brad, who had also noticed her deterioration.

"Talk to her. You're the golden boy."

"Me?"

"She certainly doesn't listen to me. 'You try losing a husband,' she said, and threw a bag of Utzes I tried to give her square in my face."

"Mom," Brad announced that evening across two roast chickens, a bowl of whole-grain rice, and a Mount Sinai of peas glistening with unsalted butter prepared by Jacintha in keeping with the dietary decrees posted on the fridge, "you need to start taking care of yourself. A little more food and a little less wine."

"You've been speaking with the great nutritionist Marvin?"

"I don't know what you're talking about."

"Spare me. I saw him murmuring to you at the flagship. What I do or don't put in my *pisk* is my business. Anyway, why should I eat? What's the point?"

By the night of his debut as Sir Toby Belch, she'd lost twenty-five pounds and was returning from the Woodmere location earlier and earlier each day to nap in the afternoons. Both Brad and Sarah insisted she attend the performance, if only to get her out of the house.

But Brad had other motives as well. Though he'd told no one, not even his sister, the experience of playing Belch, who he'd been informed by the director had the most lines in the play, had rekindled a yearning to act dormant since just before he'd started collecting coins in the third grade. The adulation for his winsomely sinister characterization of the wolf in *Little Red Riding Hood* had so overwhelmed him, he'd nearly wept from the ensuing praise. It was a losing game, he reasoned afterward alone in his room, to pursue such addictive affirmation, especially given its reliance on audiences composed of others who were bound to prove inconsistent, and eventually, should he achieve greater success, even hostile. As for the intoxicating immediacy of so much attention as he spoke words on a stage, he'd overheard his father and uncle speak of alcoholics, whose only real chance at besting the disease would have been never to have tasted a drink in the first place, or if not that, to have understood the drug's awful tyranny after a sole experience.

His mother offered acting classes on weekends, trips to the city to see Broadway shows, and of course insisted he try out for the next play, but he met her enthusiasm with resolute sobriety, only his inchoate passion for coins to help grieve the passing of his brief life on the boards.

But now, older, he was more disciplined, more sure of who and what he was, especially since his acne had begun somewhat to subside. Moreover, the director, a petite woman in her late thirties with olive skin and wild, dark hair, had begged him to audition on the day before callbacks, meaning he wouldn't even suffer the screening round.

"This character needs stature," she insisted.

"What? I'm fat?"

"Obviously not, Brad. It's your whole being. Your attitude. Your charisma."

"Ms. Revasch, please. What charisma do I have? Nobody even likes me."

"You have friends."

"Of a certain sort."

"The smart ones."

"And didn't you say this guy was a drunk? Get one of the football players."

"None of them can handle the language."

"Well, I can't handle the rehearsals. I have college applications."

"I'll give you the same deal I gave Heidi. This is Shakespeare, and we're studying him in English. It'll be worth three points extra on your semester grade. How's that for your college application?"

"Five points."

"I'll have to give Heidi five too. I just can't."

"Okay. Four for both of us. Let Heidi know I negotiated the one-point bump, and we have a deal."

"You have to get the part first. Put a little work into it."

He canceled a meet-up with a collector from Syosset to read a summary of the play that afternoon, and to the consternation of the theater clique he strolled into callbacks that night and pocketed the role.

"That's how it's done, folks," enthused Ms. Revasch. "No pauses, no straining, no overemphasis. Just the words as they were written, clearly and frankly spoken, with all the confidence that you're the person and don't have to show us."

"That's not fair. Toby is a prose part," a senior desperate to play Feste said in protest.

"Something tells me Brad would do just as fine with verse, wouldn't you, Brad?"

"I don't know," he responded piously. "You want me to read for another character?"

"I think we know where you belong in this play."

In the world of Illyria, Sir Toby lived to bring joy and decry priggery. "You're a natural at this, Brad. One of the best we've had. I'm only sorry you didn't audition for plays sooner," the director told him privately a week into rehearsals. He resolved that very night that he would pursue a theater degree in college and limit his applications to schools with reputable programs, ultimately focusing on Boston University, SUNY Purchase, and Ithaca College, where he'd thrice visited Emily. Each seemed realistic given his unexceptional grades but decent board scores.

"I'll take my GPA and my coin collection any day of the week," he explained to his parents in the year before his father's passing.

"Money isn't everything," Carl Shlansky retorted.

"Is that right, Dad? You're in the check-cashing business for reasons other than profit? It's back to your 'I provide a service no one else does'? You're a great man helping the poor? Give me a break."

"I do help them, as a matter of fact, but your larger and frankly insensitive point is exactly the one I was making. Because no, cashing checks for poor people is not at all what I was lying awake dreaming of doing when I was your age, and if I had it to do all over again, I'd have gone to college like your mother."

"Well, I'm going to college, so you don't have to worry."

"Not if you don't pass high school. And with your brains you could've gone anywhere if you'd put in a little effort."

"I've got Bs and a few Cs. What are you obsessing over?"

"Just, money isn't everything." An anxious sadness descended, about which Brad queried his mother that evening.

"If you haven't noticed," she answered, "your father has everything he ever wanted: a family, his own business, a big house. Yes, he's happy in his way, but he's also very disappointed by life."

"You're not making sense."

"I hope it never makes sense to you, which is why he said what he said. First off, we have a little depression in the family, as much as we try to hide it. On both sides. Your father, that turns him against himself. Life kicks the hell out of you, Brad. Suddenly you look around, thinking you've done everything right, but it's really just been a big joke, and the joke's on you.

Maybe you've cut a few corners like everyone else. So what? Not every-thing's what it seems."

"I don't understand."

She kissed him on the forehead.

"I've already said too much. Let's just leave it at that."

As rehearsals commenced, the other actors began to afford him grudging respect but seemed to like him less and less for his persisting ease. The Mal-volio in particular, who hoped to attend Northwestern and was considered the top actor in the school, seized every opportunity to snub or condescend.

"What did I do to you, Vince?" Brad asked one night.

"It's just the role, man. I'm Malvolio, and you're Belch."

"So?"

"They don't like each other. Do this more than once, and with a part you really have to work at instead of just stomping around the stage saying lines a seventh grader could handle, and you'll understand what I mean. It's called acting."

Heidi witnessed the exchange. "Wow, Vince, is it really pissing you off that Brad is actually good?" With reddish brown hair and kind eyes, she was easily one of the most attractive girls in Brad's class. She'd never had a boyfriend, opting instead to concentrate on theater and schoolwork. Like Brad she attended few parties, but more out of choice than exclusion. Hop-ing her intervention had more to it than her improved English grade, Brad tried to kiss her after rehearsal that night

"What is it?" he whispered when she recoiled.

"You're just not my type, Brad. It's not personal. Just don't ever do that again. Please."

Sitting alone in the car later, after his sister had long since entered the house, he sought to organize his life. With so much now within his ken—money from his coin collection, a newfound focus on theater—the truly insurmountable area seemed to be romance.

He'd only ever had one girlfriend, in the seventh grade. Precociously flirtatious, she was just coming into her own with boys, and for the three weeks he and Laurie Dwyer had gone steady, he could think of nothing but her: not his schoolwork, not his family, not his friends, not even his coins. Her father was a heart surgeon, and her mother, who didn't work, a devoted tennis player who regularly fetched Laurie from school in a blue Mercedes SL wearing court whites. Like her mother, Laurie had sandy hair, as well as a burgeoning version of Mrs. Dwyer's sinewy frame. When she spoke, which she did often, and with such a dearth of pauses one wondered when she ever breathed, her eyes flashed like headlights on a sports car.

He'd approached her in the cafeteria as she slid her tray into the cleaning rack.

"Hey, Laurie. How was your lunch?"

"Good. Yours?"

"I bring mine from home, so it's always great."

"Right. I hear your mother's a good cook. Mine doesn't cook at all. She's always back at the club until dinner, so she has the housekeeper do it. Luckily, I like the housekeeper's food more than hers. She makes pizza. The dough and everything! So what's up?" Her willingness to engage startled him. To make matters worse, whether intentionally he couldn't say, she had arched her back in such a way as to show the shape of her young breasts, her bra straps visible through a diaphanous pastel shirt.

"Earth to Brad!"

"I just wanted to know … ," he finally managed.

"Yes?"

"Are you going to Melanie's party at Grant Park?"

Her face erupted into matching archipelagos of crimson splotches on either side of her little upturned nose.

"I am. I am going to her party."

"I was wondering if you'd do the slow skate with me."

Her smile broadened as she paused to attenuate the moment.

"I will, Brad! Thanks for asking."

At the urging of his friend Paul Aiello, he resolved that during the skate he would propose going steady, but as he made his way to her during the opening notes of Lionel Richie's "Three Times a Lady," he suddenly dreaded the whole affair. While it remained true that she'd accepted his invitation, and they'd eyed each other for days since, they'd barely spoken. In fact, at times she seemed focused on avoidance. But when she took his hand, offering an eager, blushing smile, a surge of optimism prevailed. Other couples skated alongside them, but most of the grade looked on from the low surrounding wall with quiet, tugging envy. For once he was not among them.

When the song ended, she didn't remove her hand from his.

"Thanks, Brad."

"So, should we go steady?" he blurted.

"Are you asking me?"

He didn't understand her question. Of course he was asking her.

"Well, yes."

"Asking me to go steady or if I think we should?"

She needed a certain formality.

"Will you go steady with me?"

"Yes!" For the next hour they remained together, hands clasped, moving from group to group. She did all the speaking, rarely pausing to glance his way or to encourage participation beyond ornamental presence. The hyped prolixity of her enthusiasm ran through her grasp like a current as she squeezed to the rhythm of each word. His friends, and not just the hapless Simon Zeligson but Eddie Schwartz, Arthur Kim, and Jeremy Dembitzer, looked on with unconcealed astonishment.

It was Paul Aiello, however, whose appreciation most reassured him. The boy's family had just moved from Massapequa to Cedarhurst, where his father could be nearer his job as the procurement manager for a cutlery factory in Queens. Brad had eyed the boy warily on the first day of seventh grade, mostly for orienting himself toward the handsome, athletic males who played football during recess and would then mingle with the girls who'd gathered to watch. Their leader, a tall biracial kid named Elijah Henson, was already said to have had a girl's mouth on his penis, a fact Brad found incomprehensible except that the young Adonis possessed an overabundance of physical appurtenances associated with such precocity: good looks, broad, manly shoulders, a voice long since dropped, the beginnings of a beard, and a full thatch of pubic hair displayed with showy casualness in the locker room before and after gym class.

At the year's second recess, Paul invited himself into their game, with the added temerity of insisting he quarterback one of the teams. Brad left his Yeoman guide with "the coin boys," as they now identified themselves, to give what might transpire his full attention. The newcomer threw a tight spiral with decent accuracy and seemed to know just when to let go of the ball. His team failed to score on its first possession, but the playing area was narrow, and the game two-below touch, so most points occurred on long-pass plays accomplished infrequently. Elijah's team opened with a quick screen across the middle to Joey Plotkin, who was covered by a boy two inches shorter named Micah Beltzer. When the same play was executed successfully on second down—the two consecutive completions earning a first down—Paul huddled his team for adjustments, among them that Paul would now cover Joey.

On the subsequent play, Elijah dropped back to pass but then pitched the ball to Joey, who had stepped behind the line. Such trick plays, which

Brad often saw Elijah devise in his notebook during history class just before recess, could send a defense into disarray, and invariably someone would be open. In this case it was Elijah, who began streaking down the field. As he tore by to catch what would surely be a touchdown, and as the girls watched, Paul extended his leg and sent the grade's most sexually precocious boy airborne. He landed face-first, tongued his split lip, and tasted blood.

The fight that ensued introduced Brad to a level of improvised violence he had never thought possible between kids his age. Mr. Massey, the math teacher on recess duty, hastened to separate the combatants, who were taken to the hospital in separate cars. Elijah received four stitches in his lip, and Paul Aiello was treated for a concussion, having taken two punches to the head. Each was suspended for a week and required to write and read aloud to the grade five-hundred-word essays touting the importance of goodwill and the pointlessness of violence. Afterward the two penitents shook hands publicly, their insincerity palpable.

Brad had always despised Elijah and vowed immediately to befriend Paul Aiello. Doing so became especially easy when he spied the unmistakable blue of a Yeoman guide among the boy's schoolbooks.

"Are you serious?"

"Dude, you have no idea," Paul replied. "Since I was eight and got my first Walking Liberty."

"You have a '42? Or a '21?"

"Fuck you."

"Just checking."

"What's your main stuff?" asked Paul.

"I'm all over the place. In terms of silver—leaving dimes aside—I've got some Walking Libertys, but mainly Morgan dollars."

"And lemme guess: Indian heads."

"Love 'em. How I started."

Paul came to the house after school for a tour of the basement, though Brad was keen enough to know that his polish scam, then in its formative years, would never hoodwink such a seasoned collector.

"This is fucking brilliant!" Paul exclaimed.

"You want in?"

"No, I'm gonna do it myself."

"How's that gonna work?"

"With the kids in Massapequa, jack-off. Don't worry, I'm not gonna horn in on your territory." But Paul's friends to the east weren't as vulnerable as

Brad's in the Five Towns, and his polishing operation shut down as quickly as he'd opened it.

Paul also had a girlfriend, a sixth grader at his old school, and though he had yet to reach the esoteric extremes of Elijah Henson, he had felt up her breasts, an experience he described to Brad with unrelenting detail.

"I don't even know how to be around girls," Brad confessed.

"Just stop right there."

"What?"

"Never say that again. Chicks love confidence, so none of this 'I don't know how to be around them' shit. Who do you have your eye on?"

"Laurie Dwyer."

"Shit, man. I want her mom. Have you seen that fucking body?"

"I'll stick with Laurie."

"How about both of them?"

"How's that gonna happen when I can't even talk to Laurie?"

"You go up, and you ask her out."

By the time he'd summoned the nerve, Melanie Blankman's skating party loomed.

"Her saying no is not an option. Fear doesn't exist for you. It's like a stink, and girls don't want to be around it. You need to be the one in control, as if she's lucky you're even talking with her."

"I'm not good looking enough for her."

"With those blond curls of yours? Act like you're handsome, and girls will think you're handsome."

A week after the skating party, when it came time for a class trip to Philadelphia, Paul instructed that Brad not only sit with Laurie on the bus instead of with him and the coin boys but that he put his arm around her.

"Don't ask, just do it."

"Without saying anything at all?"

"She's your girlfriend now, so you put your arm around her. And guess what? She wants that. A girl wants to feel possessed, taken care of, and if you don't show her that, she's gonna wonder what's up."

Not only did she not object, she smiled, leaning in as his hand settled on her opposite shoulder. The trip would last a little over two hours, and Paul prohibited what would have been Brad's most comfortable subjects for discourse: coins, the Jets, the Giants, video games. Movies were allowed, a subject on which he was becoming increasingly expert given weekly screenings with his sisters and their friends in the den. But the subject never came up, at least not in any context that involved him. A steady stream of visitors sat nearby to whom she prattled nonstop, persistently eager, it seemed to Brad, for each to perceive his embrace. His pride swelled to such a level, he cared neither what she said nor to whom.

In Philadelphia they would first visit Constitution Hall and then the Liberty Bell.

"Let's hang out with our friends now," she said as the bus pulled in.

"Sure. Yours or mine?"

"I mean you hang out with yours, and I'll hang out with mine."

"Oh. All right."

He loathed his powerlessness. Other than asking her to slow skate and putting his arm around her on the bus, he'd not successfully initiated significant interaction between them whatsoever. Everything occurred on her terms.

"Stay away from her," Paul insisted when Brad explained her wish to separate. "Don't even check in. Let her feel what it's like to be without you."

"I don't want her to feel that."

"Trust me, you do. Then she'll beg for you to be sitting with her on the ride home, which is when it'll be dark and you can make out. Which again, how do you make that happen?"

"I don't ask, I just do."

"That's right."

By the time they reached the Liberty Bell, he'd barely seen her. When he did, a group that included Elijah Henson and Joey Plotkin surrounded her. Observing Paul's prohibition against mopey display of vulnerability, Brad laughed and mingled demonstrably with those near him to the extent that he never saw what inspired the sudden commotion. By all accounts, Paul Aiello had instigated the scuffle when another of the coin boys fixed his attentions on a seventh-grade girl from a different school, at which point a boy in a crested blazer, most likely her boyfriend, intervened.

"Leave her alone, dude," he demanded, approaching threateningly.

Paul threw the first and only punch, breaking the boy's nose. Something close to mayhem ensued, involving not only a scrum of boys more eager to threaten one another than fight but chaperones from the two relevant schools, a half dozen security guards, and an equal number of puzzled docents.

"No one, and I mean no one, talks to or comes near Paul Aiello," announced Mrs. Powers, the resolutely dowdy social studies teacher, from the front of the bus where she established a perimeter. "As far as anyone's concerned, he no longer exists."

Brad sat with Laurie for the ride home, but when he went to kiss her, she shook her head, pushing him away in what felt like disgust. Back on Long Island she skipped a good-bye, escaping into her father's Mercedes sedan, after which Brad and the coin boys found Paul grinning meekly in the back of an old red Bronco while his father conferred grimly with teachers nearby. It struck Brad that though Carl Shlansky had something of a blue-collar background, and was easily Mr. Aiello's size, Mr. Aiello would fell Brad's father and any of the other dads with the same efficiency Paul had demonstrated earlier that day with the blazer-clad boy.

"Hey, dude," Brad said, leaning into the window Paul lowered with a few winds of a crank.

"Boys. It looks like the party's over," responded Paul to Brad and the others.

"Don't say that," insisted Brad.

"I heard them talking. I'm kicked out. It's gonna be military school for me. Public school if I'm lucky."

"If you go to public school, I'm going too."

"Shut up, Brad. No, you're not."

"I'm serious."

"You're not going to public school."

"You kids get out of here. Get lost." Paul's father had returned to the car. Brad pivoted for a better look at the stubbled face, thick of jowl.

"The other kid started it, Mr. Aiello," he offered in the most conciliatory tone he could.

"You think I give a shit? Now I said get the fuck out of here."

"We'll call you, Paul!"

"Yeah, well, he won't pick up, so don't bother," Mr. Aiello answered before turning back to his son. "Roll up that fucking window." Paul obliged with a subservience Brad had never encountered in the boy he suddenly realized had become his best friend.

He waited three days until the weekend to call, hoping some degree of calm would have prevailed in the Aiello home. Paul's mother answered and said simply that her son was unavailable. In the background he heard Paul's father ask who it was as she hung up. When Brad called the following day Mr. Aiello took the receiver from his wife.

"Who is this?"

"It's Brad Shlansky, sir."

"Didn't I say the other night not to call here? And now it's twice from you already?"

"I guess you did."

"You guess. Well, let me put it this way, guesser, and for the second time: Paul is not going to be speaking to you. Not by phone, not in person, not by letter, not by radio, not by fucking semaphore. Got it?"

"Yes sir."

"You call this house again, I'm gonna come over there and break both your fucking arms."

Though it would have had uproarious effect, he didn't dare report to his parents what had been said to him. Instead, he returned the receiver to its cradle and ascended to his room, where he remained for the next several hours, occasionally parting the curtain to spy for any approaching vehicle, red Bronco or otherwise. Downstairs he made sure always to be in the presence of a parent. That night he slept in their room, feigning nausea.

Paul Aiello did not return to Woodmere Academy. It was rumored he'd been sent away, but in actuality the price of military schools dissuaded his father from such measures. After two weeks at home, he was enrolled at the public school in Valley Stream. Over the ensuing year Brad encountered him occasionally at Bill's Coins, but Mr. Aiello's less-than-salubrious interdictions dissuaded contact beyond the occasional trade. As for Laurie, the day after their trip to the Liberty Bell, her best friend was dispatched to inform Brad that the relationship was officially over.

Whatever elation he'd felt over three weeks of going steady, it couldn't approach the intensity of public shame that accompanied the breakup. Girls eyed him in the hall not with sympathy but with contempt. To make matters worse, his acne exploded. He hid among his coins, taking dinner in the basement, screaming at his mother in a fit of tearful wrath that the reasons why needn't concern her. Sarah rescued him from further interrogation by revealing what the entire middle and lower grades knew: Brad had been cast aside. In his bed at night he writhed and thrashed, wailing into his pillow so that none could hear. Until his impulsive pass at Heidi he'd not pursued a girl since.

Heidi, who remained friendly even after her rebuke of him, approached Brad at the curtain on opening night as he watched his mother find a seat at the end of the first row.

"What are you looking at, Brad?"

"Just seeing where people are."

"Is that your mom?"

"Yeah."

"I'm really sorry about your dad. I meant to go to the funeral actually, but I couldn't get the car."

"That's all right."

"It must be weird doing this play, which is all about mourning, and playing a character who tells his niece not to be sad when you're actually dealing with it in your real life." She wasn't wrong, but Brad had found Toby's zeal for life to have been helpful. In fact, he hoped his mother, in addition to seeing his return to the stage, would be inspired by some of the words he spoke. "I think you're truly amazing as Sir Toby, and I felt that even before your dad died." She paused, staring into his face. "Oh God. That came out wrong."

"I know what you're saying."

"I only meant that I wasn't just trying to make you feel good."

"You're really good too." She had the role of Maria, handmaiden to lovestruck Olivia.

"I'm fine. No Meryl Streep." She laughed.

"Do you want to be an actress?"

"I don't think so."

"Do you have a first choice for college?"

"Penn, if I can get in."

He felt the tug of old uncertainties. Had his dad been right? Couldn't he have had the coin collection *and* better grades? Had he really had to choose? But too much self-examination served only to distract. On its present trajectory, who knew what his collection might be worth by the time he finished college? Did it really matter if he ended up at BU or Purchase? Or Ithaca, like Emily?

"I want to study psychology I think," Heidi said.

"Your dad's a psychologist, right?"

"Both my parents." The Grossmans attended the Shlanskys' temple and, Brad suddenly remembered, occupied a place on that list that his mother insisted looked down on his parents for their allegedly rapacious profession.

"Two hundred dollars an hour to tell people it's all their parents' fault, and we're the ones giving Jews a bad name," she said in a rage after Heidi's mother had underwhelmed Miriam yet again with a taciturn greeting before Kol Nidre.

"What about you? Do you want to be an actor?" Heidi asked Brad.

"I think so. I mean, I know it's tough to make it and everything, and I'm not going to win any beauty contests—"

"You're handsome, Brad."

"It's ridiculous for you to say that, but thanks."

"You are. I'd kill for your hair. Anyway, there are all types in movies."

"That's actually what I'm hoping."

"And here we are. Seniors. On our way to college and then life! I mean, I know I sound lame and everything ..."

"No you don't." He wanted fervently for her to finish the point.

"I do, but ..." She paused, clearly embarrassed. "All right, I'll go ahead and say it. We can be anything we want now!" She leaned up to kiss him on the cheek. "Break a leg tonight."

The show that night could not have gone better. Between their scenes, the audience pined for Toby and his fellow travelers Maria, Fabian, Feste, and the clear favorite, Sir Andrew Aguecheek. Brad didn't miss a laugh and enjoyed as robust an ovation during his bow as anyone. Heidi made certain he was invited to the party afterward at the home of the erstwhile antagonistic Malvolio in Hewlett Neck.

"You go," Sarah insisted backstage.

"Only with you."

"Why do you need me there?"

"I don't exclude people. We're family."

"You're a good guy, Brad, and we'll always be family. Besides, I don't feel excluded. You're one of the actors."

"We're both going. It's who and what Shlanskys are."

"Fine," she responded, relenting with an unmistakable smile. "But let's get Mom to her car."

They found her still seated in the front row.

"Your father wouldn't have believed it, the way you hit every line, Brad. And Sarah, the show ran beautifully."

"Thanks, Mom. Wasn't Brad hilarious?"

"Don't deflect. I know how hard it is to make sure all the actors are where they need to be, and the lights change when they should."

"Thanks."

"I'm just so sad he wasn't here," she said, losing herself in grief.

"We are too, Mom," said Brad.

"He would have loved how you stole the show from all the fancy kids who think they've got the world on a string. I've always said you were an actor. Since the third grade when you were the—"

"The wolf, I know, Mom."

"Did you like being up there?" she asked, wiping her eyes.

"I did."

In the parking lot she couldn't make it ten steps without stopping to cry.

"Mom, you know what?" Brad finally said. "Sarah and I are going to meet you at home."

"Don't you dare, Brad. You need to enjoy this moment. Don't worry about me."

"We do worry about you."

"It's not your job to take care of your mother."

"We're meeting you at home. We'll open a bottle of white zin. But only if you eat something too."

"You're not, Brad. Please. I cry because I need to get it out. Your father and I loved each other. It was a great thing. And he would want you getting on with it, not sitting at home with your mom."

They had arrived at her car. He reached to help her. "I can do it myself." She lowered herself in, swatting his hand, then turned up to them after negotiating the buckle.

"I'm so proud of the two of you."

"Don't cry again, Mom. Please."

"And I'm proud of Emily."

"You sure you don't want us to come home?" asked Sarah.

"Be quiet coming in, and I'll see you in the morning."

At the party Brad felt more included than at any gathering of peers he'd ever been lucky enough to attend, as did his sister, who disappeared downstairs with the younger cohort. On his way from the bathroom in the sprawling home where immense panes of steel-framed glass overlooked Brosewere Bay, he was called into the open kitchen by Vince's father, who stood with several confederates around eight bottles of red wine.

"You were the uncle in the play, right?" .

"That's right, Mr. Stein."

"Call me Joel, please." He gestured to the other men. "All these assholes do. You're Carl Shlansky's kid, right?"

"Yes."

"I liked your dad. He was real people. I was at the funeral. Your sister spoke beautifully."

"Thanks. This house is amazing."

"You like wine?"

"I don't really have any experience with it."

"What we're doing here is called a vertical tasting." Brad took in the bottles. They all had what appeared to be the same label, but each in a different state of aging. "This is a wine called Chateau Latour. Did your dad drink wine?"

"Beer mostly."

"Well, he saved himself a lot of money. This is a very famous claret, from a region called Bordeaux in the South of France, but more specifically from a place called Graves, which is on the left bank of the Garonne River."

"Jesus, Joel," said one of the other men, stocky and entirely bald in a colorful madras shirt. "How long is this lecture going to go on?"

"I only want to give some context, Ray." He turned back to Brad. "So, you said you're not experienced with wine. Your father didn't drink it. I'm guessing your mother doesn't either, or if she does, she drinks white."

"White zinfandels."

"Perfect. Now, I want you to taste these three pours I'm going to put in front of you. One of them is from 1975, another from 1982, and another from 1989."

"Okay."

"Joel, is this really necessary? Among other things, it's about five bucks a sip." It was Madras again.

"What's your issue?"

"I want to drink the damn wine!"

"So, who's stopping you? And it's my fucking wine. When we're drinking the rocket fuel Cabernet at your place, you set the rules. Here, I do!"

"Forgive me for trying to expand your palate beyond one side of one river in one region of one country in Europe."

"Ignore my friend Ray, Brad. He's got the best palate of any of us, but lately he's been making us drink wine from California that's one step above what they pour at temple."

Everyone laughed, and Brad couldn't help but join. The men had an easy familiarity that didn't exclude, and Brad wondered how Vince could have such a kind father.

"It's time to learn from the next generation!" Joel Stein announced to Madras, before turning back to Brad. "Now, turn around so you don't see which one I pour in which glass. I don't want you saying you like the oldest one just because it's the oldest. This is called blind tasting, meaning you don't know what you're drinking. Just look at the pretty girls in the other room."

That Heidi appeared just beyond the threshold separating the kitchen from the living room abetted a dutiful response. She spoke with her friend Gloria Allee, a moderately popular girl who'd been in charge of props. The two looked his way as he smiled awkwardly and shrugged.

"Okay, Brad, turn around."

Before him stood three glasses, each filled no more than an inch and a half.

"Drink them in any order you like," said Joel, "and tell us what you think. Smell them if you want, too, because that's part of the experience, though the way some of my friends here describe the nose on a wine is a load of horseshit. In fact, if you mention rose petals or dark berries, or say anything about a peacock's tail, I'm going to kick you out of my house."

"I actually do smell something," said Brad tentatively. He was said to have the best sense of smell in his family.

"Oh yeah, what's that?"

"You really want me to say?"

"Now I really do," said Joel, glancing at the other men. Even Ray of the madras shirt seemed ready to be bemused.

"Well ..." Brad smelled again, embarrassed by what his brain told him and wanting to make sure before answering.

"Take your time."

"Okay." Brad smelled a third time. "It smells like a cow pasture."

"Holy hell! You mean manure! He means manure! Cow shit is what you want to say! Hah!"

"Unbelievable!" said Madras while all three men applauded.

"You're absolutely right, Brad!" announced Joel. "What you're drinking is from an area where the wines are very earthy, as you're about to taste, and they smell like shit, literally! Or if you're in good company, you say manure! You're a fucking natural! And most importantly, you're honest! You didn't back off what you really sensed, even though you probably thought it would be an insult! Why has Vince never brought you over? Now taste!"

Brad did as instructed, sipping one after another, absorbing the unmistakable taste of loam mixed with the sweet bitterness of fermented fruit. It was unlike any drink he'd ever tasted, with a tantalizing acridity undergirding the taste of dark berries. His father, "for patriotic reasons," only ever bought domestic wine from the store next to his uncle's grocery, and would describe it routinely to guests as "not exactly for the connoisseur, given the nature of the place I bought it. But trust me, it's the best they've got!"

"This is amazing," Brad said as he sipped from the third glass.

"That one specifically, or all of them?"

"All of them."

"And which do you like the best?"

Brad pointed.

"Hah!" exclaimed Madras, as the others laughed. "Now I love this kid!"

"Why?" asked Joel, seeming disappointed but keenly interested.

"Well, I guess because it tastes richer than the others, or I mean it has more different tastes in it. The ground like you said, but also the grapes, which aren't too sweet, and it stays longer in my mouth somehow."

"Which is why, as I fucking told you, Parker calls it the most balanced of the three!" exclaimed Madras in a minor fit of vindication. "And it was you, Joel who asked the kid over, not me!"

"All right, fine, fine, fine! You picked the '82, by the way, the highest rated of the three, so you've got a knack for this, though I'd do two things if I were you: Don't expect any wine you ever drink to be better; and if you do want it to be, pick a career where you can afford it!"

"Or a wife!" said Madras.

"Or a wife. And you're welcome here anytime, though I don't open the first growths every night, and usually both of these assholes have to be around. Now go be with the kids so we can be horrible and crass and talk about our wives without having to worry who hears."

Brad approached Heidi and Gloria, who remained where he'd spied them. They each held a beer.

"Was that weird?" asked Heidi. "Did they give you wine?"

"It was kind of amazing actually."

"It's so cool Vince's parents let him and his friends drink here," she said.

"And the beer is imported," said Gloria, presenting the label. "This is from the Czech Republic. You want to try it?" He took a sip, wondering how he'd get his sister and him home safely within the next couple of hours, but then opting to dispense with any concern given the frisson of the only party to which he'd been invited all fall.

"What's Vince's dad like?"

"Incredibly nice."

"Who would have thought?" The three laughed as Brad handed Gloria back her bottle.

"You were amazing tonight, Brad," she said. "I was just telling Heidi. Everyone is saying it."

"Thanks."

A trio joined them that included Vince, who handed Brad a beer of his own.

"Take this, Brad. You deserve it," he said. "And I'm sorry I've been such a dick to you during rehearsals. I really do think it was the character."

"I don't think so, Vince," interjected his friend Alex Brady, the slender and uninhibited junior who had played Aguecheek. "You just act like an asshole sometimes. Fucking own it."

Everyone laughed, including Vince.

"Fair enough," he admitted, turning back to Brad. "I'm sorry, dude. You were great."

"Thanks, Vince. And don't worry about it."

"And we're all really sorry about your dad."

Brad stared down into the label of his Pilsner Urquell, afraid condolences might lead to attenuated dialogue about his family's loss. It was awful timing, but if his father's memory needed sadness to keep it going, he'd stored up enough of that over the past ten or so years of loneliness and rejection to fuel it for a lifetime. Yet it would hardly recommend him were he too easily to deflect their sympathy.

"Thanks, Vince. We're going to miss him."

"I'm sorry I never met him."

"Yeah, well, he worked really hard."

"Brad, do you really want to be talking about your dad right now?" asked Heidi. "Because you don't have to. I certainly wouldn't in your shoes."

"I guess I don't." Why now, he wondered, among people who've never given a shit about me, am I suddenly feeling emotional, and when it could destroy everything that's happening? He took a swig of beer, which, unlike the Rolling Rock his father always had on hand, had a rich, earthy taste appropriately commensurate with Vince's father's wine. Tears seeped from his eyes as he drank. Heidi reached out to squeeze his shoulder.

"Then we won't talk about it."

"Thanks." He wiped his face with his free hand and grinned reassuringly, desperately afraid his display of emotion would repel them. "Don't go," he suddenly blurted.

"Are you kidding, man? We're actors," said Vince. "We're not going anywhere. Bring on the waterworks. Emotion's what it's all about!" While he appreciated the sentiment, it struck Brad as one of the most witlessly self-condemnatory statements, at least in the context of a person crying over the death of a parent, he'd ever heard. Perhaps he didn't want to be an actor after all if doing so meant keeping company with such self-indulgent idiocy.

"Well, I don't know about that," offered Heidi. "I certainly don't need to watch Brad mourn his dad for kicks."

"That's not what I was saying, Heidi."

"I don't really know what you were saying, but Brad doesn't want to talk anymore about his father, so let's change the subject."

"Good by me," said Vince. "I need another beer anyway." He turned to the two friends accompanying him. "You guys with me?"

"Sure, man," said Alex, before addressing Brad and the two girls. "You guys gonna still be here?"

"I guess so," answered Heidi with an ambiguous lift of her shoulders. "Sorry about that, Brad," she said when the three had gone.

"Yeah," added Gloria, whom Brad noticed had been staring at him. What he'd failed to observe, however, was how pretty she was, how tender and understanding her deep green eyes, how her hair, slightly blonder than his, curved to match the shape of her enchanting face.

"It's why I fucking hate actors sometimes," said Heidi. "Next thing you know he was gonna start talking about his feelings about your feelings. And then have us do a back-rub circle."

"Oh my God, I hated those in rehearsals," said Brad, more tears coming even as he laughed.

"Let's go outside. It's not that cold." They followed Heidi through a sliding glass door onto a wide deck overlooking a covered pool and beyond it the bay, where lights shimmered from houses across the water. As a comforting chill enveloped them, Gloria took his hand. She accomplished it so naturally, it took several steps before he realized it had happened, and when he turned to her she smiled up at him.

"Hey," she said.

"Hi," he said back, squeezing her warm palm.

"Can you believe we have another performance tomorrow night?" Heidi asked.

"I can't wait," said Brad.

"How did your mom like it?"

"She misses Dad."

"I bet he would have been proud of you," said Gloria.

"It's hard to say what he would have thought. He was a great guy. Amazing really, but more the meat-and-potatoes kind. The only times I've even been to the theater I've gone with my mom."

"You think he would want you to be an actor?" asked Gloria before stopping herself. "Oh my God, you just said you didn't want to talk about him."

"No, it's different with you guys. He'd probably have me take over his business if he had had his way. One thing about both my parents though is they put their kids and family first. Pretty much gave us whatever we wanted, but somehow without spoiling us. I mean obviously my mother still will I guess."

"We knew what you meant," volunteered Heidi, leaving him room to continue if he chose. He wondered why this triangle, so natural as to feel inevitable, hadn't taken shape years ago. He wouldn't have awakened each day with so much anxiety and dread.

"It's complicated. He wasn't very educated, my dad. He read the paper, but only for the sports and business, and he never read books. But truly, he was one of the most decent people I've ever met. The thing is, I also just found out he was cheating the government on his taxes. He must have justified it to himself in some way, but I think he was doing it like to an insane degree. Keeping cash in safes. Obviously I'm trusting you guys with this."

"Who would we tell?" laughed Heidi.

"Why am I just getting to know you two now?"

"I was wondering the same thing," said Gloria.

"Because this was the right time," said Heidi simply. "I'm getting cold," she added, not really meaning it. "I'm gonna go inside. You guys good out here?"

"Yeah, we're great," said Gloria, Brad's hand still in hers.

She initiated the kiss. Her mouth was chilled and tasted of beer. She finessed him easily, opening and maneuvering her lips in ways he couldn't predict, her tongue soft and agile. He allowed her to lead, thinking to himself this would be the measure for all his future experiences, incredulous that it had happened so unexpectedly, with this person, on this night. At some point two girls pulled open the door behind them, chatting obliviously, then pulling up short. He heard them whisper and giggle before retreating inside. He didn't care. To be the subject of gossip for what was happening was nothing short of extraordinary: he'd been waiting for this half his life.

"I'm actually getting cold," Gloria finally said after a good fifteen minutes, "but I don't want to stop."

"Me neither."

"But I have to go. I have a curfew."

"What time is it?" he asked.

"Almost one."

"Jesus. I should probably find my sister."

"Will you call me tomorrow? First thing?"

"Absolutely."

Sarah had spent her time dancing in a built-out basement outfitted with red and blue bulbs. She'd had two beers but announced she'd sweated enough to fill three bottles.

"So you glad I made you go?" he asked as he drove, careful to stop at every light and stop sign, signal for each turn, and stay five miles per hour under the speed limit.

"I heard you were making out with Gloria Allee outside on the deck."

"Who told you that?"

"Who didn't? So, what, are you guys like an item now?"

"Maybe. Why? You don't like her?"

"She's cute. Big boobs too."

"Shut up."

"Did you feel them?"

"We kissed, Sarah."

"She sort of reminds me of Mom."

"Yeah … Mom."

They drove in silence for a few blocks.

"I called Emily last night after rehearsal," Sarah finally said.

"What did she say?"

"That she talks to Mom twice a day and isn't worried. Besides, we can't make her go to the doctor, we can't make her eat, we can't make her stop drinking so much, and that it's just white wine."

"Did you tell her how much?"

"She said Mom's in mourning and it'll all level off."

When their mother didn't appear the next morning, they tried her door, which was locked but, like all interior rooms in the Shlansky house, could be opened with flatware. They discovered her facedown on the bed, a quarter-full wineglass, a spent bottle of Fetzer zinfandel, and a similarly dispatched bowl of ice cream with its spoon on the bed table beside it. When they couldn't wake her, Brad called an ambulance. While waiting, he found an empty bottle of sleeping pills and another prescription he couldn't identify from its scientific name in her bathroom, along with the mortar and pestle she'd used to grind them into a powder that was then mixed into the pint of Borden's she'd consumed with the wine. At the hospital he learned the prescription had been for a barbiturate. They pumped her stomach, but when she died at ten that morning, the doctor told them she'd effectively killed herself hours before.

"There's nothing either of you could have done," he said, taking pains to assure them.

The scene that never happened kept playing out in Brad's head: He and Sarah drove home after the play instead of to the party, arriving no more than thirty minutes later than their mother. She would still have been downstairs. Yes, she'd have already started into the wine, but he would have joined her for a glass. "'The *shiker* is a goy' doesn't apply to this family," his father used to joke. Brad would have accompanied her upstairs, where he would have sat while she removed her makeup, changed in her closet, and climbed into bed. Sarah would have joined them, all three grateful that daughter and son had preferred to be home with their grieving mother where they belonged. Most of all, and of this he was certain, she would never have taken her life with two of her children in the house.

While Sarah didn't require hospitalization as had her mother a month before, Brad did wonder if she might be headed that way. What saved her, so far as he could perceive, was rage. Between fits of crying, mostly in the arms of Emily (home to be with them now most weekends from Ithaca), his younger sister launched into philippics of such passion that Brad felt the need to defend their mother.

"She couldn't live without Dad, Sarah!"

"Fuck Dad! What about us?"

"Obviously that wasn't enough."

"And how does that make you feel?"

"Terrible, but who the hell cares?"

"And no note even? I mean who does that? What are we supposed to do now? Who's going to feed us and pay the bills? Be there for dinner to check in on how we are? All the shit parents are supposed to do?"

"We'll figure that out."

"We're fucking orphans, Brad! She made us fucking orphans! What mother does that? What kind of person does that? She left us completely alone!"

"I know, Sarah. I know."

"Who's going to take care of us? Who, Brad? Who?"

Over and over she asked.

PART TWO

TORONTO

O n airplanes David thought invariably of Adam. Though he hadn't perished at thirty thousand feet, he'd done so at the hands of terrorists, and terrorists took down passenger jets. It had been sixteen years since the bombing, but the further from it David got, the more the lost possibilities associated with memories of his friend inspired him not to squander the unlikely life he was getting to live.

Shortly after takeoff, he visited his two fellow actors who'd arranged to sit together. He couldn't stand ill-will, warranted or not.

"For how long are you guys out?"

"Me, three weeks on a pilot," responded Andrew. "Joe's doing an indie for a month. What about you?"

"Just a few days for a script meeting on something I'm supposed to direct."

"Wait, is it *Appalachian Winter*?" asked Joe.

"How do you know about *Appalachian Winter*?"

"My wife auditioned for you."

"Oh my God, that's right. I was actually going to cast her."

"It was an amazing script. What ever happened with that film?"

"It fell apart in prep. Worst year of my life."

"So, what's the new film?"

"Something that looks like it'll actually go. I didn't write it, but I did a pass. Now I get to sit in a room with the head of the company and a writer and go through all my changes page by page."

"What company?"

"Chicago Films."

"Jacob Rosenthal?"

"You know him?"

"He was going to make Anthony Calabria's movie, but he wouldn't let Anthony cast his cousin even though Anthony wrote the role for her."

"I know all about it. Anthony and I had lunch. Jacob Rosenthal is a tyrant."

"That's why Joe and I stick to acting."

His involvement with Chicago Films had begun, like so much of what he did, with a phone call in the summer of 2019.

"Are you familiar with a book called *Coal*?" asked Howard Garner, his agent.

"I read it the year it came out. Someone would actually make that? Now?"

"One guy in particular."

The script Howard sent both impressed and baffled David. Quite admirably the screenwriter, whose name was Carly Billings, had chosen a noir structure to organize an engaging but unwieldy six-hundred-page novel into a two-hour film. David recognized that he could never have come up with such a disciplining paradigm. As for the book's other challenges, namely, its refusal to supply readers with purely untainted victims in which comforting levels of outrage could reside, Ms. Billings, whom David had to assume was Black, honored Rex Patterson's impulse not to simplify at a time when that's all anyone seemed to be doing on the subject of race. Yet the dialogue constituted some of the most ham-fisted he'd ever read, especially between the LAPD detective and his love interest, the film's femme fatale, both of whom were white. Among other head scratchers, the woman, within days of being raped by her husband's two murderers, pursued sex with her liberator, which felt unlikely.

"I'm interested if they'll let me rewrite the script," he told Howard.

"Jacob says it's ready."

"Have you read it?"

"David, I don't even know who sees this movie."

"It's based on a huge bestseller."

"Do you even remember the backlash? Why do you think it hasn't been made? And bestseller doesn't mean what it used to. It also goes against every political current in our country and industry right now. You offend Black people and women. It makes no sense."

"Has it crossed your mind that because of that it's precisely the kind of movie that should be made right now?"

"I heard the same bullshit from Jacob."

"The writer of the book was Black."

"For a lot of people that made it worse."

"And those people are idiots."

"You and Jacob are going to get along great. Forget the controversy. This space is dead. There's no viable business model anymore for movies like this that cost what this one will cost to make, at least not in theaters."

Howard had represented David at United Creative Management for nearly a decade and a half, rare in an industry in which clients capriciously fired representation over even the most evanescent hiatus. Together they had witnessed a transformation in what sorts of movies got made, for what budgets, and of course how they were financed. When David had written and directed his first film in the mid-aughts, a dark thriller that sold at Sundance, foreign and ancillary domestic platforms (meaning effectively every way of exploiting a movie beyond its first run in American cinemas) could furnish enough revenue to make any film with a well-known actor and a good story a viable risk. But those markets had diminished. Cable television supplied compelling programming of its own, the video rental market had shifted dramatically with streaming not only replacing the video store but often superseding theatrical release at all, and foreign film industries were creating more of their own content.

"The whole idea of this movie is dead on arrival," Howard said.

"Then why did you bring it to me?"

"Because Jacob is obsessed. The guy's at a point in his life where he doesn't give a shit. And Jacob is tough but he's classy. I can also get you paid."

"I'm going to have to discuss the material with Charlotte."

"Jesus, I hadn't even thought about that."

"*Coal*? Two brothers rape a white woman after killing her husband in front of her?" his wife asked. "Are you serious?"

"You're not remembering the whole story."

"But how was the play, Mrs. Lincoln?"

"Very funny. A stable boy—"

"A Black stable boy. Very helpful."

"A Black stable boy whose understanding of horses is the metaphorical center of the book. Not to mention he's the only person not either in jail or dead at the end."

"Your audience, and not just a Black audience, but particularly the woke white art-house audience, isn't going to allow the movie to do any work on its own terms after two Black dudes rape a white woman who's probably going to be a well-known actress for this to get financed."

"Two words: Rex Patterson."

"Fine. Black novelist. You get a brother to direct and it's great—maybe he'll get the fucking Oscar. With a honky from West Virginia, it's going to be suicide."

"You keep forgetting the title character is Black."

"I don't care if he's Nelson Mandela. You're going to be toast. And doesn't the white detective come into the house and kill the Black rapists without due process?"

"Essentially yes."

"Ferguson, Missouri. Freddie Gray. Eric Garner. Kalief Browder."

"The detective gets killed in the end."

"Maybe I need to reread the book."

Though about to audition to play Cordelia in a production of *King Lear* that wouldn't start rehearsals until January (the English director happened to be in the country), she'd finished the novel in two days, with David agreeing to wake with their daughters and get them out the door for summer day camp three mornings in a row.

"Okay, you have to make this," she announced at 2 a.m. in the bedroom of their apartment on West Ninety-Third Street. "It's just too good. Better than I remember. You're going to be crucified if you do it right, but you've been through controversy with *Revenge*. That gave you a taste."

"Will you read the script for it this woman wrote?" he asked, sitting up.

"You need me happy and fulfilled, which means being cast as Cordelia while trying to be a mom. I read the book. Don't make me read a bad screenplay. And tell whoever it is who's got the guts to finance this in 2019 that I love him for that and he's out of his fucking mind."

The phone call with Jacob and his partner, Larry McCormick, took place at 3 p.m. in New York on a humid Monday, noon in LA.

"We want you to make this movie with us," said Jacob.

"That's fantastic," David answered.

"You sound surprised," Larry said.

"Well, I haven't really given you guys my thoughts."

"I've done my research," Jacob said quickly, as if any problems David might have were part of that research. "Plus, I said I *want* you to do the film. I can change my mind. Have you read the script?"

"I have, and I guess I have some issues with it."

"What issues? Because we'd like to start going out to actors and make this thing. As in next summer."

"Next summer?" It was already July. Given the rewrites David envisioned, it would be tight, but not impossible.

"This material is important to me," insisted Jacob.

"I'm impressed you want to take it on."

"I don't need you to be impressed. I think Rex Patterson, before he drank himself to death, had some really interesting things to say about this country. We've done John Irving, Updike, Sinclair Lewis, Philip Roth. Rex Patterson belongs with those other writers. I want to be the one who has the balls to put *Coal* out there when the studios were too chickenshit."

"What are your problems with the script?" asked Larry.

"Well, let me start with what I like."

"Why don't you not," cut in Jacob. "We don't need to be told what's good about it. We already know what's good about it. Get to the point without all the bullshit."

"Okay, I think a good deal of the dialogue doesn't work."

"Well, that's easy," answered Jacob. "You want to do a dialogue polish, that's fine, but I'm not sure we need to wait for that to send it to actors."

"Particularly with a director like you," said Larry, "You're an actor, so they trust you."

"In part that's because I never send out a script until it's ready," said David.

"You're not sending it out, we are," said Jacob. "How much time do you need?"

"I'm guessing a couple of months."

"You can have six weeks."

It was then, as he'd revealed to Andrew on the plane, that David met Anthony Calabria for lunch in New York, having heard of their collaboration.

"You want to know what it was like working with, or I should say *for* Jacob?" the director asked. "It got to the point where when he called, and I saw his name come up, I'd dread it. The arguing about my cousin was one thing. His default position is that people are always trying to fuck him— like they're luring him into a trap. And it gets worse from there."

"But you made the movie."

"He was the only one who would finance it. One thing about Jacob, he wants to make interesting stuff. Practically no one else does anymore. It's all about algorithms and data now, which you can't blame people with the amount of money that's at stake. A guy like Jacob who goes just on taste is rare. He made my film when it made no sense to. But twice I tried to quit. I wanted Andre Richardson to shoot it. 'No, he's not on our list.' I had to pick one of their guys. Costumes. For some reason he and Larry are obsessed with costumes. I don't fucking know why—maybe because Jacob's wife was a clothing designer. They made me hire this woman Lynette Jones. Then I find out they're having her send concept ideas to them before me, and Jacob is rejecting ideas I never see. I called Jacob and told him I was out. This was two months before principal photography. I said I don't care. Sue me. I can't work this way."

"And?"

"He took me to dinner and apologized, said he would back off."

"Did he?"

"For about a day."

"You said you tried to quit twice."

"The first time was when we were meeting editors. Again, I was presented with their list. And by the way, you have to edit in their offices. You have to cast in their offices. Their line producer sits in on every meeting with department heads and reports everything to Jacob. At least Jacob has taste and culture and brains. This line producer—his name is Sergei—the guy doesn't have a creative bone in his body. He hates directors because he wanted to be one and isn't—a fucking epidemic in Hollywood if you haven't noticed."

"Jesus, Anthony, I'm out. I mean, why did you make your movie under these conditions?"

"It's like all of us, David. When somebody will give us the money, we're pathetic, sycophantic, manipulative worms. Until the financing is too deep in. Then of course we become infantile brats!" He chuckled. "There are about ten directors who don't have to deal with some version of this, and I'm not one of them, so I fucking endured it."

David took a deep breath to fight his blooming nausea.

"Finish the story," he said.

"Anyway, we're meeting editors. Somehow I get them to agree to consider a couple of ideas I had who weren't on their list, and we bring in Brian Gates, who's amazing. He does all of the Peter Michael Henderson films."

"Right."

"So, Brian doesn't know Jacob. If he had, he wouldn't have done what he did, which what do you think that was?"

"He kept talking about Peter Michael Henderson."

"And Jacob hates that because Peter is a final-cut director who can do whatever he wants. But Brian keeps saying, 'Well, the way PMJ and I work,' and 'when PMJ and I were cutting *Funny Love*,' and finally Jacob says, 'Stop talking about Peter Michael Henderson.' Brian says, 'What?' And Jacob says, 'Stop talking about Peter Michael Henderson and with the stupid initials like every other pretentious moron. I don't give a shit about him, and I hate his films. They're poorly edited too, so you're not doing yourself any favors.' So Brian says, 'Well, I guess I'm not your guy then,' and Jacob says, 'No, you're not, which I could've told you ten minutes ago.' I said, I can't work with a company that treats people like that, even in an interview. And Jacob says, 'Like what? You mean not bullshitting them?'"

"Fuck me."

"Here's the deal, David: ultimately, and this is probably true for every director anywhere, you've got to figure out ways to carve out space, no matter what it takes, to do your work. Even if you have to lie, cheat, and steal. And in spite of all of it, there'll come a time, way down the road, when you might even grow to appreciate Jacob. I'm not saying you'll like him, but you'll at least be thankful he's on your side. As strange as it sounds, I'd probably work with him again. There's no one else like him, I can tell you that."

With their daughters, Samira and Anna, still in camp weekdays, and Charlotte consumed now with a callback for *King Lear*, David reread the novel, marking all parts detrimentally removed for the screenplay, while doing his best to address issues with Carly Billings's dialogue.

"I just don't get it," he told his wife. "How can a woman smart enough to structure the film this way be so hapless whenever men and women speak to one another?"

He advanced the relationship between the film's romantic leads more incrementally and wrote a version of the opening that hewed to the novel's prologue. In it a forbear of the title character endured the near-fatal experience of the Middle Passage from Senegambia on a slave ship. Given the book's provocative conceits on race, this felt essential to the story, and he struggled to understand why Carly Billings hadn't agreed.

He finished his work in just over five weeks, by which time Charlotte had been cast in *Lear*. Feeling a surge of vitality as husband to such a talented woman, he pressed Send on his laptop while performing a cameo in a friend's movie in Brooklyn. Forty minutes later he returned from set to a terse e-mail: "I said dialogue polish. You've rewritten script, and VERY POORLY. Unacceptable." Looking at the time of the transmission, he calculated seven minutes had transpired between his having sent the draft and Jacob's response.

He wrote back. "Jacob, please know I put a great deal of time into what I did, all of it specifically within the constraints of what we discussed. I'm also not sure how you came to your conclusions given such little time with the material."

Within a minute: "Opening awful. Other changes unreadable. UNAC-CEPTABLE."

Anthony Calabria's warnings aside, what provoked this treatment? The next morning he awoke to a text: "Talk today?"

They arranged to do so at 3 p.m.

"David."

"Hi, Jacob."

"I thought it best if I told you a bit about who I am and how I work. First of all, I've been a practicing lawyer, and I've been in real estate, and I've produced over seventy movies. And that's really produced, not just stuck my name on them."

"Okay."

"I make decisions. And I've gotten extremely good at that. I chose you to direct this film, but I didn't choose you to write it. I don't like how in Hollywood people come in and try to take over and grab credit and attention away from others."

David wondered how he had tried to seize credit at all, unless by adding "Revisions by David Levit" underneath "Screenplay by Carly Billings" on the script's title page, per industry standard.

"David? Are you there? Am I making sense?"

"I was just organizing it all."

"What's to organize? I think it's pretty clear."

"I'm curious about this distaste for steamrolling others since that's precisely what you're trying to do with me. You clearly didn't read all my revisions before rejecting them wholesale. In fact, you responded to my six weeks of work in a manner so perfunctory that I basically now want nothing to do with you or this project. Then there's your implication that I'm somehow trying to take the film over, which I assure you I'm not, though I will point out that in nearly every conversation you've taken pains to point out how this is your film."

"It is my film."

"Sure, Jacob, and I accept that if you need me to. All I'm trying to do is direct it in the best way I can, and that involves helping to fix the script. The opening, for instance—"

"Your opening is dead. It's not happening. Your mistake is you seem to think this film is about race, which it is, but not in the way you think."

"How do you know what I think?"

"Because I'm very good at this. You go out there and ask people about me."

"I have."

"And I bet a lot of them say I can be difficult. But it's because I actually fucking care. At every stage. About every word. Most of what you did was in there to mollify."

"What does that even mean?"

"Make the film what you think the audience wants instead of what Rex Patterson actually wrote."

"That is just not true, and I resent the thought. The opening I put back in is his, not mine. By learning about a character's lineage we learn about the character."

"In a novel, not in a movie. Prologues and epilogues are for writers who couldn't figure out how to get their ideas into the bulk of their book. Luckily in film we don't have that option. Screenwriters need to be disciplined."

"Now I'm undisciplined?"

"I'm not sure what you are anymore, and I don't like the uncertainty."

"So, pay me for the work I've done and get rid of me."

There was a pause.

"Why don't we meet face-to-face first instead?"

Chicago Films' next release was a version of Saul Bellow's *Herzog*, which would premiere at the Toronto Film Festival. Why one would make a movie in which the main character mostly writes letters, many of them to the dead, stood well beyond David's grasp, but it made him admire Jacob in spite of the friction between them. David was at the festival to support a movie called *Monstrous*, which told the story of a woman in her early thirties who returns to her New England town to deal with the alcoholism that has ravaged her life in New York. As a metaphor for the disease, she discovers that while swimming laps in a local pool, through some cosmic synergy, her movements are mimicked by a giant sea creature causing tsunamis off the coast of China on the other side of the world. If only for the sheer ridiculousness of the concept, David had agreed to play a town local.

Were the industry an ocean, and the studios big pelagic predators, the Four Seasons Hotel during the festival constituted a reef where smaller fish could mingle. These represented every one of the United States from Alaska to Oklahoma, and seemingly any country that could be named. There were buyers, sellers, investors, debtors, creditors, press agents, bloggers, reviewers, actors, directors, would-be moguls, has-been moguls, never moguls, auto-graph hounds, prostitutes, mistresses. An ecosystem all its own. David and Charlotte had a room on the eighth floor, and by the time they'd arisen and dressed, a thicket of foam-backed posters on placard stands clogged their hallway: two for movies at the festival, one for a film fund, another for a foreign sales company, another for a tax-abatement program in Sri Lanka. Suitors and press crowded the passageway.

"Why do you stay here?" asked Charlotte as they navigated their way through.

"It's a state-of-the-art look at the industry."

"More like a hucksters convention. And when you call it 'the industry' it's not sexy."

"Noted, with thanks."

The elevator opened to a packed, caffeinated lobby.

"Call me after your lunch," she said before heading to a documentary about southern Blacks in politics that featured her father. It had been made for PBS, and this would be her only chance to see it on a big screen. David regretted not accompanying her but had only an hour and hoped to spend time with the head of New Vision Films, a Los Angeles–based foreign sales company run and owned by Israelis by way of South Africa who'd relo-cated to the United States in the early eighties when apartheid seemed too resilient ever to perish.

"Why did I want to see this racism every day when it was why my parents left Europe?" Yariv Bergman, the owner of New Vision, explained to David in an impossibly thick Israeli accent when they'd met twelve years before. "I should have come to America first and skipped South Africa altogether." He had financed two of David's films, hoping for profits from domestic sales that didn't ultimately materialize, but they would likely make others together thanks to the first of their two collaborations.

"The only movie I ever make where I said I don't care if I lose money," he frequently declared about that film, which chronicled the lives of Jewish capos at Buchenwald. "You ask me what is the greatest picture I ever make, I'll tell you it's two of them: *Capos* and *Tarantula II*! *Capos* I made for my parents. *Tarantula 2* I made for two hundred thousand dollar, and we sold it around the world for five million!"

At the time he'd already compiled a library of three hundred movies, every one of which had turned a profit. He was the most successful B-movie producer in Hollywood since Roger Corman, and David remained unem-barrassed by their association. Without the profits from *Tarantula II*, along with its antecedent and six sequels, all of which were filmed in Bulgaria, *Capos* would never have been made. By now Yariv and New Vision were producing high-end action franchises that opened on thousands of American screens with A-list stars.

At the Four Seasons Yariv always occupied the same corner table at the edge of the lobby bar.

"David! How are you, my friend?"

Seated with him was his partner, Dov Delsheim, who ran foreign sales, the monetary engine of the company. He stood at an even five feet and at sixty-five had the physique of a wrestler decades younger, along with a thick Brillo of silver hair that coiled tightly no more than an inch off a wide Sephardic head. They were joined by two male assistants and a duo of Yariv's former mistresses, who now produced films together for New Vision.

"Get him a chair," Yariv urged an assistant. "David, you want a coffee? Breakfast? Anything you want."

"No, I'm great, Yariv. I just came over to say hello. I knew you'd be here."

"Always!" Dov Delsheim shouted, hubristically smacking a thick binder in front of him with the flat of his palm.

"What's in that, Dov?"

"Every number from every territory for every one of our film!" he boomed in an accent somehow thicker than Yariv's. "Even yours!"

"Well, let's not look at those."

"You still directed the greatest film I ever made," Yariv assured him.

"He loves that movie," said one of the former mistresses.

The lobby quieted discernibly as those near the elevators made way for a quintet of figures: two young women and behind them three men, the middle of whom towered over the phalanx.

"It's Charlie," said Yariv.

Charlie Gold, who with his younger brother, Rob, owned and ran Gold Films, cut as recognizable a figure as there was in film. He'd come up through the world of music, with his brother and him operating their own chain of record stores right after college in their native Buffalo. The more ambitious of the two, Charlie had always wanted to make films. As he told it, once he could take the bus downtown as a boy, he saw every movie that screened. In his teens his parents allowed him to spend summers downstate with an aunt in the city. He consumed whatever played at any theater that would admit him, from the most outlandish American thrillers and splatter movies to the works of Buñuel, Truffaut, Fassbinder, and Fellini.

He often saw three films a day while studying assiduously how they were promoted, reviewed, and monetized.

In the winter of 1985 he and Rob sold their stores and all their inventory and in May flew to Europe to attend the Cannes Film Festival. They begged, bullied, and fibbed their way into every party and screening they could, then bought smart, with Charlie's methodically acquired knowledge of contemporary, auteur-driven cinema informing each choice. They returned to America with three titles—one British, one French, and one Italian—and launched their brand. Gold Films was now a behemoth. What films Charlie wanted, he bought, and when he bought, he pursued awards with a ruthlessness that redefined the promotion game. He'd made countless careers possible but had ruined far more, entrapping filmmakers in onerous deals with unrealistic promises as he shelved their movies or simply didn't produce their scripts. Better to have artists dormant with him than active for his competitors.

David had had his own interactions with Charlie, few of them pleasant. They began seven years prior when Gold Films was set to release a highbrow teen thriller David wrote on a lark based loosely on a Jacobean revenge tragedy—Thomas Middleton and William Rowley's *The Changeling*. The idea had presented itself while he worked on sides with Charlotte for an off-Broadway production of the same play.

"What's crazy about this material," he said to her, "is that if you wanted to transpose it to present day, the best place to set it would be a high school. Obviously, all the passions are there with teenagers, but in America the lethal violence is there as well. Jesus, think of Columbine, and then add in Instagram and Twitter and Facetime. It would be insane."

"Why don't you do it?" she asked. They sat in their small kitchen, their first daughter napping in another room, not yet one. "In a weird way it might even be commercial, which wouldn't exactly hurt at this point."

He transposed the play's seventeenth-century plot to a suburban Connecticut high school, infusing it with all the violence and melodrama of the source material, inflected further by the alienation, jealousies, and treacheries of adolescence in the social media age.

Initially Yariv hoped to finance it, but this would have meant shooting in Eastern Europe, which David didn't see, so he and Howard looked elsewhere. At UCM they found a young producer from Long Island named Brad Shlansky, represented by a colleague of Howard's named Paul Aiello, who'd apparently known the relative newcomer since they were kids in neighboring towns back east. Shlansky promised to raise three times what Yariv offered, and even to shoot in the state where David had set it.

Negotiating the deal with Brad and his lawyer turned out to be one of the most contentiously awful processes David had ever endured. The producer and his lawyer seemed motivated by the most cynical view of humanity imaginable, every clause working in Brad's favor should conflict ensue. But just as with Jacob Rosenthal, David's eagerness to get his film made eradicated all reason.

Soon, however, the proclivities of the young producer most repellent in negotiations proved useful. After they'd cast an ensemble of young stars, Charlie Gold's younger brother, Rob, began pursuing the film for his genre division inside of Gold Films. Suddenly the project went from one precariously funded at three million dollars for a likely art-house release to one selling for ten million that might play at multiplexes. Unwilling to stop there, Brad pushed for a minimum of two thousand screens for opening weekend, a fifteen million dollar print and ad spend, and a theatrical release within a year of its delivery. Desperate for the film, Rob Gold agreed to it all. Solely because of Brad, David went from making a small teen thriller to directing a studio film with a guaranteed wide release.

"This is only your second movie. How did you learn to negotiate like that?" David asked Brad.

"I know how to make things look shiny," his new partner answered with a strange smile. "Now go and direct our movie!"

David did, the shoot largely uneventful, other than rumors of lost financing during preproduction that never proved true. But three weeks into his edit, Brad called David in the cutting room.

"*Revenge* is playing out right now in Montana. It's like Columbine all over again, only worse, if you can believe it."

David and his editor, along with everyone else editing films on the floor, stood before the television in the postproduction facility's common area as events unfolded live at Elysian High School in the suburbs of Billings. Because David, his production designer, and his director of photography had studied school shootings meticulously, and had sought to depict theirs in *Revenge* with as much accuracy as possible, the images on the news chronicling two Elysian eleventh graders opening fire on classmates with assault rifles stolen from the father of one of the boys seemed as if they'd been lifted from *Revenge*'s dailies. Nineteen teens (including the perpetrators, who activated suicide vests when their ammunition ran out), two teachers, and the school principal had already perished. It would be the most deadly school shooting in American history. It was being reported that at least one of the perpetrators was a Muslim, but this could not be confirmed. David closed the edit for the day. Given the circumstances—putative radicalized suicidal killers, young victims—he considered calling Sammy but didn't; the absence of Adam remained too painful.

That evening his discussion with Brad was brief: the sooner they finished the movie and delivered it to the Golds, the better. Meanwhile, more came out about the shooters and what seemed to have motivated them, offering a smorgasbord of incoherence that could satisfy the political agenda of any interest wishing to exploit it. One of the killers identified as an "Islamist," as well as a follower, via the Internet, of the late Anwar al-Awlaki, who was killed by an American drone strike in 2011. The first two classmates he killed were Jews, the only in his grade. His partner was an avowed atheist, the son of a white American father and a Filipino mother who had divorced his father and returned to the Philippines several years before, leaving the boy's raising to his unemployed alcoholic progenitor. It was from him the teens had taken the weapons, and from an Internet video the design for their vests. Their treatise referenced the wars in Afghanistan, Iraq, and Syria; the 1 percent of Americans who controlled half its wealth (an inordinate number of them Jews, who constituted the "most powerful among the powerful"); the inexorably warming planet; and finally the venality of all systems of authority—from parents, to schools, to racist police forces. They considered themselves martyrs to a revolution just beginning.

The tragedy consumed the news, with each siloed platform exploiting it to prove its respective worldview: that Islamism represented America's most pernicious foe, that the breakdown of the family was disenfranchising an entire generation, that guns were the problem, that guns were the solution, that too much wealth was controlled by too few, that a feckless liberal hysteria invested more energy in blame than solutions, that heat waves and rising seas would spell our ruin.

Within six weeks David and Brad showed the director's cut to Rob Gold's division within Gold Films. Called Parameter, it was Rob's own extremely profitable genre fiefdom. Though its films won few awards, and Rob himself hadn't ascended to the heights of respect in Hollywood his brother had, from its inception the imprint consistently led the company in earnings.

"This is a great fucking film," Rob announced. "I can't wait to show it to my brother. He's going to shit himself. This is the first movie we've had that could really go under either label, but fuck me if I'm giving it to that asshole. And it's goddamned timely too," he said, rubbing his hands together. "People are going to go nuts for this thing."

"I'm actually scared they'll think we're exploiting the situation at Elysian," David said. "They'll never know we shot it before."

"'Shot it.' That's good!"

"Not how I meant it."

"Leave that to my publicity department. Of course it's gonna be controversial, and it's also going to make a fucking mint. Controversy is good." Then he repeated, now more to himself than to David, "My brother's going to shit himself," as if little held more importance.

David considered it strange that Charlie hadn't attended the screening, but Rob's enthusiasm quelled concern. Moreover, Rob's notes were negligible, and he also offered David a three-year overhead deal for nearly half a million dollars, giving Parameter a first option on anything David chose to develop.

But then all communication stopped, and within days of David delivering his second cut, he was instructed by Rob's executives not to lock picture on the film's final third, during which most of the violence occurred. Parameter Films, he was told, might want him to reshoot the entire denouement to remove the shootings altogether.

"They can't change the plot of Middleton and Rowley," David warned Brad over the phone from the editing room in New York.

"Are you seriously thinking Rob and Charlie are concerned there's going to be public outcry over your loyalty to a drama written in, what was it, the seventeenth century by two dopes from England no one's ever heard of?"

"I'm saying I'll take my name off it."

"Just calm down. No one is forcing you to change anything, at least not before they've heard from me. They have no idea."

As all this transpired, David went to Cannes with his college housemate Noah Mendelson, where their film *Hillbilly Wedding* had somehow gotten into Critics' Week after also winning the Audience Award at Sundance. David traded his first-class ticket for two coach seats so Charlotte could join.

"It's never going to get better than this, David," she told him on their first night in the hills to the north at La Colombe d'Or beneath paintings some of modernism's greats had traded for meals half a century before. A quick perusal of the room revealed at least a dozen of the most accomplished directors and actors in international cinema interspersed, hunched over steak frites, loup de mer, magret de canard, and the like, the centuries-old room seeming to tremble in candlelight. "There's only one first time for something like this. We've got to enjoy every second." She took his hand. "This will be there for us when we're at the end together looking back."

The next morning he and Noah were drinking coffee at the Carlton Hotel while Charlotte worked out in the gym when Charlie Gold approached their table to meet Noah. Despite the imperilment of his film, David couldn't help but fight elation at being associated with someone worth Charlie's time.

"Hey, guys," Charlie said. "I saw *Hillbilly Wedding* at Sundance. We really wanted it."

"You did?" Noah answered inscrutably.

"And by the way, if you'd sold it to us, you'd be in the competition here, not Critics' Week. But I still want to work with you, and I don't say that to just anyone. I could make sure millions of people see your movies. You'd win Oscars with us. We made the way for people like you to make your movies and get them financed. You see all this?" He gestured to the crowded cafe. "We created this market."

"I'll keep that in mind, sir," said Noah.

"What's this 'sir' shit? Call me Charlie." He extended an ursine hand that Noah shook before it was clocked obligatorily to David, who had stood when Charlie approached.

"Take care, guys. And let me know if we can help with anything while you're here. Anything. My guys can take care of whatever you need."

When Charlie had left, David turned back to his college housemate.

"You didn't even stand up. The most powerful man in indie films saying he wants to make your movies."

"Didn't they offer you a first-look deal too?"

"Business Affairs, not Charlie himself."

"Yeah, you want to know something? He came to the film at Sundance and walked out thirty minutes in. They only went after it once we'd won the Audience Award and we'd already sold it. If we'd given it to him, it would just as likely end up on the shelf as in theaters. Half the time they buy movies just so they won't compete with theirs. Or they get some hack editor to recut them without telling you. He's a bad guy, David."

"I'm gonna go ask him about *Revenge*."

"I wouldn't."

He found Charlie at the curb among his entourage and touched a hulking shoulder. Charlie turned, his expression now the opposite of friendly.

"Yeah?"

"I was just over there with Noah Mendelson. I was in his film."

"What do you need?"

"I'm not sure you're aware of this, but I directed *Revenge*."

"*Revenge?*" He feigned effort to remember. "Oh. Yeah, that's with my brother's company. I learned a long time ago not to involve myself with those movies. He makes more money for us if I don't meddle. I've been wrong too many times with the genre stuff, so I haven't seen it." He turned away while remaining exactly where he stood. Effectively he'd disappeared, so emphatic was the gesture.

"How'd that go?" asked Noah when Charlie returned to his seat.

"Without you there I got a far less friendly reception."

"Until he needs something from you, or you're a twenty-year-old woman and he's chasing you around his office."

"Those stories are true?"

Two months later Howard informed David that both Charlie and Rob wanted to meet him at the New York offices of Gold Films.

"Should I go?" he asked Brad.

"Why not?"

"Alone?"

"You want to bring Charlotte? I wouldn't, but up to you."

"You think Charlie will still claim not to have seen the film?"

"Just make sure and tell them about not changing the plot of the original play, and how important that is to you and the millions of fans of ... what are the names of those two idiots?

"Middleton and Rowley."

"Middleton and Rowley. Because that's gonna be extremely persuasive, especially with Rob. He's obsessed with eighteenth-century theater."

"Seventeenth."

"Seventeenth even more! He salivates!"

David sat waiting in the reception area for half an hour perusing an array of vintage rock posters adorning the walls, presumably in reference to the source of the brothers' initial capital. On his way he'd bought an espresso served in a paper demitasse. These tiny cups constituted a fad he hoped would soon pass, mostly because the coffee tended to splatter his clothing when walking. When he was finally ushered into the conference room, the first order of business became satisfying Charlie's fascination.

"What the fuck is that?" he asked, pointing.

"It's an espresso."

"I mean what you're drinking it out of?" His tone suggested the dis-posable-cup industry should have sought his approval. He took the drink between thumb and forefinger and brought it to eye level like a grizzly examining the carcass of a bee.

"You see this?" he asked his brother.

"Yeah, I see it."

He handed it back with surprisingly dainty care. David placed it on the table without sipping.

"This is Jill Steinman," Charlie said, gesturing to his left, where a smallish woman in her fifties leaned across to shake David's hand. She had raven hair beginning to gray that she wasn't choosing to color. She wore little make-up, and her frank aspect had the severity of a person who went looking for wrongs. She reminded David of the kind of woman Adam would have dated: smart, unafraid, insistently confident.

"We asked her to be here," Charlie continued, "because she's very involved with current issues, particularly among the young, and the impact of media, social and otherwise, on the young. She's worked closely both with both Obama and Hillary."

"And Tipper Gore," she added.

"And Tipper, right," said Charlie. "Back in the day. What were you, twelve?" Jill laughed as Charlie turned back to David. "We're lucky to have her at Gold Films."

"Thanks, Charlie."

"No, thank you."

Rob remained silent.

"So, Jill," Charlie continued, "and a lot of other people incidentally, have watched your movie, and they have a good deal to say about it, and we've mainly listened, which I think is what people should do in a situation like this."

"I'm not sure I quite understand," said David. "What's the situation?"

"When you have a movie like yours."

"What sort of movie is that?"

"Already you're getting defensive, and that's not useful. Jill, you want to explain?"

"Sure." She opened a folder. "Your movie touches on certain issues afflicting our country right now."

"High school violence."

"Among others."

"And those are?"

"Terrorism, radicalization, economic disparity, social media."

"So you're conflating *Revenge* with what happened at Elysian. There's no political manifesto in *Revenge*."

"Everything is political."

"Everything is not directly political."

"I would argue it is, we just don't realize it."

"Our movie is psychological. It deals with alienation of the young in the digital age, and the violence that can result. If you want to call that political, I can't stop you."

"It fetishizes that violence."

"I don't think the film fetishizes anything. We've made the violence not only quite realistic but consequential. We studied shootings way back before the proliferation of the Internet and cell phones. Columbine, but also Pearl, Jonesboro, and others."

"Film, like all the Internet bullying you're so careful to depict in your movie, is a medium that expresses its power in ways we still don't fully understand, but for which we nevertheless need to take responsibility as filmmakers." Has she made movies herself? David wondered, repressing the impulse to ask. "What you or I might see as cautionary on screen might actually appeal to viewers not acculturated in the same way we are."

"You mean you have to have studied film theory?" inquired David. "Which clearly you have, to be able to understand a movie and whatever cultural trends it's trying to depict? Let's just stop making contemporary dramas, then."

"That's very clever, but we both know it's not what I'm saying. You have to agree that purveyors of popular culture have to examine their potential responsibility when making choices about what to put out there and when."

The patronizing tone, the weaponized aesthetic terminology had been irritating enough, but it was clear the release of his film was under serious threat.

"First of all, you act like this is a new argument. It isn't. It's been going on since Plato and Aristotle."

"We're all aware you studied classics," she said.

"I'm not flashing my credentials."

"Good," said Charlie, "because that would be a bad idea opposite Jill here. She's a very educated woman."

"Clearly," David responded. "I'm only pointing out that what she construes as an argument unique to film and our modern times actually isn't. People have been saying that the telling of controversial stories is dangerous since we started telling stories."

"No one's disputing that," Jill said with performed patience.

"Then where is this headed?" David asked, looking to Rob. The adage about the brothers—"Charlie will stab you in the back, and Rob will stab you in the stomach"—came to mind. "Rob," he asked directly, "are you going to ask me to change the film? Sanitize it? Are you even going to release it?"

Charlie answered before his brother could.

"Make no mistake, if we want to recut your film, we will."

"I think it's a bit more complicated than that," answered David. "There's a competing cut clause in my contract."

"We'll do what we want, or we won't release your fucking movie. How's that?" answered Charlie, his voice rising. "Or I decide your career is over. How would that be? But we're not going to recut anything. The film stays as it is. It's finished." The final sentence rotated slowly in the ensuing silence to reveal each intended meaning. "Frankly, I don't want to spend another penny on it. And if you were smart, you'd take all this as a compliment. We think your movie is powerful. But because of that we're going to be careful and not release it wide. As a courtesy we've brought you here to let you know that. Your movie is an art film. That's the point we're trying to make. We're going to platform it, starting out with a smaller, more exclusive release and a targeted ad campaign."

"If this is about it being an art film, why did you bring in Jill here to explain how it's dangerous?"

"Because after what happened in Montana, my company doesn't want the blood of teenagers on its hands."

"Look. My best friend was killed in Israel by terrorists."

"I'm sorry to hear that," Charlie said with impatient sincerity.

"We all are," added Rob.

"Thank you," said David. "I'd never make a movie that encouraged violence of any sort. I stand behind the film and why we made it. And I think you should too, but on that we obviously disagree—I guess extremely disagree. But as far as I'm concerned, release it how you want, particularly if you'll leave it in theaters and even expand the release if it's doing well and your fears about its destructive impact prove unfounded. After all, presumably you're going to put it out on video where it'll be seen by most people anyway."

Charlie glanced at Jill, who focused on the pages in front of her.

"We'll do everything we can," he said vaguely before rising and presenting the hand David had shaken months before at Cannes. "We appreciate your understanding."

"There's one thing you should know though," said David, not rising.

"What's that?"

"It's just, I'm not really the issue."

"Meaning what exactly?"

"Brad Shlansky has the contract with you, not me. And the contract requires a different kind of release, so unless you want actual changes to the movie, which you've thankfully said you don't, the person with whom you should really be speaking is him."

Charlie turned to his brother.

"What the fuck is this?"

"What do you mean, asshole? The film has a producer," answered Rob.

"This guy doesn't even matter!" shouted Charlie, gesturing at David. "Who cares about the fucking director if he's not a signatory?" Charlie pivoted back to David. "Why the fuck did you sit here wasting my time if you knew none of this was up to you?"

"You invited me."

"Your fucking producer is going to let us platform this movie, and for his own good, because we're not releasing it wide! You're gonna let him know that!"

"I'll be happy to, but I'll warn you, having been in a negotiation with him myself, Brad Shlansky is very serious about keeping to the letter of a contract."

"I will fucking destroy him. I will fucking string him up! You tell him that! He will not make another fucking film! He has no fucking idea what I can do!"

"Charlie wants you to know he's going to platform the film," David told Brad from the street in front of the Gold Films offices after he'd tossed his espresso and its demitasse into a public receptacle.

"And what did you say to that?" asked Brad.

"I told him you wouldn't be happy about it."

"Did you tell him about Alice?"

"I figured I'd leave that to you."

When David first learned both of Brad Shlansky's parents had died during his senior year of high school, one by suicide, and that Brad had forgone college to settle affairs and care for his sisters, it inspired admiration. Brad had overcome more than David probably ever would. But the resulting distrust of others, not to mention how Brad seemed to want so intensely to even the score with a universe that had dealt him this tragedy, put Brad beyond the reach of David's comprehension.

This became even more true when David first encountered Brad's lawyer, Alice Schaffson. Like Brad, she met opposition with overwhelming aggression once threats and dissembling had failed. What similar tragedies inspired her ungenerous worldview, David could only guess. He'd grown to dread the mere invocation of her name.

"Well then, I'm just going to have to call Alice! How would that be?" Brad would shout, as if referencing muscle in a loanshark operation.

"Let me tell you why I'm the best lawyer Brad could possibly have," she once explained to David on the phone while Brad listened in silent deference. "I work for Brad and only Brad. These other assholes out there are part of a club, and they're desperate to stay in that club, which is a fucking huge, blatant conflict of interest. I don't live there, I'm not from there, I couldn't be less interested in their world."

"You mean LA?" asked David.

"Yes, I mean LA. Where the fuck else would I mean?"

"The Golds live in New York."

"Oh please. Yeah, they live here, but they're part of that whole LA cabal. I come from Queens and I live in Queens—the good part of Queens by the way—and it's the only place I ever want to be. I don't have deals with agents and producers and directors and actors involving other clients, so I don't have to fucking make nice because tomorrow I'm going to be on the phone with them trying to do a deal for some other asshole where I'm taking his five percent. I'm not meeting them for lunch next week at the— what's that fucking place called, Brad?"

"The Cut?"

"Not the place we go. The other place. The lunch place I wouldn't be caught dead at you took me once."

"The Ivy."

"At the fucking Ivy or wherever—everybody stopping off at everybody's table—to leverage that I represent one client for my other clients. I don't have to play their fucking game. I play my game on my terms. That's why Brad has me and not one of these ridiculous so-called entertainment lawyers. You know who they're entertaining? Themselves, because they're pulling each other off all day. I can tell them all to go fuck themselves, and guess what? When I do, they don't know what to do. You should be on the phone with me sometimes."

I already am, David thought.

"And the agents. If you spent one day with me listening to the way those self-important assholes jerk themselves off in their big offices with the big windows looking out over Beverly Hills while the assistants listen in—and by the way, I love that. The assistants listening in. If the agent's a straight man, the assistant is always young and female. If the agent's a fag, young and male. A dyke, young and female. You tell me if I'm wrong. And always on the phone 'to learn.' Give me a fucking break. I tell them first thing: 'Get the assistant *off* the line. The only person who's going to *learn* anything on this call is you learning what my client needs.' If you spent an hour with me on the phone with them, you'd know more about the entertainment industry—which by the way I never worked a day in until I met Brad—than in a lifetime, because I fucking terrify them. *Terrify* them into telling the truth. We get down to the fucking marrow when I'm making a deal."

Brad had insisted she be production counsel on *Revenge* (and receive an associate producer credit), giving not only David his own experience opposite her but every other artist as well, each contract as much a rulebook for future litigation favoring Brad as a memorialization of the terms of pay, billing, and creative obligations.

She had also negotiated the purchase of *Revenge* with Gold Films.

As Charlie strode with his retinue to greet Yariv, David wondered whether there'd be any acknowledgment of their past.

"Hey, Yariv. How's the festival going for you?"

"It's great, Charlie," answered Yariv. "We got three film here, and we preselling five others. You know David Levit?"

"Hi, howya doin'?" said Charlie, seeming neither to allow nor deny that they'd had dealings.

"Very well."

Charlie faced the two former mistresses.

"Tiffany. Tatjana. How are you two?" David remembered being told Charlie and Yariv had shared time with Tatjana, a Serbian, the darker and more petite of the two.

"We're good, Charlie," she answered with piercing gloom.

"So am I," Charlie assured her obscurely. "We're having a party after our premiere tonight. I hope you guys can come." Somehow Charlie made it clear that this did not apply to David.

Yariv addressed his male assistant.

"Get the information." The young man selected from among Charlie's phalanx, then began typing quickly into a smartphone.

"Good luck with everything. All of you," said Charlie, and he was off.

"So, David, you here with a film?" asked Yariv.

"Tomorrow. I'm having lunch with Jacob Rosenthal in about twenty minutes. We're supposed to be doing something together, though I think today's meeting will determine if that's actually going to happen. Maybe I'm about to be fired."

"Why don't you make an action movie? We have all kind of script we can give you. All you need to do is get cast. You get the actors, we make the picture. I'll pay you a million dollar."

"I'll read whatever you send," David answered with a smile. Yariv and Charlie constituted a species of movie executive fast becoming extinct—Yariv mostly benign, Charlie less so. Each made decisions instinctively, often without counsel, informing startled executives only after the fact. In Yariv's case, he famously never read the scripts of films before green-lighting them, relying instead on quick plot summaries and a list of possible stars.

"If I can see the poster, then I know I can sell the picture," he would explain. "So, if you can't tell me in a simple way what happen in the movie and what the star does, and how it look on the poster, I can't sell it and I won't make it. This is better than reading a script. You don't read a movie. You watch it and tell your friends."

As he walked to lunch, David wondered why the movie business attracted such a rogues' gallery. And why so many Jews? He was familiar with the arguments regarding other professions. Centuries of arguing Torah made parsing meaning outside of religious texts a developed acuity, thus Jews in law. With banking, prohibitions against gentiles handling money exposed the field to Jews before anyone else. Medicine provided security to first-generation children of immigrants. But why film? David often remembered a conversation he had with Adam on the green his sophomore year in college not long after they'd met.

"Look at this, David" he exclaimed, flinging a hand toward the students scattered in front of them. "Out of the, say, hundred people we can see right now, a good sixty-five of them Caucasian, can you show me more than thirty-five white gentiles? You can't. And they didn't even used to allow us here. Why is that?"

"Why are you here?" David asked.

"My dad went here, which I still can't imagine. And what was I going to do, go to Princeton or Harvard and get molded into one of those ridiculous people? And even there, more than a quarter of the students are Jews. What's that about?"

"I wasn't exactly around a big sample group in Charleston."

"How many Jews in your graduating class?"

"Three of sixty-eight."

"Did your parents obsess over education?"

"My mother is a teacher."

"My parents were monsters," said Adam. "Academics over everything. They assigned us books outside of school. During the school year. My dad fucking lectured us every night at the dinner table."

"I had to write five paragraphs a week that my parents graded."

"But why? Why did my dad quote his dad and say, 'A Jew has to speak the King's English better than the king?'"

"Because it's true."

"But also true for Asians and Blacks and Hispanics. Probably more so for them."

"Different for Jews."

"How?"

"Blacks have been treated more poorly, for longer, than any other group in this country. Not even an argument. But when a Black person succeeds now, a lot of liberal educated whites are happy, even relieved in a way if I can say that, which is its own kind of pathology."

"I think you're full of shit, but elaborate."

"First of all, we're impressed because we know what the person probably had to overcome to get there. Again, we're talking liberal educated whites."

"Okay."

"Second, it chips away at how shitty we deservedly feel for the way Black people have been treated and are still treated. If there's ever a Black president, that's going to piss a lot of people off, but there's mostly going to be a big fucking celebration. A lot of whites, and you watch, I'll be right about this, will fucking rejoice. We'll say, 'See! Look how far we've come!' And trust me, we won't have come as far as we think. But it's just not like that at this point with Jews. Gentiles just get irritated by us, particularly when we fit into any of the stereotypes: pushy, overly ambitious, obsessed with money, too many of us on a college green, name the derogation. Your dad's advice works because there's just nothing delightful to gentiles about a successful Jew. So we have to be all the more adept at an ability or task to overcome how annoying we are to non-Jews. Now, make no mistake: I'd rather be Jewish than Black in America a hundred times over. What a Black person has to deal with on a daily basis—suspicion, irrational fear, condescension, and lots of other shit I'm sure we can't even fathom—adds up to more adversity than most of us, Jews included, get in a lifetime."

"So your point is that other than, say, Egypt, the Inquisition, the pogroms, and of course the six million, Blacks have had it far worse than us, certainly in America. Therefore, Black success is applauded by enlightened whites, whereas we still have to overcome how inherently despicable we are? This is your thesis?"

"Laugh, but yes. But then even if I'm right, so much of the delight people might experience in response to Black success has the taint of condescension to it, meaning it's almost impossible to win if you're Black in America."

David often remembered this conversation in the presence of Charlotte. His grandmother had described class as "grace under pressure," and by that definition, Charlotte had more of it than anyone he'd ever encountered. She simply didn't lose her cool, no matter the social circumstance. She also expected more of him creatively and personally, and certainly gave more by way of support, wisdom, and wholesale intellect than anyone in his life. Now they were raising biracial kids who identified as Black, and proudly so, but in part because society gave them no choice but to identify as *something*. They considered themselves Jews too, and were enrolled in Hebrew school, but Charlotte avoided her own associations with the religion.

"I'm Black for life," she explained, "with all the stupid prejudices and expectations that go along with that. And not just from whites. They're almost easier to deflect because they're so moronic. I can compartmentalize not being picked up by a cab or being followed in a store or being treated like I need shit explained to me, or the overcompensating wonderment when people find out I went to Sarah Lawrence and Juilliard. It hurts, but I move on. It's the 'Why didn't you marry a brother?' and 'Why are you always trying to be white?' Why do I want to add another set of expectations to that for a religion I really didn't grow up in? I'm gonna obsess over Israel and Palestine and the Holocaust and if shit's good for the fucking Jews?"

How could David, who at the time was no longer sure he even believed in God, argue with any of this? It remained a joke between them, however, that he leaned inadequately on his tribe to get her film and television work.

"All I'm asking is that you make one call. One simple call to your people out there running Hollywood."

"What about your mother's non-Catholic half? Aren't they your people too?"

"Not like your Jewish southern cracker ass. What the fuck was I marrying you for if you can't get the Conspiracy to give your wife even a week or two on one of those movies they make so much money off of so they can buy their German cars?"

"I'm trying, sweetheart."

"Would you two shut up? It's annoying, and not funny," Anna, the older and more irascible of their daughters, would inevitably protest.

"Sorry, sweetie. Your dad and I did something that was still a bit unconventional when we got married, and we like to joke our way through it."

"Anybody can marry anybody. I don't know why you guys keep making it a big deal."

"And you're very lucky to live in a city and among people where you're able to say that."

"So you keep reminding us."

"Can we just drop it, sweetie?"

"You're the one who keeps talking."

"And where I come from, I could swat your Black ass for speaking to me like that."

"Hi, David," said Jacob. He and Larry stood to greet him at a table in the back corner of a restaurant named Bosk in the lobby of Toronto's Shangri-la Hotel. "Thanks for coming to us. I can't stand the Four Seasons. I don't get from the elevator to the front door without having to talk with twelve people I'd rather avoid. Here it's quiet and simple. Expensive as hell, but no pretense. There doesn't have to be any."

"I'm not sure anyone would ever put me here."

"We would, David. You talk to anybody. We treat people well. In return we like filmmakers who come in and get the job done without a lot of self-generated drama and difficulty. We're a great experience, so long as you understand the ground rules. That's why I wanted us to meet. I can't tell with someone on the phone, but face-to-face I get an immediate sense. It's the way I am. That draft of the script you sent upset me very much."

"Before you even read it."

"What I did read was garbage. And I've read it all now a couple of times. The day you sent it I couldn't get past the first three pages."

"It's the way the novel you bought opens."

"The studio I bought the property from hired Rex Patterson to take the first crack at the screenplay, and he handed in a draft that was six hundred pages, so don't tell me everything in a book should be in the movie. The only one who ever thinks that is the novelist."

"I don't disagree, but in this case—look, you say it doesn't have to do with the main story, but spiritually I think it does."

"It's you trying to show off."

"Show off?"

"As a director. And what, you're expecting me to pay for an African unit for eight minutes of screen time? Plus, we're going to build a slave ship?"

"Were you bar mitzvahed?"

"I had no choice."

"So, you know how you have the Torah reading and the haftorah, and they relate, but only thematically? That's what I think the beginning of Rex Patterson's book is."

"I'd love to hear his response to that. And a movie isn't a fucking bar mitzvah, thank God. The prologue is not going in the movie. I told you on the phone. You're not filming it."

"You've made that clear."

"Then why are you fucking talking to me about haftorahs? A word I'd hoped never to have to hear again in my life past the age of thirteen but now you've put it back into my goddamn brain?"

"I guess by way of explanation."

"I don't need you to explain anything to me. Ever. We're hiring you to direct, not explain. To do a job like everyone else."

"But somebody has to be in charge of what the film will be creatively. I mean, isn't that why you put trust in a director?"

"I'm in charge. Of everything. Without exception. As for trust, it has to be earned. And in my experience, it rarely, if ever, is. I don't even like the word, so don't use it around me."

"The word *trust*?"

"That's right. And when other people bandy it about, it makes me not trust them, so how's that? And yes, the director is in charge. But on set. And if that's you on this film, it's only because we let it be you. I'm not interested in any ambiguity around this."

Emotional cost and debilitating compromise seemed to burden every endeavor in the film industry. Not even Noah Mendelson, who had the most unencumbered career of anyone David knew, escaped this. With *Coal* it was clear David would face repeatedly vindictive declarations, often in front of others, reminding him he had no ultimate power. He would be watched and questioned incessantly, always at some level despised. A sadness overwhelmed him because Anthony Calabria had been correct: he would put up with all of it to direct the film—the opportunity to tell Rex Patterson's provocative tale of racism and misogyny at a moment when these forces were on everyone's mind was simply too important to him.

"So, are you ready to do this for us?" Jacob asked, his face creasing into a smile that seemed to twinkle. Had David been less addled, he might have laughed at this Chekhovian turn from churlish severity to its opposite. He'd never encountered such functional misanthropy.

"Well, at the risk of upsetting you even further, I still want to make all the other changes you rejected."

Jacob stared back until Larry broke the silence.

"I actually do think he's made the script better, Jacob."

"Maybe he did, but it's not his script." Jacob didn't take his eyes off David. "This is not your script."

"I understand that."

"It's our script. And it's Carly's script. He's the screenwriter."

"Carly is a man?"

"Yes, he's a fucking man. You think a woman wrote it?"

"Well, I have to say it had surprised me," offered David.

"I don't know what that means, but we love Carly. He's a very skilled writer, and he listens. There's no ego there."

"Got it," said David, internalizing another in the fusillade of admonitions aimed his way: no ego at Chicago Films.

"So, he gets the script file back," continued Jacob. "Your writing is done on this; I don't want to read another word by you."

"I think what might be best, then, Jacob," said David, determined not to lose every penny of his dignity, "is for all of us to get into a room together, and we go through the material page by page and look at what I've proposed. I mean, presumably you want your director believing in the script he's directing for you."

"With Carly there."

"Yes."

"When can you come out?"

"I'm about to do a job in Atlanta, so not for a few months."

"A few months is not going to work."

"I'm sorry, Jacob."

"Don't worry about it," said Larry. "We've got two films in post right now and another about to start. Plus, Carly is already busy on two scripts for us, Jacob."

"Then we run into the holidays, and suddenly it's next year," Jacob complained.

"So it's early next year, and we still shoot in the summer. What's the big deal? You'll need to forgive Jacob," Larry added with a smile. "He's kind of obsessed with this one."

"You're damn right I am. I think this was really great," he then said genuinely, rising and offering a strong, bony hand. "As I told you, I need to meet a person face-to-face. Look in his eyes. And I have a good feeling now. This is going to be a good process. We'll take care of you. People who work for us in the right way always want to come back. You won't find anyone complaining."

After his lunch with Anthony Calabria, David had reached out to others, and hadn't encountered a single director who'd collaborated with Jacob who didn't describe the experience as unflaggingly humiliating. Each, however, concluded the description with some version of "But I got to make my film." Those seven words, David concluded, should be inscribed on every director's tombstone.

As with most topics, David would learn, Jacob had been right. After his acting job, a death-row drama in which he played an overzealous DA, Thanksgiving intervened. Then Carly became ill with a respiratory ailment none could identify, leading to Christmas and New Year's. In January Chicago Films was to premiere a film at Sundance, and suddenly it was February.

David asked that they put him up at the Chateau Marmont on Sunset just west of Laurel. Its uppermost floor once the redoubt of Howard Hughes, the place had a self-consciously hip drabness, but like many New Yorkers, David stayed there whenever possible. So much of Los Angeles, eager to embrace the new, repudiated an overt sense of its prewar history, whereas the Chateau embraced that past, even at the risk of seeming lusterless. It clung to the grandness of old Hollywood, with immense plastered walls thickened by decades of off-white paint always slightly mustarding or gray, and yielding to the touch in the way of surfaces never stripped of a single coat. The night he arrived he had dinner with his agent, Howard, on the patio just off the lobby under crackling torches and strings of incandescent bulbs.

"Look. Jacob is a monster. You're not going to change that. He's an old man. If he needs to feel like the film is his and not yours, let that be his problem. At the end of the day, and this is to some degree what bothers him, you're the director, and the movie will always be seen as yours. It's a director's medium, so who cares? Go in there tomorrow, be respectful, which Jacob deserves, and don't allow yourself to be baited into a fight. Make him your ally. Hopefully you leave with the script you want without worrying how you got there. That's the movie business: let everyone feel like they should get all the credit, so they don't feel like complete liars when they take it anyway."

"Deceive, in other words?"

"Call it being true enough. Jacob's money is real, he'll pay stars, and he has an output deal that guarantees distribution, so you'll be able to attract cast, and maybe you thread the needle and the movie will get seen. Without Jacob, none of that happens, so good for him. Plus, a novel Hollywood has been terrified to make? This could put you on a whole different level. You're one movie away from being your friend Noah Mendelson. This could be it."

"That's ridiculous."

"It's all ridiculous. You're talking about an industry that attracts the most desperate egos in the world for something completely ephemeral, for a product that, except in very rare cases, comes and goes and is forgotten. But still we treat every project and interaction like it's going to bring us immortality. It's completely ludicrous and childish, and we're all devoting our lives to that level of delusion. You and I included. Why would we do that? But here we are. Jacob's worth over half a billion dollars. Can you imagine what he could have done with that money and the rest of his time on the planet?"

"Half a billion?"

"He has his own building out here, his own real estate empire back in Chicago still making money, his own fucking jet, and he's bullying film-makers like a fucking maniac. And they're all like that at some level. I'd like to do a study of all these guys—Jacob, Charlie Gold, some of the people I work with, you, me. Problem is, no one would believe a word of it."

David slept well that night. Angelica, the manager, had upgraded him to a bungalow in the back, far from the bar and pool. The silence bordered on intolerable, but after half a bottle of wine he slept eight hours until his cell phone rang just after 8 a.m.

The screen read "Blocked."

"Hello?"

"Hey, David. Did I wake you?"

Dread seized him when he heard the voice. He visualized blond curls.

"Um, yeah, I guess sort of, but I needed to be up anyway."

"I figured it would be eleven your time. You're in New York, right?"

Something in Brad Shlansky's tone suggested that he knew David wasn't.

"I'm in LA actually."

"Oh. I didn't know that. You didn't want to call me? Get together? When did we last speak? Has it been a year? Seems like it. Right after Kentucky? What are you doing here?"

David knew to say as little as possible.

"What's up, Brad?"

"Oh, well, okay, I guess not bothering to call when you come out, and no polite chitchat either. You want me to get right to it. We're ready to make your film."

"Which film?"

"*Appalachian Winter.* I have the money, and I'm exercising the option. We're ready to go back into production, so I'm letting you know that. Alice is going to be sending a letter."

David paused, fighting the certainty that everything in his life was about to unravel.

"Okay."

"So since you're in LA, should we meet?"

"I'm not here on my own time really."

"You are available to start work, aren't you? Because if you're not, if you're working on something else, it's going to be a big problem, because we're ready to make offers."

"Offers, Brad?"

"To actors. I'm exercising the option. You belong to me. I just wouldn't want you to be leading anyone else on."

David thought immediately of Howard Garner's admonition that a monster be your ally and never your enemy.

"Listen, Brad. I just got up, and I've got to be somewhere, so let me call you back to discuss all this in more detail."

"Okay. I thought you'd be excited."

"Yeah. I'm excited."

"I'm gonna get Alice right into it. Tell your reps. Tell everyone. Alice is going to be calling."

The line clicked dead.

LOS ANGELES

Paul Aiello's assistant put Brad Shlansky's third call of the morning through just after eight thirty.

"I spoke to David Levit this morning. He's shitting bricks."

"Oh yeah?"

"You're finally in the car?"

"I'm running late," answered Paul.

"When I left last night there were still a dozen people there. Five of them women," said Brad.

"It's a social industry."

"Yeah, you've mentioned that."

Sometime after 1 a.m. nearly every guest at Paul's house in the Hollywood Hills had finally departed, leaving two clients sprawled on the immense sectional that anchored his living room. His designer had bought it from a boutique just west of the Beverly Center, and on nights like this Paul considered it worth every cent of the twenty-six thousand dollars it had cost, particularly since he'd persuaded his accountant to let him write off half for the amount of industry entertaining that took place at his home.

"Paul, you're so sweet to let us stay here," said Susan, the taller and younger of the two actresses as he returned through the front door from his driveway. His final guest not sleeping over, an uninvited executive whose name and studio he'd forgotten, had finally eased his Audi sedan down toward Sunset on narrow switchbacks that brought to mind the hills surrounding Florence.

"Neither of you is in any condition to drive up around here," Paul said. "And for me by myself, this place is like fucking Kane's mansion. In fact, I bought a three-bedroom so people could crash after parties if they wanted to let loose and not have to drive, not so I could wander the rooms and revel in how much space I can afford."

"Yeah, thanks, Paul," said Janine, the more inebriated of the two. "Speaking of which, I think I'm pretty cooked."

"Oh come on, guys. Let's have one more. I'm nearly done too, and I've got to be at the office for a staff meeting in"—he looked at his Heuer "Batman Bezel" chronograph—"fuck me. Seven hours. But let's just have a nightcap. Look at it this way: the two of you will be the last on my mind tonight, and the first tomorrow when everyone is going over their weekend reads."

He couldn't decide which of them was more beautiful. Janine had just been cast as a lead in the pilot for a show on ABC about an FBI forensic science lab. It would certainly go to series given the brazen tawdriness of the script (rampant 10 p.m.-slot sex on steel tables after hours involving women who could fight hand-to-hand or drop a perp with one shot) and the sultry beauty of Janine herself: half Persian with pristine olive coloring, dark eyes, and a curvaceous five-foot-six frame.

Susan, just under six feet and blond, possessed a lithe wholesome beauty he'd encountered only in two places: Northern California and Australia. Virtually a cliché, she used very little makeup on skin tanned by surfing, hiking, and running. Her simple blue tank top exposed broad shoulders and lean, muscular arms.

He'd had some experience with Janine, having met her three years before at an Italian restaurant in West Hollywood where she served as a hostess. It hadn't hurt that he was meeting his most successful client to celebrate her just having been cast as Catwoman in a new *Batman* franchise that would involve her own spin-off.

"Hi, how are you this evening?" he'd asked with his usual brio. "I was going to say 'tonight,' but the light out there is so beautiful—certainly later than afternoon. Magic hour. Though that's a bit of a misnomer because any cinematographer will tell you magic hour lasts only thirty to forty minutes."

"'Evening' works," she offered in the open way of aspiring actresses in Los Angeles hospitality jobs who never knew whom they might be serving.

I love this city, and I love my job, he thought, already laying out his strategy for ensuring she'd call him the following day.

"Listen," he said, "I'm going to want a table in the back. I'm meeting a client. Yes, I'm an agent, as if you hadn't figured that out already."

"I hadn't actually."

"Well, that's kind of you, but let's move on. Sometimes I think I reek of it, having to wear this suit every day. You'll know this actress when she comes in, and she'll say the Paul Aiello table. That's me. But do you think you could help us out? I hate to be a pain in the ass, but I put a ring around my clients, especially the female ones, and I want as few visitors to our table as possible."

"Oh, sure, I'd be happy to. And you don't need to apologize. It's sweet actually."

"Well, you're kind to say so. You're an actress too, aren't you?"

"How did you know?"

"It's my job to know. But now I sound like a cheeseball, so I'm respectfully going to end this conversation before you report me to the asshole police."

She laughed heartily from the back of her throat.

When Claire Fisher arrived, heads began to pivot while Janine brought her conspiratorially to the table.

"Your guest has arrived, Mr. Aiello. Let me know if you two need anything at all."

"'Mr. Aiello'?" said a bemused Claire when Janine had departed. "'Anything at all'?"

"What can I say? With clients like you, the secret is out. People know me."

"Yeah, right."

Paul had never dared try anything with Claire, who'd been one of his earliest clients at UCM. Now she was married with a child, while Paul was divorced without children, but thanks in part to Claire he had aggregated the best list of actresses in Los Angeles. He got them jobs, and he got them paid. They loved how he'd beat down business affairs lawyers in negotiations until, as he liked to put it, "they add the fucking zeros."

"I'm a son of a bitch when it comes to the women I represent," he told more than one prospective client. "And guess what? That's what you want: the guy who's going to leave bleeding bodies on the floor fighting to get you what you deserve. Otherwise, go get some pussy who's gonna commiserate about how your career isn't where it should be. With me there's gonna be no commiserating, because there's gonna be nothing to be sad about. You'll have more work and money than you know what to do with."

He'd helped make Claire one of the biggest stars in the world, to the point where her assent to play a role meant a movie would go forward, almost regardless of budget. The climb had been methodical and relentless, and at 10 percent they had made the agency well over five million dollars in the process, with more to come.

He insisted they split the steak Fiorentina for two, and predictably she demurred.

"Give me a break, Claire. We won't finish it, and you can eat from the fillet side. Just trust me."

"I don't have the energy to argue."

Though Paul didn't know wines, Brad Shlansky had taught him how to order them.

"At an Italian restaurant in California," he informed Paul, "with anyone under forty, always go with a Super Tuscan. Don't order the Barolo or a Brunello because they're going to be too traditional—too earthy and too tannic."

"How do you know all this shit?"

"I had my first taste at a party one night in Hewlett Neck, and I haven't stopped since."

"Fuck you. A house on the water?"

"Yeah."

"Someone I knew?"

"No. This asshole who came in ninth grade's dad, who was nice actually. The dad, not the kid. It's not worth going into, and you're not listening. People in LA like big, fruitier wines—they're more used to them—and the Super Tuscans give you enough of that without being too sweet. And if you ever see the Sassicaia, order it if it's under a hundred fifty bucks and don't think twice, but make sure it's got at least four years of age."

With that very wine on the menu and from a suitable vintage, he did so with Claire, and by the time they'd finished a bottle and had downed complimentary Muscatos they were both a bit tipsy making their way to the valet stand.

"Give them your ticket first," he told her.

"Thanks. I told Randy I'd be home by nine, and it's already ten after."

"How is Randy?"

"You'd think having the number two drama on the number one network would loosen the purse strings, but everyone's scrounging with all this new streaming content."

"Tell me about it."

"Shut up, Paul. It's great for you. More shows mean more work for more clients."

"For less money. It's a longer conversation."

"Plus, more women are getting parts now."

"That's true."

"Thank Charlie Gold."

"I'd rather not."

Had I ever somehow slept with her, Paul thought to himself, it would have ruined the possibility for this moment right here, waiting for our cars at a valet stand after a spectacular meal during which everyone snuck glances at our table, so many of them envying me, and very bitterly, for representing her. I fucking radiate success right now.

Her Range Rover arrived first, followed by his BMW i8 Roadster.

"Wait!" she exclaimed. "Is this you?"

"I got it last week."

"Are you leasing?"

"And writing it off."

"You asshole."

"I've got to look the part."

"Trust me, with this ridiculous vehicle, you do. Aren't you going to get in?"

"I'm gonna tip these guys for us. Go on. Get home to Randy."

He gave ten dollars extra to the valet to wait with his car while he reentered the restaurant and approached the hostess stand.

"You forget something?" asked Janine.

"Look. I'm not just saying this because you really helped me tonight by seating us back there."

"It didn't stop half the restaurant from going back to your table, or the other half from staring."

"Yeah, well, here's the thing. I'm never wrong about people, and I think you have something." She looked down, which he'd experienced in enough of these encounters to know not to misinterpret. Besides, he had the perfect mollifier. "Now, before you get freaked out. I don't want your number, even though my suspicion is that whatever agent ends up having it is going to make a lot of money. What I want to do is give you *my* number. Not my cell number but my office number. As in you call the agency, not me personally. My assistant answers, and you come in and we meet in the middle of the day with the door open in front of a glass window and you tell me what you're all about. Hell, I don't even know, you might already have representation, and if you do, great, so long as you like your representation, in which case lucky them and tell me to fuck off. But regardless, here's my card."

Within a week she was signed, and a month later, at her apartment in West Hollywood after a celebratory sushi dinner in a strip mall near the 405 that cost three hundred and twenty dollars on his agency expense account, they slept together. She had just booked her first job—a top-of-show guest spot on a cop procedural that would shoot in New Orleans.

"I've never done that before," he lied on this cell phone with his door closed at the office the next morning.

"Spent that much on sushi?"

"Trust me, the sushi was average price. I was talking about what happened afterward."

"I've been pretty confused. I almost didn't pick up."

"I'm glad you did. You're just unbelievably attractive, Janine."

"But are you telling me last night was not some weird—or maybe not so weird— condition of my being signed with UCM?"

"I was calling to say it will never happen again."

"That's a huge relief. We were pretty trashed, weren't we?"

"Don't say anything else. You're an actress with a tremendous amount of talent and integrity, and as gorgeous as you are, I'd still rather be your agent than your boyfriend, and I can't be both." In effect this was true, though there was no chance he *wouldn't* have slept with her. It had surprised him to have succeeded so quickly, even though in his experience the quicker the better with an actress he'd signed. In the evolving routine of representing a woman, the likelihood of anything physical receded by the week. And how had it even started the night before? He couldn't entirely be sure given the amount of sake they'd consumed, not to mention the joint they'd smoked in her living room. She had initiated contact by placing her hand on his knee. Or had he taken her hand and put it there? He supposed on reflection the latter. When he began playing with her fingers, she quietly scrutinized the developing contact.

"So, is this what we're doing?"

"That's up to you," he responded.

"Isn't it kind of up to you?"

"I don't know what that means."

"You asked if you could come in in a way that didn't seem like much of a question."

"If it wasn't a question, what was it?"

"I don't know. An expectation?"

"You need me to leave?"

"I'm just new at this I guess."

"Let me show you." He leaned in to kiss her astonishing mouth. Eventually she kissed back, and by the time the night was over they'd fucked twice.

"You're a client now. A working client. And the relationship will be professional," he said, glancing out his office window.

"I really hope so, Paul."

"Now let me get to work getting you your next job." Within ten days he had done just that, putting her on a show in Vancouver just weeks after she was to return from Louisiana. She'd rarely stopped working since, almost exclusively in network television, which meant more money than she ever imagined making, and increasingly healthy commissions for the agency.

Even before Janine, the physical need for young, emotive women had gotten to the point where he simply couldn't control it. That he encountered them everywhere and could so easily exploit his position only intensified the yearning. His looks, confidence, and no small amount of charm worked almost infallibly so long as he chose the right prospect. A cursory once-over could identify easily those who would resist his advances—no one too angry, no one who wore no makeup, no one with piercings, no one who seemed to come from wealth. He'd pass along his card to the most promising, always with the same nonthreatening, almost embarrassed speech, resulting in a phone call to the office, with intimacies days or weeks after. Sometimes he'd need an intervening meeting, sometimes not. Very rarely would he end up signing his quarry, Janine being one of few exceptions. He suspected she'd do well, so why not with him?

But of late he'd begun to feel the need for something more, if only because his methods and their results had become routine to the point of numbness, which was worse than the cravings that inspired him in the first place.

"What do you think?" Janine asked Susan. "One more before we all retire?"

"What the hell," responded the tall blonde. "I don't have anything until the afternoon, and that's a hike, where I can sweat it all out."

"I've got this insane Sauternes a producer client gave me a while back," Paul said crossing the room, careful not to mention Brad Shlansky by name, since neither would have heard of him and he wished to preserve the frisson of mystery. "I'm not going to tell you who, because it'll sound like I'm name-dropping," he added, reaching for a corkscrew, "but he's major and he knows his wine, and this half bottle I'm opening, I looked it up when he gave it to me, and it cost over two hundred dollars. And that's right. I said half bottle."

"You represent producers, Paul?" asked Susan.

"Just one. He's getting on my fucking nerves like you wouldn't believe lately, but that's another story."

"I thought you said he was major."

"For a while he owned a comic book company. A company I still represent by the way. I'll get you both meetings."

"How does a producer own a comic book company?"

"He bought it," said Paul. "Kind of."

"Kind of?"

"Then they took it back. It's complicated. He's still got a dozen of their projects set up around town, which he'll be the first to tell you. You guys'll be in them."

"I love Hollywood," said Janine.

"What's that supposed to mean?" asked Paul. He really didn't want to speak any more about Brad Shlansky, but he resented Janine's tone.

"Doesn't the director have to like the idea, and the studio approve?"

"Have I not done right by you two? Suddenly you're not trusting me?"

"We trust you," said Janine. "Or at least I do."

"As much as anybody anyway," added Susan, stretching her athletic frame along the length of the sectional. "I can't believe how down-to-earth Claire Fisher was. I talked with her for like half an hour."

"Yeah, Claire's like that. She doesn't kick the ladder down from the top. She holds it steady."

"Paul was with her the night I met him," said Janine. Paul looked up, surprised she'd had the temerity to mention their first encounter. He saw at once that she regretted it.

"Oh yeah, where was that?" asked Susan.

"At a premiere of one of Claire's films actually," offered Paul, saving them both the embarrassment.

"Which one?"

"I don't even know," he answered. "Do you remember, Janine?"

"*Friends and Family*," she improvised effortlessly, summoning a contemporaneous release.

"Oh God, she was great in that."

"And she wasn't even their first choice," said Paul as he pulled the cork from the 375 mil bottle of Château d'Yquem.

"Are you kidding me? Who else could have played that role?" asked Susan.

"At this point I don't even remember," Paul answered. "I just know I chased it like crazy, but they went with someone else. Then after the table read, they fired that actress and came back to Claire."

"That is my greatest fear," said Susan. "Being fired from a table read."

"Oh my God, me too!" exclaimed Janine. "And I've seen it happen. Twice!"

"Are you kidding me?"

"Both times at Disney."

"You have to tell me!"

With them distracted, he could reach down to the locked drawer where he'd hidden the three tablets of Rohypnol he'd ground into powder. So as to leave no trace on his browser, he'd researched options at an Internet café in East LA where he'd worn not only a hoodie but a baseball cap underneath should there have been cameras overhead. The drug flunitrazepam, particularly because of its potency when combined with alcohol, emerged as the clear favorite for its paralyzing effect without loss of consciousness. As one site put it, the user became "a kind of agreeable slave." He bought it pseudonymously, and had it mailed to a PO box in Van Nuys that he rented with cash. A week later he tested it on a woman he'd met at a sandwich counter at the Grove. On their second date, he took her to a client's film playing at the AMC 5 on Sunset, followed by pizza at Wolfgang Puck's.

"I've got these pills I want to try," he told her an hour later in his living room, "but I only want to indulge if you'll join me."

"What are they?"

"Kind of a light quaalude. I'll take it first, but like I said, only if you'll join me. I want us to be in the same place."

"Sure, I guess. What the fuck!"

The small round pills resembled baby aspirin to the point of being nearly indistinguishable, so he'd stopped off at a Duane Reade on his way to work and purchased a bottle of Bayer. He chased one with a swig of Glenmorangie in front of her before proffering the actual drug. Within twenty minutes she was utterly compliant but far from catatonic, and certainly capable of responding hazily to questions. He walked her to his bedroom, and when he kissed her, she kissed him back, if somewhat sloppily, and then allowed him to disrobe her. The sex wasn't particularly interesting until he realized he could do whatever he wanted. In the morning she remembered very little, though she did inquire with aloof shame as to certain particulars.

"Did we...?"

"The answer is probably yes," he responded, suddenly aroused by knowing more about what she'd allowed to happen than she did.

"Well, I know we did, but ... I mean did we ...?"

"You suggested it."

"Jesus, I was really out of it. I'm really not that way..."

"To be honest, neither am I. I'm sorry if you did something you regret."

"I just regret being so out control—or just feeling like I don't remember. I should never have taken that quaalude. I'm such a lightweight."

"Yeah, it's weird, it did me in too. I feel terrible about it."

He blocked her number on his cell and instructed his assistant he was to be on a conference call should she try and reach him through the UCM switchboard.

"Who is she?" the assistant asked.

"I get in these situations with actresses. I meet them and say encouraging shit because I'm a good guy and I want people to succeed. Maybe I even take a few of them out because I think they actually like me for me, but then it's quickly not about that. They think I'm going to sign them and get them in all the right rooms, change their fucking lives. It's a totally shitty industry for women out here. Why anyone would want to try to be an actress is beyond me. Unfortunately, your job is to tell them I'm unavailable in as courteous a way possible until they get the message."

Before the party he had asked Claire Fisher to "spend significant time" with Susan.

"Really, Paul?"

"She fucking loves you. Idolizes you. She's not as smart as you are, but who is? I mean, we can't all go to fucking Harvard or it wouldn't be Harvard, but she does want to go to back to college part-time, and she wants to have kids."

"What am I supposed to say to her?"

"Just help me push her in a good direction. It also wouldn't hurt if you told her to trust me the way you've trusted me."

"Fine," Claire said on the phone, and within twenty minutes of her arrival, she and Susan had stepped outside to share a joint Susan produced from the two-hundred-dollar cloth handbag Paul had purchased for a half dozen of his clients from the designer wife of a colleague.

"You really owe me, Paul," Claire said before leaving.

"She's not that bad, and she's booking jobs."

"I'm sure she is. She's stunning. She's perfect."

"You're just as beautiful."

"Now you just sound ridiculous. Anyway, I'm out of here. The half toke I had of her turbo weed has sufficiently worn off, and it's my morning with the kids."

"There's no one like you."

"The second time I experienced it," he heard Janine announce as she continued her sad chronicle of actresses divested of roles after underwhelming table reads, "was even worse. And you won't believe who it was who got fired."

"Who?"

"I'll give you a hint."

Paul dropped a first pinch of powder into one of the glasses behind the bar. His own stem waited empty atop it in full view.

"She's been in the news lately for coming out," continued Janine.

"Jennifer Carney?"

"Yes."

"I bet they regret that now."

He primed the second glass and poured, watching the powder swirl and dissolve.

"You guys ready to try this?" he asked.

"Yeah," answered Susan. "Janine is just finishing a story. This has been the best part of my night. So what movie was it?" she sat up to take the glass.

"*Tortured Lives.*"

"That piece of shit?" she exclaimed, venturing a first sip, shortly after which Janine did the same. Paul waited for any suspicion, but the mistreatment of a fellow actress interested them far more than any irregularities in the nonpareil of dessert wines.

"Getting fired from that movie should be like a badge of honor."

"Easy, I was in it. But Jennifer was just getting famous at the time. It was before the *Honeymoon* movies."

"Wait, you guys had scenes together?" asked Susan.

"In *Making Babies*. I was a bridesmaid."

"I totally forgot about that."

"The third job Janine booked, before television took her away completely," said Paul.

"We talked about that. You're getting me back into movies."

"You guys like the Sauternes?"

"Oh my God, it's amazing," said Janine, taking another sip. "Isn't it supposed to be served in smaller glasses though?"

"Yes," he answered, pouring his own, "but wineglasses are all I have. Plus, it makes it so we can have more. You can taste the chalkiness of the gravel where they grow the grapes right alongside the sweetness. It should be almost bitter."

"I see what you mean," Janine said, taking another sip.

"Yeah, it's really great," added Susan, turning back to Janine. "So, what do you mean, you saw it all happen?"

"The reading was late in the day, and we all got VIP parking passes, so I was getting into my car when the executives were coming out to get into theirs, and they were with Lani Solomon. She was running Touchstone at the time. I fucking heard her say she wanted a list of potential replacements that night, and I fucking knew."

"Who ended up getting the role?"

"Lucy Fallon, who was the best thing in the movie. She was way better than I was. I mean, she had an actual part, but still."

Sauternes, Paul determined, operated as the perfect vehicle, not only because it was to be enjoyed when the hour was late, but one sip and a person couldn't resist more. At the sink he noticed a nearly empty bottle of 2012 Chateau Talbot that could only have been brought by Brad Shlansky. He must have hated having to bring wine at all, Paul thought as he tilted it to view, calculating a good fifteen dollars in its remaining third that would be poured down the sink by the housekeeper twelve hours hence. Had he remembered to instruct her not to arrive until after noon?

Susan's words began to slur as Paul strolled back to the sectional.

"Whoa," she said nervously, "I didn't realize how much I had to drink."

"You were getting baked with Claire Fisher too," he reminded her.

"That was fucking hours ago. Jesus." She widened her eyes in an effort to summon clarity from the enveloping haze.

"Are you all right?" asked Janine.

"I'm fine," answered Paul, suddenly more anxious than eager for what was to come. The uncertainty delighted him in ways he hadn't expected.

"I wasn't talking to you." She too paused to account for what was now transpiring inside her. "Shit. Fuck! Did you put something in our drinks, you asshole?"

"Are you out of your fucking mind, Janine?" he answered.

"I'm just ... whoa ...this is insane ..." He watched as she pulled herself upright. "Fucking hell," she said, testing her jaw.

Try as he did, he couldn't get them to make out with each other. He finally walked Janine back to his room, leaving Susan on the couch, figuring that with the Viagra he'd taken hours before and at the age of thirty-eight he'd have at least three good erections in him. After sufficient time with Janine, he found Susan still on the couch, undressed her against some murmured objections, and then helped her to the bedroom. With both women now naked, he placed their faces lips-to-lips and ran their hands over each other's bodies in a coercive display, and though Janine did move a hand down Susan's back and eventually seem to kiss the actress's mouth, Susan was either too far gone or uninterested. He found his cell phone and took a few photographs that from the right angle made them seem mutually engaged. Their indifference made no sense to him: two women utterly naked, each perfect in her way, showing no appreciation for each other. He rolled Susan onto her back, but unlike Janine, who had been blearily compliant, a stubborn indifference to it all made the act far less enjoyable. He wondered if he even had a third go in him as he lay there on top of her. To his right, Janine had passed out.

In the bathroom he discovered blood.

"Shit." He returned to the bed, where more of it soaked the sheets under Susan's midsection. "Goddamn it."

He spent half an hour collecting plates and glasses before taking a shower and two Ambien. He made a bed for himself on the sectional, set his alarm for 6:30 a.m., opened a script on his iPad, and was asleep five pages in. When he woke, he spent another hour cleaning up, deciding not to address the bedroom for fear of a scene should either or both women wake with him there.

"If this is going to be a phone call where you just berate me," he told Brad Shlansky half an hour later over the speakerphone in his car, "can it please wait? I got no fucking sleep last night."

"That's my fault?"

"No, it's not, Brad, and I wasn't saying it was. You'll remember though that my workday actually starts at nine. It's eight thirty."

Paul's assistant beeped in.

"That's Jen. She knows I'm on a call, so it must be important."

"It better be."

He clicked over. "Yeah, what is it?"

"I have Susan Painter on the other line, and she's pretty hysterical."

"Yeah, she's called my cell six times already. Did she say what it's about?"

"She wouldn't."

"Have her call my cell again, and tell her I'll pick up." He clicked back over to Brad. "Brad, it's an emergency. I've got to deal with this. I'll hit you back."

"Fuck you, Paul."

"You know what, asshole? You are not my only client."

"Don't I fucking know it. Make me your next call. I'm gonna be on with Alice in fifteen minutes. Fucking call me back."

His Call Waiting beeped. He stared at the screen and saw his own name. "Fuck me," he said to his steering wheel before punching over.

"Did you call my assistant crying at eight in the morning from my house?"

"That's what you're going to say to me, you fucking … you fucking … you fucking …" He remained silent while she sobbed. "I woke … I woke

… I woke up …" She couldn't continue, wailing now, heaving for breath. This would require more of his concentration than navigating Wilshire between eight and nine would allow. He turned right onto Orlando and parked in front of a two-story Spanish mission-style bungalow with an oversized sprinkler drenching its tiny yard.

"You need to calm down and speak to me, Susan. Unless I know what you're upset about—"

"I can't … I can't …"

"You can't what?"

"I'm going to be sick again …"

He heard the phone clatter to the floor, followed by violent retching. A roomy echo blared over his Morel speakers indicating she'd moved to the bathroom off his master bedroom with the handset. The toilet flushed.

"Oh God … Oh God …Oh God … ," she kept repeating.

He waited for her to lift the phone from the glass tile floor.

"You better?" he asked. She began to hyperventilate. "Susan, we're not going to get anywhere if you don't speak with me."

"I don't … I don't … I don't want to …"

"Don't want to what?"

"Speak to you…"

"Then why have you called my cell phone seven times? Why did you call into the office from my house at eight in the morning sobbing?"

"My cell … my cell was out of battery."

"So now my assistant, and therefore all the other assistants, know you stayed over last night. Is that good for either of us? Please tell me. I've fucking pulled my car over because of the state you're in, so if you don't want to talk, let me know and I can hang up and drive to my staff meeting where I can spend time making sure it's everyone's priority to get Susan Painter her next job."

"You fucking raped me! You fucking raped both of us!" More sobbing followed.

"Susan, I want you to listen to me. I want you to listen carefully. The three of us were very drunk, in addition to the fact that you smoked a lot of pot, which everyone saw, because you did it in full view on the terrace with Claire, which is fine, people can do what they want in my house; it's a sanctuary. But you did that, and the three of us were pretty wasted, as everyone saw when they were leaving. Everyone. And we ended up in my bed doing what the three of us wanted as consenting adults. We may determine it was ill advised, but nobody raped anybody."

"You fucking drugged us, Paul!"

"What did you just say?" he asked, opting not to raise his voice.

"There was blood everywhere. You made me bleed! There's no fucking way I would ever sleep with you! You're my fucking agent, and you're like ten years older than I am!"

He sustained his even tone. "You did sleep with me, Susan, and with Janine. Last night. Obviously now you think it shouldn't have happened. We all probably regret it, but it did. Don't turn this into something it wasn't."

"Oh, Paul ..."

"Where is Janine right now?" he asked.

"She left. She said she needed to think about what to do."

"Good. Let her think."

"Paul, I'm going to the police." He began to sense a careful resolve. "I'm going to stay right here where this happened, with the bloody sheets, and the glasses you served us that fucking dessert wine in, which was clearly spiked, and the police are going to come and see everything."

"You might have noticed that I did some cleaning up this morning, so the glasses are in the dishwasher, which I ran. I want you to think this through though, because I know you have serious aspirations, and as your agent, who's building you a pretty great fucking career, I need to remind you of them in moments like this when emotions are getting the better of you. You're angry with yourself for what happened, but don't allow that to make you do things that will only make you feel worse."

"You're not my fucking agent anymore, Paul. Are you out of your fucking mind?"

"Fine. Fire me. It'll be both of our losses. I'll even say mine more than yours, but again, your prerogative, because I'm not saying we all didn't fuck up last night, which includes me. If I had it to do all over again, I never even would have had the party. That's on me. I like making people happy, and sometimes shit gets out of hand. But here's what it looks like, so we're clear. You'll go to the police and make all these outrageous fucking claims based on what we'll all agree are the facts: you and Janine were at my house at a party. You had a good deal to drink. You smoked some very strong weed. So did Janine. Everyone saw that. Maybe you took some other drugs."

"I didn't, Paul!" she shouted.

"Listen to me, because I'm not finished. You then, at the end of the night, elected to stay over. No one forced you, and no one will say or believe you were forced, because when everyone was leaving, one by one they saw you on the sofa having a great time, still drinking. All the way to the last group saw that. Then you drank more. Then the three of us had sex, and we did it consensually.'

"But we didn't, Paul, and you fucking know that!"

"I'm still not finished. What *I* will say, because it's not only absolutely true but indisputable—and I will hire the best lawyer in Los Angeles to prove, to protect my name, which is my livelihood—is what actually happened. Maybe you don't remember because you were so fucking wasted, which again I don't judge. The three of us were drinking. Janine and you were talking about actresses getting fired from table reads, and you passed out just after you said you'd had too much to drink. Janine and I started fooling around in my room, which by the way is not the first time that has happened—and she'll tell you the same thing—but you heard us going at it, and at least to me you seemed interested. Maybe I was wrong, but I walked you to my bed, because you were very unsteady, and one thing led to another and the three of us did what we did. And finally, this is going to sound weird, but I'm gonna tell you just so you know, I even took pictures of you and Janine."

"No, Paul."

"I did, just so you know. And you told me I could."

"I didn't!"

"You did. Now it's true you bled, but it was rough sex, and that happens. Like I said, we were wasted, and, whatever, I'm not small down there. Not bragging, just true. That's the version of events I will reveal—because again, it's what happened. You say it went another way. Fine. You'll have to prove it. But you need to ask yourself if you want either of these stories out. Your false one, or my true one, because neither is going to be good for you."

"I'm getting a toxicology test. Then we'll see if we weren't drugged."

"Please do. I'm begging you to. I'll even pay for it. You think I don't want you to? Like I said, I don't know what the fuck you were on last night, or who gave you what, but I sure as shit didn't give you anything, and if somebody brought that kind of shit into my house and slipped it to you without your knowing, I want to be the first to know. But let's say you *were* on something you took or that somebody—not me—gave you. People may believe you, but all you'll get from them is pity, certainly not work, because I can assure you, from experience with other clients who've tripped up for whatever reason, that no one will hire you to be in a film or TV show to play a romantic lead, which is what you are and should be, because,

Casting 101, the public doesn't want to see the drunk stoned drugged girl who stayed over at her agent's house and ended up in a threesome where she said she was raped in the movies they're paying to see. They just don't. And this is a business, so no matter how much they feel sorry for you, the people in charge will find every reason not to hire you so they don't lose their shirts. And by the way, put your brain in the mind of middle fucking America, who'll see your name in the tabloids, and ask yourself what they'll think about the rape claims of a beautiful blond surfer girl who gets drunk and stoned in a man's living room at two in the morning."

"You fucking asshole! You fucking ..." Again the phone fell to the tiles, and again he heard her retch into his toilet. He waited nearly a minute while a Lycra-clad woman who looked to be in her thirties jogged north on Orlando past his car with her dog. The toilet flushed. This time when she brought the phone to her mouth and ear, he heard only quiet, shaking sobs.

He spoke with all the warmth and empathy he could.

"Susan, what happened, happened. I'm sorry. You hear me? I'm sorry. It won't happen again. I crossed a line, and I'll say it a third time: I'm fucking very, very, very sorry. But what I want you to do now is go to the fridge, where you'll find some amazing fresh juices—I think there's orange, grapefruit, passion fruit, and a couple others that I got at Bristol Farms for like fifteen bucks a quart. All organic. Have whichever you want. Have a coffee too. There's a Nespresso to the right of the toaster, and the pods are in the drawer right underneath. Nobody's coming because I asked the housekeeper to come later. Sit out on the terrace and settle yourself down. You want to call the police then and tell your story, be my guest. Let them in through the front door for all I care. Give them some fucking juice, because I have nothing to hide. But think before you do, because it's going to be ugly and terrible and ruinous for everyone involved. I fucked up. You fucked up. We all fucked up. Don't make it worse."

The phone clicked off. What a stupid, pointless disaster. He regretted the risk he'd taken. He even regretted her pain. But she wouldn't call the police. She had too much to lose. As for Janine, knowing her, she would blame herself as much as him, even though she'd clearly figured out he altered their drinks; she'd even said it. But if he was right about the network show on which he'd booked her, she was about to make a million and a half dollars over the coming year, and more the year after that, especially if there was a renegotiation. Even should she hope to jump to other representation, the job would make doing so something of an impediment. Few agencies with any power would be eager to wait two to three years while a competitor collected commissions, especially when the client was a woman already in her late twenties whose name was in the tabloids.

He nosed down Orlando looking for a driveway in which to turn around. Brad Shlansky answered after three rings, fumbling with his phone and breathing heavily while riding his exercise bike.

"That took you long enough," he said as Paul made a right back onto Wilshire.

"Sorry. Emotional client pissed about her hotel in Vancouver. The shit I put up with."

"Poor you."

"Weren't you supposed to be on with Alice?"

"It's done. I'm gonna sue David Levit."

"For what?"

"Breach of contract," Brad responded.

"What contract?"

"I'm ready to make *Appalachian Winter*. And don't fucking tell me you didn't know this was coming, the way you were such a prick on the phone about him partnering with Jacob Rosenthal."

"You have no cast."

"You know what, Paul? I don't like where this conversation is heading. Maybe we should start over and you should just listen and deal accordingly in my interests by doing what the fuck I say."

"For starters, nobody wants to see a drama about fucking hillbillies set in the 1800s, and other than *Revenge*, David Levit hasn't made a single film that's made any money for anyone. He even lost money for Yariv Bergman. So put away the silver polish. This is a stupid proposition that only an idiot would bankroll. I don't believe for a second you have the money."

"Just keep talking."

"So, what? You're going to torpedo the movie he's set to make with Jacob Rosenthal? The other piece of shit David Levit has that no one will see?"

"I thought it was based on a best-selling book and was going to win Oscars? Now nobody will see it?"

"David Levit, by the way, who is a client at this agency? And have you ever met Jacob Rosenthal? You think that's going to be easy?"

"All I know is we're ready to go, and David Levit isn't. And I have a contract."

"Have you told him that?"

"Like I said, this morning. He's at the Chateau."

"How did you know that?"

"From Howard Garner's assistant. If you're a pretentious asshole like David Levit, that shabby-chic dump is the only place in town."

Paul was already feeling exhausted, in part because his breathing had become sympathetic with the panting in his ear from Brad's struggles with his Peloton.

"What exactly do you want me to do?" he asked.

"I want you to go down the hall to Howard Garner's office and tell him to tell David Levit that I'm fucking serious. I'm optioning his script and his services, and if he's not available, Alice is going to enter a complaint, which among other things is going to involve a courtesy call to Jacob Rosenthal to let him know there may be a restraining order on David Levit directing his big awards movie, which I read by the way."

"How'd you do that?"

"I had Jen get me a copy."

"Jen my assistant Jen?"

"Yes."

"What did you think?"

"Let's just say it's no *Appalachian Winter*, I don't care how many copies the book sold. Leaving aside the woke shit, you've got a woman in there who's just been raped chasing every guy that moves. Not so realistic, and not so timely in the time of 50.8."

"I hear he's going to be changing that."

"Who? David?"

"I think so."

"And why aren't they getting a Black director?"

"It was offered around, and no one would touch it."

"What a surprise."

"You can't harass Jacob Rosenthal, Brad."

"It's a fucking courtesy call. David Levit is not directing that fucking movie."

"Why are you doing this?"

"You figure it out." The line clicked dead.

He feels humiliated, thought Paul, and wronged, as if all of Hollywood were conspiring to further the tragedies that befell him in high school rather than supply the recompense he's convinced he deserves. And of course he needs money. He and his siblings had squandered everything they'd earned. He'd given Brad every opportunity to succeed. For a moment only two years prior it had seemed even likely he would, but Brad was now broke and unknown.

But fuck David Levit. He was a privileged, arrogant prick of the sort who made it in Hollywood by networking among others of his ilk to exclude those not deemed worthy. All of them in the habit of maneuvering con-versations craftily for quick apprehension of where you'd gone to school, followed by reciprocal exposure of their own provenance, which was their goal in the first place. The worst were the Ivy Leaguers. He hadn't met a single one who didn't smuggle in the information at the soonest possible moment. And with all this came the expectation that simply by virtue of having gone to one of those places, the entire industry should make room for them in whatever capacity they chose. People like Paul, who attended SUNY Albany, and Brad, who never went to college, might as well not exist, so comprehensive was the dismissal.

And yes, David Levit was at UCM, but Paul didn't represent him, and had no interest in doing so since he mostly lost money. He did so directly with his supercilious refusal to do television, but then doubled down by promoting his marginal art films with other agency clients who then slummed on them earning scale wages for movies no one would see. It was like losing to a team in your own division, dropping two points in the standings instead of one, both clients removing themselves from the market for a film that would get neither paid. Even *Coal*, for all its awards potential, seemed to Paul a nonstarter. He had read it months before for Claire Fisher when Jacob Rosenthal sent it to him without David Levit knowing.

"Look, it's a great role," Paul said to her. "I'm not going to lie because you're going to read it anyway since it's David Levit and he's a Noah Mendelson actor, and everybody loves Noah Mendelson."

"Everybody loves David Levit too."

"Nobody had even heard of David Levit until Noah Mendelson gave him the role in *Hillbilly Wedding*, so give me a break. And please don't do this movie. It's too grim, it's too risky, and David Levit makes films nobody sees."

"*Revenge*? And you know David went to Brown?"

"So go have dinner with him. You and all the other little boys and girls who went to fancy schools can rent out a restaurant in Silver Lake and tell each other how fucking brilliant you are. And by the way, did it ever strike you how it's mostly the rich kids who grew up with private tutors and went to all the same schools that can afford to start out as unknown actors and writers, or on assistants' wages in this industry?"

"Jesus, Paul, you've got to get over your issues."

"You do a film like this and it doesn't work, people decide you can't open a movie and it's over, meaning when the right one comes along—as in the right indie, say an actual Noah Mendelson film instead of one made by his far less talented friend—you aren't even on the list."

"I'm sorry, Paul, but I just don't think that way. It's about the material and the role, nothing else, which I think we can both agree has served me well rather than this overweening strategizing you do." He liked her least when she deployed such breezy, dismissive rhetoric, rapier words like *overweening* slashing out at him from the middle of sentences.

With *Coal* he'd been lucky.

"I want to work with David on something, but I'm a mom with a daughter now, and I'm not doing a film where I'm raped on screen. Which is tough because I loved the novel. I've got to say, though, I would have included the prologue. I'll never forget it. I almost didn't keep reading the book, it was so upsetting. Rex Patterson should have won the Pulitzer. And with everything going on in our country right now—Charlie Gold, Trayvon Martin—this film needs to get made."

"No film *needs* to get made, Claire. And especially not this one with you in it."

"Tell David I want an invite to the premiere."

Now I'm going to help Brad Shlansky destroy any chance of a premiere, Paul thought. Like so much of my life, I know it's wrong, I know it's unethical, I know it's senselessly destructive, but I'm going to put all I have behind it. David Levit has no idea what's headed his way.

BEVERLY HILLS

By the time Jacob entered his partner's office, a perceptibly anxious David Levit was seated on one end of Larry McCormick's black leather couch, with Carly Billings on the other. Larry sat adjacent chatting amiably from one of two Robsjohn-Gibbings chairs that his wife, an interior designer, had chosen for the overly decorated room.

"There he is," said Larry, rising.

"Hi, David," said Jacob, extending a hand to David as both he and Carly also stood. "Good flight in? Where do we have you?"

"I tried to put him at the Four Seasons, but he wanted the Chateau," said Larry.

"Is that why you look like you're about to throw up?" asked Jacob, not at all disheartened by David's manifest discomfort with what might transpire over the next several hours. He needed the director on his heels.

"I was up late and then got awakened by a phone call this morning."

"Is everything all right?" asked Larry.

"It's fine."

Jacob turned to Carly.

"You I saw last week, and you live here. Hell, you live in Larry's office, so I'm not giving you anything other than hello."

"Is that like 'You had me at hello'?" asked Carly.

"Very overrated movie," said Jacob as he seated himself in the chair next to Larry's.

"*Jerry Maguire* is one of the best studio films ever made," countered Larry automatically, as if such a dispute needed to happen daily in some form.

"So, you prove my point by being another moron who overrates it. Should we get started?"

Larry shouted to his assistant. "Josh, could you bring in the three copies of David's pass on *Coal*?"

They waited while Josh ferried in the small stack and deposited it on the shin-busting Mies van der Rohe coffee table between them. Per Jacob's instruction, the title page had been removed, and Jacob watched as David flinched almost imperceptibly. The brazen gambit typical of so many directors who did passes on scripts in Hollywood of adding his own name to the title page had angered Jacob before he'd read a word of the overzealous rewrite. "Revisions by David Levit" appearing underneath "Screenplay by Carly Billings" practically guaranteed David would eventually demand a cowriting credit. If Jacob didn't get out ahead of it, there'd be a protracted Writers Guild adjudication. Three names and three names only would ever adorn the title page of the screenplay for *Coal*: that of the sole screenwriter, that of the novelist, and most important, Chicago Films.

His computer facing him on his knees, Carly reached for a script, as did Larry. David opened his own laptop.

"Aren't you going to take one, Jacob?" he asked.

"I'm not touching it," Jacob responded. "And I know the original because I worked on it for months with Carly. That's right. You heard me. You won't see my name anywhere, but I was heavily involved. You're going to read everyone the changes you're proposing, out loud, and then I say if Carly makes them or not."

"Understood," said David.

Jacob found himself generally agreeing with the proposed revisions when considered individually, which surprised him, but David's manner began to irritate him immediately.

"You've got to stop talking to us like we're eight years old, and you have to simplify every fucking thing," Jacob demanded. "The condescension is unbearable. Just say the changes you want to make in as short and clear a way possible, and I'll say yes or no. A fucking lecture doesn't need to accompany every suggestion. We'll be here two days, and I'm going to despise you by the end of it, which'll result in your being fired."

"Maybe if you followed along, I wouldn't feel like I need to explain the context of each change."

"Like I said, I'm well acquainted with the fucking material. More words about what I already know makes it less clear, not more clear, especially with your annoying manner of speaking."

"I'm merely saying it would help if—"

"Stop right there. That's exactly what I'm talking about. 'It would help' is what you say by way of instructing another person, made worse with that passive-aggressive tone."

At lunch in Toronto David had shown himself conversationally agile, invoking deft nuance in moments of friction that kept him within the parameters of self-respect while still acceding to Jacob's rubrics. "He can direct the movie," Jacob told Larry afterward. "He's confident, which is good. But his weakness is what's going to save him, which is that he wants to be liked. If I bark loud enough, he'll scare."

"Okay," said David after a deliciously attenuated pause to collect himself. "My next change is on page twelve, with the dialogue between Fleet and Noreen."

"Read what Carly wrote aloud."

"Fleet: I'm gonna come in this house and we're gonna gab. Noreen: Is that the way you chat up all the dames? Fleet: No, baby, just the likes of you. Noreen: You wear your confidence a little too comfortably. Fleet: You wear your croaked husband's dough a little too comfortably."

"What's your issue?" asked Jacob.

David glanced over at Carly Billings, a man whose good looks continued to impress Jacob. At six foot two he tended to tilt down at others but never superciliously—almost apologetically in fact—with dark eyes under a thick head of cropped dreads. He had a friendly, open face, born of what could only be construed as a blessed life: investment banker for a dad, advertising executive for a mom, high school at Choate, followed by Amherst, where he played lacrosse while completing a degree in literature.

"I'm over here, David. You don't have to look at Carly. Look at me."

"Well, I'd like to—or I *did* change it to something a bit more conversational, less like a period noir."

"How is what Carly wrote not conversational?"

"So, you're asking me, right?"

"Yes, I'm fucking asking you."

"Because when I answer honestly and go so far as to explain myself, I don't want to hear how you find it condescending or pretentious or any of the other pejoratives you've grown comfortable throwing at me."

"I won't use any pejoratives you don't deserve. How about that?"

"And who determines what I deserve?"

"In this room, I do."

David took a breath.

"Okay, so—and this is kind of an overall sentiment—my issue is that I think the dialogue should still feel natural. This movie is dealing with issues of race and gender that remain current, so within interactions that should never feel like they aren't in the vernacular of the time—in other words, while always still presenting as a period film—"

"I get it. For Christ's sake, I know what *vernacular* means. And don't say 'presenting as' to me." Jacob had read on the Internet that morning that David had studied both classics and critical theory at Brown, and he was liking less and less how it manifested. "But please continue."

"It's getting difficult."

"Please."

"I don't think we want the characters to seem like they're speaking dialogue from a *movie* of that period, but rather like they're simply *of* that period. The dialogue Carly wrote feels too stylized, and in a way that's a complete departure from the novel as well. I'd like to change it to this: "Fleet: Can I come in? Noreen: That depends. Fleet: On? Noreen: Whether you're going to respect I'm in mourning"

"Carly's dialogue is better. It's snappier. Yours is boring."

"But Carly's is the way people spoke in movies of that time, not real life, which'll make the film less relevant for today when people are literally killing one another over these issues. Too much stylization lets the audience off the hook. Why make this movie if it doesn't have to do with right now?"

"This takes place back then."

"In the reality of back then, not the movies of back then."

"How do you know that's not how people spoke?" asked Jacob.

"Because I've seen other movies from that time, and unless they're detective movies about hardboiled gumshoes, it's just not what you hear. The same is true with novels—except of course detective novels—and news articles and recordings of real people from the period, which I've also read and heard."

"I actually think David is right," offered Carly.

"Fine. Change it to what David wrote."

No matter the outcome of each dispute, the director needed this firm schooling in process. Jacob had watched *Capo*, the Holocaust film David had made with Yariv Bergman, and what consigned it to being good but not great were a raft of choices, from casting to wardrobe to production design, that clearly had been David's alone under a producer who famously didn't read the scripts he financed.

More important, however, Jacob found himself beginning to like David for maintaining his dignity in the face of producorial vitality with which he was clearly unfamiliar. Jacob also sensed a burgeoning affection, or at least appreciation, coming back at him from the lanky director, no matter how sedulously Jacob tried to provoke. This was a relationship that would work, maybe even brilliantly. *Coal* was emerging, and the healthy friction between David Levit and him, mediated somehow by the confidently affable Carly Billings, was making it so.

KENTUCKY

While Jacob took nearly every one of David's suggestions, the subservient struggle, exacerbated by Jacob's imperious need for each revision to be vetted aloud for inquest, grew more and more tiresome for David as the morning wore on. In the first fifty minutes they'd reached the sixteenth page, meaning more than five hours to go. Anyone unassociated with the film industry would have marveled at how creditable movies got made at all, so needlessly cumbersome and ego-afflicted was the process.

Not least surprising in the middle of it all was Carly Billings. Given the man before him, David simply couldn't square the writer's puzzling inability to write credible dialogue for the heterosexual couple propelling much of the film's plot. Physically he was like Adam—the stuff of statuary. Unlike Adam, however, he spoke quietly and rarely—not at all typical of most screenwriters David had encountered. His voice was warm and resonant, and when he did make a point, one felt eager to take it in.

"May I ask why you wanted to write this screenplay?" David asked between notes about two hours in while Jacob took a call. "I mean obviously it's an exciting challenge, and the way you structured it is something I never would have considered."

"Well, I definitely wanted to do right by Rex Patterson, who I don't think got his due as a novelist before he died, especially from other Black folks when he wouldn't conform to certain orthodoxies. And that's even more true now. He was obviously his own worst enemy with some of the shit that he said, and on that, like everything else, he didn't discriminate. I think if he were alive today, he would have called a lot of people out though, mostly whites, and in a way folks wouldn't be able to ignore. He didn't just point out systemic racism, he shoved folks' faces in it. But because he called Blacks to the carpet too, he couldn't be so easily dismissed by white bigots, if that makes sense. The chance to do *Coal*, I mean, how could I turn it down? I honestly couldn't believe Jacob asked."

"You're a fantastic person, and those are rare," Jacob interjected, having returned to his seat.

"Thanks, Jacob," the writer responded. "If it's all right with everyone, I've got to check in with my wife. Two of our kids are sick."

"Go ahead," said Jacob. "I have a couple more calls to make myself."

David stepped into the hall and checked his phone, finding a message from Howard Garner. He called back without listening to the voicemail and was immediately put through.

"How's it going?" his agent asked.

"A lot of it is about putting me in my place. But I know that's not why you called."

"I just had a visit from Paul Aiello. Who is Alice?"

"Brad Shlansky's insane lawyer."

"Well, apparently she's going to be sending a letter about Brad being ready to make *Appalachian Winter.*"

"You know this is all bullshit, right?"

"So you were already aware of this."

"He doesn't have the fucking money, Howard. He never did, and he doesn't now."

"Getting upset is not going to help the situation."

"I'm in this meeting eating shit nonstop from Jacob Rosenthal. I haven't directed a movie in four years, and I'm about to do a really interesting one. I need this fucking thing to happen. I wish I'd never written *Appalachian Winter.*"

"Don't say that. Though I would change the title."

"What did Paul Aiello say?"

"It wasn't a good conversation. Something's up with Paul. Normally I can read him. He wasn't himself. Very unsteady."

"But what did he say?"

"That Brad owns your availability contractually. Plus a lot of shit about your fancy education and how you think you're better than everyone else."

"Can they prevent me from directing *Coal*? Can Brad force me to be available to direct a film that doesn't exist?"

"They can cause you a shitload of trouble. I've seen this before."

The assistant gestured to David from the mouth of Larry's office.

"I need to go back inside."

"I've got your lawyers calling on the other line. What do you want me to tell them?"

"You're the agent. Just whatever it takes to keep me this job. *Coal*, I mean."

David tapped off his phone, then asked Larry's assistant for the location of the restroom and if he'd need a key.

"No key and no code. It's just down the hall, through the atrium and on the left."

Even in his distracted haste he couldn't help but admire the architectural integrity of the place, though it did repeat certain fashions of the previous decade with its exposed ductwork and ceiling struts painted in bright primary colors. A large interior square of the second floor had been removed to create an enclosed courtyard under wide industrial skylights. It all cohered to the extent that David felt he could even be happy working there given Jacob's requirements that he cast and edit on the premises. Jacob might be a paranoid monster, David thought, but he does have taste. Ivan the Terrible had hired Yakovlev, after all, to build Saint Basil's.

He pushed open the door to the men's room, checked to see that it was empty, then locked himself in the farthest of three stalls, where he closed the seat and sat. He considered Brad Shlansky a sociopath. "I don't feel guilt," he'd once confided to David. "It's a wasted fucking feeling. I'm not even tempted. Nobody has ever felt guilty for me or how I feel, so why should I feel guilty about them? Other than people who are starving or homeless or maybe being bombed in a war, nobody has had it harder than me. And I don't ask for anyone's pity for what I've been through. And from way before my parents died by the way. I figured this out early on collecting coins. I go for what I want, I don't complain, and I don't feel guilt."

"Aren't you complaining right now?" David asked.

"I'm telling you who I am."

Of this David was certain: Brad intended to gore him badly. Either David would pay out all the money he and Charlotte were saving for the girls, or he would not direct *Coal*. Perhaps both. But there was little use in allowing the inevitability of any of this to hobble him before his lawyers came up with a plan.

By the time he'd collected himself and returned to Larry's office, Jacob, Larry, and Carly had waited a good ten minutes.

"Everything all right?" Larry asked.

"I had to use the restroom. Your offices are beautiful, by the way."

"Thanks," said Jacob. "But please don't elaborate."

"Yes, please don't," echoed Larry, sharing a cryptic look with his partner.

"Let's get back to it," Jacob said. "Larry and I want to take you to dinner tonight if that's all right. We'll leave from the office, unless you have plans."

"I don't."

The session, which grew less arduous the more David understood Jacob's prescribed code of conduct, finished just before six, giving David thirty minutes before dinner.

"Carly's going to turn these changes around by Wednesday—I mean, you can do that Carly, right?" asked Jacob, rising.

"Absolutely."

"And then we can make offers." He turned to David. "It's good you came out here. You might think it could have been done by e-mail or on the phone, but that's not how I like to work."

"I get it."

"It's seeming like you do."

In fact, coming out was my suggestion, David thought. In the parking lot he called his lawyers.

He would never forget his initial interaction with the first of these two ten years prior when he needed representation for his first film as a director.

"Could we meet at your office at eight?" he asked Marc Stein, Esq. "I need to be in the editing room by nine."

"That's a bit early for me," answered a voice with the rehearsed, soothing empathy of a mortician, "as I'm usually in the office late so long as LA is up and functioning."

"Could you make an exception? I'll bring a Danish."

"I'll make the exception, but I'd prefer a Dane." If only for the entertainment value, David knew immediately Marc Stein would be his attorney, and for a very long time. He was not aware that Marc had cocounsel, also gay, named George Rosen, who worked across the country in Los Angeles at one of the most powerful firms in the industry, Hirschorn, Glickman, Roberts and Fein, or Hirschorn, Glickman for short.

Taking in the exterior of Jacob's building, as striking from the outside as from within, David called Rosen first.

"Hang on. Let me get Marc." Soon the three shared the line—Stein high above Times Square in the Brill Building, where it was already night, and Rosen a half mile away from David on Rodeo Drive.

"So," began Stein, as if informing a grieving family that the embalming of its patriarch had gone horribly awry, "we've had a series of interactions with the infamous Alice today. George, would you care to take David through it?"

"Well," began Rosen, "we got a letter from her early this morning exercising your option to direct *Appalachian Winter*."

"Which I still aver to be the best script you've ever written," interjected Stein.

"Well, you can thank Charlotte for that."

"And why is that, may we ask?"

"She taught me to write truthfully about where I'm from. It goes back to something she said when we started dating. In a lot of ways *Appalachian Winter* is about me leaving West Virginia and coming to New York."

"Well, we hope you get to make it."

"Not with him. He has no financing."

"They say he does," said Rosen.

"So, does that mean they're going to pay me?"

"If you remember," said Stein with dulcet care, "the option payment kicks in only when you're a week from production, not when he exercises the option. Alice stipulates, per the contract, that Shlansky can own your services without imminent remuneration."

"Who the fuck agreed to that?"

"You did! We told you not to!" barked Rosen.

"We told you a lot of things concerning the *Appalachian Winter* contract that you ignored."

It was true. In David's credulous enthusiasm he had accepted a welter of disadvantageous terms, along with language regarding payment sched-ules and creative rights so tortured with ambiguity that little of it bore actual meaning other than to obligate Brad Shlansky to very little while giving him complete power over David's material.

"He could at least introduce you to his funding source!" Rosen shouted at the time.

"Brad says only when he has the option."

"So, you see what's happening here," interjected Stein. "He's getting exclusivity on your material based on his word alone, and we all know him to be, shall we say, less than forthright."

Even Noah Mendelson, who wanted David to act in an adaptation of Flannery O'Connor's "The Life You Save May Be Your Own," instructed him not to go back into business with Brad.

"Instead of working with me you're trusting that coin collector guy from Long Island who sues everyone?"

"He raised the money for *Revenge*."

"And sued Charlie and Rob! Who does that?"

"He won."

"And *Appalachian Winter* is not *Revenge*. Tell me the plot again."

"A boy and his family walk across West Virginia before the Civil War."

"Right. And the big climax?"

"They make it to Ohio."

"People will be flocking to see it. They'll need to rent out stadiums."

"Have you read *As I Lay Dying*? Family walks across Mississippi. Big event in the end is a burial and the old man gets a set of teeth."

"Leaving aside the implication that you're somehow Faulkner, on a Friday night when someone in Charleston or LA or Chicago or New York is figuring out what to go see, and they've got a Marvel movie, the latest studio comedy, the latest studio thriller, two or three action movies with serious body counts, and a couple of art films with bigger budgets and more, shall we say, eventful endings than yours—not to mention they can forgo all that and stay home for what's on Netflix—what are they going to choose? Answer: not your abstruse West Virginia fucking period drama with a title like *Appalachian Winter* and its scintillating Faulknerian cadence. You're being lied to so this guy can go fish for money he'll never get."

But David had turned down the role Noah was offering and instructed his consternated lawyers to send him signature pages, convinced that with all his maneuvering Brad could at least sell the material in ways David couldn't. The contract signed, they hired a casting director, production designer, art director, a location scout, and a line producer, and set about building the film.

A month into preproduction in Kentucky no one had been paid, including a local support staff of six. There was also no longer any money for rental cars or even hotel bills of sixty dollars per night in the small town where they were to base production. Brad Shlansky, who never set foot on location, blamed everyone else: the line producer for failing to provide timely documentation for a completion bond, the actors and their representation for haggling over deal points, and of course David for constantly querying when funds would arrive.

"I have a mind to take the money elsewhere and put it into a project that actually deserves it."

"What money, Brad?"

"The money I'm on the verge of getting if I didn't have to be on my cell with you complaining every hour. Do you understand I'm a producer with a dozen other projects set up around town?"

"What do you mean 'on the verge of getting'? When I signed the contract, you said you had the money."

"You're saying I was lying?"

Soon Brad wouldn't allow himself to be on the phone alone but was always accompanied by his sisters, whom David could hear scribbling notes. Alice frequently joined from New York, and David suspected they were being recorded. But in call after call Brad refused to shut the movie down. He would listen to the line producer's woes, insist he was "working on it," and otherwise yield to silence, allowing others to suggest remedies. Finally, when he forbade them to use the credit card that had been issued, and it was wondered aloud by Brad's younger sister how transportation home would be covered, the line producer, whose name was Michael Stewart, succumbed.

"If that's the case," he said, looking across at David from the speakerphone around which the team in Kentucky huddled in David's cold and dingy office, "then I don't see how we can continue out here."

"What are you saying, Michael?" asked Alice.

"That we have to shut down."

"You're shutting the production down?"

"Your client is."

"I didn't hear him say that. I heard you say that, Michael. Isn't that what everyone else heard?" Brad's sisters corroborated Alice's read with a kind of morbid enthusiasm, while Brad remained silent. He had once advised David, "When you get what you want, the conversation is over. Don't say another word."

"Fine," said the exasperated line producer. "I'm shutting the production down."

"You're making the call," clarified Alice.

"Sure, Alice. If that's how you want to construe it. Or you could say I'm actually being the adult in this whole process. But those are just words."

"Words are all we have," she snapped back.

"We certainly don't have any money to make *Appalachian Winter*," said Michael.

They departed Kentucky two days later, informed that should anyone contemplate suing for wages, he or she should first call Alice. In response she would describe what would be Brad's countersuit referencing their erratic behavior on location, a mendacious cash flow, and that it had been they who shut down production, and not Brad. David returned to New York in June, and in July Jacob Rosenthal called his agent about *Coal*. It was now February.

"Here's the thing, David," said Rosen. "He can exercise the option for *Appalachian Winter* with only a letter. That's all he needs to supply per the contract everyone told you not to sign."

"For the film he failed to finance," interjected Stein. "We're frankly not even sure what he wants other than that you not work."

"So he's got me?"

"Insofar as he can exercise the option for *Appalachian Winter* just by saying he's doing it, and then claim you're unavailable to anyone but him, yes."

David looked for a place to sit, choosing the curb near a spotless Aston Martin of British racing green backed into the space nearest the office's entrance. That must belong to Jacob, he thought, beholding the sun's reflection along its elegant lines. California was so indescribably perfect as to make one sick, David thought. In New York he'd at least be on the move, trudging soot-flecked snow, his feet lacerated by the cold. He could find comfort in the meteorological echo of his gloom. Here one felt ashamed for any setback, with no excuse for anguish given such indescribable comfort day after day, not to mention the proliferation of sports cars to ogle.

"So what do I do?"

"You're going to have to hire a litigator," answered Stein.

"Can't you guys handle this?"

"We're transactional lawyers," said Rosen. "We're not equipped for this sort of thing."

"Or you can back out of the film with Jacob Rosenthal and make yourself available to Brad Shlansky and see if that mollifies him."

"For a movie that isn't real? Then I'm just effectively sitting around. Indefinitely. He won't raise the money, and if I try to direct or act in something else, he'll just do this to me again. Plus, we're really onto something with *Coal*."

"Thus, our encouragement that you hire a litigator," said Stein. "May we suggest one?"

David didn't respond.

"David, this is serious. Alice is crazy, but she's relentless."

"I've got it covered."

"May we ask by whom?"

"You won't know him."

"But he's a lawyer, specifically a litigator?"

"Last I heard. It's been a while. We've kind of been out of touch since our best friend died in a terrorist explosion in Israel."

VAN NUYS

Brad Shlansky met Alice for the first time when he walked into her down-town Manhattan office in the winter of 2009 after the worst financial crisis to afflict the United States since the Depression. They'd spoken briefly by phone the week before after Brad's great-uncle had given Brad her number.

"She's the most viciously unscrupulous lawyer you'll ever meet," he crowed. "And that's who you want on your side when it comes to our sort of businesses. Trust me. Better on your side than the other!"

"I just need a transactional lawyer," Brad responded. "This is about more than the IRS. I'm selling the stores."

"You're what?"

"You heard me, Uncle Julian."

"That's not what your father wanted."

"Well, he died, and that's not what I wanted, plus a lot of other things he did, so I guess that makes two of us."

"I wish I weren't the age I am, or I'd buy them. Or buy them for my son the layabout, but a cash business is the last thing he needs. Your parents didn't know how lucky they had it with you and your sisters. But look, transactions are when you need a litigator the most. I used to tell your father the same thing. Better to expect trouble with language that favors you—that way you always win if you sue or get sued. And always have a lawyer who's going to scare the shit out of people. It makes for better deals. Go meet Alice. In two seconds you'll see what I mean."

The offices of Markey, Schaffson and Roos occupied eight hundred square feet on the ninth floor of a building near the courthouse in lower Manhattan. Three attorneys shared two assistants, an arrangement Brad never stopped resenting when he'd call and no one would answer, sending him careening through a labyrinth of voicemail options. He brought with him a bottle of 2000 Chateau Duhart-Milon he'd purchased in Woodmere for thirty-four dollars.

"What's this?" she asked.

"For seeing me."

She placed it on a desk littered with paper and the remains of an egg sandwich without registering the bottle's label, instead looking him up and down. He'd dressed as he always did, in a button-down shirt tucked snugly to emphasize his relatively trim frame under the wool jacket his mother had bought him weeks before his father died.

"Take off your coat and take a load off," she said, "Tell me your story and how I can help."

Having seated himself in one of two green leather club chairs, he chronicled the demise of his parents and their business while she took page after page of notes. Before he knew it, he told her, it would be a decade, and by now he'd ascertained that more faced his sisters and him than he could ever have imagined, so impenetrable had been the battlements of deception erected by Carl Shlansky.

"So tell me about now," commanded Alice.

"I'm not sure I understand."

"How are you and your sisters? This is quite a story."

"Me and Emily are in the house in Woodmere. Emily graduated awhile back. Sarah, our younger sister, is at college in Delaware. She took a year off after our parents died."

"What's she studying?"

"Theater. And literature. I'm incredibly proud of her."

"That's a lot to say when you decided to forgo college yourself. You're an amazingly generous person."

"I'm not sure about that, but I love Emily and Sarah."

"Clearly."

"They didn't deserve what happened. None of us did. Not just losing our parents, but you can see in the papers I brought that the government has a pretty good case."

"Was this an arbitrary audit?"

"We think they were tipped off by a pissed-off employee who sensed stuff wasn't right."

"So tell me specifically what you'd like from me."

"Well, for starters we need someone to negotiate a settlement with the IRS, otherwise we're wiped out completely. We want to sell everything, including the house, and leave all this behind."

"When you say leave all this behind ..."

"Go to California."

"What's in California?"

"We want to make movies."

"Wow."

"Me'n my younger sister did theater together in high school. I was gonna study theater in college."

"Theater isn't movies."

"We also want a change of scenery. And watching movies was a big deal in our house as kids. Movie nights with pizza, that kind of thing."

"Do you have connections?"

"One."

"I hope he's a good one, because I hear that's important out there. Very important."

"He's good, and we go way back. In terms of the stores, five of them are on leases the landlords would be happy to get out of even with the real estate crash. The other two buildings we own. Give or take, we've got about four hundred and fifty thousand in the safes, and maybe fifty thousand or so in hard assets in the locations. There's also the Shlansky's Same Day brand, though we'd like a carve-out for our production-company name."

"Your production-company name?"

"Same Day Films."

"I see." She continued writing.

"The house is worth about four hundred thousand now, I think, which would be highway robbery. I mean seriously. One of the nicest streets in Woodmere. But that's what the appraiser said. The two store locations we own would fetch a little over two hundred thousand. Not exactly blue-chip even in good times. The government wants one and a half million, which obviously isn't going to work, particularly since the commercial real estate was bought at a discount, meaning even now the taxes are going to murder us on the sale. Same thing with the house. They know it and we know it."

"Where did you learn to talk this way?"

"Pardon?"

"I know fifty-year-old businessmen who don't have the command you do."

"I guess I've had to grow up fast. Plus, my dad. And I've kind of been in business on my own since I was in middle school, but that's another story."

"Well, I'm not a tax lawyer. I'm a litigator and a litigator, in that order."

"Uncle Julian said maybe someone in your firm, but you would oversee it all and also do the deals on selling the house, the stores and the business. And that you'd look after me and my interests like no one else."

"That's very kind. My partner has experience with the government and knows people at some good tax firms. It's a nightmare dealing with the feds, but they've always got a settlement floor in mind so they can clear it off their desk and deal with the next poor schmuck."

"So given your experience, and what your partner can do, what do you think?"

"I think this is a very ugly situation. I mean, just doing the math in my head based on what you told me, particularly if the government has your parents dead to rights—sorry, that was ill conceived—"

"No problem."

"But if the government has a case, you'll maybe settle for ninety cents on the dollar, plus asset forfeiture—"

"The two stores?"

"And everything in them, absolutely, if they're owned by the entity. And as you've pointed out, this is an awful time. And can you really sell the company? I mean once you've sorted all this out and indemnified any purchaser?"

"I can think of at least two buyers. The financial crisis has actually been good for our business. The banks are shittier to our clientele than ever."

"Okay. The sale with the best possible return and good language is where I can be of use. I mean direct use. I can organize a team for the rest, and for that I won't charge you."

With the help of her partner and outside counsel, they initiated settlement discussions with the government that exposed more inculpating details the longer negotiations went on, resulting in a steady hardening of the IRS position. It turned out that Carl Shlansky had been hiding money from Marvin Liebner as well, with a third set of books locked in a concealed drawer in Carl's desk, a fact that transformed the untitled and underpaid CFO from a reluctant government witness to a vindictively eager one, supplying analysis so forensically complete as to render any defense pointless. Finally, the two Shlansky's Same Day locations under company ownership, along with the house in Woodmere Park, were discovered to have mortgages.

"My father hated owing anyone anything!" Brad exclaimed to Alice.

"Apparently he got over it."

"How much worse is this going to get?"

Through it all, his mother's suicide continued to haunt Brad. He fixated on the party. He could have forced her to come along, just as he had Sarah. After all, there'd been other adults present. Instead, while his sister danced in a basement under colored lights, he had sipped first-growth Bordeaux (subsequent research had taught him as much), reveled in adulation for his performance in *Twelfth Night*, and then made out with a girl. At the most consequential moment in his life, he, to whom nothing was more important than family, had failed.

But toward his father, whose death had seated him for this test of filial love, there began to prevail a confusion of responses from bewilderment to anger. It wasn't the tax evasion per se. To loathe the government, resent its intrusions and self-dealing inefficiencies, this he could understand. Without a college education, and by sheer sweat and smarts, Carl Shlansky had built a venerable business all his own. Why should so much of it have been taken from him just to pay government salaries or be redistributed to the "less fortunate" to whom his business was already catering? Besides, it wasn't that his father had paid *no* taxes but rather a carefully considered fraction of what was owed, demonstrating at least some measure of appreciation for safe streets, water, sewage, a fire brigade, a strong defense, and yes, succor for the neediest. This became clear to Brad once he'd reconciled the three sets of books and had a look at the government's case. To Brad's astonishment, no matter the year, his father never dipped below 17 percent of his earnings going to the government, almost as if he belonged to a religion that tithed that canonized proportion. In several instances in fact, when the man might have concealed an especially good year simply by mimicking the books of the one previous, he instead fabricated to *increase* his liabilities, manifesting a strange kind of rectitude.

It was more the inanity of his father's methods that confounded Brad, just as did both his parents' seemingly aggressive indifference toward health and longevity. For a man who'd been so diligently hardworking and shrewd, it seemed as if his abdications had been almost intentional. Brad himself had swindled others, finding justification surprisingly easy. But he'd done so with care and forethought, and knew gradually to curtail such practices when his trading peers attained an age and acuity that rendered them no longer vulnerable. His father had taken not only his life's work but the very future of his family and, through willfully careless deception, caused it to amount not only to nothing but to an actual burden for his survivors. Who would do that? What sort of man?

"You're going to need to come into the city so we can go over all this," Alice warned on the phone once the lawyers had finished their initial work. "And bring your sisters."

"We're talking right now," Brad responded. "Why do I need to—just tell me what's going on. It's over an hour to get to you. Or can't I at least just come see you in Forest Hills?"

"It's an hour you're going to spend. Tomorrow morning. Ten o'clock. My partner and Rafferty need to be there, which is the reason for the office."

Norman Rafferty, a squat man with thinning red hair and an ill-advised beard of compensatory density, was the litigator dealing with the government. Brad had begun to despise him for how thoroughly he seemed to relish his work. The more sordid Carl Shlansky's malfeasance, the more titillating to Rafferty. With increased merriment his lower visage would broaden into the shape of a thickly bristled bell.

"I absolutely love this shit," he announced on nearly every call.

"I'm glad you're amused," Brad would offer quietly.

"The fed lawyer was breaking my phone speaker, he was shouting so loud. Just spitting with rage. I had to ask him if he was all right. I was almost disappointed when he calmed down."

"Good for you."

"I'm not going to lie: your father was one of a kind. I'm sorry never to have met him. He really put the 'fuck you' in tax evasion. The seventeen percent rule is killing me!"

Though Brad, Emily, and Sarah, who was home from college, arrived ten minutes early, Alice, Rafferty, and Alice's partner Philip Roos already occupied three of the six mismatched office chairs surrounding a small conference table inundated with documents. The seats at the end nearest the door stood empty, rotated forebodingly away, as if cautioning them not to enter. When the siblings did, the room quieted as all three attorneys stood to greet them.

"Wow," said Sarah.

"All of you, thanks for coming in," Alice said.

"Sure," Brad responded as he sat in the end chair. Emily and Sarah took those on either side of him.

"As I said on the phone, we thought it best we go over all of this in person. Norman has made what seems like a final deal with the government that's pretty good, all things considered."

"To cut to the chase, it's eighty-eight cents on the dollar," said Rafferty. "I tried like a motherfucker to get it down to eighty-five, but we were lucky to get them off ninety. It's an example thing. They want to pillory you guys because these cash businesses, with so much flow-through and the completely unsupervised record keeping, people just cheat, cheat, cheat. Your father was wildly aggressive in what the government considers an already unscrupulous business." His lower face began to broaden. "And when I say wildly aggressive—"

"We're aware," said Brad.

Alice seized a manila folder lying separate from the other documents and handed it over.

"This is our accounting. It's all detailed. You're going to want to take it home, obviously, because it's a lot, but the top sheet tells the story."

"Should we look now?"

"The quicker we figure all this out, the quicker you and your siblings can get on with your lives. But if you'd rather it be in private—"

"No."

From Marvin's quick tutorial on his first day with the Same Day books, Brad knew the most salient figure he was about to encounter would lie nestled inside parentheses, meaning debt. The only mystery lay in the magnitude.

"For Christ's sake, Brad, we can understand your trepidation," said Rafferty. "You are not going to like the number you guys are about to see. Should I just tell you?" He turned to Alice. "Should I just tell them?"

"Please don't," said Brad.

"Are you going to open it already?" asked Sarah.

"You know what? I didn't have to bring you guys."

"I didn't say anything," said Emily.

"Just give me a second."

"The news isn't going to get any better."

"I know that, Sarah."

He opened the folder, and under a bold heading centered atop the page that read "FMV Holdings, Carl and Miriam Shlansky/Shlansky Same Day Enterprises," twelve columns of numbers appeared. Atop each stood a year date, left to right, from 1997 to the present one of 2009. On the left margin was a list of holdings, from "Real Estate" to "Cash/Cash Equivalents" to "Office Equipment" to "Art" to "Automobiles," even "Guns."

"What's this?" asked Brad.

"Apparently your father kept a pistol in every store."

"I never saw any. Did either of you guys know that?" he asked his sisters.

"I think Mom might have mentioned it once."

The image of his father fumbling with a firearm accosted him suddenly, until he recalled they'd actually gone once to a range to fire one, a memory he didn't savor.

"I assume you'll want to sell them. They'd need to be registered in California."

"Yeah, of course."

"Of course?"

"Sell them! What do we need with guns?"

Two titles occupied final spots: "Tax Liabilities" and then finally just "Liabilities." At the very bottom of each row amounts appeared in bold for each year. They increased exponentially left to right, all in parentheses, like a death march.

"You're going to want to look at the number on the bottom right," offered Alice. It read: ($98,548.33).

"So you're saying, if I read this right, that even if we take all the cash from the safes, sell the store and all the real estate—the house and the two locations Mom and Dad owned, and even all three cars, we owe almost a hundred thousand dollars? Add up every single asset, including the fucking guns, and we owe six figures?"

"That's the situation, Brad," said Alice. "And that doesn't include our work so far, or any of the closing costs for unwinding all this, which are incremental and not insignificant."

"Your father, I gotta tell you—" began Rafferty.

"Will you please just stop it with that?" shouted Brad.

"Of course. I understand."

"So how does this work?" Brad asked Alice. "I mean, how does a person— or a family—exist with this sort of debt, which includes our being homeless even to get to that number, and still we owe. We'll have no place to live and no way to pay rent."

"Well, one option is not to sell and to work your way out of it. Your father was running a profitable business. A lot of this debt accrued because of the hole he dug for himself with taxes he owed on earnings. Like Norman said, it just compounded, and that gets very ugly. But you can declare bankruptcy, take the protection, and work your way back to solvency. It'll take some years, but you can get there."

"I don't want to be in the check-cashing business, and neither do my sisters."

"That's fine, but just be aware you're going to have this albatross of debt around your necks. No bank is going to loan you money for whatever else you might want to do, and that goes for California too. Just turning over all stones, is there some asset your parents kept secret that's not listed?"

"It wouldn't surprise me," offered Rafferty tentatively.

"Norman, please," Alice interjected.

"Not that I know of," responded Brad.

"What about your coin collection?" asked Sarah.

"I don't think a coin collection's going to make much difference," said Alice, "though I wouldn't mention it when we meet with the government if it's important to you. They go after everything."

Brad sat staring at the page in front of him.

"Brad?" said Sarah.

"Sarah has a point," he said finally.

They called Frakes and Bowman's from the conference room phone. "These guys are tops," Philip Roos had insisted. "Seven years ago I was handling an estate in Great Neck, and the beneficiaries couldn't stop bickering about the fucking coins their father collected, so we ended up deciding just to liquidate the whole thing and have them split the money. These guys made it unbelievably easy. They'll even send an appraiser to your house."

At first no one would be available for an on-site visit for five weeks, and Brad was told to supply a list in advance to expedite the process.

"Or you can bring them in."

"That's going to be difficult."

"How many coins is this?"

"Thousands. I don't want to seem like I'm bragging, but it's a serious collection."

"And you say you're out on Long Island?"

"Woodmere."

Brad pressed the speakerphone option while he waited on hold. After several tinny minutes of what Alice's partner informed them was Aaron Copland's *Fanfare for the Common Man*, an older man clicked on while Emily, Sarah, and the three attorneys listened in.

"Hello, this is Jamison Bowman. I understand you have quite a few coins."

"I do," Brad answered.

"Have you ever been to one of the auctions or in our store? Why have I never heard of you?"

"I guess I've just been doing my own thing out here."

"My girl said. Five Towns?"

"Yeah."

"That's a whole world of its own. My wife's from the North Shore. When can we send someone to look at what you've got?"

The unfathomably slender gentleman dispatched by the auction house, with the unlikely name of Wiley, first name Edwin, projected little kindness as he accepted Brad's offer of a glass of water, "No ice, please." He set to work in the basement without otherwise speaking except to ask where he could situate his light, loop, and ledger. He tarried over each specimen with the practiced fastidiousness of a museum antiquarian rather than the dirty-knuckled dealers with whom Brad was familiar.

While the man examined and scribbled, Brad's disdain for the collection grew almost unbearable. He pondered the plurality of life's hours spent growing and organizing its number, not to mention the mental energy allocated to devising trades, whether willful swindles, shrewd pressings of advantage, or, as was mostly the case of late, equitable swaps to complete certain subsets of the larger whole, such as the attainment of his final Morgan dollar—the ever elusive 1885 Carson City—just before his first meeting with Alice. Really, he thought to himself, as Wiley hovered over what looked to be an Indian head from the mid-1870s, this could end up being the great accomplishment of my life. At twenty-five not only did Brad not have a girlfriend, he remained a virgin, a fact he blamed mostly on his persisting acne, especially given his recent focus on fitness as a repudiation of his parents' indifference to it. Yes, Alice was right to observe, I've taken care of my sisters, sorting the mess Mom and Dad left behind, but so what? These coins—not a degree, not any hope of a career that might interest me, not any prospect of a family of my own—are all I amount to.

After four and a half hours, during which Wiley took breaks every twenty minutes to climb the stairs and step outside to inhale a brown Davidoff cigarette down to its filter, the reckoning was complete. He uttered a perfunctory good-bye without shaking Brad's hand, though he did proffer his card, along with the catalogue for a forthcoming auction.

"Are you in a position to give me a sense of what it all might be worth? I mean, I have my own ideas, but—"

"I'm not at liberty."

"It's pretty impressive though, wouldn't you say?" he queried, already hating himself for such cloying desperation.

"For a basement in Woodmere I suppose." He turned toward his car before Brad could humiliate himself further, a record of every rare coin Brad would ever own tucked under his arm. Brad was done, just as he was done with parents and their self-destruction (whether through malfeasance, the stress that resulted from it, or suicide), with the downtrodden who couldn't get bank accounts, with the very state in which he was born and raised and its hot, humid summers. With winter of any kind.

Twelve days after Edwin Wiley left with an accounting of his coins, Brad answered the kitchen phone and found himself speaking once more with Jamison Bowman.

"Good morning, Brad. Edwin has had a look at your collection."

"Yes. I watched him."

"And he's had a chance to tally what I'd call the take price for what you've got, meaning the minimum it should go for. Now we have two versions of that, which we can also discuss—one for the entire collection, and one for it being sold piece by piece, which can take longer, but over that time can yield results that are more robust. I'm assuming you're willing to sell every coin you put in front of us."

"That's correct."

"Our floor price then is $188,000."

"Okay," responded Brad with some relief.

"Edwin said you're young."

"Well, I'm not old."

"That's a decent collection to have amassed without having spent a lifetime doing it."

"I'm going to want to sell it, and soon, so how does that work, and what do you guys get?"

"Well, we can simply buy the collection from you for eighty percent of the price I quoted, or we can put the collection up for auction and share a percentage."

"Which would be?"

"Five percent from you, and seventeen and a half from the buyer."

"But effectively all from me," said Brad, "because all parties know that going in and it's still a hit I take."

"You're not wrong. Everyone who works with us trusts our appraisals, and they trust our curation. That has to be worth something. Many would accurately describe the fees as paying for themselves."

"What would you advise I do?"

"It sounds like you don't want to sell in separate lots for risk of not all of it going quickly, and the process getting attenuated."

"That's essentially the idea, yes."

"I'm going to try to think of both of us right now, Brad. I don't wish to upset you, but we've sold some important collections out of this place, and yours is not going to shake the numismatic world."

"Understood."

"One of two types of entities is going to want your coins in toto: either a shop with equity but not a lot of stock, so maybe one starting out. Or a speculative collector who covets certain of your coins—just scanning the list, the Carson City dollar, your '55 double die, the '43 copper Lincoln head, the '23S Walking Liberty, to name just a few—and is interested in purchasing the rest to put away as an investment or sell or trade. And if you get several collectors bidding against each other, you'll be in a good situation—exceeding the two and a half percent more than if you just sold to us outright."

"So, you're saying I should be a little patient and auction the collection rather than sell to you now."

"That is what I'm saying, again thinking in terms of what would benefit us both. I think you're going to do better than Edwin's low number. Forgive me for saying so, but we're very good at this."

The auction would take place in late July. Brad and his sisters spent the summer doing what they'd somehow avoided for years, "settling the affairs" of their parents, a term Brad found bewilderingly anodyne given the physical and emotional toil of cleaning out the home in which they'd spent their lives. Sarah wept unceasingly, to the extent that he wondered at the biology of a seemingly fathomless reservoir of tears. Emily anesthetized herself with food, adding more than twenty pounds to an already beleaguered frame. For two full months, closet by closet, box by box, item by item, they assayed decades in a fugue of sadness, anger, and gluttony.

Daily calls from Alice, Rafferty, and Philip Roos updating him on the sale of assets, as well as the papering of the government settlement that included documentation from Frakes and Bowman's as to the value of his collection, served as his only relief. Liquidation, after all, would not only mitigate the impact of family tragedy but underwrite their escape from it as well.

Regarding the coins, the self-promoting Jamison Bowman proved prescient in every respect: Brad had indeed chosen the right house, and their estimates had been low. When not two but three collectors, including one from Melbourne and another from Hong Kong, had finished bidding, the fruits of his childhood obsession sold to a collector in South Carolina for $205,000.

Not eager to attract further attention as the tax-cheating son of a tax-cheating father, Brad enlisted Edwin Wiley to help determine a cost basis for his collection. With scant documentation—would he hunt down Simon Zeligson and every witless subsequent trader?—the challenge became to fabricate a number low enough to discourage need for proof. As Rafferty cheerily advised, "You don't want to give these assholes a number so aggressive they come after you. Lose a thousand bucks so you don't lose ten, not to mention another year of the IRS having its dick up your ass."

They settled on an amount just over $130,000, though it had in truth been a third of that, meaning a taxable profit of $75,000, with the remainder unmolested.

In the winter of 2009, with the government and lawyers made whole, Brad, Sarah, and Emily climbed into their late father's Yukon with just over forty thousand dollars and drove west.

"I've got a feeling you're going to do interesting things out there, and if only out of curiosity, I want in," Alice announced over a celebratory dinner at Smith & Wollensky's, assuring a continuing presence in his life. "Plus, the movie business? You're going to be dealing with some of the most dishonest fucking shysters on the planet. Trust me when I say, you'll need me more than ever."

Brad had read in *Newsday* about a successful screenwriter who outlined his first script at the age of twenty-three driving from North Carolina to Hollywood by stopping at rest areas along his route to scribble scene descriptions and bits of dialogue on index cards. On reaching Los Angeles, he billeted himself for two weeks in a studio apartment off Highland to flesh it all out, and within a month he had signed with an agent who sold the script for six figures.

"We're gonna do one better," Brad instructed Emily and Sarah in the weeks leading to their departure. "First of all, we don't need to go looking for an agent because we've already got one. Paul Aiello works for United Creative Management."

"The one who sucker-punched the kid on the school trip?" asked Sarah.

"He represents Selena Machado and Claire Fisher, smartass. And he's already talking about us with everyone. And secondly, we're gonna produce the script we write."

"What do we know about producing?" asked Emily.

"What did I know about coins when I started? And I just sold my collection for two hundred grand. Paul's gonna help us, and Alice is gonna protect us. And we're gonna produce because we'll generate the material. The credit will get us the access to learn as we go, and by the end of the process we'll be ready for the next one. It's how it fucking works."

"Brad, we're just three schnooks from Woodmere whose parents were in the check-cashing business," said Sarah. "You really think we're just going to go out to Hollywood and suddenly produce a movie because you were able to cheat eighth graders by shining coins with silver polish?"

"First of all, I don't like that word you just used. I didn't cheat anyone. Nobody forced anyone to trade coins with me. Secondly, did you and I not bust open the theater clique in high school, with you fucking president of the drama club by the time you were a senior, and me getting a lead role the first time I tried out? I will sell us. We're Shlanskys, which means we're smarter than everyone else, and we stick together. Five years from now, LA won't know what hit it. Now please, let's use these brains that were the best thing our parents gave us and write a great fucking script!"

By the time they'd reached Pennsylvania they'd settled on a horror film about a serial killer who preyed on the lonely. It would be called *The Recluse*, and its antagonist would be just that, a basement dweller haunting bars in search of plus-size women to dismember. A hundred miles into Ohio, Brad suggested the psychological dimension of the detective pursuing him being a diabetic.

"That's ridiculous, Brad," shouted Emily from the backseat.

"It's not," argued Sarah. "Having a guy checking his glucose levels while he's chasing a killer is funny and weird—the kind of shit horror fans love. And the detective having a physical issue makes it more interesting and dire."

"Fat women are getting slaughtered every ten minutes. How much more dire do you want?" asked Emily.

"Dire for the protagonist," answered Sarah. "Harder for him. He's disadvantaged, but in a way that allows him to relate to the victims. It's a great idea, Emily. You're outvoted." For good measure they added a health-obsessed wife for the detective who berated him about his diet, sending him into the arms of a corpulent undercover policewoman, herself a lonely heart who ends up becoming bait in pursuit of the murderer.

In Nevada Brad called Paul Aiello, with whom he'd been speaking by phone for months.

"Get ready to send this out. We're almost done with the outline, and it's gonna be fucking fantastic."

"It better be, so I don't look like an asshole the way I've been selling you guys."

Paul's assistant had found them a cheap three-bedroom apartment in Venice, where in a joyous frenzy they finished a draft and revised it twice within three weeks. It was the happiest Brad had been since before the death of his father, his confidence vindicated by Paul's response.

"Not only am I gonna sell this ridiculous piece of shit, you're gonna get it made," he said on the phone. "There's nothing better in Los Angeles than to be new, and especially in horror, which is very sought after right now. I gave another speech about you and the project in our staff meeting this morning. And I've got just the actor to play your fucking diabetic detective, which is fucking hilarious by the way. And we'll put a hip director on it too, which it needs. Partner you with a producer who knows what he's doing and get this thing started so we can make some real money."

"It's all happening so fast," said Brad.

"You've done the hardest part. It starts with getting the first one sold. Then you have something you can take out and dance on the table so that people want in on your next one. Everyone makes the mistake out here of waiting until a film comes out to strike, but a movie is never as good as people say it's gonna to be. You've got to get the next job before the piece of shit you're working on comes out—while people still think you're going to win the Oscar or gross a hundred million. I hate lying, but I love fucking exaggerating. I'm going to fucking drown you guys in scripts."

Paul optioned *The Recluse* to a video-driven genre company called Vulcan Films, which allowed Brad and his sisters to come on as producers, including an "In Association with" card for Same Day Films. As he'd promised, the agency packaged it with Paul's client Sam Parker, a network television star on hiatus, as the detective.

"It just shouldn't be this easy," Brad said with a chuckle.

"Is your script *Citizen Kane*? No. But I'm great at what I do, which in this case was to get people to think that maybe, just maybe, it's gonna be the *Citizen Kane* of horror movies involving fat female victims and a diabetic detective, which, by the way, you might have to change because Sam is cut and he's not dropping any muscle."

"One thing. Why is Sam Parker making more than me and my sisters?"

"Promising them Sam Parker is how I got Vulcan to bite, asshole. Without Sam, if your script was optioned at all, it would still be in development, and that's no knock on your script. We're threading a needle here. With the material alone you and Sarah and Emily are just genre creators. Add Sam into the mix, suddenly you're hip. It's like you get what horror films are on another level. Suddenly you're artists. So trust me, this is just the warm-up. A few more films and we're going to crash the Oscars like the fucking Golds. You're gonna be on that stage one day thanking me for all I did for you. Because let me tell you something. No one should have to go through what you and your sisters went through. Whatever happens to you in Hollywood, whatever we do together, you deserve it, because you guys picked yourselves up from a tragedy, studied up how to write a screenplay, put in the work, and decided to make the world do right by you. You've fucking come out here, and now you take, because it's about to be your turn. By the way, I love this Alice woman, your lawyer. She's a fucking terror."

A young music video director in whom the agency had fervent hopes came on to "helm" the film, as was announced in an industry publication Paul called "one of the trades." Brad, who'd been reading the *New York Times* business section since the week his father died, found in these some of the most peculiar journalism he'd ever encountered.

"I need a fucking lexicon. It's worse than the Robert McKee book," he told Sarah, referring to the screenwriting manual they'd consulted before moving west.

Vulcan Films rented production space for *The Recluse* in a shabby two-story building in Van Nuys, where Brad and his siblings were given a cramped office to share noticeably far from the director. There Brad began to immerse himself in observing how the film was being put together, doing his best to manage suspicions that the process inhibited any impulse toward quality. It brought to mind the auction of his coins. Based on "take numbers" for foreign sales and pre-sales, which would largely be brokered at European film festivals, the movie was projected to fetch just over $2 million so long as it was at all creditable. Given the financing entity's expectation of a 20 percent margin after fees, it needed therefore to be made for no more than $1.5 million, but really for less, as the budget held back a "contingency" of 8 percent it was made clear the filmmakers must never invade.

"It's very simple, Brad," his father had answered when Brad, at the age of ten, asked how a person made money cashing other people's checks. "Of course we charge them for the service. That should be obvious. But back up and think of it more generally. Every business of a certain size needs to do one thing and one thing only: bring in at least, *at least*, a dollar and ten cents for every dollar it spends. So, say I have to lay out a hundred dollars to pay Marvin and Cheryl and Draymond and everyone their salaries, and to keep the lights and heat on, and the air-conditioning in summer, and pay the insurance and everything else. What do I have to earn?"

"A hundred and ten dollars."

"And that ten dollars is my profit. And again, that's bare minimum. Ten is really just enough to keep going—you're surviving and nothing more at my scale."

"So why not just charge more, or take more from each check?"

"First of all, the State of New York has a say in that, and second, because then my clients go to the other guy. But no matter what you do in this world, I don't care where you are and what it is, ultimately it boils down to that—bringing in at least ten percent more than you lay out. If you don't do that, you're up a creek. A creek of shit!"

The Recluse was getting made because Vulcan Films determined that for the million and a half dollars it would cost to produce, within a year they'd have brought in at least two million, well more than Carl Shlansky's 10 percent profit. It was a paradigm no different from that of a place that cashed checks, sold groceries, or made toasters.

"And that's what people forget," Paul Aiello confirmed on the patio of a restaurant overlooking the beach in Santa Monica. "They get caught up in the fact that it's movies, with all the bullshit of seeing their pictures on billboards or their name in the paper or having a statue for their shelf, getting the good table at the right restaurant, you name it. And meanwhile there's serious money to be made, and they're not making it because they're focused on the wrong stuff. Most of these douchebags out here would be far richer and far happier if they just did something else." He took a sip of the 2004 Chateau Meyney Brad had ordered that would be charged, along with the casually extravagant dinner, to UCM. "But I've got to tell you, serious pussy, Brad. Like you wouldn't believe. And if you have power, it's like revenge of the fucking nerds."

Brad had already begun to experience this on his own set, and with one woman in particular. He'd noticed her during the third week of photography when she, along with a soundman, a camera operator, and two grips, set up director's chairs and a tent of black duvetyn in an area adjacent to the stages where the film was shooting for the remainder of the schedule. Her resemblance to Gloria Allee startled him. Like her, she had sandy hair, fair skin, and a curvy body. But what most reminded him of the young woman who'd given him his first romantic kiss was the open friendliness of her face.

"Is she with us?" he asked one of the assistant directors.

"Yeah, she's doing EPK."

"What's that?"

"Electronic press kit. They interview everyone—the actors, the director, you guys."

"What do you mean 'you guys'?"

"You and your sisters. You wrote the movie, right?"

"Yeah."

"Well, so they interview you and it gets put in with the movie as an extra, or when people are promoting it. You know how you see the promos on airplanes or maybe the movie's website before it comes out with the people talking? The making of? You'll be interviewed for that."

For days he awaited his invitation, but it didn't materialize. One after another the actors, the director, even the director of photography were ushered into the tent, but never Brad and his sisters. With only a week left of principal photography, he approached the first AD.

"So, Rick, am I gonna be interviewed for the EPK?"

"Honestly, Brad, I was trying to protect you from it."

"What do you mean?"

"Most people hate those fucking things. You sit there for twenty minutes instead of being on set or going home, and no one ever watches it."

"Yeah, well, I wrote the movie. Me and my sisters. Plus we're producers."

"I know."

"So I think we deserve to be interviewed, don't you?"

Later that afternoon he was summoned, along with Emily and Sarah, to the tent where the woman had arranged three chairs in front of a Canon digital camera and two chimera lights.

"Hi, I'm Amanda," she said in a voice that was deeper and warmer than Gloria Allee's. "I was wondering when you guys were going to show up. I've been bugging Rick in fact. Your script is insane. Everyone loves it."

"Thanks. I'm Brad obviously, and this is my little sister, Sarah, and my older sister, Emily."

"It's really great to meet you guys. You're from New York, right?"

"Yeah, Long Island," answered Emily.

"Well, I'm two states over. Pennsylvania. Pittsburgh."

"The Penguins," Brad said inanely.

"What, you're suddenly a hockey fan?" asked Sarah. He wanted to punch her, but she was right. He had no interest in the sport whatsoever but wanted to say something to cover his sudden anxiety.

"That's so funny," Amanda answered. "I actually love the Penguins. I used to go to games with my dad."

"You don't anymore?" Brad asked.

"He died actually."

Brad looked at Emily and Sarah, who returned his uncertain gaze.

"Well, I'm really sorry to hear that," he offered. "We have something in common."

"Wow. This got deep real quick," she said, laughing. "I mean, I guess I shouldn't make light of it, but life deals what life deals."

"I'm just lucky to have my sisters," said Brad, put at ease by the woman's easy charm.

"And they're obviously lucky to have you," she volunteered, holding his gaze. Since the moment he'd entered the tent, other than the glance to his sisters, he hadn't taken his eyes from hers. As for the interview, he couldn't remember a single question afterward, other than that most had been directed at him. Nor could he recall his answers. Just keep speaking and smiling, he told himself as it was happening, and don't let her know she's one of the most amazing women you've ever encountered.

"So what the fuck was that?" Sarah asked once they were clear of the tent.

"What are you talking about?"

"You and that woman were practically making out."

"What, she didn't ask you and Emily enough questions?"

"You think I give a shit about that? She's cute. Reminds me of Gloria Allee. Are you gonna ask her out or what?"

"She works for us."

"That you're gonna have to explain."

"We're producers. We hired her."

"Cut the shit, Brad. Man up."

"Excuse me?"

"First off, she does not work for us, because, if you haven't noticed, we're producers in name only. Nobody asks us about shit, not even our script. And secondly, Vulcan pays her out of the budget. We didn't even know she existed until they asked us to go in and do that interview no one will ever see."

"It's still not a good look, Sarah."

"Well, I've got news for you. We were her last one."

"How do you know that?"

"The sound guy told me when he was putting on my mic. You were too busy slobbering over her to hear. So as of thirty seconds ago she's no longer on the job you supposedly hired her for."

Twenty minutes later, on his way to his and his sisters' trailer, he saw several grips dismantling the EPK tent and, nearby, Amanda chatting with her soundman. Before he realized he was no longer moving, she began to walk toward him.

"I loved what you had to say about the horror genre."

"Me and my sisters watched a lot of movies growing up."

"Are you enjoying this whole process?"

"I'm mostly just surprised by it. But we want to keep doing this."

"Clearly."

"So, would you want to maybe go out sometime?" Just as with asking Laurie Dwyer to go steady, the words escaped his mouth before he'd assessed the risk. It was as if his soul had given his brain no choice.

"I would love that, Brad."

She left him with a scrap of the day's call sheet with her phone number.

Meanwhile, Paul delivered on his threat to send more scripts than Brad and his siblings would have time to read. Sarah vetted them all, dispensing with those that failed to interest her after twenty pages.

"You can really tell by then?" asked Emily.

"You want this job? And guess what? Yeah, I can."

Among the plethora of cynically raunchy comedies, nonsensical thrillers, and derivative horror films not a tenth as inventive as theirs, one script stood out, demanding to be made. Sarah finished it in one sitting over coffee in the catering tent on the very day Amanda gave Brad her phone number, then marched across base camp to the AD trailer to have two copies printed.

"You both need to leave set right now and read this," she said. "This is the next movie we're going to make. We need to commit to it today before anyone else sees it."

Brad stared down at its cover: *Revenge*, screenplay by David Levit.

BEVERLY HILLS

Not once in the preceding forty-eight hours had Paul Aiello roamed the halls of UCM, as was his wont, so effectively had Susan Painter's threats and the two days of silence that followed shaken him. While he'd been convinced that morning of the efficacy of his arguments, a certain resolution in her voice gnawed at him. He'd effectively stripped his home of all that could implicate, but should she go after him, the inevitable publicity of being brought in for questioning, even should no evidence support her claims, would be enormously disruptive. He regretted signing her. On a deeper level—and he couldn't quite name or even describe the intuition—he had for a time sensed a disquieting change in the susceptibility of women to his advances, not to mention a restiveness in their aftermath, successful or not.

Thankfully, the Jake Baker deal had arrived Wednesday morning while he was still in his car.

"I've got Jamie Ungerman from Fox," Jen informed him, referring to the studio's head of casting for television. "She says you can't call back."

"And why's that?"

"If you don't take her call now, you'll go right into the staff meeting and then it's at least two hours before you'll get back to her, and by then they'll have moved on."

"Put her through."

"Good morning, Paul."

"What's this emergency?"

"You been online yet?"

"I haven't even gotten to the fucking office, which you know."

"Jesus, what's with the mood? You want me to call someone else with this offer for a series lead and a guaranteed thirteen? I can go to the next actor on my list."

"Sorry. Rough morning."

"Well, that makes two of us. When you do get around to reading *Deadline*, or when you get to your staff meeting, you're going to hear that Skeet Thompson got arrested early this morning for beating up his girlfriend."

"I told you not to hire that asshole."

"Well, Skeet's girlfriend's bad night is Jake Baker's good morning."

"You're a woman. Aren't you supposed to be sympathetic? Or at least outraged?"

"I'm a sixty-five-year-old woman. You have no idea what I went through when I was young. It's terrible, but Skeet is ruined and the girlfriend will get over it."

"You should have offered the role to Jake in the first place." Paul's client had gone to network against Skeet Thompson for the pilot Fox was producing.

"Jake was always my first choice."

"Because you knew no one would be better for it, especially not Skeet Thompson."

"Yeah, well Skeet and Damon went way back."

"That doesn't change the fact this was always Jake's role. I told you that. He helped his daughter through addiction. She's now up at UC Santa Barbara majoring in marine biology." In the show—written and to be executive produced by Damon Kelley, one of the most successful showrunners in network television (hence the guarantee of at least thirteen episodes)—a wealthy neurosurgeon whose teenage son dies of an opioid overdose in an understaffed ER forsakes his practice to run that very same ER. The pilot script had a sharp, morbid humor to it, and far more cynical narratives had been rewarded with multiple seasons. Paul joined his colleagues at UCM in predicting years of pickups. It could be career defining for his client, at least in television.

"You know that this conversation doesn't start, Jamie, unless we're talking about six figures with the first of those being the number three."

"We were paying Skeet two hundred, and this is not 1995."

"I'll say it again: if you want Jake, you pay him three hundred fifty per episode, or I tell him to pass."

"The offer is two hundred thousand, which is what it was in the deal he already signed to go to network, and it expires end of business. We start shooting in eight days. If it's not your guy, I move on, and I mean by lunch. Either we have a deal, or we don't. I don't have time to fuck around."

By three o'clock they'd closed at $250,000, meaning Paul had brought in $325,000 to the agency, and in all likelihood far more, from this one phone call. Of course, he admitted to himself, I've been chopping wood for three years on Jake Baker, so it was a hell of a lot more work than the one offer. But once again, he had invested his time and reputation in the right client, and this one atypically not an actress. Mostly, however, he wasn't obsessing over Susan Painter. She still had not called, and had ignored three e-mails he'd sent personally with auditions for the following week. But perhaps she was considering his advice. She sought success and understood she couldn't do better than him and UCM for representation. As for Janine, he'd called in a favor with a producer friend and lined up a meeting with a creative VP at HBO to discuss their optioning a book she'd read about the shah of Iran. In their halting conversation, Janine hadn't once mentioned Susan or the events that had transpired at his house.

He decided to circle the floor with the katana given to him inexplicably by his brother for his seventeenth birthday.

"Back in a few, Jen." His current assistant, twenty-four years old, was from Boston. She'd studied English in college somewhere in Maine and had followed that with an MBA at UCLA. He preferred well-educated overachievers on his desk, mostly because such provenance made dictatorial control of them nothing short of delectable.

"So, how's that for your Stanford degree?" he'd asked one. "I bet you never imagined you'd be bossed around by a dumb mook from Long Island who went to a state school. Aren't you glad your parents spent sixty grand a year on that, what was it, art history degree?"

"Philosophy actually, and I'm paying off ninety thousand dollars in student loans," she responded, fighting tears. He'd been lambasting her all morning.

"Yeah, then you're even stupider than I thought."

"*Stupider* is not a word," she replied, after which he fired her.

He liked Jen, however. She rarely cried or lost her cool and certainly wouldn't dare correct his English. She even seemed to enjoy working as an assistant, rather than treating it as a demeaning necessity for advancement. Her father, it surprised him to learn, had been a Pentagon correspondent for ABC News after twenty years in the service. Perhaps because of the military upbringing she projected an imperviousness to the sort of abuse he normally meted out, and though slender, athletic, and sly in a manner that suggested she'd be somewhat devious in the sack, he didn't dare try and sleep with her.

"I'll only be fifteen minutes," he said, "but if it's fucking Brad Shlansky, tell him at least an hour."

"He's not going to believe me."

"Well, you have to do a better job convincing him. Look at it as today's challenge. I just need a quick walk-around to remind everyone I'm here."

"I was wondering. I haven't seen the sword since last week."

"I was feeling a little under the weather."

"You've had a lot going on. The Jake Baker negotiation, whatever the deal was with Susan Painter."

"Susan's going to be fine. Jake's gonna make over three million dollars. Life's great."

He turned to stroll the gauntlet of smartly dressed young assistants penned with their headsets and computer screens in cubicles to his left, and the offices of senior agents on the right.

He'd joined UCM as a partner upon moving to Los Angeles from New York City in 1997 after two years in the music business. Already back east he could credit himself with an eye for young talent, culling his first clients from the ranks of dancers in clubs and rap videos to fill what he perceived to be an underserved market for female headliners in the male-dominated and mostly misogynistic urban music world. Of the dozen or so he signed, eight landed record deals, earning him enough money and status to strike out on his own. In particular, a crass and savvy Puerto Rican from Queens named Selena Machado demonstrated not only the talent, sex appeal, and moxie to become a star but a relentless, downright wrathful ambition that at times terrified him. But he'd harnessed and guided it, and together they'd turned her into a worldwide brand. He'd always understood, however, that she'd move on from him, so he continued to represent other clients even when she asked him to work exclusively with her. Together they agreed she needed an agent for the films she'd begun to be offered, which brought him to Los Angeles and UCM. The agency's desperation to sign her leveraged his position considerably.

"How do you like that?" he said to Brad Shlansky on the phone the day UCM offered him a contract. Brad was the sole friend from back east with whom he maintained any contact, which had only increased when he'd learned of the deaths of his old friend's parents. "I've got my own double-lot office in one of the biggest firms in Hollywood—and I got it within three months of landing out here. You should see the way these saps who've slogged it out into their forties and fifties look at me. I did at the age of twenty-five what they've spent decades working for."

And none could argue with his eventual results, particularly after he'd managed to gather some of the most talented but demanding women on the company roster under his name.

"How the fuck do you do it?" a mystified Howard Garner asked. "Not just Claire Fisher. You've practically got everyone."

"I let them know I'm gonna go out there and fucking kill for them. And I mean literally. I don't get on the phone and stroke their egos and shovel shit or try and be their therapist. I kill very big game, and I bring it home for them to eat."

"What does any of that even mean, Paul?"

"It means I get them more work than they have time for, and I get them paid like men."

Among the agents at UCM, Janet Liebowitz loathed him most, and he her. Given her appearance, it frankly astounded him she was an agent at all, and one of the most feared in the building. Much like Paul (if you took away the distraction of sex), she lived for her clients, a fact that should have rendered her and Paul allies. Instead, she had oozed hostility since the morning he entered the building to be interviewed.

"What're you? Puerto Rican?"

"Italian American."

"I don't understand. How did you become Selena's manager, then?" she asked. He'd noticed her the second he sat down at the long conference table. No younger than sixty, and emphatically Jewish, she wore one of the most cumbersome wigs he'd ever seen, composed of waxen synthetic hair piled high in broad curls and canted preposterously from being too large for her head. "I mean, what, are you even twenty yet? This is the most ridiculous thing I've ever seen."

"Maybe I should just leave," he volunteered.

"Be my fucking guest," she said. To his surprise, everyone laughed.

"Don't mind Janet," said Murray Luthnow, one of the agency's founders. "In fact, try and be like her. She's more loyal and aggressive than anyone I've ever met. There's not a better agent in this building, nor will there ever be."

One of the highlights of his daily rounds was to linger at her door.

"Hey, Janet."

"Paul, I don't have time. Could you shut it, please? I don't know why Paige left it open. *Paige!*" she shouted. "I told you to close the fucking door when you leave my office!"

Paul remained. "I actually needed to talk to you about a limited series on HBO Brad Shlansky wants to offer Joe Moore."

"Joey's not doing television. You know that."

"We're making the offer, so you're gonna to have to pass it on."

"You put those words in the wrong order. You mean 'pass on it.'"

"Very funny."

"Don't be an asshole. And to be an offer it needs to have dates and the words 'pay or play,' which please don't do, because it'll be a lie."

"You don't want to look at it for your other clients?"

"Do you know how big my stack is for this weekend? I don't want to read it. Joey doesn't want to read it. My assistant doesn't want to read it. The fucking janitor doesn't want to read it. I don't even want to waste five minutes looking at the coverage."

"It's HBO."

"It's not fucking HBO! It's your lame-ass client Brad Shlansky trying to attach my client so he can go fishing at every goddamn place. Joey gets paid fifteen million dollars a picture, and he's booked for the next year and a half. It's a pass. Now leave."

"Movies are dead. TV is the future."

"Good for TV."

"You have a good day."

"*Paige! Shut the fucking door!*" The trembling assistant rushed to close what Paul had left open.

The remainder of his loop didn't furnish nearly the delightful stridency of that interaction, though almost every assistant said hello, hoping he'd antagonize their taskmasters in like fashion. With complete certainty he recognized himself as the most popular agent among the floor's subalterns.

"How do I get Brad Shlansky to leave David Levit alone?" asked Howard Garner from behind his desk.

"You tell me. Brad is pissed."

"I get that. But what's his end game? Obviously, he doesn't have the money to make *Appalachian Winter*."

"He says he does."

"Come on, Paul."

"What he says is what we have to go on. He did buy a comic book company."

"Yeah, you've mentioned that a time or two."

"Went out to Austin and bought the twelfth-largest comic book company in America that had never even winked at Hollywood."

"Okay. I know that's working out for you—"

"And the agency."

"But how's it working out for Brad these days? I ran into him in Santa Monica a month ago, and he didn't seem too excited. Not about that, UCM, or you, for that matter. You guys got him booted off the Sony lot."

"You don't see it, do you?" Paul began to lift and drop the flat end of his katana rhythmically into his left palm. "Brad wants respect."

"And David Levit wants to make this film," said Howard. "*Coal*, I mean. It's going to be a big deal for him. A really important movie."

"When people say a movie is going to be important, I want to throw up."

"Didn't Claire Fisher read it?"

"Wasn't interested."

"Fine. But David needs this. He's not trying to piss anyone off."

"Then he should make nice with my client."

"And I'm asking how he does that."

"Maybe start by apologizing."

"Apologize for what?"

"For going into business with someone else without discussing it first with Brad after all Brad has done for him."

"Are you out of your mind, Paul? Is your client? I mean, do you even believe what's coming out of your mouth? Brad stiffed an entire crew David brought out to Kentucky because Brad said he had money he didn't. It was the single biggest setback of David's career. He almost didn't recover."

"It seems like he's recovering fine. Didn't you just say how important *Coal* is going to be? And Brad made *Revenge*. Are you forgetting that? And everything that did for David?"

"Why does that mean David needs Brad's permission to work? And would you stop it with the sword?"

"It's a katana."

"Would you stop it with the katana."

"What am I doing with it?"

"You're smacking it threateningly in your hand."

"You feel threatened? That isn't my intention at all." He continued with the weapon in a steady beat of audible smacks. "David needs to take Brad seriously. Very seriously. Do you want me to leave your door open? Janet wanted hers shut."

"Gee, I wonder why."

This had been a good stroll. He'd riled up Janet, and he'd let Howard Garner know Brad meant to squeeze his client hard. Unnerving Howard had been especially gratifying. Everyone said decisions in Hollywood were made out of fear and greed. The second of these worked in obvious ways: people's need for wealth and power was limitless. But with fear, everyone had it wrong, associating trepidation with missing the big project or deal. Few understood how anxiety could be exploited more instinctively. Howard

Garner, with all his years as an agent, with all his reputed wisdom and erudition, was as pathetically vulnerable as anyone he'd encountered when it came to getting sliced open with a samurai sword by a potentially unhinged colleague.

When Paul rounded the corner, Jen was standing, which she never did unless rising to meet a visitor or crossing the thoroughfare to Paul's office. Her eyes widened from puzzlement to mild urgency as he approached.

"There's a detective from the LAPD who needs to speak with you, and he was being difficult about leaving a message."

"Did he say what it was about?"

"I tried to get that out of him, but he said it was a private matter."

"Whatever the fuck that means. I guess you shouldn't listen in."

He entered his office and closed the door.

MISSISSIPPI

"**N**o characters looking into wide-angle lenses."
"You realize, Jacob," David answered, "that I didn't need to write the sequence that way. The assault happens. I could just shoot it as I describe, on the day, as part of the coverage."

"But you won't be able to. I'll be there or Larry or one of our guys to tell you to move on. You'd be wasting your time, the crew's time, and my money."

"Which you could say about any shooting strategy that attempts to do something more interesting than three-camera television."

Carly and Larry stared at the floor.

"I'm going to ignore you just said that," said Jacob.

"Believe it or not, I actually thought you'd like this. It costs nothing to achieve other than a lens swap and an added setup, and if it works, it could be incredibly evocative. We get inside a guy's head while he beats the shit out of someone."

"The audience for this movie, other than a few pretentious filmmaker friends of yours, and some second-rate critics who wish they were direc-tors, doesn't care about evocative. They just want a good story told in the way it needs to be told without any embellishment. Look at Rex Patterson's prose. It's clean and clear. This POV sequence is nothing but you jacking off so a few dozen irrelevant people can say how brilliant you are. Meanwhile, I'm out twenty million dollars."

"Twenty million dollars?"

"The budget of the goddamn movie."

"If one shot that may or may not be used can torpedo the whole film, we have a lot more to discuss, Jacob. You know I'll shoot it both ways, which any director you'd hire would, so why not let me do this? If it doesn't work, we have the other way of editing it. And am I really having to argue with you about one setup? Is that where we're at?"

I guess we are, Jacob thought to himself. "Fine, put it in the script, Carly," he said. "But David, if you're running behind that day, you drop the shot."

"Sure."

"Sure, yes, or sure, right, as in you're being fucking ironic?"

"Sure yes. I'm aware you're not an irony guy, Jacob."

"That's right. I'm not an irony guy."

"For what it's worth, I think it'll be a cool sequence," offered Carly.

"Then you pay for it. I've certainly hired you enough over the years for you to be able to afford it."

At least we're all getting along, Jacob thought later as he drove his Aston Martin to meet David and Larry for dinner. In Chicago and for his first few years in Los Angeles he'd only driven Porsche 911s, but the sleekness of the DB11 had captivated him from the moment he first saw one at the valet stand at Gladstones in Pacific Palisades years before. The following week he bought his first, and he'd owned three since, trading them in every few years. Paddling into fourth gear down his favorite stretch of Wilshire, he credited himself for assembling three smart people, each with particular accuities, to argue for what *Coal* would be. David brought insight to be sure, and the collective striving with Jacob as final arbiter would ultimately make the difference.

No amount of schooling could match what Jacob had learned during his days down south as a defense attorney, then in Chicago afterward, and now in Hollywood. People either wanted to dominate you to achieve their own ends or they wanted something you had badly enough to allow you to dominate them. That was it. Otherwise, they wouldn't bother to be around you. And once a person had been put into one of those categories, you needed to decide whether they were going to pursue their interests deviously or straightforwardly. This applied in business relationships as well as personal ones, and you then dealt accordingly, never taking it personally when you got fucked. If you understood this, you had no one but yourself to blame when others surprised you with deceit. Taking responsibility in this way added singular power to the decisions Jacob made regarding those with whom he would associate, particularly in business. David Levit wanted to direct *Coal* badly enough to allow himself to be dominated by Jacob, but he still craved a level of authorship that would discourage fecklessly inept direction, bringing the right balance of subservience and authority.

Jacob was first to arrive. When the waiter came by the table he ordered a bottle of 2005 Caymus, his wife's favorite.

"Is this going to work for you?" he asked after David and Larry settled into their chairs, knowing it was a bullshit question but enjoying the two men announcing their assent with predictably clumsy enthusiasm.

"So, where do you live in New York?" he asked David, eager to avoid the topic of *Coal* and also learn more about the director personally.

"We're on the Upper West Side."

"That's you and your wife?"

"And two daughters."

"Tell us about your wife."

"Well, she's from New Orleans. Went to college in the East and then Juilliard, where we started dating. Her parents met in Alabama during the civil rights movement."

"May we see a picture?"

David produced his phone and scrolled with little difficulty to a flattering image. He presented it to Jacob, who stared for a full twenty seconds.

"Your wife is very attractive," he said, indifferent to how David might take his surprise that an ungainly walleyed Jew had managed to marry such a beauty.

"She's smarter than she is attractive. I know everyone says that, but it's true."

"What does she do?" asked Larry.

"She's an actress. As good with Shakespeare as anyone I know."

"So mainly theater?"

"Almost exclusively. She pretty much walks in the door and gets the job at this point, which is obviously beyond what she ever expected."

"I'll say," Larry submitted. "My daughter is out there trying it, and she can barely even get auditions."

"Your daughter doesn't look like his wife," offered Jacob.

"Thanks, Jacob," said Larry.

"Charlotte is amazing with text," said David. "And she's got a regality to her that's like nothing I've ever seen. She's actually in rehearsals right now to play Cordelia in *King Lear*."

"Does she do any film?" asked Larry.

"Not much. I think with trained theater actors there's a learning curve in terms of understanding that stage acting and film acting have plenty of overlap when it comes to what's going on inside but involve completely different skill sets as to how that all gets shared. She's too shrewd not to figure it out though, if that's what she wants."

"Have you put her in your films?"

"I've tried with every one, and she's done a few, but she'll only take a role if she thinks the part is right. And she likes working onstage more. There's something about how plays rely more on the words that appeals to her. Like I said, she's very brainy."

"You know ... ," said Jacob, staring into his glass. David and Larry waited for him to continue, and eventually he did. "I know something about being in an interracial relationship in this country. Yes, it's different now than when I was younger, even with all the shit that's going on, but no matter what anyone says, there are aspects that aren't at all simple. And you're from West Virginia, right? That can't be easy when you go home."

"Yes, and like I said, she's from Louisiana. I've got to be honest, though, we get some looks and the odd comment, but it's ultimately not much of an impediment for us. We think about what some of her relatives have dealt with—even her parents—and it's hard to get too outraged at the stuff we face. Plus, I take my lead from Charlotte, and she's really tough and determined and wise, and she just doesn't ever let us play the victims—certainly not herself. As for me, I get to spend my life with her, so how could I ever feel anything but lucky?"

David and Larry waited for a response from Jacob, but none came. Larry reached to grasp his partner's forearm, resting on the table.

"Jacob?"

"I'm fine, Larry," he growled incisively, pulling his arm away. His time in Mississippi had escaped significant rumination for perhaps a decade. Now a face on a smartphone and a loving encomium from a man nearly forty years his junior brought forward quite unexpectedly all the pain associated with leaving the town of Carthage. This was not just because David's wife was Black but because of other similarities: the intelligent eyes, the broad, vulnerable smile radiating oxymoronic strength. "I think you're a decent and honest person, David, and I'm glad we're working together. I also think we're going to make a terrific movie. You could have played the card of who you married countless times while we've been working on this—I mean because of all the racial overtones in the script. You could have tried to back me into a corner about this or that, particularly with how aggressive I can sometimes be, and that you haven't says a lot about you."

"I appreciate your saying that, Jacob, but like I said, I take my cue from her. And I really have no leg to stand on with a lot of this stuff, especially since I didn't marry her because I'm some good or evolved person or wanted to right any wrongs. I married her because I was in love and couldn't imagine life without her."

Jacob nodded, not wishing to pursue the conversation further, particularly in front of Larry, who might ask questions he wasn't eager to answer.

"So, it's now Wednesday," Jacob said. "I think we should keep you out here if that's all right, and meet tomorrow in Larry's office to go over offers and crew. I want you here for all of that."

"Crew?" asked David.

"Department heads and seconds. We get very involved."

"Right."

Jacob turned to Larry. "Let's extend him for a few days. Have him leave Thursday afternoon."

"I've got to call my wife," said David. "Like I said, she's in the middle of tech rehearsals, so it's a tricky time for us in terms of childcare."

"Call her. I want to push this forward. As I think I've told you, I've lived my life in stages. But I've never been better at anything than what Larry and I have accomplished. I'm also going to say this, maybe because I'm feeling a little mellow from the wine I wish we could have shared with your wife: I don't have many movies left in me. I'm getting to the end of it—"

"Oh, come on now, Jacob."

"Shut up, Larry. I don't have many films left in me. You know it and I know it. And if we do this right and this is my last movie, that's just fine with me. A film that's actually about difficult, ugly, and truthful human interactions made for thinking adults right now. A film dealing with race in America that isn't ultimately about race in America but about America it-self." He paused to look at David. "You know Larry and I met Rex Patterson."

"You never told me that."

"Like you never told me about your wife. We drove up to Seattle and took the ferry out to Orcas Island. He was well into drinking himself to death at that point, and as he described it, he'd moved to the edge of America so he could hopefully fall off it. You know what he said to me?"

"What?"

"He said what pissed him off most—and why after embracing all the publicity, he suddenly shunned it—was that no one seemed to understand the real issue in America wasn't race, it was class. That race warfare was just an expression of class warfare, and that that had been true since abolition."

"Doesn't that sort of ignore Jim Crow? Which is when his novel is set?"

"But who's the smartest character in *Coal*?"

"Coal himself."

"A Black character who by the end owns a racehorse sired by the stud he used to feed and groom. Rex told Larry and me that if he wrote a sequel, he'd make the now wealthy Coal a rapacious monster."

"But everything in the book deals with race."

"That sort of statement right there was Rex's problem. Everyone was so caught up in what the Blacks did versus what the whites did—the way they are right now—they missed the larger point, which is that slavery might be our original sin, but it was born of something deeper, which was the human lust for power over others. And sure that involves race, but it also transcends race. That was the point of the prologue you wanted to put in the movie."

"So why didn't we?"

"Because you needed it in the novel but not the film. Except for Coal himself, everyone in the movie, just like in the novel, is ultimately corrupt. Like humanity: each person both victim and perpetrator. That's why the Black community turned on Rex Patterson. One Black writer summed it up perfectly. I forget his name, but Rex sure didn't. He said something to the effect of 'Rex Patterson may be on to something writing about flawed and violent Black people, but he's working against our cause, and that we can't allow. *Coal* might as well have been written by a white nationalist for all the damage it'll do by way of confirming the Black stereotype.' Rex grew up on James Baldwin and Stokely Carmichael. Can you imagine him dealing with that kind of backlash?"

"I can't."

"We saw it and it wasn't pretty. So, let's you and me and Carly and Larry and whoever we get to play Coal do this right."

"Does it bother you that three of the four of us are white?"

"It does and it doesn't."

"Meaning?"

"Two things. I learned to despise the issue of race—hate it like you couldn't imagine, and from all sides—the hard way. I saw it wreck Rex Patterson too."

"And the other thing?"

"I'm the last person you'll meet who'd ever say racism doesn't exist. And that's why I have to make this film, no matter what fucking color I am."

CARTHAGE

B y his senior year in college Jacob had already decided on law school. It was 1966 and in spite of having a now deceased father who'd served, he opted not to enlist but to complete the education that same father had coercively predicted for him.

"I'm the first person to go to college in this family," Isaac Rosenthal had declared. "My father didn't even finish high school before he came to America. And his grandson is going to go to law school."

Desperate to leave Illinois and all the confining midwestern mores associated with it, Jacob also craved space to test the "freedoms" about which he'd heard so much, few of which had made it to Illinois colleges with the same potency he'd read of elsewhere. After no small amount of research, Berkeley and only Berkeley beckoned, though he had grades and LSAT scores that could have gained him admittance anywhere.

"Not even Harvard is out of the question," complained his incredulous mother, suddenly expert on higher education though she had barely finished high school. "And you want to go out there and study with all the crazies?"

"That's exactly what I want to do."

"You think you're going to waltz into a law office with that hair and beard and they're going to be begging to hire you? Showering you and your Berkeley degree with offers? I don't know which your father would hate more, the hair and the clothes or not fighting for your country."

"You really want me in Vietnam?"

"I wasn't talking about me. I'd kill you if you signed up."

"I'm glad you clarified that, because you seemed to be complaining about my hair and beard and using what might have been my dead father's opprobrium to prove your point. And by the way, he sure as shit wouldn't have wanted me in Vietnam, where we have no business anyway."

"Enough. You're not a lawyer yet."

Berkeley, while he enjoyed the climate, and particularly the winter fog, along with the wild unpredictability at any hour of the day along Telegraph Avenue and the phenomenon of women bedding him on the same day they'd met, ended up a decidedly mixed experience. Yes, he'd embraced the counterculture movement in clothes and grooming, but aspects of its ideology proved his midwestern upbringing in the house of a domineering father had more of a hold on him than he'd imagined.

First, there was the preponderance of liberal Jews, most of them from California, who seemed to be working out mind-numbingly uninteresting issues with their upper-middle-class parents. They spoke and dressed down expensively, haranguing professors and one another about justice, the war, racial and gender equality, the military industrial complex, and most of all the venality of corporate America. They would understand the law in order to tear it down. Then, predictably, he watched the opportunities awaiting Berkeley Law graduates temper their revolutionary fervor as one by one the overwhelming majority matriculated in partner-track positions at white-shoe firms.

Jacob underwent a different transformation. While his peers were being seduced by opening salaries of high five figures leading to partnerships that could make them millions, a class in criminal justice had inspired him to fixate on *in*justices perpetrated against the disenfranchised. Specifically, the more cases he examined, the more clear it became that to be a rich criminal in America usually meant exoneration, and to be a poor but accused innocent, incarceration. Moreover, when it came to criminal justice, it was if the civil rights movement hadn't even begun, and the more certain of this he became, the more agitated it made him. For the first time in his life he began to experience the deep-seated anger his father had always predicted for him.

In a nod to his childhood interest, he went to movies incessantly because only there, lost in the dark within the stories of others, could he find any semblance of respite. The theater was on Shattuck Avenue off Dwight Way, and he could walk there from campus. The films, many of them foreign, and curated by the film critic Pauline Kael, not only exposed him to cinema as an art form but also, in a plurality of cases, confirmed that the sorts of inequities that pervaded his own country existed elsewhere. At least, he said to himself, these writers and directors are deploying what they've learned for some good.

Midway through his second year he changed his focus to litigation, and specifically criminal defense, figuring that even should he end up returning to transactional law, the skills he'd learn as a courtroom lawyer might prove invaluable to clients in potential disputes.

"You're one of the top students in the class, Jacob," his contracts professor said to him late in his third year. "And you haven't taken a single interview.

229

You could go anywhere. To any firm—certainly in the state of California, or back in Chicago even. Wasn't your father in real estate?"

"The family still is."

"So?" A black-and-white photograph of Earl Warren with the professor as one of his young clerks loomed behind the man's head. The juxtaposition struck Jacob as comical. Why is this asshole wanting me to sell out? he wondered.

"I don't want to work at a firm."

"What are you going to do?"

"I'm going to find a small town, probably somewhere in the South. I'm going to open a practice there, and I'm going to charge defendants what I think they can pay."

A silence ensued as the professor took this in, followed by four rhythmic nods.

"That's going to be one lucky town," he said quietly.

In July of that year Jacob moved to Carthage, Mississippi, the seat of Leake County, north of the Pearl River. It had a population of approximately three thousand, around 40 percent Black. One of the largest chicken-processing plants in America stood just out of town, the county's most prolific and reliable employer. The brick courthouse, which stood on the main square, was rebuilt in 1910 in a style anticipating the art deco movement that would take hold late in the following decade. Its architect had been the head of the local Klan. Jacob set up an office within walking distance. He often felt as if he were in his own spiritual Vietnam, so remote and unknowable was the culture he encountered. His clients, and they arrived in a constant flow from the moment he set himself up, were almost without exception poor, if not outright poverty-stricken, and mostly Black.

The other attorneys in Carthage soon both appreciated and despised Jacob. He relieved tremendous pressure, since the destitute seeking an alternative to public defense no longer burdened them with their unprofitable and desperate predicaments. Jacob turned none away. A person presented pay stubs, and together they'd determine a fee. While in rare circumstances he did work pro bono, he generally required remuneration of some sort to discourage inefficient use of his time. So far, so good. But opposing Jacob, whether in a courtroom or outside of it, became an ordeal no local attorney or prosecutor wished to endure. He fought viciously and precisely, building relentless arguments with clear reasoning so inventively deployed that the opponent or judge often had to pause before responding.

For those he represented, the only downside was his impatience with dissembling of any sort. Expecting unconditional advocacy, they'd instead find themselves interrogated with a ferocity that often went beyond what they'd undergone when arrested or sued.

His second week in town, a Black woman in her early forties entered his office.

"My boy's over in the jail on murder, and he ain't done it."

"All right."

"And my auntie said you came to town to represent folks like that."

"That's right."

"Well, I just told you he's over there locked up right now, what you waiting on?"

After negotiating a fee of seventy cents an hour, Jacob visited the young man, whose name was Raymond, at the jail. Given his size, it didn't surprise Jacob to learn he'd played offensive guard at Mississippi Valley State before blowing out a knee. This had also kept him out of the war.

"I ain't killed nobody."

"Raymond, I've looked over the case the DA has on you, and I have to tell you I think you're lying to my face."

"Say what?"

"Fingerprints, a witness, PCP in your system the night they picked you up. Plus motive. Don't bullshit me."

"Yeah, I had a motive, but that don't mean I did it."

"Raymond, if you think I'm going to walk in that courtroom and argue that your fingerprints on a murder weapon aren't yours, and that a nine-year-old girl who saw you knife this woman is lying, you're out of your fucking mind."

"It's your job."

"My job is to give you fair representation before the law, which means if you murdered someone, which I believe you did, making sure that all the mitigating circumstances—do you know what that means?"

"Yes."

"Again, I don't believe you. What does it mean?"

"It means that can get me off."

"It means facts in the case motivating your behavior that should be considered in lessening the severity of the charge—potentially execution or life without parole—against you. And if I'm wasting all my energy telling moronic lies, I don't end up protecting you, I end up hurting you, not to mention looking like an asshole. Now, I'll poke holes in the state's case wherever I can. I'll do it doggedly, and with only your interests in mind. But I'm a guy who likes to know everything. I don't want to fall down a hole I didn't realize was there, let alone one that's in plain sight. Now, did you kill this woman? And in front of her daughter?"

"Yes."

"Why?"

"I was crazy jealous."

"On the PCP."

"On the PCP."

"Okay. Now you seem to be saying you took the PCP before you learned of your girlfriend's infidelity."

"Yeah. He told me after."

"Meaning you were high when you heard."

"High as a goddamn rocket ship."

"And that's when you went to her house?"

"Somethin' like that."

Harlan "Bully" Weathers, who stood at about five foot eight and seemed to weigh well north of two hundred pounds, met Jacob the next morning at the courthouse. He wore a muted plaid Oxford suit with no tie over a pastel-blue Brooks Brothers shirt. His face was ruddy and wide.

"How'd you come to be called Bully?" Jacob asked as they shook hands.

"It's a Mississippi State thing. Bulldogs. Went there—undergrad and law school—and everybody says I look and act like the mascot. It's nice weather. Should we step outside?"

They ventured onto the square with their coffees.

"We all get to know each other pretty well around here. Even with the hair and the beard, from what I hear it's sounding like you're going to fit in just fine, sir. The other lawyers say you shoot pretty straight. It's tough to come into a new place, especially one this small, and not ruffle feathers."

"Well, as for my hair and beard, the former used to be even longer, and the latter I'm now trimming close every day, so it could be a lot worse."

"You were at Berkeley?"

"That's right."

"And moved here? With no people draggin' you back kickin' and screamin'? Not even a girl you were chasin'?"

"That's right."

"That I've never heard of, but good for you. So, let's get down to business. You want to make a deal for your nigger."

Jacob had heard the word spoken plenty by whites, and not only in Chicago but in California, which often surprised him, but never deployed with such careless ease. The district attorney might as well have substituted the word *man*, or *client*. Jacob felt his rage begin to flex. He also understood that to show offense would do the opposite of helping get Raymond a few decades outside of prison at the end of his life.

"I do think us coming to an agreement regarding Mr. Stiles might serve everyone's interests, certainly in gaining you your conviction quickly, with minimal cost to the state in time and money."

"Capital case. Very easy for us."

"Well, I don't know about that."

"Which is what he deserves. But please go on."

"You may or may not be aware my client was impaired at the time."

"Horse tranquilizer. An illicit substance in the state of Mississippi. I believe on the Berkeley campus as well, or were the students there able to get PCP legalized?"

"Not as of the time I'd graduated, but you never know."

"You'll fit in great down here, Counselor. We like to keep it jocular."

"But you're right. Mr. Stiles purchased the PCP himself, and took it himself, but it will be perceived by any jury or sentencing judge as an impairment."

"I'm not worried about that. And you know I shouldn't be."

"It was also after he'd taken the PCP that he learned Ms. Rochambeau had been associating with another gentleman. A mutual friend of theirs in fact."

"You're telling me that your nigger learned of this while impaired. Or in any case that's what you're going to argue? You have proof of this? Which would have to be the person who'll swear he or she informed him of this at a time consistent with his impairment? And probably implicating himself as well, assuming he wasn't present simply as an observer."

"That is all correct."

"Have you spoken with this person, or are you just hearing this from your ni—"

"Mr. Harlan—."

"Bully, please."

"Bully, I'm going to have to ask you respectfully to afford my client the dignity of using his name. Raymond Stiles."

"You'd like me to use his name. A boy God gave the gift of size and athletic ability that got him a free ride at one of our state's top schools where he could play division one football and get his ticket stamped to the NFL, where he'd be given every opportunity in this so-called racist country to earn in a few years more than many will in a lifetime? Not to mention fame and notoriety the likes of which you and I will never know?"

"Yes, that's what I'd like."

"Well, you don't get that because he doesn't deserve that courtesy from me. He certainly didn't give it to the woman he killed or her daughter who had to watch it. But I'll tell you what. If you can show me a deposition of whoever told your client about the deceased's situation vis-à-vis the other man and when it was revealed, along with one from a witness to the drug use and when that occurred, and I can depose that witness as well, then we might have something further to discuss."

Jacob drove to the processing plant the following day to meet a man named Trey Slausson, who had not only sold Raymond the PCP but exposed the infidelity of his on-again, off-again girlfriend.

"Go see him on his lunch break, 'round eleven," Raymond advised. "Our shift out there starts at six a.m. They ain't gonna let him off the line to talk to you otherwise."

To his surprise, Jacob encountered a white man in his late thirties, scant of build, elaborately shifty in his movements, and above all, a profligate talker. The guy wouldn't shut up.

"You bet your ass I told him. I'll tell you what else. I also told him not to be goin' over there. And not because I figured he'd kill her. Knife her or whatever. Never crossed my mind. I mean, Raymond's a big guy. Big as three houses and a shed. But he's a sweetheart. I wouldn't want to be between him and a quarterback, but he don't even play no more. Which is a whole other deal. Think about it. You was gonna be in the NFL, for sure, and now you're workin' out here for a buck eighty-five a hour? How's that work? But the reason was, I just didn't want him goin' over there in case Anfernee, who was the feller she was fuckin', or at least I think she was fuckin', was there, because Anfernee carries a pistol."

These words, delivered in syncopated bursts between furtive glances everywhere but at Jacob, took some time to unpack.

"A moment ago, Mr. Slausson—"

"You call me Trey, now. I ain't your girlfriend's daddy."

"Trey. You said a moment ago you weren't even sure that Ms. Rochambeau, and I think you said his name was Anthony—"

"Anfernee. I don't know if it's the schoolin' or what, hell, maybe it's just the pressure of bein' in the hospiller, or the excitement at havin' a baby, but either way, his mama, Anfernee's I mean, likely got up in there with the nurse, wanted to name him Anthony, but she just spelled it how she says it, and so that's the way all folks got to be pronouncin' the name from then on out."

"So Anfernee and Ms. Rochambeau might not have been sleeping together?"

"Well, that I got to kind of doubt, just on account of you're increasin' the odds against you. Most folks get her done and then they're outta there. No shuteye involved in the deal."

"Point taken."

"But was they ballin'? It sure looked like it on account of Anfernee was at my place a couple maybe three days before and said he was on his way over to Janeese's—"

"Ms. Rochambeau's."

"That's right. So he was on his way there, which got me to thinkin'. I'm always studyin' people, because you got to do that in my line of work, I mean my other line of work when I ain't here."

"You're talking about selling drugs."

"I ain't said that. You said that."

"But weren't Ms. Rochambeau and Anfernee friends?"

"Well, sure, but who goes to a lady's house by hisself who ain't up to no good?"

"Friends, maybe? I'm not really sure."

"Answer me this. You think if Anfernee was to have fetched up at her place and she shows the tops of her legs, he wouldn'ta jumped on that? Because I know Anfernee, and I knew her."

"Okay, look, what's important to me is that you told Raymond they were having sex, and *after* he had taken the PCP. Is that the case?"

"It's took you this long to figure that out? And let me get this straight, you're his lawyer?"

Jacob had long passed the point where further dialogue with this creature would aid Raymond's defense. While Mr. Slausson had confirmed having told Raymond of his girlfriend's infidelity when Raymond already under the influence of the drugs he'd sold him, the infidelity might have been imagined. Yes, it would still obtain that Raymond *believed* her infidelity a fact while impaired, but if in reality it hadn't been, Bully Weathers could adduce the deranged fantasy as further proof that Raymond was unsuitable ever to live in society.

Luckily the prosecutor had deposed Trey Slausson on another case.

"I swear to you, after six hours with that man, I left the room stupider than when I'd gone in. I've a mind to set your client free rather than spend a minute with Trey Slausson, but I'll give Mr. Stiles—and I said his name for you—thirty to life, eligible in twenty."

"Fifteen."

"I said twenty. Hopefully I'll have retired to Florida by then."

They settled on seventeen.

"I like the way you handled yourself, Counselor," said Bully after sentencing.

"All right," responded Jacob.

"I've got a good sense of people. If I promise to watch my language, would you care to join me for my weekend hobby?"

"That depends what the hobby is. I'm kind of a movie buff, but that's about as elaborate as I get with my free time."

"This ain't movies."

Jacob paused to consider. He'd made few friends in Carthage but didn't in any way despair over this. He hadn't moved there for the social scene, and in a sense in defiance of it, which his interactions with Bully only vindicated. That said, the better he knew the enemy, the more effective he might be.

"Where shall we meet?"

The gun range lay four miles east of town and had both an indoor and outdoor component for operation year-round. On the east-west span inside a fenced perimeter stood a prefabricated building approximately half the size of a football field made of steel siding painted a dull yellow, with an isosceles roof of corrugated metal at an angle so obtuse Jacob wondered why the designer hadn't simply made it flat. Inside stretched one of the largest stores of any sort Jacob had ever encountered. He thought immediately of his father in the Marines and the contretemps over the cleaning of his M1 Carbine.

"If you're not careful, you might start to think in clichés," said Bully as they entered. "But if you look at it another way, it's all controlled. And these folks don't cater to the bad guys. Ninety percent of the clientele is military, retired military, law enforcement, and hunters."

"I hope so," responded Jacob.

"Hey, Bill!" Bully addressed a slender, bearded man in an Atlanta Braves cap presiding over a seemingly endless glass counter that alone contained more firearms than Jacob had ever figured he'd see in his life. "My friend here from up California way has never shot a gun before, and we're gonna fix that. Let's start with ear protection."

They outfitted him with soft orange plugs and black industrial muffs.

"Does he need a weapon, Bully, or will he use one of yours?"

"Needs a weapon. Loaned my other pistol to my married son who's having some trouble with a fellow at work," Bully explained vaguely.

"All right, why doesn't he join me over here." Bill moved twenty feet down where about five dozen pistols varying in size and shape lay in three rows on a carpet of green synthetic turf.

Jacob pointed to a smaller one.

"What's that?"

"A Walther TP. German. Nice weapon but not great for target shooting. Very light, so she gets snappy on the recoil. Short sight radius too. More for close quarters. Give this Browning HP a feel." He reached down for one of the larger weapons. "I've got one in the back we can rent you. Good weight, clear sighting. She'll give you tight groups right out of the gate."

"What's HP stand for?" Jacob asked.

"High power," Bill said. "Based off a design from Mr. Browning himself in the mid-twenties before he died, and then made by the Belgians mostly. Great firearm. Check out the profile of those sights." Jacob took the pistol, surprised by its easy, balanced weight. "Feels good, don't it? Give a look down the top with whichever is your good eye."

Jacob used his left to line two vertical protrusions just above the grip with another at the pistol's nose. He sighted the face of a hearty redheaded man holding a rifle in a Remington poster on the wall behind the salesman.

"And with the mass of that weapon, more of the kick is absorbed. Good smooth action too. Great squeeze, and she's right back ready to go on that gorgeous rail. I think that's a better gun than the 1911, which is more what Browning's known for."

As in the presence of any expertise, Jacob felt himself immediately drawn in.

"Let me give you a quick tour," Bill continued, taking the gun back and manipulating it deftly. "We start with the most important part, which is the safety." He switched a lever twice on the left side of the pistol just above the grip. "Every piece of this weapon is engineered and machined with QC like you wouldn't believe." He moved his thumb to a round button with a waffled tread. "This right here—and there's no plastic on this gun by the way—drops the magazine." He mashed it, and the grip's interior leapt into his other hand with a friendly click. "Cartridges go in here one by one. Nine millimeter. Bip, bip, bip." He mimed the loading of bullets between two sloping shoulders at the top before reseating the magazine.

"Once she's ready, you chamber your first round." Holding the grip in his right hand, he seized the top of the weapon with his left and ratcheted back what appeared to be the entire upper housing, before releasing it back into place. "And there you be. Thirteen shots. First of that capacity. Made for the French military. No cocking. Semiautomatic, which is what I was saying about the tight groupings. Negatives? A little trigger bite while you get used to it." He pointed to the webbing between his thumb and forefinger. "So just be aware. Safety's a little stiff. But that's pretty much it. Feels as good in the hand as any gun out there." He passed it back, presenting the grip. "What do you do?"

"Jacob here is on the other side," Bully answered with a chuckle. "He's a defense attorney. But we don't hold that against him."

"Well then, esquire," said Bill, "you want to rent one of those for the day?"

"I want to buy one," answered Jacob.

"Buy one? He said you've never shot a gun," responded Bill, laughing with Bully.

"You say it's the best one for me, I believe you."

"Well, good then. Bully here is a Colt man like every other hick around here, but that right there," he said, pointing, "is as good a shooting weapon as you're ever gonna buy."

Firing it thrilled Jacob, connecting him to a need to release frustrations heretofore only articulated with words. But to both Bully's and Bill's astonishment, he left the weapon on the premises.

"The point of having a firearm is to protect yourself," Bully announced.

"Maybe for you," Jacob responded. "If someone wants to do me in, I don't think my having a gun I barely know how to use is going to make a difference. Besides, what does it say to my clients if I'm carrying a pistol around?"

He became a regular on weekends, usually riding out with Bully but socializing with other law enforcement officials as well, including, to his relief, many of the Blacks on the police force. Bully seemed at ease with everyone.

"We all bleed blue," he offered. While this hardly expiated the prosecutor for his epithets, or those of many of the other whites in town, it made friendship with men who probably denigrated Jews nearly as much as blacks at least tolerable. Nor did Jacob wish to waste energy battling prejudices far too deeply ingrained to take on individually. Better to befriend, if even superficially, where he could while working vigorously within the system to protect the most vulnerable.

Eight months into his practice a woman walked into his office seeking help for her husband, who'd been arrested for armed robbery and attempted manslaughter a few towns over in Meridian. Her skin was dark, accentuating the whites of big eyes set wide in a warm, almost maternal young face.

"We can pay you," she said in a confident, sturdy tone. "I'm not certain what you charge, but if it's not more than other lawyers, it won't be a problem. I'm here in other words because of your reputation, not because of the pay scale everyone talks about."

Under the law, her husband had indeed participated in a robbery and assault, a fact he freely if reluctantly admitted. He'd grown up in Philadelphia, a town between Meridian and Carthage, and had not objected early one evening when his brother and two cousins insisted he pull his recently purchased used 1967 Ford Galaxie into the parking lot of a liquor store just closing. He had not driven away when he sensed commotion inside, nor when the trio came tearing from the establishment's interior, its white owner chasing them with a baseball bat. A cousin shot the man twice in the stomach—wounds from which he had barely recovered. The brother and cousins tumbled into her husband's car with $267 in cash, and at their urging he had driven away, leaving the wounded man bleeding in the parking lot. Her husband cursed the three of them all the way to his brother's house, then sped to his own, where he perfunctorily greeted his wife, who was getting ready for her night shift as an administrative nurse at the very hospital where the liquor store owner was already being treated. He rushed into their bedroom to call the authorities. This brought the police to his door the following day, and soon after, he, his cousins, and his brother were arrested. The prosecutors were trying them separately but not treating the reluctant driver any differently from those considered his accomplices.

"Let me tell you something," she said, her eyes narrowing. "If my husband were white, and I were white, the police over there in Meridian would be saying he drove the car because they had guns to his head. Instead, it's like he hatched the idea with them."

"What about the fact that he called the wounded man in?"

"They say he did that to get himself off. That if he really cared, he would've stayed to help him, or even called from his brother's house. By the time he did call, the man had been at the hospital for twenty minutes anyway."

"I'd like to meet your husband. You don't have a pay stub from where you work, do you?"

"I already told you I want to compensate you what you'd charge anyone. Anywhere. No more, no less."

"Well, that's complicated."

"Not if you don't make it complicated. Just, what's your hourly fee?"

Her husband, whose name was Gray Bradley, was a resident at the hospital where she worked. He might even have helped treat the store owner had he been on call. They had moved to Meridian when he'd finished medical school at Ole Miss, where she had attended nursing school. They had no children. Like his wife, whose name was Violet, he spoke with care, as if each word might be scrutinized for errors in grammar. Unassuming but confident, he had gentle eyes and round features in a face that made you feel safe in its presence. He radiated decency.

"They gave no indication they were going to rob the place when they asked that I stop there. I didn't even know they had a gun."

"This is going to sound like a strange or maybe unfair question, but did you know any of them owned a gun?"

"Yes. But that's how a lot of people are in Philadelphia. We just grew up that way. Not my brother and I, but most folks generally figure they can protect their homes and their families better than the police can. Or will, frankly, unless you're in the white part of town. No offense."

"None taken, and I'm sure what you're saying is true."

"Because it is," said Violet.

"Will your cousins and brother confirm what you're saying? That is, that they made no mention of their intention to rob the store when they asked you to pull over?"

"The police told me that Derrick, that's my brother, said we all planned it together."

"Do you believe your brother said that?"

"That he would lie about that? Absolutely not. It's the police who are lying."

"They're saying whatever they need to implicate Gray as much as possible," interjected Violet. "That's what they do, if you haven't figured it out yet. It's like they want Black people to commit crimes so they can get us behind bars and off their streets. Out of their towns."

After more than half a year in the county, during which he'd met nearly every law enforcement official and prosecuting attorney, he didn't doubt a word they were telling him. To be Black meant living by entirely different standards of rectitude. One bad choice, whether intentionally, unintentionally, by omission or accident, could mean the end of your life as you knew it.

Most certainly Gray Bradley would go to jail, quite possibly for ten years or more. He would have a record that couldn't be expunged, limiting severely the sort of medical practice he could ever have, should he be permitted to finish residency anywhere at all. Jacob was also convinced that were Gray white in Mississippi, Jacob could get him off without serving a day; there wouldn't even need to be a trial.

Violet was furious with her husband. She had grown up in Jackson raised by a single mother and a loyal, nurturing stepfather. She had never met her father. As her mother described it, they had spent seven hours together, "and it was the stupidest and luckiest night of my life." She was seventeen and drinking with friends at a bar in Old Dixon when the soldiers came in in their uniforms. Four hours and too many daiquiris later, she was in the backseat of his car. If she'd learned his name, by the next day she'd forgotten it, and when she discovered she was pregnant he was on the Korean Peninsula, based on the vague description she and her parents were able to give the CO of the two dozen or so Black men in their early twenties who'd been at the bar that night.

"And when you go wonderin' about whether there's a God, you just look into a mirror, because trust me, at eighteen I sure didn't want to have a baby, and don't you think for a second that in 1948 a Black girl couldn't get a problem taken care of. But your grandma and grandpa were having none of that."

Growing up, Violet had despised her mother for her obsession with schoolwork, strict prohibitions against alcohol or drugs of any kind, and undeviating curfews. But a National Merit Scholarship took her to Ole Miss, where she graduated magna cum laude. She stayed on for nursing school, where she met Gray, who had been an undergraduate at Duke but wanted to attend medical school closer to his mother and her cooking, both of which he missed in faraway Durham. On their first date she knew they'd marry.

"How does a man allow himself to make a mistake like that? Why do you even let two stupid country-ass delinquents in your car, I don't care if they are family, when you know damn well they're gonna have guns? What idiot does that who's got so much to lose: a career ahead of him, a woman like me at home, parents who love him? His mother broke her back for Derrick and him." She asked this over dinner the night before Gray's sentencing. He'd been found guilty as an accessory and was to spend three years in Parchman. "And I'm sorry, but now I'm gonna be another Black woman with a husband in prison. I know that's selfish of me to say, but seriously. Anyone I meet who sees my ring will say, 'And what does your husband do?' 'Oh, he's in prison. It's complicated. He was driving, but he didn't know they were going to rob the liquor store and shoot the white owner.' 'Where did this happen?' 'Just right down the road in Meridian. You probably pass it every day!'" She began to weep.

It was his first time out at night in Carthage with one of his clients, and people stared. They were in her part of town, and he was the only Caucasian in the establishment.

"You're gonna say what you're gonna say," Jacob offered quietly. "And with any luck he's gonna be out in two years, maybe even sooner. You two can move somewhere then and get on with your lives."

"That's what's going to happen, Jacob? You've got it all figured out?"

"I do know he won't serve all three years. I'll make sure of it. And besides, what choice do you have?"

She wiped her eyes. "Why did you come down here?"

"Because I couldn't not come down here."

"And then what?"

"What does that mean?"

"You're going to stay in Mississippi? Run for mayor of Carthage? I don't like your chances."

"Honestly, I haven't thought that far ahead."

"We're practically your only paying clients. How are you affording it?"

"My family has money."

"Your family?"

"My father is dead, but he left a profitable real estate business intact."

"So, you're doing your Freedom Rider thing?"

"Does that look like what I'm doing?"

"I'm not complaining."

"Good."

"But people who have money can do whatever they want."

"To an extent."

"Is this that?"

"For now."

"And then what?"

"I don't know."

"Well, you should. Why waste such a blessing?"

"I've never thought of it that way."

"You should."

"Besides, this doesn't feel like a waste to me."

"What do you love more than anything?"

"I don't know." He laughed. "Movies?"

"Movies?"

"Yeah. When I was a kid, then in college."

"So why not do that?"

"It's a long life."

"That it is, Jacob. That it is." The way she said it he wasn't sure she was speaking to herself, to him, or both.

Two weeks later she appeared at his office wearing a dress he'd never seen on her in months of meetings and court dates.

"I'm not handling this well, and there's no one I can talk to."

"You don't have any friends, Violet?"

"I have you."

On the first night she drove him to her place, but on subsequent ones he would drive there himself, park four or five blocks away, and walk to the complex where she and Gray had made their first home near the hospital. Carthage being Carthage, word spread. Though each had much to lose, they couldn't stop seeing each other. He despised himself for the cliché— carrying on with the vulnerable wife of the client he'd failed to keep from prison—and he despised her for the callousness of betraying her husband. Yet he thought about her by the minute and called her incessantly. As she allowed him in, a hardness about her began to fall away, enabling a physical connection less angry and desperate than in their initial fervor.

Well over a month into their relationship, just as they were falling asleep, they heard a knock at her door. She opened it to two police officers, one Black. Jacob stayed in the bedroom, recognizing both voices from the gun range.

"Ma'am, we're sorry to disturb you, but we've had a complaint from your downstairs neighbor." It was the Black officer.

"What kind of complaint?"

"A noise complaint."

"I wasn't playing music. No one's here. The television wasn't even on."

"A complaint was made."

Most in the complex were white, but not all, a rarity in Carthage, which remained quite segregated. A plurality of the residents, Black and white, worked at the hospital and were under forty, a few with young children. Many were just starting out, either as singles, cohabitants, or newlyweds. A white married couple resided in the apartment below, the wife a pediatric nurse with whom Violet had had friendly interactions, both at the hospital and in the complex. They had even coordinated grocery runs to save on gas. She and her husband, ten years her senior, sang in a church choir.

"I just bet you have a beautiful singing voice," she once said to Violet. "We're always looking."

"I'm gonna stay with my Black church, Carrie, if I can ever get Gray to go with me."

"Well, you let me know if you change your mind."

Now the relationship cooled, becoming quietly hostile. A week after the visit from the police, Violet found taped to her windshield a sign reading "Stick with your kind."

"That was not written by Carrie or her husband. It wasn't written by a white person either, I can tell you," she informed Jacob. Though he'd found the previous week's visit mildly amusing, he now became livid. Yes, this was a relationship he shouldn't under any circumstances be having, but professional ethics didn't seem to be animating community objections from either side.

"People will screw you, Jacob," his father told him routinely when he was growing up. "Sometimes it's personal, sometimes it isn't, it doesn't matter. You're either in the way, or them thinking you're in the way is a distraction from their own bullshit. So if they use a stick, you use a mallet. They use a mallet, you use a sledgehammer. But always hit back."

In this case, he didn't know how, other than to continue with Violet in ruthless defiance of what might come. And come it did. In spite of his proven results and sliding rates, business dwindled. Few whites had ever breached the threshold of his office, but now none did. The number of Blacks diminished by more than half.

"It's not that you're carrying on with a sister—well, I mean it's that too—but it's that you're carrying on with a married sister of a man locked up," one of Carthage's Black lawyers told him. "It just doesn't sit right with folks. And why the hell should it, Jacob?"

"I'm not expecting you to understand."

"Well, then you'd better figure something out, because if you can't make me understand, and I still like you and am out here having lunch in public with you God knows why, then you've put yourself in a very difficult spot, because any way you cut it—white or Black—what you're up to is wrong, wrong, wrong."

Bully Weathers agreed but did little to mask deeper objections. "Jacob, you're taking every bit of goodwill this town has to offer a liberal Jewish lawyer coming down here to stir things up, and you're just pissing it away."

"Why is it anyone's business?"

"There's a level of decorum that needs to be respected."

"Is that about her husband or the color of her skin?"

"I think you know the answer to that."

That afternoon a brick came through the window of his office. For the first time he wished he hadn't left his gun at the range.

The sheriff, a tall, red-faced thirty-year veteran named Joe Queally who liked to brag that he cut his own hair once a week with a number four clipper, appeared with a deputy two hours after Jacob's call.

"You see who it was?" he asked languidly, avoiding any eye contact.

"I saw a wood-paneled Mercury station wagon."

"Yeah, a lot of those."

"Surely not too many, Sheriff."

"Quite a few."

"So?"

Joe Queally inclined his head to the shards strewn across the linoleum. "It's your mess, Counselor. I reckon you better start cleanin' it up."

After sweeping the glass, Jacob walked two blocks to Clayton's Hardware to ask about a new window. He had represented its owner two months prior in a dispute with his landlord over the size of his refuse bins.

"Yeah, Jacob, I'd sure like to, but we're backed up here like you wouldn't believe. I got Lester and Jessie out on jobs clear into next month, and ain't nobody else around here can cut and frame. What I could do is sell you some plywood as a temporary fix. Joey can help you drag a sheet from out back."

"Can he help me put it in?"

"Thing is, I'm gonna need him here at the store."

He left without the plywood, cursing all the way to Thomastown, where he hired carpenters to travel back to Carthage and install a window. It cost him twice what it should have.

Violet retreated into herself. This, combined with his anger, did little to sustain what had brought them together, or even their resolve to have it restored. She wanted to hide, he wanted recklessly to defy. One night when he came in a manner she found purposefully audible, she slapped him across the face. Instinctively he struck her back, apologizing profusely as she wept. No one had ever hit her. It felt unnecessary to say he'd never struck a woman either; he'd done so now, which was all that mattered. The town is going to win, he thought when he let himself out well before dawn.

That week she quit her job and moved back to Jackson to live with her mother. In a letter hand-delivered by a friend she thanked him for all he had done for her husband. She had loved Jacob for a moment, she wrote, but needed to love Gray for a lifetime. What they'd done was wrong, but she didn't regret it. It had taught her, albeit painfully, where her priorities needed to lie. He marveled at her self-assured clarity, and also thought to himself that even she, like her husband one of the more resolutely decent people he'd ever encountered, had betrayed someone in service of her own needs, as of course had he. Moreover, Bully was right: he had ruined his practice, thereby depriving meaningful representation to the very disenfranchised he'd moved to Mississippi to serve. What he'd done was bad, he understood that, but the opprobrium from both sides had little to do with the reasons why, and it enraged him that he'd given himself no footing to object.

The last person he saw in Carthage was Bully. Jacob stopped by his house with the Browning pistol, restored to the box in which it had been purchased.

"Seems to me you'll need this in Chicago more than here, even with all the nonsense you got yourself into lately," the prosecutor said.

"I'll have no use for it there."

"I'm gonna miss you like a son of a bitch," Bully said, taking the box before the two shook hands. "No matter what came of your time down here, you're a truly good man, Jacob. One of the few I've ever met."

"Yeah …" was all Jacob could think to say, wondering if Bully meant a word of the appraisal.

The week of his return to Chicago he took his mother to dinner.

"I want to know the extent of Dad's holdings."

"Suddenly you're interested?"

"I never said I wouldn't be."

"Daniel handles all of that," she informed him, referring to her sister's husband. Daniel was one of the few people Jacob had ever met whom he liked instantly without that opinion eroding into some form of tolerable contempt.

"When you say handles…"

"We pay a fellow at a firm Danny trusts to manage the properties for a fee. He says it's a fair fee, and worth it for all the time it would take. He's even made a few purchases along the way according to Danny. Conservative ones, or so I'm told, but the numbers have only improved. Really improved, actually. Your father took very good care of us."

"And Danny can put me in touch with this individual?"

"You own a third of it, Jacob, and when I go, you'll own half. What choice does he have?"

Jacob could only marvel at his father's knack for buying distressed assets in neighborhoods few perceived would gentrify. And Danny had indeed chosen the right steward in a hard-nosed Irishman named Sean Nichols, who came from a family of cops on the South Side and had gone to business school after receiving an architecture degree from Notre Dame.

"No one," Danny had been told by a friend at the synagogue, "knows the city better than Sean Nichols, and trust me, as a Jew that's hard for me to say about an Irish Catholic."

In 1971 when Jacob returned to Chicago, the holdings were worth just over fifteen million dollars, throwing off an income, net of taxes and fees, of around seven hundred thousand dollars a year. With his sister's and his mother's consent, he took over the portfolio, hiring Sean Nichols full-time at 120 percent of his brokerage salary, and sweetening the deal with 5 percent ownership of Rosenthal Real Estate Holdings. The partnership was almost magical, combining Sean's understanding of buildings, zoning, and urban trends with Jacob's dogged pursuit of sellers in promising neighborhoods. They bought aggressively and shrewdly, culminating in a spree during the savings and loan crisis that turned what Jacob's father had begun into one of the city's largest private firms. By the time Jacob left Chicago in the spring of 1988, two divorces behind him, and with notions finally of doing as Violet had urged and trying his hand in films, it was worth $400 million, and had not a penny of debt.

HOLLYWOOD

Jacob came to Hollywood with two advantages: an uncorrupted love of movies, and what the industry called "fuck you" money. He could set his own terms with those of his choosing and have only himself to blame when poor decisions were made. And since succumbing to his attraction to Violet Bradley there'd been few of those. Even the two failed marriages he left behind in Chicago no longer felt like mistakes, each decidedly transactional, an aspect of marriage he had come to believe inevitable. Thankfully he had understood this at the outset, demanding prenuptial agreements in both. He dissolved the first when he simply could no longer stand to be in his wife's presence, and the second when wife number two could no longer stand to be in his.

She let him know this by sleeping with the construction foreman for the house they were renovating in Lincoln Park. He had to credit her for the vindictive clarity of the act itself, which would barely pass muster in a melodrama: she and the builder had been carrying on in the very bedroom in which she and Jacob were soon to cohabitate. He suspected this two months before they would move in when she traipsed him through the upstairs to reveal the progress that had been made and he noticed one of her hair ties just under the newly installed bed, which inexplicably had already been outfitted with linens. Pocketing it quietly, he planned a surprise visit the next afternoon just after the daily call he'd begun to receive from her at his office right after lunch. He parked his metallic gray Targa a block away and entered the house from the back, passing two finishing carpenters who betrayed no alarm at his presence, causing him to wonder whether his suspicions might be unfounded. When he discovered the door to the bedroom locked, he waited outside rather than knocking.

He'd known the foreman for about seven years and had watched him climb the ranks at Klingman Construction, the company founded by his grandfather Jerome Klingman during the postwar residential construction boom financed by the GI bill. The grandson, Tom Klingman, was muscular and handsome, with the effortless confidence of someone who's been complimented on his looks all his life. At twenty-eight he was well more than a decade younger than Jacob and the same age as Jacob's wife. Her name was Justine, and Jacob had met her in the wake of his first divorce at a bar on Rush Street. He had come in with two younger colleagues from his office to avoid yet another night alone in his kitchen with a ribeye and a bottle of Cabernet.

"Look! An actual grown man," she'd exclaimed upon seeing him enter the bar normally frequented by brash young commodities traders. When he left, he asked for her number, which she'd already written on a slip of paper, a simple hubris he found seductive. He presented her with a two-and-a-half-carat brilliant-cut diamond on the anniversary of their first date.

"Oh my God, is this three carats?"

"Just over two and a half. A D flawless."

"You didn't want to have me help you pick it out?"

Two days and five thousand dollars later they'd exchanged the stone for one a half carat larger, and the ring itself to platinum from white gold.

"Hey, Tom," he said when the younger Klingman exited the room as if he'd been checking a punch list.

"Shit! Jacob!" the foreman responded, closing the door behind him.

"Everything good in there?"

"Yeah, great, but we're going to have to rehang one of the bathroom cabinets."

"Why don't you show me?" When Jacob opened the door, she was making the bed.

"Hi, Jacob," she said, as if expecting him. For some reason it gave him a modicum of comfort to see that she wore both her wedding band and the three-carat diamond.

In spite of that marriage's failure, which in part he attributed to age disparity, his third wife was twenty-one years his junior. He was convinced, however, that this one would last. She came from Cleveland and had moved to California to attend Pitzer College, where she had majored in studio art. Within its fourth year a clothing label she'd founded gained shelf space at Fred Segal. It had just been valued at forty million dollars when they were seated next to each other at a dinner party in Brentwood. He thought nothing of it when she turned to face him, pulling her legs up in her chair to sit in what had been referred to as tailor fashion by his grade school teachers. They spoke almost exclusively to each other for the entire meal.

The party's hostess reached him the following day at the sprawling Lantana office complex in Santa Monica where he'd set up for the year while his new space in Beverly Hills was being remodeled.

"Well, you really fucked things up last night."

"How's that?"

"Laila Gershon wants your number."

"Who?"

"The woman sitting to your left at dinner last night? I was trying to set her up with the guy on the other side of her."

"The writer?"

"Showrunner actually."

"Right, the detective drama."

"That pays him three million a year."

"Good for him."

"Better for him and for Laila if you hadn't been drooling all over her."

"I don't drool, Ella, and certainly not last night. She's too young for me anyway."

"I agree, but she doesn't think so."

"Then give her my number. I'm certainly not calling her."

Two hours later his assistant put Laila through.

"I hear you refused to call me."

"I'm not a lech."

"Neither am I."

"I'm not sure how you could be in this scenario, but I trust you all the same, and that doesn't come easy with me."

They dated for three years, and she advertised almost relentlessly what she wanted from him and why—stability, honesty, intelligence, wisdom, humor, and if all continued to go well, a child—even insisting in a stubbornly rational way that she was also falling in love with him.

"I honestly can't understand why or how that could be," he told her.

"Aren't you falling in love with me?"

"You're young, bright, and beautiful. A man of my age and looks isn't supposed to be allowed in the same room with you."

"Shut up, Jacob. First of all, I'm thirty-seven, not in my twenties. And I'm divorced. And if you want to understand it, it's because I've never met anyone so clear about who and what he is, no matter the consequences."

"Isn't that why you should stay away from me?"

"I always know where I stand with you, and that's what I want. Plus, I've got about a minute left to have children. I want them to have your morals and your brain."

"Your brain's plenty fine, trust me. And my morals, as you call them, have been hard-won and weren't always what you think."

One day I'm going to understand what made her turn to me at that dinner party instead of to the guy on her left, he thought as he pulled into his space at Chicago Films the morning after his dinner with Larry and David Levit. He stopped, as he often did, to behold his building, one he had begged over the years to purchase from its owner, the City of Los Angeles. Built early in the preceding century as a police station, complete with contiguous stables, it had been repurposed over the years into a storage facility for city records, an elementary school, and finally municipal offices, before he took it over and, along with an architect named Rand Davis, invoked a design strategy that had won more than a few coveted awards.

His favorite line of thinking praised, in spite of Jacob's resolutely capitalist sensibilities, the building's postmodern aesthetic. The etymology of this nonsense, he soon learned, derived from his fascination with the building's original elements. During an initial inspection, he'd looked beyond the false ceiling lowered below the maze of ductwork to see the thickness of the single-cut support beams and the riveting on the steel framing. Immediately he demanded it all be exposed. Apparently, this bore immense political meaning. A paragraph from *Das Kapital* even made its way into one publicly delivered panegyric that described the architect's "almost reverent exposure of not only the human work that went into the building, but the persisting, straining muscularity of the edifice itself." This proving insufficiently laudatory, the speaker elaborated: "The original utilitarian structure now serves empirically to demonstrate both the cost and honor of labor. As much as any building interior in Los Angeles, it is itself a testament to collective endeavor, though originally devised as a place in which the oppressive laws of a burgeoning industrialist system were inflicted on the underclass—a police station. Rand Davis has restored this integrity and all its attending irony with an aesthetic decency all his own, laying bare the sweat of the anonymous and long dead."

This had actually been spoken without humility, irony, or embarrassment to a room of 250 morons nodding sagaciously at a benefit masquerading as an awards ceremony, then was reprinted in a trade periodical that Jacob framed for his office wall to test visitors on their level of sycophancy. On one occasion a screenwriter whom Larry had tapped to adapt a Norman Mailer novel stopped to read it without the usual urging. That the young writer had pitched up in front of it felt like a sign.

"What do you think of that?" Jacob asked offhandedly.

"I agree with every word."

"Is that right?"

"In fact, I know this is going to sound weird, but it's exactly what I was thinking."

"Well, this has been a useful meeting."

"Pardon?"

"I know what I need to know."

"Does this mean I'm not—"

"What the fuck do you think it means?"

Larry appeared at his door within minutes. "What happened in here with my writer?"

"No one is 'your' writer.' And I don't want him near the words of Norman Mailer is what happened."

"I already worked it out with his agent. There's a deal in place."

"He's a pussy and he's full of shit."

"Jacob—"

"He doesn't work for us. No discussion."

"You don't do that, Jacob."

"Well, I just did. And the more you tell me how things are and aren't done, the more I want to do the opposite."

He had met Larry on the first film in which Jacob invested, a psychological thriller about a professor enlisted by detectives to help catch a serial killer who composed verse to toy with haplessly unschooled authorities. The twist involved the inevitable suspicion that the hired expert was actually the murderer, only for it to be discovered that one of the detectives, a former student who'd taken the case to his mentor in the first place, was the true culprit. Larry was the film's line producer, and Jacob loved his opening question when they met for dinner.

"Why on earth are you putting money into this piece of shit? It's utterly ridiculous. Who's going to want to see it?"

"You think no one?" asked Jacob with a laugh.

"People who like serial killer movies don't read poetry, and people who read poetry don't see violent thrillers. It's a bad mix. Not to mention the fact that the guy's a professor. If he's so smart, and so knowledgeable, how can he not suspect his own student? Which isn't even to mention, how many detectives have you ever met who studied poetry in college?"

"You're wrong on all of it, except maybe the last point," responded Jacob. "People like to be entertained, but they also like to feel smart. This movie does that but without ever being pretentious. None of the poetry in there is particularly challenging, other than the one by Wallace Stevens.

And really, how the fuck do you and I know what detectives study in college?"

"I'd never even heard of Wallace Stevens. Had you?"

"Had heard of him but never read him and never will. But who are we to say there's not a detective out there who doesn't go home at night and crack open a volume?"

"Please."

"The movie is suspenseful and fun. You watch, it's going to do well. I wish I could invest more. Also, I've looked at the comps and it's a bargain."

"This isn't real estate, Jacob."

"Don't ever say that to me again. It's insulting."

"Okay, but just know that these guys out here are a lot more squishy with their books than overvaluing properties for purchase loans. If this is a success, you're going to have to fight for every penny."

The film grossed $67 million domestically, driving foreign sales that nearly equaled that number. As warned, Larry's company sought to withhold from Jacob every dollar it could, mostly through overhead expenses Jacob had to challenge line by line.

"No, I really want to know why, two years before we even went into production, and a year before I moved out here, there was a fifteen-hundred-dollar dinner at Dan Tana's."

"We took the writer out to discuss the script."

"Who did? The whole office and everyone's spouse? What was discussed that required a thousand-and-a-half-dollar meal that's now being deducted from my profits?"

"It's a social industry, Jacob."

"Yeah? Socialize on your nickel. Remove it. I'm not paying for it."

"It was already paid for."

"Exactly, so don't now fucking charge me for your stupidity after the fact."

There were inflated marketing fees, interest payments on money the company loaned to itself, office equipment charges, personnel fees, and a litany of amorphous "development costs" that if legitimate might have had the original script predating Hammurabi's Code. What had been presented to him as a film with a negative cost of ten million dollars had suddenly ballooned to nearly three times that once the studio was compensated not only for all of this but for prints and advertising, and of course its first-position premium. By Larry's clandestine accounting Jacob should have tripled his investment of two million dollars. Instead, his projected payout over four years would total just over three.

"Jacob, on your first movie you're going to get a hundred and fifty percent back. Why are you busting our balls?" asked Nathan Gordon, Larry's soon-to-be-ex-boss.

"I'm not busting your balls, I'm going to fucking sue you."

"You do that, and no one's going to want to do business with you. This might look like a big town, but it isn't. We all talk."

Without engaging lawyers, they settled on another million dollars for Jacob, still not what he was owed, but he had better ways to spend his time than eking out another million when he intended to make far more in the ensuing years. They agreed to the number at an Italian restaurant on Barrington over a dinner Jacob was confident would be charged to some other investor on some other film.

"And by the way, I'm taking Larry McCormick." he said as Nathan signed for the meal.

"What do you mean by that?"

"You haven't renewed his contract, so I poached him. He's going to tell you tomorrow."

Larry arrived the next morning to a locked office and his personal effects boxed by interns.

"Jacob, why the fuck did you tell Nathan I was leaving? My God."

"Because he's an arrogant fuck. He knew he'd ripped me off for over a million dollars even after the settlement. Sitting there drinking his grappa, fondling his Monte Cristo. I wanted that smug look off his face. Not having you there is going to cost him, and a lot more than what he still owes me."

"You should have let me leave on my own terms."

"I saved you having to sit in his office and explain yourself. You're pissed at me now, but this is going to be a great partnership. We're going to have fun."

After all of it, if it is going to be my last film, why *Coal*? Jacob asked himself as waited in his office for Larry to arrive to review the day's agenda, which would start at 10 a.m. with David Levit to go over crew. I employ over forty people in a company named after the city of my birth with a library that now includes franchise movies, horror films, romantic comedies, dramas, adaptations of literary fiction, even an Oscar for Best Picture. It's been an incredible run. To end with *Coal*?

For starters, it was the most exciting piece of contemporary fiction he'd read in twenty years, especially in the context of what he'd been through in Mississippi. Had it been written by a Caucasian, it surely would have come and gone, or worse, never been published for fear of uproar, but Rex Patterson was Black and had made both himself and the novel a nexus for discussions about America that Jacob had been waiting half his life to hear. In response to critics who questioned why he'd begun his novel with the trope of Black-on-white sexual violence, Patterson had responded, "I wanted to shove an extreme manifestation of white fear in the audience's face, and then tell a story to help them get over that with a lot of self-examination about this country along the way. And by the way, there isn't a Black man in America, with all we put up with in terms of the looks and the avoidance and the fear, who doesn't at some point want to do violence against whites. And I mean murder some motherfuckers. If we didn't have those fantasies, we wouldn't be human. Let's get real on both sides."

Jacob also understood the book on a level deeper than the racial issues that seemed to animate it at a time when every interaction was being seen through race. Like any significant work of fiction, its more controversial aspects were actually a sideshow. This wasn't ultimately a novel about Blacks and whites. Its characters came at the reader suffused with concealed needs that required cold cynicism and artful dissembling as they navigated 1950s Los Angeles. It was a milieu in which trust led to very dangerous, often violently lethal places. The skin color of the characters informed their individual strategies for sure, but not their basic impulses, and that, as he'd explained to David the night before, was ultimately Patterson's point. Another way of putting it: human beings were basically shitty, no matter the color, and as his father had taught him long ago, wanted one another to fail. Redemption, if there ever really was any, came in the form of that rare individual who could navigate such perfidy without betraying the scant potential for decency lurking within each of us. The character Coal Runner, who happened also to be Black, personified this hope.

"If we're going to do this, we have to hire an African American director," Larry insisted the day Jacob purchased the book. "I know you hate thinking in these terms, but this is tough material, written by a person of color. "

"Why can't you just say Black?"

"Because I prefer the terms used by the people I'm talking about to describe themselves. It's a matter of respect. With a director of color we can inoculate ourselves against the racism accusation."

"Why do I need to be inoculated against a disease I don't have?"

"I said the accusation. And by the way, everyone is racist."

"Jesus."

"You don't believe it?"

"Obviously everyone is racist. People say it to sound evolved when it's completely redundant. Like saying wet water."

"Then what's your point?"

"How about this? Since everyone is racist, including Blacks, then there's some other condition that's more virulent in which racist impulses are given free rein, and whatever that is, I'm the opposite. But fine. Inoculate us against rampant stupidity. Hire a Black director, which, by the way, is also racist."

After three had passed, they pursued a man named John Riddle, who'd made and starred in a biopic about Dizzy Gillespie that had come out earlier in the year. Mr. Riddle also demurred, without reading the script, describing the novel as "sensationalist and pointlessly dark."

"In other words, he's a moron," Jacob told the agent on the phone. "Will he at least come in and talk with us?"

"I'll get right on that, Jacob. I always want my clients meeting with producers who think they're morons."

"Give him a few hours with Larry and me, and we'll smarten him up."

"What about David Levit? He's also my client."

"The gawky actor from the Jacob Mendelson movies?"

"He directs too, Jacob," interjected Larry. "But he's not African American."

"At this point I don't give a shit. What has he directed?"

"That you would have heard of?"

"No, Larry, tell me the ones I haven't heard of, so I'll really want to hire him."

"He made *Revenge*," said the agent.

"Did that movie even work?"

"Depends what you mean. Did it make money? Yes, a lot, and for everyone, including this agency. Watch it and decide for yourself. It was very smart, and very timely."

"How could something called *Revenge* be smart?"

"Ask the critics. Or all the people who saw it. It dealt with teen violence and social media, so in terms of controversy you'd be getting a director who's been there."

"Who released it?"

"Bay Bridge. It was bought by the Golds though."

"He survived Charlie and Rob?"

"Oh, did he ever."

"Send him the material."

Someday I'll tell David about Violet, Jacob thought as Larry entered his office.

THE BEVERLY HILLS HOTEL

Hunched in a chair on the balcony off their bedroom in Los Feliz, his hands buried in his blond curls, Brad Shlansky could barely contain his rage. That his wife had spent five hundred dollars on a pair of shoes and fifteen hundred on a dress didn't help. Her mother was in town from Pittsburgh, and she and Amanda had been at Fred Segal all morning. God only knew where they'd had lunch and what that had cost.

"You seem to forget it's my money too," she offered bluntly.

"And you seem to forget we're married."

"One thing doesn't have to do with the other. Or actually it completely does."

After working out and showering that morning he'd read every article the Internet would disgorge about Jacob Rosenthal. The old man had been born into money, and he'd come to Hollywood willing to spend it, building what amounted to his own studio. If Sarah and Emily and I had had his resources, Brad quickly determined, we wouldn't be in this situation. David Levit wouldn't matter. Nor would Paul Aiello or those assholes at Lone Star Pulp.

"I'm your wife with my own bank account," Amanda continued. In the context of Jacob Rosenthal's advantages, this only made him angrier.

"We have expenses, children," he said, referring to their twins who were not yet two.

"And so?"

"What about them?"

"It's my money, Brad."

The same argument had tormented them since their first date.

"There's something I want to make clear," she'd said. "I do fine on my own. I'll expect you to pay for dinner when we go out and treat me the way a man's supposed to treat a woman traditionally so long as we're dating because that's how I was raised. But in terms of the rest of it, we're who we are separately, and we'll be together because we choose to be."

"Why are you saying this?" he asked.

"Because you're a producer and I was working on your set. Your little sister was right. I just don't want this to come off like I'm some kind of gold digger."

"Yeah, well, you've got the wrong idea on that one. There's no gold. At least for now."

She was almost as tall as he and, in spite of her ample frame, nearly as fit. The sex, which she initiated by inviting him in after their third date, generally followed her lead. He looked up at her the first time, finding the entire situation unfathomable: such beauty, such gloriously selfish freedom, such sexual prowess in a partner had seemed beyond fantasy. She had the softest skin he'd ever touched.

He'd finally lost his virginity before leaving New Jersey, and had even had a few girlfriends, but he'd succumbed long before to the conviction that carnality would come to him only by way of luck, obligation, or largesse, and with women who settled for him because they couldn't do better. Yes, in spite of acne that had receded but not abated completely, in LA he'd sensed interest from women he'd never encountered back east, but early on Amanda represented a being so unimaginably seductive to him that he began almost to resent her presence in his life, plagued by dogged certainty of its evanescence. Why would a woman like her stay with him? It would be better, he determined, to find a way to distance himself rather than yield so much control.

Several months after their parents' deaths, Sarah and Emily convinced him they should see therapists, and as this well preceded any suspicion that the federal government knew of the debt owed to it, he acquiesced in spite of the prodigious hourly fee.

"Honestly, both my fucking parents died," he announced in a plush but musty office in Hewlett. "One by suicide in our house while I was at a party fifteen minutes away. Talking to you isn't going to change that." The psychiatrist, an older man in his late seventies named Pollard, referenced Freud with punishing frequency, and though Brad often couldn't identify with concepts such as transference and sublimation, one theory made perfect sense: that of childhood mastery.

"Early on, our parents go away from us," Pollard explained. "Moms work or go to lunch with friends, or parents can drive to dinner leaving the kids behind with a stranger. It's all natural in the modern world but way beyond what we're built for psychologically. The two-year-old has no context to understand that the parent will come back. To him or her it seems permanent. Freud observed children take their favorite toy and throw it from themselves, saying things like 'Go away!' or 'Leave!' And he determined that the children were simply trying to exert some sort of control over a world in which these all-important beings were perpetually leaving them. Far better to have something go away with you making the choice than having to feel left behind. It's a kind of first flirtation with power, and of course it comes from being powerless."

As his relationship with Amanda entered its seventh month and *The Recluse* had been delivered to its optimistic financiers, he couldn't resist picking fights with her in ways that reminded him of this doctor he saw but thrice. It only exacerbated matters that in addition to his certainty that she'd leave him, he felt himself ceding more and more authority—the very opposite of what he wished might transpire. He, who'd assumed responsibility for his sisters, agreed to leave the three-bedroom apartment they shared and move to Amanda's two-thousand-square-foot mid-century home in one of LA's trendiest neighborhoods.

"You rent this?" he sputtered when first invited in.

"I got an amazing deal. It's a sublet from an actress who's shooting in Atlanta on a series for the year, but I'm hoping I can buy it from her one day."

"So you must be doing well."

"My dad left me some money. But yeah. Producers like me."

"I guess they do. How'd you get into EPK? I mean, it's a pretty specific field."

"I was working for this firm as an intern, and we were on this shoot for Warner Brothers of this thriller that I guess they'd subcontracted out because their team was busy. My boss got food poisoning at lunch, and I got thrown in to ask the questions, which was also when numbers one through five on the call sheet were scheduled. And I don't know, I guess it caught some people's eyes, including the actors. I got promoted and have been doing it ever since."

"For that same company?"

"No, they went exclusively into personal representation, and that woman, my boss, handed over her accounts to me, so I'm on my own. Just starting out. That's how you guys were able to afford me."

"You have your own company?"

"I've been trying to tell you."

"I'm not getting it," he said.

"Please don't ask 'Why are you with me?' again. It's getting pathetic."

"Especially now. It makes no sense."

"As maybe you guessed, I've been with more than a few guys in my life."

"It's not something I try and think about, but yeah, the thought has crossed my mind."

"Almost all of them vain assholes. You're not like them. Well, you're not vain anyway. I mean you do seem to work out a lot—"

"For my health."

"Understandable. And I've seen you be a jerk, but it's because you don't care if people like you. It's almost like you sometimes want them not to like you. You're a lot like my father was."

"You realize I'm a Jew."

"You're a blond Jew."

"I'm being serious."

"My dad put family above everything. He planned for us, even before he knew he was going to die. It's how I could rent this place, buy equipment, but also I could get on my feet after college, which I graduated from without any debt. The way you take care of your sisters, I can see you're gonna be the same way."

"I hope so. But given the fact that you're a gorgeous upper-class shiksa—"

"Whoa. Who said upper-class? My dad left me a hundred thousand dollars, half of which I've spent. After that, I'm on my own."

"My mistake."

"It was something, and I'm not complaining, but let's be accurate."

"I'm a kike from Long Island whose parents were in the check-cashing business. My point is, it's unlikely that your father was anything like me, as flattering as that is."

"You act like him. You're a hustler. In a good way. And also like you, he never finished college."

"I never went to college."

"So, neither of you had college degrees, but you didn't let it stop you."

"Why didn't he finish?"

"His dad lost his job and the family needed him to go earn a salary, so he left before his final year. He started working as a warehouse clerk at a freight company, and after twenty years he was part owner."

"Was he honest?"

"He was shrewd."

"Meaning?"

"He did what he had to do to get what he wanted. I don't think he ever harmed anyone, but he outsmarted plenty." She shrugged. "I think the story of a guy who didn't have a lot of advantages to begin with but who never complained about that and just got on with it is a pretty good story."

Brad thought about his own father. Had he ever heard him complain, other than with non-lexical grunts when rising from a chair or easing himself behind a steering wheel? As he worked sixty-hour weeks until the day before his death, all while concealing stacks of cash from a covetous government, Carl Shlansky only ever projected steady optimism in a tough business he navigated ruthlessly. But unlike Amanda's dad, he'd left only liabilities behind.

"It is a good story," he finally answered, emotion welling unexpectedly as it only could when thoughts drifted to his late parents.

"And by the way, are you honest?"

"What?"

"You asked that about my father."

He thought for a moment.

"I'm honest with myself."

Their relationship deepened with an alacrity that astonished them both. But with it grew the resentment that he simply couldn't control. Her self-sufficiency maddened him; even as he admired it, he also feared it. He chided her for the amount of makeup she wore, the time allocated to hair care and skin care, the way she walked, drove, spoke to strangers, closed a car door. None of it had the devious psychological effect intended, and to make matters worse, she even intuited its poignant source.

"You can be as petty as you want to drive me away," she announced one night after he'd belittled her over dinner with Emily and Sarah for not catching a reference to Springsteen. "But if that's what you're after, you'll just have to have the guts to break up. Either that or sleep with someone else and then I will dump you and you'll kill yourself with grief."

"I don't like remarks like that. You don't know a fucking thing about suicide."

"Sorry. That wasn't nice. But we both know you're never going to get close to matching what we have when you're nice. All this stupid criticism does is point up how scared you are, and that makes you look weak, which is the opposite of what you should be given all you've overcome in your life. You're an amazing guy, Brad. Just admit it to yourself."

How could she be so confidence-inspiring and emasculating all at once? It was a poetic feat. Within a year of their having met, as his criticisms gave way to admiration and even grateful appreciation for what she saw in him, she began to suggest marriage.

"I love you, and I'm not interested in messing around. I don't want anyone else, and you don't want anyone else. Besides, maybe it will finally put your paranoid mind at ease. I want to have kids, and we'd make great ones. You'll be a wonderful dad."

"Do it," insisted Sarah when he revealed Amanda's wishes to her.

"There's just shit between us that's still unresolved," he confided in response.

"Yeah, your issues, not hers. What's your fucking problem? She's beautiful, she's smart, she's loyal. You're going to let that get away?"

What choice did he have but to agree? Sarah was right: he couldn't break up with her, and any serious issues between them clearly stemmed from the vulnerability of loving her as he never imagined he could love anyone. But even after a wedding in Pittsburgh for which her mother flew his sisters and Paul Aiello first-class, with rooms at the Fairmont Hotel and three days of festivities the exuberance of which frankly embarrassed him, he couldn't entirely vanquish his anxieties. In fact, the entire weekend only inspired new vexations. Not only had Amanda's father left his family with a surplus rather than debt, Amanda's mother had done what his mother had not: she had chosen to live, and clearly with Amanda and her younger brother in mind. Why had Miriam Shlansky allowed her grief over losing a husband to be more important than a future with her own children? Fifteen minutes into the dinner he wanted the whole night to end. It wasn't that he didn't love her but more that he was trapped inside of that love.

"Honestly, name me any adversity you've ever really faced," he asked after the anemic first weekend grosses had come in on the platform release of *The Recluse*, along with reviews adducing the "laughably derivative" and "cynical" writing as the primary reason to avoid seeing the film.

"Is that a joke, Brad?"

"I know, your father died, which trust me, I understand. But you got to be at his bedside when it happened."

"Yeah, that was a real thrill."

"Your family prepared for it is what I'm saying. And your mother picked up the pieces, not you."

"We really don't want to be having this conversation. Your feelings are hurt because of what a few critics wrote, but that's no reason to attack me."

"This has cost me millions of dollars."

"How do you figure that?"

"In profit participation. And what we could be paid for the next film if this one had been successful."

"My father always said that money you expected to make is money you never had."

"I'm not your fucking father!"

"I was just making a point. What is your problem?"

"I could spend a lifetime explaining, and you'd never understand."

Instead of mollifying him with the institution's nominal assurance of permanence, marriage only made the inevitability of their demise more devastating. It would mean he was divorced, worse than a breakup, left behind in disgrace. Laurie Dwyer all over again. Someone else would come along, and she'd see Brad for the insufficient dolt he was.

Then, as a result of making David Levit's *Revenge*, everything changed. In producing he discovered the occupation for which he seemed to have been preparing his entire life, one that called on his every acuity and strength. By way of maximizing this, he had shifted the balance within Same Day Films, instructing Alice to draw up new articles of incorporation. He became sole president and CEO, Sarah, vice president of development, and Emily, vice president of production.

"You're demoting us?" Sarah asked.

"I'm giving us each our accurate titles, though I don't know what Emily understands about production, unless it means texting guys on her cell phone between trips to the craft services table."

"He should have the title, Sarah," offered their older sister. "Coming out here was his idea. Without Brad we'd still be in Woodmere."

"Does this mean you can order us around?" Sarah asked.

"That's exactly what it means. And guess what else? It's going to be better because decisions will be made quicker. We'll make more movies."

"I'd be happy with just *another* movie. But if I'm vice president of— what was it?"

"Development."

"Development, that means I actually do that."

"It's what you already fucking do. You read scripts and meet with the writers."

"And help decide what we make."

"You and Emily both. But the final decisions are mine, and I do the selling and the raising of money and the setting of terms."

Brad had already begun to formulate the new structure during production on *The Recluse*. First and foremost, he and his sisters would no longer write. When examining the situation with any candor, he had to agree with the critics: *The Recluse* had ultimately been a cynical exercise. He and Emily and Sarah had gleefully chucked one cliché on top of another in a hyped frenzy hurtling seventy-five miles an hour toward LA in a Yukon, and while they deserved credit for getting their first film made, they also earned derision for its absence of originality. Moreover, when he reminisced about making the film, the writing, to his surprise, had brought the fewest rewards. He despised the bickering, especially with Sarah and her propensity to haul in references to books she'd read in college or the professors who'd assigned them. Emily would either side with Sarah or abstain, which was almost worse. Every decision constituted a battle, and even though he won most of these, he had no desire to repeat the process, particularly given the shared credit.

Before they'd been clapped in the critical stocks, he made this clear to Amanda.

"Trust me, it says screenplay by the three of us, but I'm the one who wrote the fucking thing. I read the McKee book, not them. I structured it all, and I rejected all their bad ideas. It should be 'story by' the three of us, and 'screenplay by' me, and even that would exaggerate their contributions except for arguing with me at every turn. But it's fine. Like with everything else, I'm going to do all the work while they get two thirds of the benefits. Ask Sarah, who of the three of us dealt with all the bullshit over the Same Day stores and then took only one third of the estate, which ended up being mostly my coin collection. I found Alice, I made it so they could get their college degrees, I dealt with the government, I sold the house. But it's fine. I'm over it."

"It doesn't sound like you're over it."

"At the end of the day, I love my sisters. Like with everything, it's complicated."

"It doesn't have to be."

"Maybe not for you."

During actual production of *The Recluse*, when he imagined he'd finally enjoy some say as the originator of the material, he learned how little power being screenwriters actually conferred.

"You and Sarah and Emily will have no say over anything. You understand that?" Alice warned going into the deal.

"I understand that's what they think."

"No, Brad. It's in the contract, and what's in a contract is what people will do. You're going to get your script made, but creatively you and Emily and Sarah no longer exist."

"Paul says the language is standard."

"Of course he does. They're all in collusion out there. He wants his ten percent. On this one and the next one. He doesn't care about you or your film."

"He does actually."

"Let him prove it. Tell him you're not giving away all these approvals—Jesus, over director, casting, editing, even your goddamn script—the script you wrote they can change! I've never seen anything like it!"

"Paul says they won't give that stuff away to any writer, and I trust him. We go way back, him and me. And besides, no one is going to push us around."

Brad soon discovered that, producer and screenwriting credits aside, he and his siblings exercised less power on set than not only the actual producers but the director as well, whose easy way with actors and crew furnished a fleetness with decision making—from where to put the camera, to what an actor would wear, what sort of car an actor would drive, how an actor would move or say a line, to the look of a room, the color of paint on the walls—that effectively discouraged any input from Brad and his siblings.

"Ted," he complained on one of many occasions to Ted Brody, the congenitally arrogant twenty-eight-year-old executive assigned to represent Vulcan Films' interests on set, "this is not how me and my sisters imagined this scene being played at all."

The moment to which he referred involved the first, and therefore tone-setting murder in the film.

"What's your issue?"

"Well, for one thing, there's supposed to be humor in it. Half this stuff we wrote with our tongues in our cheeks."

"That you're going to have to explain."

"It's referencing other horror movies."

"So, go tell Andrew," Ted said, referring to the director.

"He never listens to me."

"Exactly. Nor do we want him to. It's Andrew's film. Trust his vision."

"Yesterday you said it was Vulcan's film."

"Because it is our film. And lucky for us too, because Vulcan is not in the business of making a yuk-fest about fat women having their stomachs sliced open. Now go back and sit on your chair by the monitor and feel lucky your script is getting made at all. I'm tired of your badgering me ten times a day."

At that moment Brad resolved always to be in Vulcan's role and never again his own. He certainly didn't wish to direct, and it frankly mystified him that more people craved that title than that of producer, where the real power lay. In fact, the director was the most pathetically deluded person on a set, and Andrew was a perfect example with his utterly specious presumptions of authorship. Though he existed at the whim of Vulcan, and directed a script not his own, he bestrode the locations chummily tyrannizing everyone, effecting changes with a self-satisfied smile as if everyone had matriculated to serve him and him alone. To Brad and his sisters he said "Good morning" at the start of each day and "See you tomorrow" at wrap, but other than that he rarely acknowledged them, apart from occasionally to ask with feigned understatement apparently meant to charm, "Did I thank you yet for writing this script?" as if Brad, Emily, and Sarah needed his patronizing encouragement. Most infuriating was his policy of moving everyone, even Brad, Emily, and Sarah, away from his monitor so he could be sequestered from all oversight. The whole process constituted one big dupe. For all his and his sisters' work conceiving the story and script, others seized the attention, power, authorship, and eventually profits.

But rather than sulk three rows behind the secondary monitor, Brad roamed in pursuit of knowledge. His own issues aside, the movie set struck him as a truly miraculous enterprise, with laborers specific to specialized tasks answering to seconds who answered to department heads who answered to the director and producers, mostly without resentment or rancor. The level of expertise, combined with enthusiasm for the work, even on a low-budget horror movie, simply made him giddy. Very few of those he encountered seemed to want to be anywhere else doing anything else, the work itself and the hours dedicated to it so arduous that it could be no other way. Why else would people work sixty-hour weeks laying dolly track, setting flags, fixing collars, powdering faces, holding a boom?

Paul Aiello visited frequently, usually with an aspiring actress in tow.

"Where do you find these girls?" Brad asked.

"Trust me, they're not girls. And I find them all over. But make no mistake, my blond friend, they call me, not the other way around. Did you read the two scripts I sent over yesterday?"

"Sarah did. She passed the one about the pregnant teenager along, and Emily is reading it. If she likes it, I'll read it too."

"What're they, your assistants?"

"Don't say that to Sarah. I'll be hearing about it for a month."

"Just find one you like already."

"Sarah gave us copies of *Revenge*. She's nuts for it."

"She should be, which is what I told her when I sent it. And that guy is a client."

"Yours?"

"Please. God forbid. Howard Garner's. But still."

Within six weeks Alice was papering the deal.

"So, to be clear," Brad asked Paul Aiello and Alice on the phone, "if Sarah and Emily and I come in with the financing, we get to make this thing whatever we want it to be? We call the shots?"

"It'll be what those assholes from Vulcan had on your movie," Alice assured him. "You approve the casting, the crew, everything. The fucking locations if you want. You'll even have final cut. In fact, you should have final cut. A movie you put together and finance is your movie."

"But doesn't the director always try and get that? And David Levit wrote it too."

"Have David Levit show us his Oscar, and then we can talk," answered Alice. "And tell me an industry in America where the CEO lets the product designer determine what a fucking product is going to be. You think that at Ford or Maytag or fucking Hoover Vacuum Cleaners the designer or product engineer gets final say? No. He does a design and gets compensated. It's your fucking money. You're going to raise it. I'm learning a lot about this business, and there's a fucking reason on the Academy Awards it's the producer who takes home the Best Picture statue, not the fucking director who got hired by the producer."

Brad made naming Amanda as unit publicist a condition of financing, going so far as to have Alice memorialize it in the contract. David Levit's outrage surprised him.

"I told you in our first meeting you'd have to hire her, and you agreed, so what difference does it make?"

"Brad, I can ask the same question back. If you know we're going to hire her, why do you need her name in my contract?"

"Because people go back on their word."

"Under what circumstances would that happen here?"

"Maybe you meet some woman who fucks your brains out and decide you want her to do the booklet and the EPK."

"I'm married, Brad. That's the craziest thing I've ever heard."

"Then you need to get out more."

Working with Amanda on a set he commanded provided a balance that allowed their marriage finally to make sense to him. He could look across the catering tent at the hundred or so gathered and know they were there because of him. He had taken David Levit's script back east to his contemporaries now running the chain of check-cashing stores that had bought

Shlansky's Same Day and had returned with their promise to fund production. Yes, the film had nearly shut down when this same group balked after the opening weekend numbers for *The Recluse*, but by then Rob Gold and Parameter had promised to buy the film for nearly three times its negative cost, not only eliminating all risk but assuring a substantial return.

"Are you proud of me?" he couldn't help but ask Amanda one night on their way home from set.

"I always knew you had this in you, Brad, so I was already proud of you. I've got to admit though, I didn't know how much patience I had left. You'd become a total monster."

"I'm sorry. You haven't deserved any of it. You make me feel incredibly lucky, and you're amazing at what you do. Please don't ever leave me."

"There's stuff inside of you that you need to look at."

"If you ask me to go to therapy again—"

"That's exactly what I'm asking."

"Success is my therapy."

"And when that goes away?"

Because the Golds had purchased *Revenge* for so much more than its negative cost before a frame had been shot—this in spite of David Levit's insistence that they close the deal for far less out of fear it would vanish—Same Day Films and their equity partners were set to make more than a 150 percent return net of fees within a year of shooting the first frame. But Brad also understood the need for the film itself to make money, which would give Same Day access to entirely new levels of filmmaker, financing, and distribution. With this in mind he and Alice had forced the Golds to guarantee a wide release.

This also meant that David Levit would need to overcome any impulses to impress his film-theory buddies from college and deliver a mainstream thriller people actually wanted to see. In spite of a great script and impeccable casting, this was by no means guaranteed. Not only did David refer constantly to filmmakers and writers no one who'd see the film would ever have heard of, his insistence that with every decision in life he thought about a friend of his who'd died in a terrorist attack had Brad more than concerned. The adage that films were made three times: first in the writing, then in the directing, and finally in the editing, took on singular relevance.

But the first cut of *Revenge* captivated Brad and his sisters from its opening images to its bloody conclusion—made all the more compelling by its taking place in the wake of Elysian.

Brad called David immediately.

"You're my fucking hero."

"You know this movie is going to upset some people."

"Kids are shooting other kids in high schools in this country. Not to mention shopping malls and dance clubs. We made a film about it."

"Elysian wasn't Columbine, Brad. The culture is different now. There's no middle ground. We're going to be caught up in all that because of those stupid kids and their crazy manifesto. And no one will ever know we made the film before Elysian. They'll think we're piling on or taking sides, or worse, capitalizing."

"It's going to be great publicity."

"Who're you, Rob Gold? Did you really just say that?"

"And guess what? You were thinking it."

"I'd rather have a movie that means something than one that does well at the box office."

"This is America. If it doesn't do well at the box office, it'll never mean anything, and vice versa. And by the way, if your script wasn't provocative in a way that could make money, I wouldn't have made it and the Golds wouldn't have overpaid for it. So how about this: let's hope it's relevant and also makes a hundred million dollars."

"Fine."

"And finish it already, because every day past Elysian we're not putting it out, it's hemorrhaging the relevance that's so fucking important to you. The guys at Parameter are going crazy."

But soon neither Brad nor David could get Rob Gold on the phone, their calls instead returned by Barry Shamus, Rob's top lieutenant.

"Why all of a sudden am I on the phone with you?" Brad asked.

"That's how it works at this stage."

"What stage is that?"

"Where we're figuring out what the movie is."

"Three weeks ago Rob loved the film."

"And he still loves the film," said Barry, the pace of his words decelerating as if addressing a toddler. "All I said, both to you and your director, is you can't lock the last half hour."

"Here's the fucking deal," responded Brad. "I gave you a script and a package with a director and actors. We filmed that script, with an ending you approved, with those actors, and edited it in a way that we have on record as Rob loving. The only thing I can think that has changed is that now Rob's brother has watched it. So this obviously has to do with him. So put Charlie Gold on the fucking phone and let him tell me and my director what he doesn't like about the film his brother said was gonna make a fucking mint."

"Charlie is not getting on the phone with you." It was as if Brad would sooner get an audience with God.

"Then do me a fucking favor. Don't call me until you can tell me when my director gets to lock picture and we can deliver this film for a release date I want in fucking writing. And on two thousand screens with fifteen million dollars for prints and advertising like the contract says!"

He called Alice. They patched in Paul Aiello and David Levit.

"I want to make this very painful for them," Brad insisted.

"Oh, we're going to make it painful," Alice assured him. "Trust me. They have no idea."

"Please don't sue anyone," said David.

"That's not your decision," Alice snapped. "You're lucky Brad's even letting you on this call."

"I'm with David on this one," said Paul.

"Why's that?" asked Alice.

"Because Brad's going to want to keep doing business out here."

"Let me explain something about business," said Alice.

"Oh God, please don't," Paul begged.

"What matters is getting your due. You do that, the rest takes care of itself."

"This industry is different."

"Every fucking industry says that. And you know what? I haven't experienced one where success and power don't go hand in hand."

"Alice—"

"Shut your face and listen for once. It's very simple. If Brad lets the Golds fuck him, nobody is going to give a shit about Brad Shlansky and his sisters as producers because nobody will have heard of them. Their movie will come and go in a few theaters if it gets released at all."

"Isn't Brad your first and only client out here?"

"That's right. And I can sit here in Forest Hills and know more than you in Beverly Hills. Go figure. So you're going to back the fuck off and let me do my job."

"Listen to me, Alice. Please. If you sue Charlie, it'll bite Brad in the ass."

"Well, it'll be his ass, not yours."

"You're right about that."

"Which is the fucking problem. Your friendship with Brad only goes so far."

"I've known him a lot longer than you have."

"Then fucking act like it, you goddamn pussy."

Alice began with a demand letter to Gold Films Business Affairs that effected a meeting in New York with the Golds and David Levit in which Charlie discovered the director had no power in the LLC. That afternoon Brad answered a call from Charlie's assistant. Charlie would be staying at the Beverly Hills Hotel the following week and hoped Brad could join him for breakfast.

"What do I do?" he asked Alice.

"I bet it's fantastic. You can probably have an omelet with whatever the fuck you want in it. Beluga caviar and a lobster tail. Juice squeezed on the spot for you by twelve naked virgins. And he's paying. I would go. But park on the street so you don't have to pay the valet like the last time I was out. That was larceny."

When Brad arrived, Charlie was already seated with two young assistants, one male and one female, the table littered with smeared plates and a surfeit of condiments, creamers, and sweeteners. At the sole empty space some lucky soul had enjoyed a serving of eggs Benedict, should the shrapnel of Canadian bacon and poached egg glazed with hollandaise sauce be trusted.

"Sorry. We just had Ridley Scott here. Someone'll clean that up. I never said you should be on time!" Charlie smiled, not rising. "I assume you're Brad Shlansky."

"I am," said Brad, seating himself.

"Thanks for coming." Charlie barked at a nearby waiter. "Hey, you want to get someone to clean this up? I've asked twice already."

"Right away, Mr. Gold."

Soon the table had been cleared and reset and the waiter hovered solicitously.

"Go ahead," said Charlie to Brad. "Anything you want. On or off the menu. You say it and they'll bring."

"Can you do a lox plate?" Brad asked.

"Bring him a lox plate," said Charlie. He turned back to Brad. "What kind of bagel?"

David addressed the waiter.

"You have onion?"

"Yes sir."

"So bring him the lox plate with an onion bagel, and an everything and a plain in case he changes his mind. Plus a pitcher of the orange juice." He addressed David again. "You like orange juice? It's fucking amazing here. Not like the shit we get in New York. The oranges were picked yesterday ten miles from here."

"Sure."

"So the pitcher of orange juice too and a fresh glass for me. And refill my coffee."

"Yes, Mr. Gold."

When the waiter had left, Charlie gestured to his two assistants.

"This is Gabriella, and that's Christian. They work with me."

"Hi, I'm Brad. Nice to meet you."

Each smiled diffidently, nodding without speaking.

"All right," said Charlie, "like I tried to tell your director. What's his name again? The guy who was in the Noah Mendelson movie and got famous for a minute and a half?"

"David Levit."

"Right. He's very smug that guy. These fucking directors. Without us, no movie. We make it happen, people like you and me. While the director gets all the credit, we take all the risk."

"That's certainly true."

"I knew you were one of the ones who get it. I could tell as soon as you walked in. Long Island, right?

"Yes."

"I love it. Anyway, as I tried to tell your director, we're going to platform your movie—start exclusive and small. Basically what we do with our Oscar titles. And we'll do that sometime next year. He tried to say you'd object, but it was clear he didn't know what he was talking about, so I thought I'd sit face-to-face and make sure you agree it's what's best. I like your film very much, by the way."

"I appreciate that."

"Good."

"The thing is, we have an agreement that says you've got to release it wide."

"Yeah? I don't even know about any of that. My brother made the deal."

"Okay, so it's two thousand screens and fifteen million dollars for prints and advertising."

"You and I both know that's ridiculous for a movie like this."

"That may be your opinion. It could even be mine, but it's what the contract says."

"Even though it's not in the best interest of your film? Do you really want to do that to your project? Have an art film get torn apart by mainstream critics, then flop on two thousand screens and disappear in a week? Then where are you gonna be?"

"If I thought *Revenge* was an art film, I never would have asked people to invest in it."

"Those investors have already made a lot of money from us."

"So obviously you don't think it's an art film either, or you wouldn't have paid so much."

"I didn't. My brother did."

"David Levit said you brought up issues about the content being dangerous."

"People are taking sides in this country. On all sorts of issues. It's a moment. Turn on Fox News. Race, gender, politics, social media. We're not interested in making matters worse."

"That can be your opinion. But we still think the movie should be released wide and with real support, which is why we negotiated that in the contract."

"You keep talking about the fucking contract. It's beginning to piss me off."

"Contracts are important to me."

"I don't care about what's important to you. I also don't give a shit how you think what's now my film, having paid ten fucking million dollars for it, should be released. I own it. I'm the fucking distributor, not you and your fucking dentist investors from Ozone Park."

"Most of the money came from one of the biggest same-day lender chains on the East Coast. They bought my parents' business."

"How the fuck old are you?"

"I'm twenty-nine."

"So on your first movie—"

"My second."

"Your second movie you made a goddamn killing, and it's going to be released by the best company in the business, ever. You hit the fucking jackpot. Let me release this thing how I want, and we get on with our lives. What do you care at this point?"

"I'm trying to make a name for myself. Whatever you say, you know and I know a wide release helps with that. Plus, my investors and I have a back end, so we want a big release."

"For all it would cost us to put this movie on two thousand screens— fifteen million dollars *minimum*—this film is never going to make the kind of money where you and your investors—what is it you said? Same-day lenders? Jews?"

"Yes, as a matter of fact. So am I."

"You're blond. That's lucky."

"Because?"

"You can pass."

"Not with the name Shlansky."

"And your family were same-day lenders too?"

"We were in check cashing." Brad knew what was coming, especially from another Jew, so he did what he could to forestall further innuendo. "My dad operated in locations whites wouldn't dare set foot in."

"I respect that."

"Good."

Charlie turned to the male assistant.

"You have that bag?"

The assistant reached under his chair and produced a small dark-blue duffel with an Adidas logo. He passed it to Charlie, who held it on his lap exposed to view.

"There's a lot of money in this bag. I can assure you more cash than you've ever seen in a single pile, no matter what business your parents and your investors are in."

"My parents are deceased."

"I'm sorry about that. Me and Rob were close to our parents, so I know how that feels. I can also tell you this is a lot more than you would ever make after we're done with our accounting, which we're very good at in terms of proving how much we're out on a movie."

"We can ask to look at your books."

"I'm told your father did some creative bookkeeping of his own."

This Brad had not expected.

"How do you know that?"

"I have good people working for me."

"Meaning you also knew my parents are deceased, as well as what they did."

"Correct."

Brad waited.

"So, this is a million dollars," Charlie said, patting the bag. "And I frankly don't give a shit what you do with it. It's cash, so you take it and distribute it or don't distribute it, report it or don't report it. Put it in a fucking safe in the back of the store if you want." Charlie paused to allow Brad to absorb the reference. "I never gave it to you, in other words, so far as anyone else will ever know. Your fucking investors don't even have to know. And if you're wondering about Gabriella and Christian here, assistants at our company sign very strict NDAs where basically we murder them legally if they break it." He paused, pivoting a hand. "Gabriella?"

She handed over a manila folder that Charlie opened, exposing a two-page document.

"This is a release, with no mention of a payment, that says we can distribute your movie however we think best. I want you to sign it. We've got a notary standing by. He's enjoying a soda in the lobby."

"I sign it and you give me the bag."

"What bag?"

"Does that piece of paper specify what sort of platform release? Is there any guarantee at all as to number of screens and P&A support?"

"This is a million dollars, Brad. I think that's worth us getting to do what we think is best for a movie like this."

"Meaning shelve it if you want."

"We're not going to shelve it."

"But you can if you choose."

"I guess that's fucking right."

Brad knew Paul Aiello was right: to make an enemy of Charlie Gold could decimate him as a producer. Conversely, in a single stroke he could both placate the man and finance Same Day Films—including salaries and development—for two years, perhaps more, no one, other than perhaps Emily and Sarah, the wiser. Yet memories of his father's malfeasance, coupled with the implication in Charlie's offer that Brad could be bought, simply nauseated him. He had swindled unsuspecting peers out of coins, dissembled to the government as to the cost basis for those coins, even proffered some helpful untruths to the investors in *Revenge,* but Brad had always been true to himself. In this moment he had to do what was right, and taking money at the expense of his investors and his future simply wouldn't represent the person he wanted to be. Moreover, if Charlie didn't consider parting with a million dollars to be advantageous somehow to Gold Films, he wouldn't be offering it, meaning perhaps Brad could get more, and not in the form of a bribe.

"So, my problem is this," he finally said. "Effectively we delivered the movie months ago, and you still don't have it on your release schedule. There's been no long lead press, there's no trailer. Nothing. You're really already in breach of contract."

"If you mention the contract one more time, I'm going to punch your fucking lights out."

"I can understand why you wouldn't want me mentioning it, but that still doesn't mean you aren't in breach. If I take this money, at the very least it's going to save you the fifteen million dollars in prints and advertising you don't want to spend. This is the movie business where we dress up profit seeking, or fear of losing a shitload of money, with good morals whenever possible. I'm guessing bad publicity and maybe lawsuits if someone shoots up a high school and blames *Revenge* is what's causing all this. Meanwhile, you're probably already covered on foreign sales well more than the million you're offering me."

The assistants stared at their plates.

"Do you have any idea what I can do to you?" Charlie asked.

"I have an idea what you think you can do to me."

"A few phone calls and no one finances your movies, no one sends you scripts, no one sends you actors. Your fucking phone goes silent, and your calls aren't taken. You don't exist because I make it known I don't want you to exist. Understand that every fucking film of any real fucking substance you see I've either made or decided not to make. I own the journalists, I own their publishers, I own the fucking paparazzi. I own the moviegoer, which means everyone because everyone in this country bows down to the movies, and I *am* the fucking movies. And when you're done in movies, I will follow you into whatever you try and do next. Go back to cashing checks for *schwartzers*, go try and sell fucking diamonds. No matter what it is, I will make you die there too. A fucking immediate death, like I shot you in the fucking brain. That you're even sitting across from me getting minutes of my time makes this the fucking most meaningful day of your life."

"I still want my movie to be released like it says in the contract."

Charlie thrust the bag back at the assistant who had presented it.

"You'll regret not letting this end here like you'll regret nothing else in your life." Wanting to set his own terms for departure, Brad rose as Charlie continued. "Because if you think we're going to settle, let alone for anything close to what was in that bag, you're out of your fucking mind. I have a dozen lawyers on payroll. While you're buried in legal bills, or your fucking ambulance-chasing contingency lawyer is screaming uncle for the shit my guys will put him through with countersuits and motions to delay, I'm not going to be paying a nickel I wouldn't have been paying anyway. This is going to be nothing for me. In fact, I'm going to love it."

"Now the fun starts," Alice told Brad when he reported what had transpired. "And he'll *wish* I was a man."

It astounded them both how quickly the private investigator she hired began furnishing information. Upon seeing the film, a fearful Charlie had shown it to friends in government. When several confirmed his fear that it might inspire more violence, he determined not just to bury the movie but never to release it domestically. Even more surprising, the entire saga followed the same pattern as a Shakespeare adaptation with a young producer from New Jersey that was to have been released in the wake of the Columbine shootings. Charlie had endeavored to squelch that release as well, and with a bribe in cash its producer had also refused.

"How do we know all this?" Brad asked from his exercise bike.

"E-mails, calendars, the screening room schedule down there. You name it."

"So, because a few senators didn't like my movie he can break his contract?"

"Not just a few senators. A certain former first lady who wants to be president. Charlie thinks he's a fucking Medici."

"What does that mean?"

"He's not only gonna try and control the movie business, he's gonna choose who gets to be pope. I'm told he wants to enter politics himself one day, which, trust me, ain't gonna happen once you hear the rest of what I've got to say. We have names, Brad. Names."

"Names of what?"

"Women—models, actresses, assistants—women Charlie has settled with over the years for sexual assault, sexual harassment, and get this: goddamn rape. The guy's a fucking pig."

"What does that have to do with us?"

"A settlement NDA, no matter how much changed hands, doesn't muzzle in a court of law. We can compel them to testify."

"But why would we do that? Charlie didn't rape me."

"We show a pattern of criminal behavior and the willful attempt to quash it by any means. Figuratively he tried to fuck you, you said no, he threatened to ruin you, then offered you money. Same thing he did to the guy ten years ago after Columbine. And these women, Brad, at least one who he accosted in her own apartment, and when she threatened charges, he tells her how he can make or break her career, and when that doesn't work, he pays her off. Trust me, this is never going to trial, and you're getting a lot more than the million he offered when they come begging to settle. And by the way, you think my guy I hired is an animal, you're not going to believe who was digging up background on you on Long Island, where they found out about your father."

"Who?"

"The Golds have ex-fucking Mossad guys on their payroll they sick on anybody who crosses them. Mossad, Brad! For the fucking movie business!"

"Jesus."

"I hear fear in your voice. Stop it with that. *Revenge* is the best thing that ever happened to you, and the asshole public hasn't even seen it yet!"

Gold Films settled for $2.5 million and agreed to release the film per all contractual stipulations through a rival company, protecting Charlie and Rob from blame for any negative "real world" ramifications, while still satisfying their obligations to Brad. The film took in $15 million domestically its first weekend, and $37 million before the release effectively ended two months later. As Brad had inferred, Gold Films retained rights for all foreign markets, where the movie grossed $58 million outside of the United States and Canada. Not a single person or entity, so far as Brad could tell, lost money; in fact, everyone, including the Golds' net of the settlement, did well.

As for Same Day Films, Brad and his sisters suddenly had more than $400,000 in their bank account, the rest going to the film's investors.

"Fuck the money, which trust me, there's three of you, you'll burn through it," Paul told him. "The point is, now I don't have to chase scripts for you, they come to me. Though I will say—and I told you this would happen—Charlie Gold has put out the word on you."

"So what."

"It's the sort of thing that can follow you for years, Brad."

"Didn't you just say you don't have to chase scripts?"

"Maybe without the shit he spreads we'd be getting *better* scripts. Just trust me. The dust hasn't settled on this yet, and you can tell Alice I said so."

Same Day Films moved out of the apartment Sarah and Emily still shared and rented an office in Studio City. They hired an assistant and took on an intern to help Sarah read scripts. Unfortunately few interested her, in spite of an inexhaustible succession of meetings that always involved lunch or early-evening drinks.

"The food and beverage industry is going to put up a plaque out here in your honor," Brad told her. "You do know this job is about making films, not wining and dining out-of-work screenwriters."

"It's a social industry."

"If I hear that again, I'm moving back to Long Island. And meanwhile a bunch of shitty movies get made. I wonder if there's any connection."

"I'll give it a think."

"You do that. And bring back a receipt."

When Sarah did bring him projects, he was exceedingly careful, perhaps to a fault, given that months passed without their pursuing material beyond discussion inside the office. Scripts that did intrigue proved difficult to finance, lacking either a star or a concept worth the expense. And when he'd try to attach stars, agents were slow to respond, taking months to read the scripts, if they bothered to at all.

"Did you tell them who I am, Paul?"

"Who's that?"

"The guy who made *Revenge*?"

"You shouldn't have sued Charlie Gold."

"Until you have proof that's what's going on, I don't want to hear that asshole's name."

"You're experiencing the proof."

"We're burning through our money."

"I told you. Maybe I get you in an overhead deal where a studio pays your bills."

Finally, one project, a thriller about young white-collar criminals running a drug ring out of an LA hedge fund called *White Pill*, excited him sufficiently for Brad to make an offer to the director and producer during their first meeting at the Same Day offices.

"They said it's a five-million-dollar movie!" Sarah erupted, incredulous, when the filmmakers left. "Where the fuck are we going to find that?"

"Paul and I will figure it out," he told his sister. "And did it ever occur to you that if I hadn't made the offer and we don't start papering it, the script goes away? The only actually commercial project that has interested us in the last month? Let me do what I fucking do."

To finance *White Pill* he deployed the same tactic he had with *Revenge*, which was to have Alice tie up the property for as long as possible without his having to spend meaningfully, abiding by an early lesson he'd learned from Paul Aiello: in Los Angeles, if you can look like you're making a movie, you're making a movie. Accordingly, all payments, including the option, needed to be deferred until production began. As further insurance, this required that negotiations with the writer and director be attenuated for as long as possible, and with contractual language always favoring Same Day. In the meantime, Brad could announce the film in the trades to attract acting talent, which would in turn help him secure financing. He could open offices, hire a casting director, location scouts, and designers, all on the promise of payment in due time.

White Pill, however, did not demonstrate the appeal with actors and their representatives that *Revenge* had, particularly with so many agents, per Charlie Gold, now wary of his name. Nor was its director as persuasive aggregating talent as David Levit had been. Within a month of opening production offices, for which Brad and his sisters had been paying two thousand dollars a week in Thousand Oaks, without a single creditable financing lead, Brad closed the film down. Invoices materialized for staff, rental cars, office furniture, and a cascade of other liabilities totaling over sixty thousand dollars, with more surely to come.

"Exactly what I said would happen," Sarah offered unhelpfully.

"Shut the fuck up. Maybe I'd listen to you if you had actually done a thing for the past four weeks but complain, spend money, and order people around."

The line producer pestered him daily.

"You do know we have outstanding bills? To the casting director, the production office coordinator and her assistant, the office PAs?"

"The movie didn't get made."

"I don't think that matters to them."

"Maybe it should have."

"They were filling out time cards! They worked for you!"

"Have them try being orphaned at seventeen."

"I think I'm going to throw up."

"You're not going to throw up."

"You haven't paid me either, Brad. Eight weeks I've been on, plus the budget I did. And so much of this with my vendors." It wouldn't end. He'd answer one question, and she'd conjure other liabilities. He and Sarah began pretending bad connections.

"Sorry, I'm in the hills on the way to the valley. I'm losing you."

When they stopped hearing from her, a letter arrived itemizing invoices she had paid personally, totaling just over twenty thousand dollars. He instructed Emily to call and promise she'd be reimbursed the moment they got financing, and with that Same Day Films escaped further obligation, *White Pill* dematerializing as if it had never existed. Should they have paid every bill, it would have wiped them out. Enough money remained from *Revenge* to last them three months.

In the meantime, Amanda's phone rang morning and night with other people's movies to publicize. He couldn't be in bed with her, have a meal, see a movie without interruption, every ring a dagger of humiliation. She hired an assistant, as well as another team for interviews.

As could only happen in Los Angeles, an incoming call changed everything.

"You're phoning *me*?" Brad asked Paul Aiello, who since the implosion of *White Pill* had been keeping his distance. "If it's about Charlie Gold trashing me again, you've made your point."

"I'm sending you a box of comic books by courier. You need to have them read by tomorrow night."

"Why's that?"

"We're going to dinner with a couple guys I met."

Within six months Brad and his sisters were buying furniture for space on the Sony lot, with a development stipend thrown in, and all the writers, directors, and actors at UCM as their personal stable. He had never entirely believed Paul's prognostications for their partnership, even though he'd often parroted them to his sisters and Amanda, but what his oldest friend predicted was actually materializing. *The Recluse,* before it had failed as a film, had led to *Revenge,* and (*White Pill* but a minor diversion) *Revenge* had led to Lone Star Pulp, an Austin-based comic book imprint whose material Paul arranged for Brad and him to control entirely for film.

He could only laugh, therefore, when just as this transpired, David Levit called with *Appalachian Winter,* a nineteenth-century drama set in the director's home state of West Virginia. The actor/director bragged that it was the best script he would ever write. Brad took it home that night at Sarah's urging, where Amanda snapped it from his grasp the moment he walked in the door. She appeared from upstairs inside of two hours.

"You need to make this film, Brad. Read it and make it. I'll do unit publicity for free."

"Are you kidding me?" Brad asked Sarah the following day. "Fifteen million dollars?"

"That's the number David gave Emily."

"It's nineteenth century," his older sister explained. "Antebellum. Everything has to be either removed or built. Plus you've got period buggies, costumes, props—"

"Don't explain shit to me I already know," said Brad.

"*Revenge* did well," offered Sarah. "He wants to step up."

"Don't fucking compare this to *Revenge. Revenge* was a present-day genre picture."

"Picture?" asked Sarah. "Who are you? Louis B. Mayer all of the sudden? It's called a fucking movie. We're from Long Island."

Narrated by a twelve-year-old innocent as his family traveled across West Virginia in the late 1850s, David Levit's Gothic drama fell into the category

Brad had heard described during his eight years in LA as "execution driven." Yes, the plot had picaresque elements as the family patriarch conned and swindled at every stop, building to tragic violence, but the film also relied on an abstraction of rural vistas and the eccentric misfits who inhabited them. Brad knew, therefore, that he'd need to negotiate terms that gave Same Day ultimate creative power to safeguard against such obfuscatory conceits. He and Alice would exploit David's desperation for financing to retain control of budget, crew, casting, scheduling, and the edit with a lattice of ambiguous provisions that would cause his attorneys to weep. Most important, however, they would ensure complete control over the director and his material for as long as possible, indefinitely even, without having to spend a penny until those pennies weren't Brad's.

Inside of ten years in Los Angeles, he would have all the status he'd imagined for himself and more: not only what surely would be tentpole films with Sony and the comic book company, but perhaps an Oscar with David Levit—not out of the question given the material, subject matter, and period setting. Plus, he liked David Levit, and David Levit liked him. Now let Sarah deride Brad for using the word *picture*. Let Charlie Gold try and ruin him.

That same week Amanda informed him she was pregnant.

"Call David Levit's people," he instructed Sarah. "We're putting *Appalachian Winter* on our slate."

FILM FORUM

"I have to make this movie."

"Do you know how many times I've heard you say that, David?" Charlotte asked. "And why does your 'having' to make *Coal* necessitate your staying in LA two more days? Aren't there telephones? Isn't there e-mail? Skype?"

"It's what Jacob Rosenthal wants. None of this is my fault."

"Don't say that."

"What?"

"It's not your fault. Invariably that means the opposite. This always happens when you go out there. Now I've got to hire a babysitter for two more afternoons and nights. And you understand I'm in ten-out-of-twelves, so I won't get home until after midnight. And then I'm waking up with the girls while working on one of the toughest roles I've ever played, and you're not here."

"I'm sorry."

"You're up with them for a month straight when you get home."

"Two months."

"Deal."

He took the two flights of stairs from his suite down past the pool and up to the patio restaurant where he chose a table in semidarkness under the eaves. He couldn't remember a succession of worse days since Adam's death. On his deliberately careful drive back to the Chateau after dinner the night before in Beverly Hills where he, Jacob, and Larry McCormick had finished two bottles of wine, he was searching for KCRW on the dial in his rented Mini Cooper when his cell phone rang from a blocked number.

"David, it's Brad."

"Yeah, Brad? I'm driving."

"Alice was on the phone with your lawyers today, and I've got to tell you we're getting nowhere."

"I don't know what to say about that."

"After all we've been through, after all I've done for you, you suddenly don't know what to say. Well, I'm going to have a lot to say, you can count on that. And so is Alice."

He'd had too much to drink to be having this conversation. For that same reason he couldn't restrain himself.

"Brad, why are you doing this?"

"Trying to make the movie you begged me to produce?"

"If you were trying to make *Appalachian Winter*, I would have heard from you in the seven months since you pulled the plug on us in Kentucky."

"I didn't pull the plug, you guys did. We have contemporaneous notes."

"Just let me get on with my life. I'll make this movie with Chicago Films, and then I'll make *Appalachian Winter* with you if you really have the money, but in the right way. Not like last time. Please."

"You want me to wait around with my dick in my hands for two years while you get to go make movies with Jacob Rosenthal?"

"One movie, Brad."

"Which will lead to another and another. You think I don't know how this works? And you fuck me over like everyone else out here?" Brad was sounding unhinged. David wondered if he might be drunk. What had happened to the producer who owned a comic book company and claimed stewardship of more projects than he had time for?

"I don't have anything to do with everyone else, Brad."

"You're available to *me, right now*! You're mine! Not Jacob Rosenthal's. Not anyone else's. Mine!"

"Show us your financing documents. Let us look at them. And if I can actually even meet with the financier—"

"Where in the contract does it say you get to meet anyone or see a single fucking document? Nowhere! You want Alice to send over a copy? I raise the money, you direct the fucking movie!" He was shouting, unmoored from anything close to rational. "That's why you came fucking begging me to make it in the first place when everyone out here was my best friend! And now you think you get to leave me behind like everybody else and go make some other movie unscathed?"

"You think I'm unscathed? My reputation was spotless before *Appalachian Winter* fell apart. None of those people you didn't pay will ever work with me again."

"Who's the one with the opportunity to make another film right now after promising me *Appalachian Winter* was the most important movie he'd ever make and then leaving me with all the bills?" As in many of their conversations David felt himself succumbing to a burden of falsehoods so crushing that they began to seem true, so depleted was his strength in parsing them. "You're going to be available, and I don't care how long it fucking takes! You'll sit on your ass for twenty years! I don't give a shit, because if I don't work, you don't work!"

"You can't do this, Brad."

"Alice has written up the complaint. She's calling Jacob tomorrow."

David wondered if Brad knew Jacob Rosenthal, guessing no, that he was merely employing the habit endemic to the film industry of using first names to connote familiarity where there was none.

"I'm gonna shut that fucking movie down!"

David eased back onto La Cienega and ascended the steep incline toward Sunset, where he made the right toward the Chateau. As he passed the Standard Hotel with its upside-down sign he wondered if he should call Sammy again and wake him in New York.

"First of all, did you really write a film called *Appalachian Winter?*" Sammy had asked the day before.

"I'll probably change the title."

"And who the hell did this contract? And who told you to sign it? This is the most willfully sloppy legal writing I've ever seen. I can't even understand it syntactically."

"I think that was the point. Like I told you, he has this attorney—"

"This Alice woman I spoke to?"

"They beat you down."

"David, didn't *you* have an attorney? I mean, this is a bloodbath."

"I had two attorneys. I still do."

"And what, they engaged in an attempt to out-idiot each other? They should both be disbarred."

"They told me not to sign it."

"None of this is making sense."

"You'd have to be a filmmaker desperate to get his movie made to understand."

"What're you David, suddenly a moron?"

"It's what happens to people out here; they let themselves get preyed on."

"Aren't you vaguely famous?"

"Getting to direct the movies you write is different than acting in ones you didn't, though an acting career comes with its own indignities, trust me. But yes, I've been very lucky; it's not lost on me."

"Let's talk about his lawyer."

"Alice."

"She hyperventilates on the phone. And she subjected you to all manner of ad hominem attack. Says you're like everyone in Hollywood."

"I'm glad this amuses you."

"She says you use people up and leave them behind for your own advancement. That her client effectively handed you your career by financing *Revenge*. I'm just looking at my notes here. Ah, and now you're famous and he's in debt, lost his comic book company, whatever that means, and you don't give a shit. Adam would love all this, by the way."

"I'm sure he would, but Sam, I want you please to listen to me—"

"Why would I listen to anyone stupid enough to have signed the document I just read? I mean, seriously, I think I lost ten IQ points just having it on the screen in front of me."

"Because you're going to stop it with that and listen."

"Only as a thought experiment."

"What Alice told you, Sammy, is complete fantasy. You know I'm not like that. I'm not that person."

"I know. Simple guy from West Virginia. You and I haven't exactly been in touch since after Adam died. What do I know what Hollywood does to people, with your limousines and pool parties?"

"You're joking around, and this guy is threatening to destroy me."

"No one is going to destroy you, David. We're going to get you through this."

"We need to talk about your fee."

"You can't afford me."

"What does that mean?"

"First of all, I made a promise a long time ago to both you and Adam. Half in jest at the time, but a promise is still a promise. Secondly—and I'm not trying to belittle you or exalt myself, I'm just stating fact—I litigate for corporations who have so much at stake, they'll compensate at a rate beyond what a person like you, or me for that matter, could ever pay."

"Then it all turned out like you hoped."

"I guess it did, David."

Sammy's pursuit of a law degree had occupied much discussion between Adam, David, and Sammy, with none doubting Sammy would be accepted to the school of his choice. Early on, his father— who still occupied a seat on the federal bench in Philadelphia—had taken to calling his youngest son "the Rottweiler" for his combative arguing style during dinner-table disputes.

"If you don't become a litigator," he announced when Sammy was in the seventh grade, "God will have squandered some real abilities," to which the thirteen-year-old retorted, "That assumes the existence of God, which I'm not prepared to cede."

At the time of his acceptance to Columbia and every other law school to which he'd applied, it seemed Sammy could've done anything with his life. He was even fronting for a band playing songs he'd written at various fringe bars in the East Village, this after his semester studying history at the Sorbonne, from which he returned with a French girlfriend.

"You do understand that people would kill to have your options, Sammy," David remarked at the time.

"Here's the truth," Sammy confided. "I don't want to struggle downtown playing music in bars chasing labels like a desperate fool, and I don't really want to spend my life in the academy and have to put a lot of time in teaching kids like us history on a professor's salary. Add to that that I've got a woman I'm going to marry who's got fancy tastes, and we're going to have children. I guess what I'm saying is I'm gonna get the law degree."

"Did you write Adam and tell him?"

"He made me promise to represent him gratis in any and all disputes. A pledge I'll make to you as well. By the way, he's coming home before Christmas."

Four years later, Adam dead for nearly as long, Sammy faced another choice, this one curiously not unlike the previous one, but mooted with Adam absent over lunch at an Indian restaurant in Midtown where Sammy had requested he and David meet. Sammy had performed well at Columbia, editing the law review and finishing third in his class. Though recruited by many of the top firms in the country, he'd accepted a clerkship with David Souter, where he'd spent the customary year. Back in New York he was offered both a partner track at Proskauer, Rose and an associate professorship at NYU Law School, where he could either begin to publish and pursue a teaching line or bide his time for a judgeship.

"It's like you breathe different air than the rest of us," said David.

"Oh, shut up."

"Like if when I got out of Juilliard instead of being unemployed, I'd been offered a network series and the Bond franchise."

"Enough."

"It seems to me though that once you've gone the corporate law route, from what I understand of it, while you can go back to teaching, it's going to be difficult really to do that with any meaning."

"And why is that?"

"I don't know. Isn't corporate law a whole world you have to throw yourself into completely? Particularly if you want to make partner? Mergers and acquisitions, hostile takeovers, poison pills."

"What's your point?"

"Unless you were going to do all that work then give it all up, and the salary that's going to go along with it, you wouldn't ever be a full professor but an adjunct, and that would be that in terms of an academic career and judicial scholarship. Are you really going to want to wake up at age fifty and say to yourself you gave your incredible mind to corporate law?"

Sammy stared down at his plate.

"How about you give this a think, David," he said finally. "I wake up when I'm fifty with a wife and two or three kids on a professor's or a judge's salary, and I'm barely able to save to put them through college and have anything left over, and I'm constantly having to think about money while I'm training lawyers to make two million dollars a year at big firms. Or I can be a lawyer at one of those firms and raise a family while doing the work I trained for, which is to litigate. And did it ever occur to you, while you make your banal generalizations about corporate law and poison pills, which is a term you're throwing around probably without even understanding what it means, that I might actually become really, really good at that sort of work?"

"I never doubted it for a second."

"With the challenge of hundreds of millions of dollars at stake in any given case, and arguing against brilliant minds in front of other brilliant minds in the fucking crucible of capitalism, and getting paid really well for it, and that I might even really enjoy that?"

"You make a lot of sense, Sammy. But it sounds like you've already decided, so why were you asking me?"

"I was asking because I thought you might actually have something, *anything*, to say that I hadn't already thought of." Voiced with quiet rage, it constituted one of the more cruel remarks ever directed at David, if only for the sheer simplicity of its implication: that he simply wasn't smart enough, not just on the topic at hand but on any topic, to enlighten his friend.

"I'm sorry, David," said Sammy. "That was an awful thing to say. I didn't mean it."

"Of course you did," David responded. "But it's all right. I wish I could give you what you need—what we both need—which is Adam here." This only confirmed yet again what David already suspected, and what Charlotte's mother had warned. Adam had perished, but their past together would never relinquish its hold.

David and Sammy saw each other less frequently. In spite of Sammy's apology and the acknowledgment of its deeper poignancy, these kinds of interchanges seemed to proliferate between them. Moreover, whenever David would dare argue with Sammy, no matter the topic, he'd find himself attacked viciously, out of all proportion with the particular dispute. They hadn't seen each another for nine years—since David's wedding to Charlotte in New Orleans—before David picked up the phone in Los Angeles the day Rosen and Stein insisted he hire a litigator.

"Look, I didn't want to bother you with this, Sammy. I know you're not an entertainment lawyer, but I just couldn't think of anyone else."

"It's all right, David. What's up?"

"Well, it's complicated and a bit involved, but also fast moving. Do you have a few minutes? I can be as succinct as possible. I know things must be insane there. I heard you made partner."

"I did."

"Are you happy about it?"

"It's really interesting work. I imagine a bit like you, with new cases and challenges coming along with enough frequency so that shit doesn't get old. At least I imagine that's what it's like with each new part. You've certainly been doing well. Acting, writing, directing."

"Well enough."

"I'm happy for you, David. I really am. Adam would be too. I know he would."

"I still think about him constantly."

"So do I, David. We didn't realize how good we had it."

"No, we didn't."

David wondered if calling had been a mistake given the pause that followed.

"Tell me what's going on, David," Sammy finally said.

"Well, I don't know if you saw my film *Revenge.*"

"Saw it and read about it and liked it. Good movie. I'm sorry I didn't call. A lot of controversy around it. And Gold Films. You wrote a piece in *New York* magazine."

"You read it?"

"The movie got delayed because of the shootings at Elysian. I'm sorry I didn't call. I think to, and then—"

"I know. It's all right. So the guy who produced that is named Brad Shlansky, and he's this sort of Dickensian character from Long Island who came out to LA to produce movies with his sisters."

"Okay."

"Both their parents died when Brad was in high school, and he's got the kind of outlook on life that that sort of tragedy can engender in a certain type of really rotten soul."

"Jesus, David. What did this guy do to you?"

"Yeah, I guess that was a little harsh."

"This poor guy's parents died. I've never heard you speak that way."

"I'm just really frustrated, and I guess more importantly extremely scared. Obviously he doesn't have a rotten soul. In fact, in certain respects, I kind of admire him."

"But he's after you."

"When it came to making my next film, I took it to him—"

"Because you trusted this Fagin fellow?"

"Fagin?"

"Nefarious Dickens character, also Jewish."

"I did. And unlike with *Revenge*, he didn't actually end up raising the money."

"So you want to go after him."

"No. He's going after me."

"What am I not getting here?"

David explained his opportunity to move on from the ruins of *Appalachian Winter* and make *Coal* with Jacob Rosenthal.

"*Coal*, the Rex Patterson novel, *Coal*? How has that not been made into a movie already?"

"It's complicated. Tough material right now for the money it would cost, but this guy Jacob Rosenthal is unorthodox."

"It sounds like you're trading one unscrupulous Jew for another."

"I wouldn't call Jacob unscrupulous. In fact, he's the opposite. What the two do have in common though is a virulent mistrust of the world."

"I think you could've used a bit more of that yourself. So, what's Fagin's lawyer's name again?"

"Alice."

"Alice what?

"Schaffson." David heard Sammy's keyboard clicking.

"Right. Got her right here. She looks a bit unstable, David." There was another pause, accompanied by more clicking. "She went to Fordham, which is no fly-by-night institution. Send me the contract you signed, and have Fagin—"

"Brad Shlansky. A blond Jew from Long Island."

"Have Brad Shlansky from Long Island give her my number."

"So, what you're saying is I'm toast?" David asked Sammy later that day when his friend had had a chance to review the contract and finish berating David for having signed it.

"I don't really know. They seem to have an option on your script, which then leads to the directing services as related to that option, and once they exercise one, it triggers the other, but with no real defined term. It's insane, unless the understanding is that they can basically hold you forever, which will make no sense to any judge, meaning the entire contract could be voided, no matter how stupid you were for having agreed to it all. If your question is if this went to trial would we win, my answer would have to be yes, but it's always a risk. This Alice could get there in front of the judge and start waving her hands around and hyperventilating—did I mention the hyperventilating?"

"You did."

"And the judge could respond to that. Plus, it's the movie business, and even judges are susceptible to certain prejudices in that sector because of what movies are in the culture. The other question is, are they even counting on a judge or jury hearing on this? Or are they bluffing?"

"In poker you bluff to win the hand."

"Exactly."

"What is winning here? Surely it's not making the movie. I told you he doesn't have the financing. He couldn't possibly with no cast. In other words, he'd be winning my availability for something he has no way of accomplishing."

"So, he wants to punish you or he wants a payoff. Alice said you humiliated him. That he's tired of everyone humiliating him."

"Should I call and apologize?"

"Are you being serious?"

"My agent said to. I just want this to go away."

"Let me make this clear, David. Under no circumstances call this guy. Don't talk to him at all. And under no circumstances apologize. You can't project any suggestion that going out and getting other work is wrong. This whole thing is crazy."

"Like you said a second ago, this is the movie business. At a certain point normal standards just don't apply."

"So why the fuck are you in it?"

Just before Laurel he made the hairpin left across the westbound lane on Sunset to reach his hotel. He eased by the tented valet station up the short driveway to the garage, where one of the same two harried attendants who'd been working the impossibly cramped area for decades took his car. He passed a bickering couple seated on the low bench facing the street and made his way up the dimly lit stairs to the lobby to retrieve his room key.

Turning toward the elevator, he considered having a Cognac in the sunken expanse that stretched away down a few descending steps to the left of reception. In a far corner he saw an older Australian actor named Nigel Gleeson, who had starred in Noah Mendelson's last film, sitting alone behind a high-shouldered bottle, his nose in a hardback. David moved past the low tables and overstuffed couches on which sat the usual complement of slender, hip men and lithe women in varying states of dishabille. The room glowed from small table lamps and wall sconces, all fitted with small Edison bulbs at the minimum setting on their squeezers. Three or four dozen *ofrenda* candles flickered from every available surface.

"Hey, Nigel," David said. "What are you reading?"

The Australian looked up.

"David! My God. I was hiding back here. I couldn't stand it up in my room—too much splendid isolation."

"Should I go?"

"No! I'd talk to you any day! You're only twenty years younger than I am, so we'll actually have something to say to each another."

"Walking back here I was thinking youth has its advantages."

"Well, I'm having a rest from that. At least for tonight. You want a sip of this? I can get another glass. I'm not going to finish it. Well, I was, but shouldn't, so you'll be doing me a favor."

"Sure, what is it?"

"Oh, some California rubbish. Decent enough though." He hailed a young waiter in the customary white shirt and black shawl-collared vest. "Could you just bring an extra glass here for my friend? Thanks so much. Sorry to be a bother." He turned back to David. "So how's our friend Mr. Mendelson? He out here as well?"

"No, happily back in Brooklyn."

"Tell him he's got to put us in his next movie together. Damn, I had a good time with him. I tell you though, I'd like to be in one of your movies."

"That would be incredible."

"*Capos* was absolutely harrowing."

"Thanks."

"And you? What are you up to out here? Acting?"

"No, writing and directing, but just for a series of meetings. I was supposed to leave today."

"Mate, that's my bloody life, may it never abate. It's gotten to the point now where I leave my departures open-ended. I just take the cash and have my manager book the flights, because frankly they just won't let you go."

"That's not necessarily a bad thing."

"It's a bloody great thing!"

The waiter appeared with David's glass.

"Thanks for that," Nigel said, looking up. "You want something to nibble on, David? On me."

"No thanks. I just came from a big dinner."

"Of course you did." He looked once more to the waiter. "That'll be it for now, with any luck, thanks so much."

"Just let me know if you need anything else, Mr. Gleeson. Oh, and your wine was covered by Mr. Abelson."

"What? Is Fred here?"

"Yes. Outside."

"Oh, that's lovely of him. Tell him thanks, and that I hope he'll stop by on his way out."

"I'm with UCM too, and Fred never buys my wine," David remarked with feigned umbrage once the waiter had departed.

"Win an Oscar. Everything changes."

"I'll keep that in mind."

"That's the thing about this place," Nigel said as he gave David a healthy pour. "It's so relentlessly, fucking interminably, diabolically seductive. Obvious thing to say, right? But even before my success. We're treated ludicrously well, staying in these hotels, where"—he gestured expansively—"there's beauty all around us all the time, our needs are catered to, at least when there's the work. And as if that wasn't enough, we're so far away— me from Sydney, you from New York—we've none of the hassles of our actual *lives*. Even the bloody time differences create space for us. Honestly, just look at this place. It's unreal, down to the twinkling lights. And I'm sitting back here reading Bulgakov with a bottle of wine my agent just paid for, though I've got literally piles of per diem cash upstairs just as pocket money for my seven-figure job. How did it bleeding happen?"

"Yeah … that seven-figure part. Not exactly my reality. Certainly not as an actor, and come to think of it not as a writer/director either. Not even close."

"Like I said, that Oscar, mate."

"I'll get right on it."

"Or try concentrating on one or the other. Be an actor or a writer or a director! Jesus, not all three! Are you mad? But seriously, you know what else it is about this place? What turned it around for me?

"What?"

"Again, not exactly an original thought, but you've got to give me credit for boiling it down to a simple aphorism."

"Which is?"

"Everything in Los Angeles, and I mean *every* interaction, is business. Meaning every bloody thing you do, every place you go, every person you meet, every decision you make. Absolutely no exceptions. Business."

"You're out in public to have a taco, no matter where it is, everyone goes everywhere, someone can see you and offer you a job. I've heard it before."

"Yes, of course you have, so sure, start with that. But it happens mostly without us even knowing it. I've been out one night, and my agent's rung up the next day with an offer because the director or producer had been at the same restaurant. Never came over to say hi or introduce him or herself, but just saw me and boom, I clicked for a role. But that's the obvious stuff. Go deeper. That waiter who brought your glass and told me about Fred getting the wine. He's quite probably a writer or an actor or a director already. Aspiring, I mean. All of them are. That's why they're out here. He's twenty—what?—five now, but by the time he's thirty-five he's going to be on with life and hopefully doing what he really wants to do. Is he the next Noah Mendelson? David Levit? Charlie Gold?"

"I don't see him as Charlie. No one is Charlie."

"Who the fuck knows? And I'm not stopping there. He's got friends, and guess what they all talk about when they get together? Who they fucking waited on in their humiliating fucking jobs serving the toffs. Who's nice and who's a prick. Who tips and who doesn't. Who looked like shite and who perfectly spiffy. So you better bloody well know: my interaction with him?"

"Business."

"You bet your ass."

"Pretty cynical, Nigel. And exhausting."

"Being nice is cynical? I find it bloody invigorating. And look at us here. In a minute Fred Abelson, one of the most powerful agents in Hollywood, who just bought us our wine—"

"Bought you our wine."

"By virtue of this interaction, the one between you and me, that you came over for a confab and I obliged, he bought both of our wines."

"So, this too is a business interaction between you and me?"

"Of course it bloody is, David. I just told you I'd be in one of your films. And there's nothing wrong with that. I love the work, I love the life, I love the pursuit. And presumably you do too, or choose something else to do, because the bloody bullshit we also put up with, particularly early on when we're being rejected relentlessly? It ain't worth it, mate."

"It certainly isn't."

"So, Fred's going to come over here, and because you stopped by to have a drink with me, and you're looking successful there in your boots and black jeans and snazzy blazer—what is that? Paul Smith?"

"Yes."

"Your Paul Smith blazer. And he sees you're with good old me, and I'm with good old you, he's going to think better of both of us. Two of his clients out quaffing at the bloody Chateau. He'll talk about it in the staff meeting tomorrow—who's your main guy there?"

"Howard Garner."

"Howard's a cunt. But he'll mention to everyone that he saw you with me last night, which'll make Howard happy, and Howard will push just that little extra for you with the studios tomorrow, and on it bloody goes."

"Is that actually why you're down here? Like some kind of a Venus flytrap waiting for us bugs to land on you?"

"Fuck off. Good one though. I'm down here because I love being down here. And why—and here's the point—I'm well dressed wherever I go and whatever I do, and why I'm unfailingly nice and gracious to everyone. It's also why, as I was describing, I tend to have more work offered to me than I have time for."

"There's also the fact that you're one of the most talented actors in the world."

"What a bleeding crock. If you think we're where we are just because of talent, you're fooling yourself. It's the smallest part of it. Loads of people have talent. Did you go to drama school?"

"Yes."

"I went to NIDA in Sydney. And were you one of the top actors in your class?"

"Absolutely not. Considered the weakest by everyone."

"Not so different than me."

"I don't believe that."

"Well, you're going to have to, because it's true. I mean, look, the truth? I was fine, but I could name half a dozen as good or better—and not subjectively, but objectively better in terms of whatever it is you think makes an actor: transformation, emotional honesty, movement, clarity with text, vocal range, imagination—you name it in whatever order. A few of them are still working, most of them aren't."

"So, you schmoozed your way to the top?"

"I haven't schmoozed for a moment in my life actually, and if that's what you think I mean, you haven't heard a bloody word I've uttered. It comes down to understanding that you need to be a decent, reliable bloke wherever you go and whatever you do. Does that make me a schmoozer or some sort of poncy fraud the way the word implies? You be the judge. Like your man Lincoln said: 'charity to all and malice toward none.' And that, as much as whatever talent I've got, is why I go from job to job to job, and eventually I won the coveted statue that led to the sweet taste of free Cabernet on your tongue."

The smugness aside, David couldn't disagree with the essential premise as to how the business operated in Los Angeles, which furnished many of the animating reasons for Charlotte and him remaining in New York.

"Forgetting that I actually prefer working in theater," Charlotte said, "I don't want every time I go out to have to be worrying about what I'm wearing or how my makeup looks. Actresses have no choice out there. And what's even more irritating is that women in that sort of predicament end up looking at each other even more than they do already. I don't want any part of it. And I don't want to have to perk myself up if I'm in a bad mood so I don't seem down or bitter or unsuccessful. Better to be here—so long as we don't live on the Upper East Side or in SoHo or Tribeca—and be fucking invisible."

Nigel Gleeson could also, David knew, deploy his strategy because he came by his charm honestly. David didn't have such permeated affability.

"And by the way, David," Nigel asked, "what's the bloody downside of being stubbornly gracious and dressing well?"

As if on cue, a smiling Fred Abelson and a woman David presumed to be his wife appeared before them.

"Fred! You bought our wine! If I'd known, there was a Barolo at twice the price! Don't encourage us!" Nigel exclaimed with a grin David could no longer entirely trust.

"You *should* be encouraged!" exclaimed the nattily dressed agent. "Hello, David! What do we have you in town for?"

"I've been meeting with Jacob Rosenthal."

"Oh, right. Howard Garner was mentioning that. Jacob's tough, but I respect the hell out of him. Everyone does. What's that project again?"

"Coal."

"Yes. It's all coming back. Your adaptation?"

"No. Something Howard brought me."

"Good for him," said the agent. "Anything in it for Nigel?"

"Jesus, Fred! Shameless!" laughed Nigel.

"Doesn't every film have a part for Nigel?" queried David, grinning as he realized Nigel's theory was being proven now quite tangibly right before their eyes, and he was playing the game.

"Well played, David!" said Nigel with a wink.

"Is that the Rex Patterson novel?" asked the woman with Fred.

"It is," said David.

"That's quite a book."

It relieved David to observe that she was in her mid-fifties.

"I'm sorry, David," said Fred, "you've never met my wife, Jane. Jane, David Levit, one of our clients. Acts, writes, and directs."

David rose to shake her hand.

"Nice to meet you."

"Jane is a writer," said Fred. "Not screenplays, but a real writer who tolerates having a movie-business husband. We're spending our first year with no kids in the house, and we were sitting over there rejoicing and weeping simultaneously."

"You probably didn't know this, David," said Nigel, "but Fred is one of the normal ones. Actually stayed married, raised a family with his first and only beautiful wife, who stands there before you, the whole bit."

"You two enjoy yourselves," said Fred, taking Jane's arm. "And the tab will remain open, Nigel, if you want that Barolo."

"I think the expense account is safe, Fred, but thanks. You're a legend. Truly."

"I'll speak with you in the morning. Two projects came in."

"You mean I might not be headed home next month?"

"Not unless you want to!" said the agent. "Take care, David. Good luck with *Coal*. I assume you've been in touch with our below-the-line guys?"

"I will be."

"And let me know if you need any help with casting or the deal or anything."

"I will," said David, knowing Brad Shlansky also to be a client, and wondering if Fred would or even could exert any pressure on Paul Aiello.

"So, I've got to ask," David said to Nigel after the agent and his wife had left. "How long have you actually been here?"

"You ready? In the US, mind you. Going on fourteen months. Was scheduled for three."

"Jesus."

"Started out on a Marvel movie, which was twelve weeks in Atlanta. Then went to North Carolina for a month and a half on a very weird thriller for Screen Gems, then back to Atlanta for an HBO thing, and now here for this one. A bit of time between each."

"And the one here is what?"

"A studio comedy. Playing a mean rich dad to a girl following her heart with a rudderless ne'er-do-well who ends up designing an app that sells for tens of millions, so the dad gets his. Useless fluff, but couldn't say no when they backed up the Brinks truck. Nearly all my scenes shoot on the stage at Paramount, so I don't even have to get on a highway or go over the hill, which is nice. And mostly three-day weeks. Lots of time off to read and chase the Sheilas. Ends in a month, then who knows? There's the bloody virus they say might gum up air travel, but I don't believe a word of it. And anyway, it seems like from what Fred said there'll be another vine to catch hold of. Anything to avoid real life, right!"

David shook his head, incredulous.

"Don't be jealous, mate. Doesn't become you."

"Come to think of it, I'd miss my wife and daughters."

"My kids, yes, I do miss them, but they're obviously grown, so even when I'm in Sydney we mostly speak on the phone. And as for my wives—I had three of those—it's best not to see them. They've taken too much of my money. Tends to breed resentment."

David rose.

"You off, then?"

"I've got an early-morning phone call to New York."

"Sounds ominous."

"Have you ever been sued?"

"Didn't I just say I get along with people? Well, except those wives."

"Good night, Nigel. And thanks for the wine."

"It was Fred's pleasure."

Under the Chateau's use-softened sheets, he shuddered imagining what had been cleaned from them over the years, or from the walls and carpets for that matter. Yet he appreciated the refusal to mask the dingier, more sordid aspects of the hotel's history: Howard Hughes's seclusion, John

Belushi's death, Fitzgerald's heart attack, Nicholas Ray bedding an underage Natalie Wood, the Jean Harlow affair, and more recent tales of overdoses, fifty-thousand-dollar room service bills from twenty-something stars, and every manner of assignation and assault.

He considered the life of Nigel Gleeson, devoid, it seemed, of all the complications that riddled his own: sharp, needy daughters, a talented but tirelessly demanding wife he still loved, his own acting, writing, and directing aspirations and the challenges associated with each. And now the threat of a lawsuit that could stymie it all, including his ability to support his family. Nigel, with his performed charm, could relish the always replenishing reality of an actor going from offer to offer, utterly content with its unassailable and extremely remunerative simplicity. But did he want to be Nigel, thrice divorced, cosseted and solitary inside a life that seemed to resist any sense of home? Surely not. In fact, the very prospect felt unrewarding in its way.

He woke twice in the night, once to piss and another to take aspirin. Each time, a few pages from the James Baldwin essays he'd brought along as research for *Coal*, and he was blissfully out.

"Good morning Mr. Levit, it's seven a.m."

"Thank you," he said into the receiver next to his bed.

He'd missed calls from Sammy and Charlotte on his silenced phone. He rang Sammy first.

"You spoke with Brad Shlansky."

"In the car last night. It was a blocked number."

"You gave them a huge amount of information."

"You've already spoken with Alice?"

"She hyperventilated at me for twenty minutes. I had to give her several breathers. You need to phone Jacob Rosenthal before she does. She's liable to make the guy believe anything."

"Jacob is extremely sharp."

"Don't take any chances. How he responds is going to determine a lot. Call him in an hour. That'll be eight. You have his cell number, I assume."

"I do."

He tried Charlotte, who did not pick up, but as he exited the shower his phone chirped.

"Sorry. I was in a yoga class," she said. "I can't get back to sleep after dropping the girls off. Please tell me you're not delaying your trip home again."

"I'm not."

Though he'd want privacy for his call with Jacob, he needed out of his room. A quadruple espresso in the morning air would keep him keen and alert for what he feared would be a difficult exchange.

Given the early hour, the patio was mostly empty but for a breakfast meeting involving two investors and a too-loud pitchman for what sounded like a film fund in the far corner, and a half dozen single guests scattered haphazardly, staring languidly at phones, a few of them no doubt waiting for others to join. David took a seat in the back to the left near the busboy station and ordered eggs scrambled with jalapeños and spinach along with a side of chicken sausage. He tried to settle himself with a Thomas Fried-man piece in the *New York Times* about the Blue and White Party in Israel but thought only of Adam. Lately news of the virus in China seemed to be nipping at terrorism's heels, but he could always count on at least one op-ed to address the Middle East. Once, he and Adam and Sammy had gone to Film Forum on West Houston to see a Palestinian film set in Ramallah during the second intifada. Afterward they'd stood outside discussing it when nearby three older couples, the two men wearing yarmulkes, stood doing the same.

"It didn't seem interested in the impact of terrorism on Israelis, only the other way around," one of the men said. "Meanwhile, the terrorists are the cause of everything."

"And of course the *New York Times* loved it," said a woman David presumed to be the speaker's wife. "Anything against Israel they love."

"Well, of course," insisted another of the women, "Israel is always in the wrong. Anytime Jews show strength."

"I can't listen to these people." Adam was seething. "They're like a parody."

"Don't say anything," Sammy urged. But Adam had already stepped over.

"Did it ever occur to you that there's a problem with Jews occupying land that no world body recognizes as exclusively theirs?" he asked them.

"Are you Jewish?" responded one of the men.

"Oh God, could you possibly be more predictable?" asked Adam.

"You look Jewish."

"Does it fucking matter?" asked Adam.

"Of course it matters, and I would appreciate your not using that sort of language."

"You seem very angry," offered the other yarmulke wearer.

"Answer my question," demanded Adam.

"No world body recognized the Holocaust when it was happening."

"Did you really just say that?"

"What's wrong with what I said? Don't you want Israel to exist?"

"Of course I do, but not to the extent where we're inhabiting land that wasn't part of the mandate. And what the fuck does that have to do with the Holocaust?"

"So it never happens again!"

"Oh, fuck you! Do you even know what you're saying?! Do you know this is why people hate us? How this makes me embarrassed to even be a Jew associated with lazy fucking thinkers like you? I wish you all would die! Do you hear me? Die! Just fucking die so the rest of us can get on with actually trying to solve the problem!"

"Don't you dare speak to my husband that way!" shrieked one of the women, in tears now as Sammy pulled Adam away.

Over slices on Carmine Street, Adam apologized.

"I'm sorry. I don't know what gets into me."

"Urging them to perish was somewhat extreme, Adam, not to mention the fact that without the Holocaust there probably wouldn't be an Israel," offered Sammy.

"Maybe I need to go there." It was the first time he ever mentioned it, David suddenly remembered. It must have been the moment he decided to go.

A publicist and a client about to experience her first junket took the table next to David's and began loudly vetting a press schedule.

"They were going to pair you with Jillian, but I told them absolutely not. You'd never get a word in, trust me. I used to work with her. And you like Tom, right? I mean, Tom is nice, and people love him. They love him because he's nice. You need to be with someone who's not going to dominate. Jillian dominates. Not Tom. Tom's nice."

"Yeah, Tom's nice."

David couldn't help but wonder if this assessment of Tom were true given the pair's inculcative need to assure each other of it. He checked his watch—7:50—but decided to call Jacob anyway. Leaving his iPad with his half-finished food, he stepped with his espresso to a central area where a careful geometry of outdoor couches stood empty.

"Aren't I seeing you at the office in two hours?" asked Jacob without saying hello.

"I need to discuss something beforehand. Do you have a few minutes?"

"Let me grab my coffee and go out back. My wife's doing the crossword."

David heard the slide of a heavy glass door. He pictured a back patio looking out over Bel Air and Beverly Hills beyond. Perhaps a pool.

"Have you heard about these wildfires, David?" Jacob asked.

"Yeah. It's been all over the news."

"Half of Brentwood is evacuating. I'm staring at a haze like you wouldn't believe."

"There were a lot of people checking in to the hotel yesterday."

"Larry and I had a good time with you last night. It's great to learn more about your life, and the more I know, the more reassured I am. I think you're just the director we need. We should have fun this morning."

"I hope so."

"What's on your mind?"

David chronicled his dealings with Brad Shlansky, concluding with the specific threat to *Coal* and Chicago Films.

"So, they're going for a TRO?"

"What's that?"

"A restraining order. To stop you from directing the movie?"

"I guess that's right."

"Meaning basically they want to be paid off, which I'm not going to do."

"I wasn't asking you to."

"Good."

"And I certainly can't pay. I mean, if that's what they're after, which I'm actually not sure—"

"David. Stop. It's what they're after."

"This guy is different, Jacob. He's a little off. He's had some success out here, but I'm not sure Hollywood has treated him so well."

"You say he doesn't have a cast?"

"Correct."

"With all due respect, you're not a director who can get a period movie about West Virginia hillbillies financed without a cast, or you wouldn't be involved with this asshole. Hell, you probably wouldn't be involved with me if you had that kind of power."

"That's actually not true."

"This Alice woman is going to call me this morning you said?"

"Yeah."

"Well, I'll whack her across the head with a two-by-four and see what happens."

"May I ask what that means?"

"It's what you do with low-life bullies like this guy and his lawyer. Hopefully they'll call before you get to the office and we'll have a sense of what's what."

"I'm sorry about this, Jacob."

"You know how you know you're successful in America? Some loser says he's going to sue you. And that goes double in the movies. That doesn't mean this isn't going to be a problem, but you have no reason to apologize yet, except maybe you signed a contract you shouldn't have."

In spite of all he'd endured from Jacob by way of insult and humiliation, had they been sitting opposite each other David would have thrown his arms around the old man in a fit of despondent gratitude.

AUSTIN

P aul Aiello had recently calculated having spoken to Brad Shlansky on average half a dozen times a day for the decade Brad and his sisters had been in Los Angeles, meaning easily ten thousand phone calls. In the last several months none had been pleasant.

"You're going to walk down to Howard Garner's office, and you're going to tell him to tell his client he will lose representation at UCM. That the agency is dumping him."

"David Levit has been with UCM forever, Brad. Way before you or even I got here."

"I want you to look up his earnings from last year."

"We established fifty calls ago he's not a big earner. Hell, I told you that years ago. But by the way, buddy, neither are you lately."

"I bought a comic book company you still fucking represent thanks to me. How about what you've made off me as a result of that?"

"For the last time, you didn't *buy* the company, no matter how much polish you put on that coin."

"Don't ever say that to me again."

"I was at the dinner. I fucking arranged it. I found the company. Stop saying you bought it or that it was ever even partly yours, or I'm going to start hanging up on you."

Two years earlier Paul had accompanied a young woman to Austin, Texas, with whom he'd started a dalliance after she helped him select T-shirts at the boutique where she worked. He preferred the simple cotton variety, but with hip conversation-starter images for working out at a gym down the hill on Sunset that was popular with actresses. He'd stayed over the previous night with the hostess from a restaurant in Culver City called Swallowtail, and after leaving her apartment on North Curson decided to take a morning stroll down Melrose before heading home. At least three T-shirts in the window interested him: one with Slim Pickens astride the atomic bomb, another of Captain Kirk in his mustard top speaking into his communicator, and finally a white vintage Clinton/Gore from 1992.

"Hi, I'm Grace. Is there something I can help you with?"

He noticed her tattoos immediately but not optimistically. Generally, a preponderance of ink inhibited appearing in front of the camera, meaning dangling the prospect of representation was unlikely to interest her. She was lean and strong, a tautness visible across her back and shoulders under the gray tank top she wore. She chided him easily when he shared a preference for garments that wouldn't fit too loosely.

"You think that's what the ladies want?"

"How do you know I like ladies?"

"It's pretty obvious."

"I guess I should take that as a compliment. Nothing against gays, but a guy wants to be known for what he is, right?"

"I guess."

"Obviously you're not an actress, though I'm not going to lie, lose the tattoos and you could be."

"I'm a first AC."

"You go to film school?"

"Fuck that."

"Completely agree. Total racket. Learn by doing. That's what most of the greats did. So, do you want to shoot someday?"

"Yep."

"I bet you're very good."

"What makes you think that?"

"I'm paid to be right about this sort of thing. I'm with UCM. We do below-the-line, by the way."

She knew the sous chef at a restaurant in Venice called Merguez that specialized in Moroccan fare with a street-food bent. None of the chairs or tables matched, and the walls were covered with graffiti, some in English, some in French, some in Arabic. Other than one older couple who'd surely read a review, the clientele reflected his date's penchant for body art and piercings. She surprised him at the end of dinner by inviting him to her apartment nearby to stay over.

"Did you really just ask me that?"

"I don't like ambiguity. Besides, I have some really good weed."

To his surprise, even as they began to see each other with some regularity, he could not interest her in representation.

"You're below-the-line talent. I wouldn't even be involved."

"If it's going to happen, it'll happen, but not because I fuck an agent. That would be a little disgusting, don't you think?"

"I'm not sure how to take that."

"Plus, I only work on stuff that interests me, and where I can operate, which they'd never let me do on the sorts of films you're talking about."

"You mean films people see?"

"Aren't you a little young to be such a fucking reactionary, Paul?"

He was beginning to like her. He couldn't help himself. He'd even stopped dishing out his card, if only because most free evenings he found himself at one of their places. She invited him to Austin to see a friend's band.

"I'll go, but I'm going to expense it and we'll stay at the Four Seasons like the fascist I am. I'm thirty-four. I don't stay on friends' sofas anymore."

"You don't have to persuade me. I fucking love hotels. The nicer the better."

The weekend ended up a disaster but for the party they attended the first night after the show. The house was near Lady Bird Lake and not far from South Congress Books, or so she told him, her tone implying he should care.

"So, what, we should go browse fiction in the morning with our cappuccinos and fucking scones?" he asked.

"Jesus, man, you've been acting like a complete dick all night. What is it with you?"

"I didn't like the music, I hated Sixth Street, and I can't relate to your friends."

"At least you're being honest. I don't like some of them either. But it started when we were at the airport. It's the agency thing, isn't it?"

"I'm just saying meet with the team."

"I don't want to, and I don't fucking need to. And I mean seriously, Paul, look at me. It makes no sense."

"How the fuck do you know?"

"It's the commoditization of everything I love."

"It's what I do all day. Am I just fucking repulsive to you or what?"

"Obviously not."

"Or the fucking hotel with the view of the river and the nice sheets that practically gave you an orgasm earlier that my agency paid for?"

"The hotel was your fucking idea! What's this really about?"

"Me wanting to give you a leg up."

"Did it ever occur to you that this isn't transactional?"

"What the fuck is that supposed to mean?"

"You obviously think I'll only keep fucking you if there's career advancement in it for me, which by the way is a pretty pathetic way to think about yourself."

"Oh bullshit."

"It's what you fucking led with when we met. You couldn't get your lame-ass UCM card out fast enough."

"I got news for you. If there's one thing that's true in life, it's that everything has a price."

"Which basically means you think I'm a whore."

"You said it, not me."

They didn't speak for the entire party, other than her informing him she'd stay the weekend on a friend's sofa and pay for her own ticket home on a separate flight. She asked that he pack her suitcase and leave it in the hotel lobby for her to collect the following day.

"So, what the fuck am I supposed to do here now?" he asked, wondering how, yet again, he'd managed to sabotage something healthy and good.

"Hand out your card. I hear the staff at South Congress Books are hot. Doesn't UCM have a literary side?"

Abandoned and unaffiliated, he'd commandeered an opener and a six-pack of Shiner from the kitchen and found a seat on the living room sofa. The house, a small late-forties ranch, was strewn haphazardly with mismatched vintage furniture on floorboards that creaked audibly, even with the Decemberists blasting. Christmas lights framed a picture window overlooking a fenced-in yard where partygoers languished on lawn furniture.

Halfway through his third bottle, two guys in their late twenties dressed nearly identically in trucker's caps and worn plaid button-downs left open over what looked to be concert shirts stood over him.

"These free?" one asked, referring to a chair to Paul's left and the loveseat adjacent.

"As of about ten seconds ago. I thought I was being pretty charming, but the two young ladies begged to differ."

"Well, our luck. We tend to find a place at these parties and park it, so you'll have to be pretty fucking offensive to get us to leave."

"I'd offer you both a beer, but it looks like you brought your own. What is that?"

Each was bearded, the heavier of the two more so, as if they'd organized a correlation between girth and amplitude of facial hair.

"Well, I'm a porter guy, and this is Lobo Midnight." He presented a darkly opaque bottle with a label of blue and black with white lettering on which a wolf dressed in a suit and tie stood holding a filled goblet.

"I'm Eitan, by the way." He switched his bottle to his left hand to offer his right. Paul shook it, the clutch confident and coldly damp.

"And what do you have?" asked Paul of the sparser beard, adding, "I seriously feel like a pedestrian here with my Shiner, which is probably to you guys what Fosters is to the Australians."

"I'm Reggie, and yeah, almost. Shiner's is pretty rancid except for their bock, but remember where you are. Plus, me and Eitan are beer snobs even for here. We're pretty ridiculous." With that he presented his six-pack. "This is an IPA I like called Jabberwocky. It's brewed in Magnolia."

"Fuckin' nerds is what we are!" Eitan added with a chuckle.

"What do you guys do?"

"We have a comic book company."

"Are you fucking serious?"

"Why, are you into comics?"

"Well, kind of, these days. I have to be. I'm in the movie business. Not many dramas in theaters lately."

"The movie business? In Austin?"

"Los Angeles. I came out here with a woman who's in the other room right now not speaking to me."

"This isn't your night, dude."

"Until now. What kind of stuff do you publish?"

"You're going to love this coming from where you do," said Eitan. "Everything but the superhero shit. We're cultier. More underground. You ever read *Watchmen*?"

"Saw the movie but didn't read it."

"So that—the original graphic novel—to us is the high-water mark of what a comic can be. Except for one character, there are really no superpowers."

"Or *Batman*. We love Batman," added Reggie. "Because he's a deeply fucked-up, vengeful guy, not some idiot in a cape—"

"Well, he does have a cape—" said Reggie.

"But he's not an *idiot* in a cape who's half spider or turns into a green anger thug when he's pissed or can fly into space or some shit."

"Basically," Eitan said, "we're a couple of misanthropes, and our comics are about deeply troubled people. Vigilantes and spies, and assassins, and secret agents who are either psychopathic or really depressed."

"So, who says there isn't a place for that in Hollywood?" asked Paul. "I mean if your stuff is good and popular, which I have to imagine it is, given the expensive beer."

"Some of our stuff definitely has a following," said Reggie.

"So, like in the Austin area or nationwide?" asked Paul.

"Some of it worldwide."

"And no one has approached you about adaptations?"

"We've been flown out three times by different studios, and it just felt like bullshit. I mean, there was one option that kept getting picked up, but it amounted to nothing, and it paralyzed the writer. All he did was call about whether the movie was gonna get made. He couldn't think about anything else."

"That's Los Angeles," said Paul.

"It wasn't for us. We kind of like minding our own business."

"Do you even have representation there?"

"You mean like an agent?" asked Reggie.

"We have to deal with agents all the time," said Eitan. "Why would we inflict that on someone else?"

"So that your trips to Los Angeles wouldn't be a waste of time anymore but actually enormously, obscenely fucking profitable for you and your writers."

"I take it you're an agent?" asked Reggie.

"I am. With United Creative Management."

"I've actually heard of them," said Eitan.

"We represent a lot of the producers and directors of those superhero movies you hate," Paul offered with tactical honesty. "Look, I'm going to make this easy for you. I want you to send me—what would be a good number?—six of your favorite titles. I don't even give a shit if you think they'd make good movies. Just for a sense of what you guys like—what kind of material you're drawn to. If I like them, I'm gonna have UCM fly you out and put you up. The worst that would come of it is a free weekend to try out the brewpubs in LA."

On Tuesday via FedEx he received not six but a dozen comics, all printed on paper a grade above newsprint. As advertised, the subject matter veered toward destructively high-stakes and often macabre human interaction, rather than the use of special powers. Several titles caught his eye. The first, called *Hellish*, chronicled the escapades of a scantily clad large-breasted vigilante who'd been sold into slavery as a child after watching her mother get killed. She now traveled from town to town across Texas in search of injustices to rectify, always with a violence twistedly out of proportion with what feckless legal authorities might have meted out. Happily for both her recruits and readers, she satisfied ravenous sexual appetites as well, with both men and women, doling out one-night-stands even more generously than her rough justice.

"I got a fucking hard-on just reading it," Paul exclaimed to Brad on the phone. "Seriously, I almost went into the bathroom and jacked off. I would've if it weren't for all the assistants and their headsets."

Another, titled *Berlin Girl* and also featuring a female protagonist, was set in the Second World War and told of an Allied spy who used sex to infiltrate the shadowy world of the Third Reich's high command. Like her counterpart in *Hellish*, she too spread the sex around, but more for subterfuge than enjoyment. Her murders were precise and quick, proving herself more of a surgeon than a brawler.

His favorite, however, concerned a private investigator in Houston whose alcoholism and cocaine addiction both interfered with and inspired his work for clients, who were mostly women. He was an unmarried loner, meaning plenty of nookie with every type of partner. Eitan and Reggie did seem to understand what sold, no matter the protagonist's gender.

"Seriously, these guys must spank it ten times a day. There's sex on every other page of these fucking things," he told Brad.

By Thursday afternoon Eitan and Reggie were in Paul's office.

"You guys don't know it, but you're sitting on a gold mine, and I'm gonna make it so you don't have to do a goddamn thing but count money if that's how you want it. In other words, you can be as involved in the film-industry *commodification*"—he'd been using the word with profligate vengeance since Grace had impaled him with it in Austin—"of your product as you want. The key is to get you a guy on the ground in LA—not me, but an actual full-time producer—who can connect the material to actors and production companies and studios. In other words, who can go around and flog it without you guys having to think about anything but putting out your books."

"Okay, but what's this guy you're talking about going to want out of it? And, I mean, can we meet him?" asked Eitan.

"Jesus! You have to meet him! You need to love him, otherwise this doesn't work! The guy I have in mind, who I've known since we were kids collecting coins on Long Island, isn't gonna want much, other than a piece of the films and obviously getting to produce whatever gets set up. The studio pays his fee, not you guys. And the beauty of this of course would be that it would all be in-house. You'd be my clients, he's my client, we'd cast the projects with UCM actors who are the types of stars the studios have hardons for. This *Hellish* comic, for starters—I can think of three actresses off the top of my head who'd kill to play that part. My clients. I have the best list of actresses in the business, and you can ask anyone that. You can fucking look it up."

"We did."

"What I'm talking about is very different than what you described happened to you last time. I'm a fucking doer, not a talker."

"What's their company called?" Brad asked.

"Lone Star Pulp. This is gonna be fucking huge. This is the big fish we've been after, Brad. Your troubles are over."

The four met for dinner that night at Mastro's on Canon Drive in Beverly Hills.

"You're not going to believe the steak here," Paul announced as they took menus. "I know, you're thinking, we're from Texas, but trust me. And don't fucking think of ordering anything but the strip or the ribeye. It comes on a fucking two-hundred-degree plate. The steak is practically still sizzling while you cut into it."

"You two like wine?" asked Brad.

"They're serious beer guys," said Paul. "Like you with the vino. Connoisseurs. Although I still can't believe you became a fucking wine expert. Seriously." He laughed, turning back to Reggie and Eitan. "I know where this asshole grew up. Not exactly a region of high culture even if you lived on the fanciest street in town like he did and went to the snooty private school."

"You mean the one you got kicked out of?" asked Brad.

"Let's not dredge up the past," said Paul.

"Fine by me."

"You guys went to school together too?" asked Reggie.

"For a time," said Brad. "Until Mr. 'I'm not fancy' got booted for reasons I won't divulge. And while we're at it, he got to go off to college while I had to stay home and take care of my family, so don't be fooled by the woe-is-me routine."

Paul knew he'd offended, but sometimes he couldn't help himself. Yes, unlike Brad he'd attended college, but a state school he'd mostly paid for himself by working days in the cafeteria and admissions office and nights bartending. Had Paul's tyrannical father perished like Brad's, he'd have counted it a blessing.

"But when you grew up where we did," Paul said, hoping to mollify, "and the way we did, the bonds are pretty tight. There's no one, and I mean no one, I trust more than this guy sitting next to me. But fuck that. We're here to learn about you two."

"Yeah," said Brad. "I mean, I've spent ten hours straight with your comics, and I could spend twenty more. You guys are fucking insane."

"Thanks," responded Reggie.

"I'm serious. This stuff is genius," Brad continued. "You're putting out stuff for people buying comics *now*, the way Stan fucking Lee was writing for kids buying comics in his time, and that's the kind of company I want to produce for. Not the movies of today, but the movies of tomorrow."

Paul listened astonished. The penultimate sentiment alone, with its implication of sufficient options that Brad could cater to preferences, represented mendacity as unashamedly dispatched as any he'd encountered during his dozen years in Hollywood.

"My point is," Brad continued, "that you guys are why I picked up and came out here, which, by the way, was not easy. Me and my sisters drove across the country with barely enough money for gas. You can ask Paul. We literally wrote a script on the way out, and within less than two years, thanks in part to Paul, we had it sold and shot. Then we made *Revenge*. Have you seen it?"

"We have. It was amazing," said Reggie.

"I studied that play in English lit in college," added Eitan.

"Well, that was us too," said Brad.

"He's right," Paul said. "Brad made *Revenge* happen. It wouldn't have even been released without him. The Golds were going to shelve it. David Levit, the director, gets all the credit, but without Brad here not only raising the money but negotiating a great contract and then forcing the Golds to honor it while David Levit was quaking in his fucking boots, the movie never would have seen the light of day after Elysian. Which isn't even to mention all the script notes. I don't even want to get started on those."

"Not to take anything away from David," said Brad by way of assurance. "But I look at producing as a complete, hands-on fucking job. I don't show up and sit there texting. I make the movie. Like Paul said, I work on the script until it's right. I'm there for all of preproduction. On set I'm the first one arriving in the morning and the last to leave."

"After the fucking grips."

"The grips work harder than anyone."

"We love the grips," Paul confirmed.

"And I'm in on casting, budgeting, and picking crew," continued Brad. "Then the editing. All of it. My job will be to make sure nobody fucks up your comics, because you guys are the ones who originated the material."

"Well, not us to be clear, but the writers and artists who actually wrote them," corrected Eitan.

"Sure, but you know what I'm saying."

"We do," volunteered Reggie.

"But before any of that, I'm going to be in and out of the studios on your behalf. With Paul's help I'm gonna leverage the relationships me and him have made all over town. And you guys are going to be my top priority."

"*Our* top priority," Paul corrected. "Any star worth anything at UCM is going to know about your comics. Me and Brad are going to get them attached to properties so that when he walks into a studio it's with an A-list package."

"Trust him when he says that," said Brad. "But it's even better, because not just UCM. Me and Paul have relationships everywhere, so the other big agencies too. With the actors we can attach, you're going to be swimming in offers."

"But what does that mean exactly—offers?" asked Reggie. "Because we had that the last time."

"You want to take this one, Paul?" asked Brad, projecting amicable patience so the novitiates might be brought up to speed.

"Sure," said Paul. "A studio meets with Brad. You guys aren't even there. You're down in Texas doing what you do best, which is to run your fucking amazing company finding and publishing the most interesting comics around so you can drink your craft beer at night."

"Go on," said Eitan.

"Cut all the Hollywood bullshit, I get it," said Paul. "So, a studio meets with Brad, and he's brought in not only *Berlin Girl* but my client Claire Fisher to play the lead."

"*Catwoman* Claire Fisher?" asked Reggie.

"I've been practically her only agent. One of my first clients."

"I mean, we saw her on your list—"

"Oh, trust me, she'll flip for *Berlin Girl*, only I haven't sent it to her because I have fucking scruples and don't want to get ahead of myself. Another agent would have given it to her already to dangle her in front of you tonight. Wouldn't be good for her or you. That's not me."

"That's not Paul," confirmed Brad. "I know this guy a long time, and he's what he says he is, which is rare in this business."

"Enough, Brad!"

"Sorry. They should know."

"We're selling ourselves hard because we love your comics. So, the studio listens to the pitch, which at this point is just a concept, meaning your comic as a film: sexy, badass Allied spy fucking and killing her way through Nazi Berlin played by one of the biggest stars on the planet. The second Brad leaves, the studio calls me with a hard-on, because seriously, Claire Fisher in that role? With a German accent? And I tell them we're at three other studios simultaneously, but we want to make it with them, which by the way is what I'm saying to all *four* of the studios—"

"Hey," interjected Brad. "I just said you had scruples!"

"Not when it comes to getting my clients what they deserve, prick!" Everyone laughed. "And we get a bidding war going, and it's so fucking insane, even you guys who don't give a shit about any of this—which is why I fucking love you—don't know what to do with yourselves. Finally, I call and say Warner Brothers has optioned the property for a hundred and fifty thousand dollars against a million three."

"Meaning?"

"Meaning a hundred and fifty thousand dollars to own the underlying rights for a year and a half, and if they make the film, you and your writers get another million-one-fifty."

"Okay," said Reggie.

"We get a great screenwriter on, a director, designers to help come up with concept, and pretty soon it's a project with a script, a cast, and a team ready to go."

"And with Claire Fisher attached, you think they aren't gonna green-light that movie?" asked Brad, taking over the narrative. "I'll be telling them to fucking calm down, which is what I mean by the way when I say it's my job not to let them fuck it up. In other words, spending the time to get the script right and the look right before a frame of it is shot. The thing about the studios is they don't fucking care. They just want product. I'm here to make sure the picture actually works and has some fucking integrity."

Again, Paul had to marvel. The idea of Brad, so broke he was on the verge of returning to Woodmere, exercising any meaningful influence over a studio's choice as to who would direct a wide-release film, or who would design, shoot, or act in it, struck him as so ridiculous, he wanted to howl. And yet precisely because of that audacity, he also understood that his friend had every chance to become just the sort of producer he now so desperately aped. The story seemed to tell itself over and over in Los Angeles. Hyperaggressive, unfathomably ambitious, and natively intelligent young men, and sometimes women, came west unencumbered by conscience or morals and seemed to will themselves into the very status they pretended early on to have but manifestly didn't. Those derided one day ran successful companies the next. And this was why, when Brad had called to say he was considering moving to Los Angeles to begin anew after the death of his parents, Paul had done all he could to encourage it.

"If I can give you one piece of advice out here," he instructed just days after Brad's arrival, "it's that yes, it's important to get along. You have to, in fact, so people will keep hiring you, working with you. But more important than anything, if you want to *do* the hiring, is not just to make people like you but to make people want to *be* you. In fact that's more important. And it starts with playing the part. You figure that out, your fucking coin collection will be nothing compared to what you'll do out here."

By the time the rib eyes were consumed from plates that burned to the touch as advertised, it had become clear two deals would occur, so long as Brad and Paul prevented Eitan and Reggie from seeking representation elsewhere: one with UCM and the other with Same Day Films.

"You guys are making a smart decision," Brad said, raising a glass of Sauternes after three bottles of 2008 Chateau-Figeac had been drained to the tannins, all charged, along with the steaks and profiteroles, to Paul's perpetually overdrawn UCM expense account. "I'm just a poor schmuck who came out here from Long Island and got lucky. Somehow, I can now drive onto any studio lot. Go figure that one out. But this guy"—he pointed to Paul—"this guy is as good an agent as you're ever going to meet. He'll fucking take a samurai sword to the jugular of anyone who fucks with his clients. You think I'm joking."

"No, we saw the sword this morning," Eitan said.

"He makes millions of dollars for people. Millions. He fucking gets it done. Your heads are going to be spinning, you'll be so tired of success."

"All right, Brad," Paul cut in. "You can shut up now, or nothing I do is going to surprise them. Give me some room to exceed expectations!"

Ten minutes later, Brad called his sisters from Paul's car.

"You guys are on speaker. We just bought a comic book company."

The description startled Paul, but not as much as it did Sarah.

"What the fuck is that supposed to mean, you bought a comic book company?" she asked. "I thought you were meeting to talk about producing. And how can you buy something when you don't have any money?"

"We're getting a piece of the company, if you'd shut up and listen. As a part of the deal. It was Alice's idea. And by the way, you're fucking welcome, Sarah."

"Are these guys dumbshits?" she asked. "Paul, are these guys dumbshits?"

"I don't think they are, Sarah." He couldn't get enough of the bickering that went on between Brad and his younger sister.

"And what the fuck do we know about producing comic book movies?" she asked.

"You know what, Sarah? Keep underestimating me. And by the way, thanks for reminding me why you weren't invited to dinner. Because if you ever want to back out of this company, be my fucking guest."

"That's not happening, asshole. I'm still waiting for my cut of the coin collection."

"You and Emily effectively got a third each, if you don't remember. But if you want that reduced to the two percent I gave you when you were ten, you can give me back the thirty-one I overpaid." She didn't answer. "Yeah, I didn't think so. Be at the office early tomorrow so we can all be on with Alice."

When detailed the following day, the deal made more sense to Sarah. Same Day Films would indeed take a stake in Lone Star Pulp, but only 7 percent, and solely for the duration of the partnership, at the termination of which the percentage would revert fully, free and clear, to Reggie and Eitan, as no purchase cost had applied. What Brad was representing as outright ownership, with the implication that Lone Star Pulp was now Same Day's and Same Day's alone, was, to say the least, highly provisional.

"I'm not objecting on moral grounds," Paul cautioned. "It's just, what're folks gonna say when they find out it's bullshit?"

"How is it bullshit?"

"You didn't 'buy' a comic book company, Brad."

"In terms of movie deals, it's my company. I control all the properties. And I did buy it, I just didn't pay any money."

"All the other bending of truth aside, that one you're going to have to explain. If not money, what changed hands for the less than ten percent of it?"

"I'm paying with my fucking time and my sweat. And do me a favor, dickweed, instead of analyzing my every move, why don't you actually start setting up the actor and studio meetings you promised. We need one of these deals to work. There's no money coming in. We can't keep our lights on."

"Forgive me for getting you access to more than fifty titles of IP. And I told you to save some of the money from *Revenge* and the Golds, and not to try and do that piece of shit *White Pill*."

"There's three of us over here, plus an assistant. Get me my meetings."

"You don't think I want one of these titles to work more than you? I've got this."

Paul set about inundating UCM's most significant clients with Lone Star Pulp titles. The strategy began with a visit to the lead agent for each star.

"I've got a great property for Johnny Ryan," he told Janet Liebowitz from her doorway.

"You do know he's booked for the next twenty months?"

"Gee, Janet, you sound like you're doing me a favor by considering an offer."

"And he doesn't have time to read."

"It's not a script, it's a comic."

"Oh my God. Brad Shlansky's lame-ass company. Johnny is working. He doesn't read when he's working."

"He can look at it between setups. Trust me, he's gonna like it."

"Just send it over so I don't have to listen to you any longer."

"He likes it," she said on the phone a month later. "But he gets a producer credit."

"Fine."

"And script approval, director approval, and costar approval."

"Done."

"Don't you have to ask lame-ass Brad Shlansky?"

"Brad knows how the game works."

"I'm also gonna need to know where you and lame-ass are taking it."

"Please don't call him that."

"Tell that to Charlie Gold. I don't want any foreign-sales bottom feeders on my phone sheet. Just the major studios. That's it. If Yariv Bergman calls me, I'm going to walk down the hall and burn your office down."

"He's not gonna be on a backlot in Bulgaria."

"If a studio is making it, I don't care where the fuck he is, and neither will Johnny if they pay his quote and a big fat producer fee and give him the approvals I said. It'll be you and Brad Shlansky's faces it blows up in if you don't abide by what I said, and to the fucking letter. I'm putting it in an e-mail just so it's clear."

With Johnny Ryan attached to *Dagger*, a dystopian thriller set in an unnamed future metropolis where marauders swept neighborhoods in search of organs to harvest, Paul gained meetings for Brad at every studio. What neither he nor Brad had considered, however, was that these same executives were awash in titles from every mainstream and cult imprint in the world. The attachment of stars did set Brad somewhat apart, as the majority of competing producers were counting on their material alone, but the bidding wars they'd predicted didn't materialize. Nevertheless, deals were made, and within five months Brad was volunteering that he "had a dozen projects set up at the studios."

"I keep telling you," warned Paul, "you've got to calm it down."

"Please explain to me how that applies here."

"It's a very loose use of the term 'set up.'"

"How the fuck would you put it? They've hired screenwriters and concept artists and directors they're paying development fees, and they've bought the options."

"Let's just say I don't think Johnny Ryan and all of our other clients are clearing their schedules yet. It's all good, just don't get ahead of yourself."

"And why is none of this fucking money coming to us?"

"You've got to make the movies, Brad."

"I'm doing all the fucking legwork, and the option fees are being sent to Austin—after you take your ten percent of course. Or to these screenwriters getting paid five hundred grand a pop to fucking transcribe comics, with you again taking ten percent. Me and my sisters could transcribe comics."

"I'll suggest it to the studios."

"Where's our fucking money?"

"One of these titles will get made. That's all you need. You'll pick up a big fee, which'll lead to bigger fees one after another, and you'll be thanking me instead of yelling at me."

Such interactions increased in number and intensity as months passed and Brad suffered more and more the realities of what the industry called "development," whereby projects that seemed inevitable languished in script form while more immediate priorities superseded them. He read the trades so voraciously that Paul wondered how he had time to do anything else.

"Everyone's getting their movies made except us," Brad complained. "I want to hurt somebody, I'm so fucking pissed."

"If people get a whiff of this insanity, they're not going to trust you to make anything."

"Let them try and not let me make the fucking movies I own. I'll have Alice on them so fast they're not going to know what hit them. Because at this point, I don't fucking care."

"Alice on them for what?"

"Breach, asshole. They sat in their fucking studio offices—I can think of five or six of them—and said they were making these movies."

"Who?"

"The fucking executives. Sarah sitting right beside me."

"Executives can't green-light movies, Brad. Only the studio head can."

"They said we were moving forward. Shook my hand and said it, then started writing checks to everyone but me."

"Just stop it."

"We need that goddamn overhead deal you were talking about then, because otherwise I'm gonna be doing this from Sarah and Emily's living room, and how's that gonna look?"

"Fine, but that's not necessarily in the interest of Lone Star Pulp."

"Why's it bad for Lone Star?"

"Because, dickweed, it means whatever studio gives you offices owns first rights on everything Reggie and Eitan have and everything you have. It's going to be an all-in deal and therefore no leverage for negotiation if it's a really good property. All the price corridors will be preset."

"Can't the deal just be for Same Day Films and leave Lone Star out of it?"

"So they can own fucking *White Pill*? Or what is that script you just sent over? *Hillbilly Winter*?

"*Appalachian Winter*, and laugh now."

"I know. You and David Levit already have tuxedoes fitted for your night at the Dolby Theater. The only real value Same Day has is Lone Star Pulp's IP. And another thing. The office is going to be against your fees and the properties, and trust me, they will ream you on the overhead, and then if you ever leave, or if they don't renew your deal, that overhead will still get booked against the IP, no matter where you make the movies. Nothing's for free, particularly not space on a lot."

"Just make us a goddamn deal. You work for me, not Lone Star Pulp."

"Technically not true."

"You work for me first. Make us a fucking deal. We're strangling."

Against Paul's advice, Brad and his sisters took first-floor offices at Sony and once again hired an assistant, all costs deferred to future earnings. The studio now effectively owned every title not already spoken for, but still none advanced beyond development. As Brad described it, Sarah burned through their expense account on breakfasts, lunches, dinners, and drinks with creatives. Emily kept the kitchen stocked, did crosswords, and scanned dating sites to little avail, a source of deep frustration to her given the fact that Sarah seemed to be consorting with every interested twenty-something male in Hollywood. Between phone calls to Paul and Alice, Brad waited for scripts to come in on which the studio would then give notes, causing further attenuation, not to mention commissionable step fees for UCM writers. Even their most promising title, *Dagger* with Johnny Ryan, couldn't find its way. When the screenplay finally satisfied the studio, the star had taken two films that would have him unavailable for as many years. It didn't help when Brad read that Universal was developing its own dystopian thriller with organ theft as an animating story point.

"You're not suing Johnny Ryan, Brad," said Paul wearily.

"I've spent hundreds of hours and hundreds of thousands of dollars based on his word, and now he's suddenly unavailable?"

"Hundreds of hours? Please. And the studio spent that money, not you. His word is subject to his availability, as was always made clear. Plus, if you remember, he's a producer on the film with a say as to when, where, and how it's made. Take special note of that word *when*. Why do you think Janet Liebowitz got him the title, and his lawyers negotiated the stipulations that go with it? Alice isn't the only clever fucking lawyer around. You made Johnny your partner for better or worse, which, by the way, is a good thing because without him and the other stars attached to these comics you don't have a studio deal and your nice little office. Plus, you sue one actor, and no other actor will come near you. It'll make the shit Charlie Gold is spreading about you—which has not stopped by the way—seem like nothing. At least people secretly hate Charlie. Actors are different."

Ten months after Same Day moved into their offices, the executive in charge of the Lone Star catalogue was fired for suggestive e-mails sent to female colleagues, his remit handed over to a far less enthusiastic, one might even say avowedly uninterested replacement.

"This girl doesn't even like comics!"

"Don't call her a girl, Brad. You've got to be careful. Everything is changing."

"She's younger than Sarah."

"She must have impressed someone over there."

"I wonder how."

"That studio is run by a woman."

"Yeah?"

"Brad, I'm not continuing with this conversation."

"I want a different executive."

"She's the only one who would take you guys."

"Are you fucking kidding me?"

"And only because she's from Texas and liked the name. Let's just say that unless you can somehow convince her you have a movie the studio might actually do, your days there are numbered. Enjoy the offices while they last, and don't buy any furniture you won't be able to take with you."

Brad and his sisters decamped with over $2 million against Lone Star properties and another $150,000 of overhead booked to Same Day Films spread out over those projects—meaning they were substantially in debt against their most valuable IP without a movie to show for it. Considering that the pretentious and unfinanceable *Appalachian Winter* also didn't get made, costing Brad tens of thousands, and that now David Levit would skate on from that embarrassment and direct for Chicago Films without even the courtesy of a phone call to Brad, Paul certainly understood why Brad would focus his rage on the one figure he could actually harm.

"You're going to do exactly what I say!" Brad shouted into the interior of Paul's car.

"I've got a lot of other shit I'm dealing with right now, Brad."

"I want David Levit, his boolah-boolah lawyer, you, and Howard Garner in a conference room at UCM on Friday."

"What is this, a fucking shakedown?"

"It's whatever I want it to be. Friday morning."

"I'm getting off the phone now."

Paul left his car underground with the valet, then ascended thirty-two floors in an elevator of pink Italian marble to the Century City offices of Martin Lasher, the attorney he'd retained the previous afternoon. They met in a conference room with a view over Santa Monica to the ocean. The day was clear, and he could just make out Catalina Island, suspended in an azure haze.

"Sorry I'm late. On the phone."

"No worries," answered Martin, handsome and in his sixties, dressed crisply in a navy Valentino suit. "I hope a good call."

"Someone I've done nothing but favors for who only brings me grief."

"Well, now you're here. So, I've spoken with the police, and I've spoken with lawyers for both of the women." Martin's face relaxed within its moisturized creases into a practiced and friendly neutrality. "One you're going to be fine with. It looks like money and some other doable demands will make her go away. But Ms. Painter is quite eager to cause problems."

"Meaning what exactly?"

"When I talk about a settlement, I get nowhere."

"Does she really think she can claim what we did wasn't consensual? The last people to leave saw her smoking weed and drinking and probably doing blow for all I know earlier in the night. She was still on my couch, half plastered, after one in the morning."

"She had a blood test done and found traces of a sedative."

"So the fuck what? Does that mean I gave it to her? How would I even do that? And can she prove it? Can anyone?"

"If they subpoena the other woman who will claim the same thing?"

"Did Janine have a fucking blood test?"

"Not that I know of."

"So, they took them together if that happens. Or it was someone else. They're lying, Marty. Lying. They obviously woke up in the morning, found themselves in my bed together, regretted what they'd done, and decided to come after me. Concocted the whole fucking thing. I'm no saint, but those two stayed over at my house and did what they did very willingly. One of them I'd slept with before."

"She would admit to that?"

"Janine? Yes. And others would corroborate. My friend Brad Shlansky, who I told at the time, for starters."

"And she continued being represented by you?"

"Very much to her benefit."

"That's useful."

"And let them say they didn't go at it with each other too. Which, and Susan knows this, I have photographs on my phone by the way."

"You took photographs?"

"What? Now you don't want to represent me?"

"I didn't say that."

"So fucking tell the lawyer that, yes, I have pictures of their willing participation, if Susan hasn't told her already. And that I'm going to let that shit out if they fucking push this. See what their careers look like then when they're online."

"Don't go there, Paul."

"I'm fighting for my life here."

"I won't be a party to it. And per her lawyer, Ms. Painter no longer wants a career."

"Well, she should think that through, because this is about a lot more. Wherever she goes, all anyone will have to do is type her name in on the

Internet and this story will come up. How she was in a fucking threesome on booze and weed and God knows what else. What did you say was in her blood? A fucking sedative? I will not let my livelihood be destroyed by an actress—an actress by the way I've worked my ass off for—just because she feels a little guilty for fucking her agent with another girl in the bed."

"I'm sure she's already aware of that, Paul. But listen to me, if you get the two of them saying you slipped them drugs, and corroborating each other, your situation changes completely, and to the DA it's no longer just one person's word against another's. And if Ms. Rouhani hasn't been tested, I've got to find out what was in Ms. Painter's blood and learn when traces of it can no longer be detected."

"But Janine is saying she'll settle?"

"Yes. And I know her lawyer. Patricia Murray. Comes off very white-shoe, but she's as tough as they come. Here." He passed over a list of five names on a sheet of paper. Paul recognized each immediately.

"What the fuck is this?"

"In addition to the money settlement—"

"Which you haven't said the number."

"I'm getting to that. Ms. Rouhani, who it seems *does* still want a career, would like to continue to be represented at your agency but not by you or any of your male colleagues. She wants you to pass her off to one of the women on that list with whom she would then meet for assurance as to level of enthusiasm."

"Oh, fuck me."

"Can the attorney tell her client this is something you're prepared to arrange?"

Paul gazed at the names. None liked him in the least.

"Tracy and Shani and Diana, it would be a nonstarter. If it were Claire Fisher, that's one thing. Maybe Esther or Janet." He paused, thinking it through. "I can try with Janet. Fuck. Yes, tell her I think I can make it happen. Janet would do it to spite me."

"As for the money, they came in at seven hundred. I think we knock it down a bit."

Paul suppressed nausea.

"Paul?"

"I heard you."

"It's a negotiation. Everything is a negotiation."

"I get it. It's how I make my fucking living."

"But unfortunately, as I said, they've got all the leverage. Do you have that kind of liquidity?"

"Of course I don't."

"It doesn't have to be all in one hit, particularly if you can demonstrate you don't have it on hand. What do you have in the bank?"

"About four hundred thousand. But I've got to live."

"You make an initial payment of a hundred and fifty or so. The rest you pay out over the next five years. On a schedule. What about your house?"

"Fucking Christ, Marty."

"Again, my sense is I can get Ms. Rouhani and her team down, plus signing with someone on that list. The other woman, we'll just have to see."

LOS FELIZ

B rad Shlansky sat forward in the Aeron chair, a remnant from the year at Sony, in his office at the house in Los Feliz thinking about his father. It was just after 9 a.m. He'd completed his half hour on the exercise bike, followed by a circuit of weights, and had eaten a breakfast of granola with yogurt. Thankfully Amanda sensed his mood and was avoiding him, meaning scant interaction since the twins had awakened them at six fifteen.

Should he and his sisters have stayed on Long Island? Would Carl Shlansky have preferred it? They would never have made two films. Brad wouldn't have met Amanda, who, for all the tension between them, he still loved and knew he always would. He wouldn't now have twin boys with her. He wouldn't have had his company name on a studio lot door. And yet it amounted to so little: scant recognition for Brad and his sisters, while those with whom they were connected, Lone Star Pulp and before then David Levit, received all the attention, remunerative and otherwise. *The Recluse*, a movie he once believed would establish his siblings and him with a measure of permanence, ended up being such an embarrassment that they left it off the company website, which itself had cost seven thousand dollars to build for what had dwindled to fewer than a dozen clicks a day, most of those, he suspected, from his sister Emily.

"I sit here waiting for the phone to ring," he'd complained months before to an increasingly unsympathetic Paul Aiello. "If I'd stayed in Woodmere and kept my father's stores, I could've made a deal with the government with a long payment schedule and fucking gone to town. Those assholes who bought us sold to a bigger consortium and made a goddamn killing. They earned six times more off *Revenge* than we did. Why am I suddenly bankrupt and no one takes my calls?"

"Unfortunately, about twenty minutes ago your day just got worse."

"How could my day possibly have gotten worse?"

"Reggie and Eitan called, and they want to end their agreement with Same Day."

"We have a fucking contract."

"A two-year contract, the term of which ends in six weeks. They're sending a letter to Alice, but they wanted to let me know first as a courtesy."

"You and not me? Why are they doing this?"

"I can tell you what they said, if you really want to hear."

"I want to fucking hear."

"This is Eitan talking, not me. They got tired of nothing happening beyond the scripts getting written and a lot of talk. So, he started calling the studio directly."

"Suddenly the simple guys from Texas who didn't want to be involved in the movie business are calling the studio behind my back?"

"Things change when you get a taste. The studio told them they were ending their deal with you. When they asked why, Debbie said they didn't anticipate moving forward on any of the properties." Debbie had been their new executive, a short and humorless brunette from Dallas who chewed gum incessantly and always seemed to be frowning, a combination Brad quickly had begun to loathe. "You've really rubbed her the wrong way. And by the way, she used to work for Charlie Gold."

"That should have made her love me!"

"Charlie gave her her start."

"I'm calling Alice."

"Per your contract, Lone Star can terminate with notice, Brad. So just shut the fuck up about Alice and enjoy your final months of 'owning' a comic book company, because if you haven't forgotten, that reverts too."

"Why are you being such a prick?"

"Because I don't have time anymore to manage your fucking paranoia. It's always the same: everyone's going to get a call from Alice, who if you ask me was the worst thing that ever happened to you. If you'd listened to me instead of her back when you decided to sue Charlie Gold, you might not be in this mess."

Week by week, the disappointments had only aggregated, with David Levit now epitomizing all the indignities Paul Aiello found so easy to dismiss. While the director, with his acting career handed to him by a college housemate, gamboled from project to project, Brad languished. Without *Revenge*, who would even know David directed movies? If Brad didn't prevent it, David would soon have an Oscar, and once again, gifted to him like every other aspect of his career, this time by Jacob Rosenthal. In David Levit's world, everyone else committed the resources and expended the sweat, while David took the credit. This was Hollywood.

He'd left the first message for Jacob Rosenthal at 9 a.m. and was told the producer was on a call.

"Well, let him know he's going to want to speak to me," he told the assistant, who sounded uncharacteristically to be in her fifties. When Jacob hadn't called by 9:30, he dialed again.

"This is Brad Shlansky again. Is Jacob available yet?"

"He isn't. I'm sure he'll call you when he can."

At 9:50 the phone on Brad's desk rang. He allowed three rings to give the impression of industry.

"This is Brad."

"This is Jacob Rosenthal," came a gruff, Chicago-accented voice. "You wanted to speak with me?"

"Jacob! How are you?"

"I'm sorry. Have we met?"

"We have a lot of people in common."

"I can't imagine who they could be."

"Well, David Levit would be one."

"Right. I spoke to your lawyer about half an hour ago, not to mention David himself. What seems to be the problem?"

"They didn't explain?"

"I'd like to hear it from you."

"Okay. It involves a project of yours. We were calling as a courtesy because I know what it's like to be down the road on something and have it all fall apart."

"What the fuck is that supposed to mean?"

"David Levit is contractually obligated to direct a film I've just green-lit."

"Green-lit? Are you running a studio?"

"No, but we do have a number of projects. I own a lot of IP with a comic book company in fact. I'm sure you've read about us in the trades."

"I avoid the trades."

"As I said, this is a courtesy call. I'm not out to prove anything or litigate anything with you. You're a lawyer, I know."

"Was."

"So, I wouldn't be so stupid. But you can trust me when I say that once we exercise the option for David's movie with us, which we've in fact done, he's exclusive to Same Day Films."

"If you've already done it, why are you calling me? Why, in other words, do I have to be listening to you do this big-shot act when I'm trying to run a company that actually makes movies instead of trying to stop other people from making movies?"

"So that's the way you want to play this?"

"Does somebody write these lines for you? Christ almighty."

"What lines?" Brad felt himself begin to falter. He'd never encountered such quietly effortless aggression.

"Look, you and your lawyer back in New York might be able to scare other people," Jacob continued. "I heard about your thing with the Golds, and some other threatening actions you've taken over the years with nitwits susceptible to this sort of nonsense. I'm making *Coal*, and with David Levit. What? You had a movie with him fall through? Boo-hoo. It happens to everyone. It means you had a movie at all. You should spend your energy trying to get a new one off the ground and leave everyone else the fuck alone."

"Now you're going to tell me what to do?"

"No, I'm not 'going to,' I just did. And it's the last you'll hear from me, because I'm hanging up now." The line clicked dead.

Brad smashed the receiver into its cradle repeatedly until the entire apparatus had splintered to shards, the circuitry and wiring exposed.

"*Fuck fuck fuck fuck!*" he screamed, as Amanda appeared.

"What the hell is wrong with you? The boys are sleeping, and I'm on a call."

"Then close the fucking door. I'm going to be on with Alice."

CHATEAU MARMONT

D avid sent a text to Charlotte confirming he'd be on the 1 p.m. plane the following day. He would have called but knew she'd be no-where near her phone, which in all likelihood lay silenced on her dressing room table on Lafayette Street as she endured the tedium of her last ten out of twelve. In truth the wine list downstairs interested him more than a phone conversation with anyone, especially Charlotte, who would detain him for at least an hour describing every anxiety, ache, and slight as the production lurched toward its first audience. He simply didn't have it in him.

He'd called to reserve a seat at the outdoor bar several hours before leaving the Chicago Films offices, where he and Jacob and Larry had spent the day going over names not only of actors but of department heads as well. Normally this level of input from a financier would have irked him no end. So long as a designer or cinematographer could boast an A-list resume and had worked successfully with a director before, why should there be any question as to their involvement?

He stepped onto the patio, where a stand of torches threw a lambent glow, and took a seat toward the middle of the bar, counting three empty stools on one side and four on the other. Just after he sat, a woman and two men took those to his left.

"Mr. Levit, can I get you anything?" asked a tanned server with a strong and impeccably stubbled jaw.

"Yeah, thanks. A glass of the Cabernet, please, and I think I'm going to get the steak, but let me have a look at the menu first, if that's all right."

"Certainly." The bartender handed one over, then folded a napkin into a right triangle he placed in front of David, its hypotenuse hugging the bar's lip. The wine appeared as David scanned for options to the steak.

"Have you made a decision?"

"Yeah, I'll stick with the New York strip, rare, and start with the beet salad, please. And thanks."

He opened his journal and began to write.

At the Chateau Bar. Just ordered a steak. Per the instruction of the resolutely polite Nigel Gleeson, I was almost performatively gracious.

What's happening to me? With all my so-called education, with all my seeming toughness as an actor and filmmaker who has somehow sustained a career, why does the prospect of an unhinged Brad Shlansky and his deranged lawyer render me so useless? The ugliness and rage that motivate him are simply paralyzing. Does this mean I consider myself his opposite? Like anyone, I pursue my interests. But not in the manner of Brad Shlansky—bullying, aiming to destroy. And then there's Jacob Rosenthal, suddenly a kind of savior, who nevertheless will scour every choice I make and impulse I have for signs of deception. I can't stop thinking about Adam, not least because he would have loved both these guys as characters. I seem to live my life to prove something to a guy who died in a fucking bus explosion. In a sense FOR him, as if I was given his place. He was smarter than I, more talented. And generous with it, inexhaustibly so. We never fully understand the people or situations that are going to form us when we're actually experiencing them. All those long interactions in college and NYC admonishing me to do better.

David took his last sip of wine as the waiter brought his beet salad. "Would you like another glass?"

"That would be great."

"Hi, sorry, is this taken?" came a female voice to his right. Without his having noticed, a second trio had taken the stools on her far side, leaving the one empty perch.

"Uh, no."

She looked to be in her late twenties, about five foot six, with a wide, friendly face, light green eyes, and sandy blond hair. Her shoulders and arms were toned in the manner of someone who spends time daily in some form of exercise, probably supervised.

"Wait, are you David Levit?"

"Yeah."

"I loved *Revenge*. Don't you live in New York?"

"I do. This is a hotel."

"Right. Obviously. Sorry. Not a stalker. I have friends there who've seen you on the subway. We all thought it was so cool you still ride the train."

"I think you probably have the wrong idea of what sort of money I make."

"You're staying at the Chateau, aren't you?"

"Not on my nickel."

"Does that mean you only ride the subway because you have to?"

"I love the trains. When they're not crowded anyway. And they're usually faster."

"So seriously, do you mind if I sit here?" she asked as the bartender refilled David's glass. "I was supposed to meet a friend, but she bailed on me. I already valeted my car and was on the patio when her text came in. I have a book with me, so I won't bother you."

She lifted a plastic bag he recognized from just down Sunset.

"Book Soup," he announced.

"I had an hour to kill after an audition."

"Back before iTunes I never came to LA without going there and to Amoeba Music. Now I just go to Book Soup, though I haven't had time this trip."

"I'm the same way. I can do music on a phone or my iPad, but I love actual books."

"What did you pick up?"

"You're gonna say I'm a cliché."

"Only if it's Murakami."

"Oh my God. Fuck you." She took *The Wind-Up Bird Chronicle* from the bag. "I haven't ever read him, but all of my friends have, so I thought I'd try one. How is that wine?"

"It's good. My favorite here by the glass."

"You have a favorite here?"

"I guess I do."

"I think I'm gonna order a white. Excuse me," she said, motioning to the bartender. "Could I get a glass of white wine?"

"Certainly." He placed a list in front of her.

"There's a Chardonnay, a pinot grigio, a sauvignon blanc…," she announced.

"Don't ask me," said David.

"You don't have a favorite white here?"

"Just a red, and it was trial and error."

"A glass of the pinot grigio, please," she told the bartender before turning back to David. "So, what are you doing out here? Other than staying at this hotel on someone else's dime?"

"Nickel."

"Nickel."

"I'm directing a film—or I'm getting ready maybe to direct it. I was meeting with the financiers and the writer, figuring out some of the cast we're going to make offers to, and the crew, which is premature, but everyone does stuff differently."

"Why is that premature? I'm sorry. You want to eat your dinner and write. I'll read my book."

"You're not bothering me, and I'm done writing. It's just meandering shit anyway."

"A journal? Do you go back and read it?"

"Rarely, and I'm not sure I ever want others to. I had a friend who said he wrote his 'for the biographers.' I'm certainly not doing that, so I don't really know what the purpose is."

Her wine arrived.

"Could I see a menu, please?" she asked. After the bartender had obliged, she fixed her eyes once more on David, her interest sincere and keen. "So why is it premature to talk about crew?"

"Because movies for movie theaters are hard to get made right now. We get so excited at the possibility, we act like it's real before it is. Illusion about illusions. The movie I'm out here for won't actually be financed—even though I've been flown out and they've spent almost half a million dollars optioning a book and having a script written—until we cast the leads with actors who can offset the risk of the twenty or so million it'll cost to make it. And that's a pretty limited list."

"Stars, in other words."

"That's the less verbose way of putting it, yes."

She offered a smile that showed two rows of straightened teeth the brightness of which one rarely saw outside of Los Angeles.

"Anyway, I don't like to get ahead of myself with crew until a film is actually happening," he continued. "People rearrange their lives to do a movie because often it means going out of town, and even if it's in town it's four-teen-hour days, and they have wives, husbands, kids, dogs, and I only like to say there's going to be a disruption if there actually is going to be one. I've had one movie fall apart with crew on board, and that one time was enough."

"Have you decided what you'd like?" asked the bartender, placing a folded napkin before her to match the one in front of David. The sky had darkened to a deep violet. Behind her, lights from kitchens and living rooms in the houses ascending into the hills glimmered warmly. He grew suddenly anxious over how perfect their interaction was beginning to seem.

"I'll have the octopus salad," she told the bartender. The choice, which he found funny for some reason, felt like a life preserver tossed from the deck of a retreating ship.

"Why are you laughing?" she asked, doing so along with him.

"I guess I wouldn't have figured that's what you'd order."

"I'm having to watch you eat a plate of beets."

"I might even want to try a bite of your salad. I've never had it here."

"Pretty quick to be at the sharing-food stage, don't you think, David?" she asked in a manner that reminded him suddenly of Charlotte.

"You're safe with me," he offered, raising his left hand. "Happily and resolutely married."

"I saw it before I even sat down, which is why I started talking to you in the first place."

"Meaning?"

"I really have to explain?"

"Even these days? After 50.8?"

"Please. Sometimes I even carry a fake wedding ring of my own with me, but I didn't expect to be stood up tonight. It's a whole thing, because then I have to take it off for auditions."

"Why's that?"

"Please. What a male question. A wedding ring on a woman adds five years, minimum. Plus, if you're single and the decision makers are male, it ups your chances not to have one."

"Is that really true?"

"I'm sad to say it is. But now that that's out of the way, we can try each other's salads."

"So obviously you're an actress."

"And a temp, and a personal trainer. And ashamed of none of it even though it's so fucking typical."

"How's it going? I guess well enough if you can come here."

"I have an agent now, which is more than a lot of my friends. And a manager. Neither very powerful, but still. I've done a few national commercials, about five plays no one has seen, and some TV guest spots. A couple top-of-shows."

"Did you study acting in college?"

"UC Irvine. Stayed close to home."

"Los Angeles?"

"That would be too close. Mill Valley. My parents are still there."

"Are they supportive?"

"They worry about me. Here I am, after all, with a strange married man at a bar."

"Exactly."

"It's weird though. I mean you're not that much older than I am—"

"More than you think."

"But you've been through it."

"I'm not understanding. Through what?"

"The stage I'm in right now. Even a night like this where I was going to meet a friend and she canceled. That I could just go up to a bar and decide to get a drink. It's so fucking crazy—yes, I'm thirty—"

"You're thirty?"

"You thought I was younger or older?"

"Am I allowed to say?"

"You're required."

"Younger. No wedding ring."

"I actually wish you'd said older."

"Because?"

"I guess it relates to what I was talking about. Being an adult is just so surprising sometimes."

"But you like it?"

"I fucking love it. I'm my own person. Taking risks, doing what I feel like doing. Very first world, I know, and my parents gave me my car, but I pay my rent, pay for my groceries, my phone bill. I'm doing it. Living my actual life. No boyfriend, which is a bummer."

"Is that hard out here?"

"Hard to meet guys who are smarter than they are self-centered or fucking repulsively ambitious? Yes. Like even the fact that you knew who Murakami is. People out here don't read. They're too busy perfecting themselves."

"Didn't you say your friends turned you on to him?

"First of all, women friends, and second of all, the two who did now live on the East Coast."

David shook his head.

"Yeah, but I just don't buy that about LA," he said.

"I'm going to have another glass of wine. You?"

"Sure. Thanks," he said to the bartender, then turned back to her. "People here live off telling stories. You can't do that and not read."

"But what? Scripts?" she asked. "The trades online?"

"Book Soup stays in business."

"That's true."

"And I'm working with a producer right now who's as well-read as anyone I know in New York." His steak came with their drinks, and he requested a second plate. "I'm giving you some of this."

"It looks fantastic. Are you sure?" she asked.

"Yes. And by the way," he said as he forked over a wedge of sirloin. "I'm gonna get your wine and your salad."

"No way," she said. "I'm not letting you."

"I was flown out here business class and given a per diem. Thank Chicago Films. I hope you work for them someday. As an actress, that is. Not as a temp or a trainer."

"Hah. Thanks, David."

"I don't know your name."

"Iris," she answered. "Iris Wood."

"Well, it's great meeting you, Iris. In fact, this has been one of the only good parts of my trip."

"Better than talking prematurely about making a movie?"

"That definitely has been the opposite of pleasant. Mostly I've been having to defend, unnecessarily, all of the choices I want to make."

"Aren't you the director?"

He wondered suddenly if her interest was compelled by a desire that he give her work. He shunted the idea aside, caught up instead in the chance to explore out loud the predicament in which he found himself with Jacob.

"When I was solely an actor, I never fully understood what was really going on in terms of the actual making of a film in production. I would walk onto a set, and yeah, I'd see a big crew, and the producers gathered around their monitor, maybe a screenwriter, obviously the DP and some-times the star, but mostly I thought, well, this is the director's show, because of course he's the one—or actually I should say *she* because my first movie was with a female director—"

"Who was that?"

"A woman named Penny Marshall."

"Laverne!"

"You know who Penny Marshall was?"

"My mom used to show me all her favorite shows on DVD."

"That's a good mom."

"So, go on," she urged, leaning forward.

"Why are you so interested?" he heard himself ask, regretting it the moment he did. But something about her persisting attention, coupled with the unenhanced beauty of her, continued to set him slightly on edge.

"I guess maybe I'm like you were. Just curious about it all. I mean obviously you were a lot more successful than I am—"

"Not always, trust me. I did plenty of commercials and plenty of plays."

"Plays in New York. Big difference. Was it hard for you to get work out of school?"

"Not in theater. But in film and on television, yeah. I got lucky."

"I don't believe in luck."

"Why's that?"

"It allows for its opposite. People start saying they're unlucky and that becomes an excuse."

"That's smart."

"So, are you going to tell me about when you were on a set as an actor?"

"Right. What was I saying?"

She laughed. "A little too much to drink, David?"

"This conversation just keeps going in unexpected directions. Though I have gone a bit beyond my limit."

"You were remembering working with Laverne."

"Right. I had this vision of the director as this benign dictator—that all the decisions ultimately rested with him or her. I would go onto each set after that and think, I want to do that. Every actor hits that fork in the road, I think, where they feel the way I felt, or they say to themselves, no fucking way, I love acting and that's all I ever want to do."

"Put me in that category."

"And my friend Noah said—"

"Noah Mendelson?"

"Sorry. Yeah. Noah said, well, if you want to direct, and you can write, write your own material, because trust me it's the only way you can have anything close to the control you're describing. But the thing is, and this is what I eventually learned, you don't ever really have complete control. Not even Noah does. When you get people to give you millions of dollars, which of course isn't a donation but an investment in an extremely risky field, you can't really blame them for getting anxious about some of the choices you make and fighting you about certain things. It's kind of the deal. But at the same time there's nothing in my life more rewarding, especially when I've written the script. I'm frankly living a life so beyond where I thought it would go that I can't even fathom it at times. Which isn't to say I've made all the right choices, but somehow here I am, kind of like you were saying, in the middle of it getting to sit here with you at this bar, tomorrow morning meeting with a financier I begrudgingly really respect, and hopefully keeping the wolves at bay."

"What wolves are those?"

"Not worth going into other than to say that not everyone out here wants everyone else to succeed."

"You have people like that?"

"Of course I do. And as you succeed, and trust me you will—"

"How do you know that?"

He paused.

"You're too manifestly appealing not to."

"Manifestly appealing. Wow. I'm gonna carry that one with me forever."

"Sorry. I was choosing my words. Trying not to—"

"It's all good."

"The point is, it'll happen for you as an actress, and if not that, something else. And there will be those who'll resent that. But you've got to keep moving forward without allowing it to distract you. You do that, always promoting optimism and being disciplined in what you do, you can have a pretty decent life."

She stared back at him.

"What?" he asked.

"I came up here, a total stranger, and you've given me probably one of the most reassuring conversations I've had out here in months."

"Sitting across from you, or next to you, isn't so difficult."

"Because I'm manifestly appealing?"

"Sure. Something like that."

"So, you want to know what I've always wondered?"

"What is that?"

She reached for his hand.

"What the rooms here are like."

His breath caught.

"No strings attached," she continued. "I know you're married. You have a life back in New York. That's all great. This doesn't have anything to do with that. It *won't* have anything to do with that. I just don't want this right here, right now, to end. I want to spend the night with you here in this hotel. I want to be close with you and then send you on your way and you send me on mine with what I suspect will be an amazing secret between us. Nobody will ever know."

"The problem is, I'll know."

"Yes, you will." Her eyes didn't leave his.

When he woke the next morning, she was on the way to the shower, her unblemished body moving with languid ease. This couldn't suppress the overwhelming guilt that had hobbled him as soon as he'd made it for the first time the night before, though the experience itself had been extraordinary. Her utter control of him, the responsiveness of her body to everything she seemed to guide him to do astonished him as she let herself go in vocalized bursts, shuddering uncontrollably as she climaxed. They'd repeated the act twice more before falling asleep, his growing disappointment in himself no match for her beauty and the abilities associated with it.

"You're up already?" he asked.

"I've got to meet a client at the gym in forty minutes."

He thought of Charlotte and his daughters and wanted nothing more than for them not to exist, never to have existed, so he could start a life with Iris Wood, their single night together stretching into a lifetime. Yes, he loved his wife and cherished his children, but he needed the woman standing impossibly naked in front of him to come back into the bed.

"Forty minutes? Where?"

"Westwood, unfortunately."

"You can't be a little late?"

"Sorry."

He heard the water go in the bathroom and noticed her phone lying atop the nightstand, where she must have placed it after setting an alarm. This reminded him to check his, where predictably he saw four missed calls from his wife, the last just after 2 a.m. in New York. Three texts interspersed themselves, the last one reading "Going to bed." None seemed frantic or even remotely querulous.

Iris emerged from the shower within minutes, wrapped in a towel.

"Sorry about this, but I can't be late," she said.

He watched as she reached into her bag for sweats and a sports bra into which she scooped each perfect breast. She covered this with a simple green T-shirt that hung halfway down her front, exposing a flat midriff.

"You had those clothes with you?"

"I told you I came here from the gym to meet my friend."

"From an audition."

"Before that I was at the gym."

"So, is this it? I mean, can I get your number? Do you want mine?"

She came to the bed and sat, leaning over him, her immaculate skin catching drops from her hair.

"We agreed this would be one night."

"We did."

"I'm not a homewrecker. I'm just a woman who found a guy attractive. This was great, but it's not good for either of us if it goes any further. Trust me. I may look great to you right now, and you might have enjoyed what happened, but long term, I'm not for you, and you're not a guy who wants to be cheating on his wife."

She leaned down and kissed him, and as he began to lose himself in it, she broke away.

"Take care of yourself."

She snatched up her phone and was gone.

He lay in bed, shame enveloping him, replaced quickly by fear. He rushed naked to his jeans for his wallet, which was still in his front pocket. He checked it for his credit cards and cash, all of which remained. He looked to his nightstand, where his watch also lay where he'd left it. I'm a heel for not trusting her, he thought. But what if she'd fleeced me? How would I explain that? Not to mention that I wore no protection, and never even asked if she was on the pill. For one night, one night, I risked everything I have. He reached for his phone.

"What happened to you? I kept calling," Charlotte asked without saying hello.

"I went to the bar downstairs and forgot my phone, and then I ran into Nigel Gleeson."

"Again?"

"Yeah. We talked until eleven thirty, so by the time I got up to my room you'd gone to bed. I didn't want to wake you."

"Tell me you're packed and you're going to be on that flight this afternoon."

"Not packed yet, but yes. Absolutely, completely and totally enthusiastically yes."

"Okay, that's a little strong."

"How was the dress last night?"

"We're going to need every preview."

"How are you and Rafe getting along?"

"You mean is he still directing me? Yes. Upstaging me? Yes. I hate older actors."

"Did you talk with Dexter?"

"He promised he'll deal with it, but not now. The same old shit. He actually said to me, 'The guy has won two Tonys and an Olivier, what am I supposed to do?'"

"Did you give him your look?"

"I did."

"Charlotte?"

"Yeah?"

"You're going to be amazing. I love you. Thank you for being with me."

He heard the pause before it even happened. How could he have been so stupid?

"Did you fuck somebody last night?"

"What?!"

"I asked, did you fuck somebody last night?"

"I told you I was with Nigel. I can't tell you I love you?"

"The way you told me was not of the daily variety but more of the I-feel-guilty-as-shit variety. Plus, the over-modified description before of how eager you are to get home, which didn't seem to be the case when you kept extending your stay because of a movie no one will see."

"You encouraged me to do this movie. And people will see it."

"You're not answering my question."

"I *do* feel extremely guilty. You're going through techs and dress rehearsal and waking up with the girls without me there. It's not fair to you, which I was just reminded of when you were making sure I'd be on the flight tonight. That's why I'm overdoing it."

"Uh-huh ..."

A call beeped in, and "Blocked" appeared on the screen.

"You have another call?"

"Yeah. Probably Brad Shlansky, but I'm not taking it."

"I loathe him," she said flatly.

"Not as much as I do."

"So, you didn't sleep with some beautiful woman last night. Some blond California girl with perky breasts and no children who wants to be in one of your movies?"

"Obviously I did not, Charlotte," he answered, marveling at her accuracy.

"Just get home, David."

"I'll see you late tonight. Am I allowed to say I love you?"

"You can say it when you're at the airport. Just pack your damn bag."

ALBANY

After not finding her in her office, Paul Aiello reached Janet Liebowitz in her car on Sunset two miles east of the 405.

"Yeah, I usually do Wilshire this time of day," he tossed out amicably, hoping to mask his misery in needing something from her so desperately.

While he'd never gotten along with Janet, he'd always respected her, and at one time could consider her something of an ally. But the business into which he'd matriculated well over a decade before bore little resemblance to what it had become. Back then information changed hands freely in staff meetings, with an esprit de corps defined by a certain type of client and the sorts of agents to whom they appealed. UCM, though slanted toward television and comedy, could also identify itself as a home for artists who perceived and created defiantly. Even as one of the top four agencies in Los Angeles, it still enjoyed a sense of itself as chic and iconoclastic. Its agents had protected this image and one another.

But downward pressure on the earnings of writers, directors, and actors not at the very upper echelons had of late effected a transformation. Yes, with so many platforms now desperate for content, new opportunities proliferated, but this expansion demanded more work for less margin. Larger agencies innovated by exploiting their scale to fashion revenue streams separate from those of their clients. They became, as a kind of side business, producers themselves, either through packaging deals that charged percentages for aggregating talent around a project, or through the actual formation of financing entities for which they took fees. Even while their clients' earnings remained static or in many cases declined, they could now effectively force studios to pay for access to their talent. Particularly in television, which included not only actors but writers and showrunners, profits increased to such an extent that they attracted private equity partners into the agency business, who in turn could capitalize expanding overhead to service that talent.

For individual agents this brought a new stratum of oversight, one that focused on sustaining and even increasing short-term returns, with less appreciation for the careers of so-called prestige artists, who might take longer to develop. Initially Paul appreciated these new metrics. Definable terms such as the magnitude of earnings under one's direct control made determining one's value within the company far more tangible. Too many of his colleagues failed to understand that the word "business" followed "the agency" when naming the field they'd chosen. Paul finally understood this in an epiphany one rare night alone in his bed in the hills. All that matters, he told himself, is how big that number under my name is. He brought his katana to work the following morning and took immediately to standing with it while negotiating deals. Soon it accompanied him as he roamed the floor.

"It's my thing now," he announced to Brad Shlansky. "Half of them think I'm going to bash in their coffee tables, and the other half that I'm gonna decapitate someone."

"It's hilarious, but what's the point?" asked Brad.

"They hate me anyway. Now they'll understand that I fight on a whole different level. It's fucking MMA with a samurai sword."

He had to give himself credit. Since Centaur Capital Partners had purchased 20 percent of the company and a less ambiguous earnings calculus was applied, he was shown to have bested nearly every one of his colleagues with their MBAs and law degrees and all the supercilious posturing associated with them. Not only could he bring producers and studios to their knees like none other, he could convert the toil of others to profit almost effortlessly. Uniting Same Day Films with Lone Star Pulp was but one example. Without a single film being made, the partnership had turned into a minor gusher. The agency reaped commissions on every property optioned and every script written, since he managed to keep development almost exclusively in-house with UCM writers, directors, designers, and actors. Should a film get made, agency fees would easily reach seven figures. Yes, Lone Star had severed ties with Brad Shlansky, but at least Same Day had enjoyed the status associated with a bungalow on the Sony lot. Nor was it Paul's fault that Brad carried himself too hubristically around studio executives, or that his gouging of Charlie Gold, no matter how justified, had so damaged his reputation. As for Paul's relationship with Eitan and Reggie, it had only improved since they jettisoned Brad. They'd just sold a new title to Warner Brothers with a replacement producer whom Paul had also signed. Professionally Paul had never felt more vital.

None of this made him popular among the other agents on the floor, however, nor did the increasingly virulent rumors concerning his habits with women.

"What the fuck do you want from me, Paul?" Janet barked into the phone after, at Paul's insistence, her assistant had been absented from the line.

"Is that the way we're supposed to talk to each other, Janet? Don't we still work for the same company?"

"I'm in the middle of rolling calls; I'm late for my granddaughter's fucking horse show; I'm in standstill traffic; I just heard on the radio that if this stupid virus spreads, they'll close down restaurants, which, *just kill me now*; and half of Los Angeles is on fire. What's so fucking important?"

"I'm calling to do you a favor."

"Unlikely."

"You know my client Janine Rouhani?"

"The ABC forensics pilot. What about her?"

"Well, first of all, she's amazing."

"Yeah, I bet she is."

"What's that supposed to mean?"

"Go on, Paul."

"She wants female representation."

"I'm not sharing a client with you. Find somebody else."

"I'm not asking you to share her."

"You're passing her on? Why would you do that?"

"I told you. She wants a woman."

"But why not just a woman on her team? She's firing you?"

"Janet, this is what she's asking for, okay? I can't get inside every actor's head. The client comes first. Once we start making it about ourselves, we're no longer serving the artist."

"I'm sorry, could you just hang on one second." She made the sounds of retching violently. "I'm back. So basically you fucked her, and it's awkward now?"

"You know what, Janet? Out of all the women at the agency, I picked you to hand over six figures in commissions minimum per year. Thanks for considering. I'll ask Shani."

"Yeah, right. Like Shani has time for another client. And six figures under my name? Bullshit. She's gonna be tied to the network show you put her on. The commissions will be yours without you having to lift another finger. Basically, I'll be working for you until her show gets canceled."

"Not during her hiatus. That'll all go to you, and she likes to work. Plus, by the time that show's over her Q will be through the roof."

"Did you really just say *Q?* What is this, 1995? Were you even born then?"

"Use whatever word you like. She's gonna be a fucking golden goose. You'll also like her. She's a hard worker, she's honest, decent, smart, reads fast, and she gets the jobs she goes up for. She even wants to produce."

"Of course she does, they all do, which, by the way, is a time-sucking headache. Suddenly it's not just scripts, but articles and novels, then talking with them on the phone only to learn they don't understand a word they read. You know what you do when an actor wants to start a production company? You fucking drop them."

"Janine is different."

"You're saying she goes from you to me? You're no longer involved? Clean and simple?"

"And if for some reason her pilot doesn't get picked up—but it will—she's all yours in every respect. I won't be involved in the least."

"Split the commission with me on the TV show, and I'll take her."

"Are you fucking kidding me?"

"Oh, give me a break, Paul. You know I'm gonna have to be dealing with every little complaint, scheduling issue, and slight for every week she does on that stupid show. 'It's too much work,' 'It's not enough work.' 'I hate the writing.' 'I hate the wardrobe.' 'It's too many sex scenes.' 'Why can't I get a better story line?' Plus, the upfronts, the TCAs, and every appearance and interview—"

"She'll hire a fucking publicist. And she has a manager."

"You think I'm a goddamn moron? I'll be on conference calls with those vampires every other day."

"I'll give you two and a half percent."

"The full five. Half the ten."

"Fuck. Fine." She fully perceived her leverage, and he had no time to put up any sort of front.

"So, can I go now? Or are there other so-called favors you want to do for me?"

"It would be great if you called Janine. Instead of waiting for her to call you. Just so she can feel like—"

"Of course I'll fucking call her, Paul."

Now if Marty could just get the actress and her lawyer to agree to a number under half a million dollars, and Susan a number not too far north of that, along with payment schedules he could manage without having to sell his house outright, he could set his life straight. He would pull back on the sex, the drinking, the drugs. One by one he'd watched his colleagues jettison old habits as they married, had children, and anchored themselves professionally. Yes, they'd usually relapse during periods of divorce or separation, but each invariably understood that to have longevity they couldn't sustain the hedonism of years past. It was all too much of a business now.

"All right," he informed Martin on his next call, which he made from his cell. "You can tell Janine's attorney Janet Liebowitz will take her."

"Good, but that negotiation has changed a bit."

"I'm not talking about Susan. I said Janine."

"Me too. They moved the goalposts on you."

"They can't do that."

"You have no power here, Paul. We're at their mercy."

"What the fuck happened?"

"The women talked. The one told the other she wouldn't even entertain taking less than a million if she took anything at all."

"Susan Painter? Who ever said a million for her? I never agreed to that!"

"You haven't agreed to anything, but that doesn't mean her lawyer hasn't put that number in her head, so that's what Ms. Painter told Ms. Rouhani."

"So now Janine wants a million dollars too?"

"Eight-fifty, plus the agent switch, which somehow they figure is worth one-fifty, don't ask me how, not that I objected."

"I can't take this, Marty."

"The allegation is nonconsensual sex, Paul. Rape. With two women."

"I keep trying to figure that out, and it makes me more and more angry. A nonconsensual fucking threesome? I mean, how does that even happen? I'd have to be twice my size and have six arms."

"Leaving aside their claims as to how, let's just one more time go through the ramifications of this being exposed even if it was consensual. Do you or do you not represent the two of them?"

"You don't need to—"

"No, Paul, obviously I do because we always end up here. You can fight the one, Ms. Rouhani, and say you'd had relations before, which weakens her case, and yeah, the two of them flame out if this goes public, but they take you along with them. No agency post–Charlie Gold and 50.8 is going to keep a guy who did what you did, even accepting your version. As it is, it wouldn't surprise me if Ms. Painter actually sued UCM too. But right now, unless you want to day-trade or sell real estate, I'm sorry, but you're going to have to man up and pay."

"How is that manning up? And I don't have a million eight five!"

"That's not going to be the number. More like a million and a quarter between the two is my guess. Now, you say you got Janet Liebowitz to agree?"

"Yes."

"I'm going to get back into this and start countering."

Paul had spent an hour on the phone that morning with his bank, and an appraiser would visit his house in the coming days to confirm what he already knew from a perusal of comps: a second mortgage could yield him in the neighborhood of six hundred thousand dollars. If Marty could attenuate the payments to the women over five years, that might just be manageable, so long as he retained his job, which of course would depend on Susan Painter neither pressing charges nor suing UCM.

How had he gotten himself here? He loathed introspection of any sort. Human beings sought pleasure and avoided pain, and any forensics on the matter—of the sort that invariably involved what happened when a person was seven and got left behind with a mean babysitter, or even, as in his case, flayed routinely by an alcoholic father—always seemed like time-squandering distraction. You couldn't alter how you were raised; you could just get over it, and Paul had done that with a vengeance. But why did he always end up miring himself in peril, the very opposite of life's putative aim?

After the ill-fated seventh grade trip to Philadelphia, he'd have gone straight to a military academy had his father not balked at the price. Instead, he ended up in public school, where he fell in with a dissolute, hard-drinking cohort and barely scraped by. His parents lost all hope by the time he reached tenth grade—too exhausted from their jobs even to bother clocking when he came and went, if he showed up nights at all.

"What're you gonna do when you graduate?" his father wondered in October of his senior year. "*If* you fucking graduate, I should say, with the turds you're laying in every class."

"I'm gonna go to college."

"What college is going to accept you? And who's gonna to pay for that?"

"I guess I will."

"Because you're not getting a penny from me, that I can tell you."

He had a C– average going into his senior year but a more than proficient score on his SATs thanks to lax proctoring and having been sat next to a studious-looking girl whose answers he cribbed. With this he gained acceptance to SUNY Albany, along with a financial aid package, calculated based on his parents' earnings, that mitigated yearly tuition to just over six thousand dollars, half of which he could cover with summer work and the remainder with a local serving job the coming year.

"Three thousand dollars. That's all I'm gonna need from you guys. Fifteen hundred a semester," he told his parents.

"If your mother wants to take it out of her paycheck, that's her business. But not me. Bite me once, you're to blame, bite me twice, I'm to blame."

"Jesus, Dad, it was fucking seventh grade."

"Yeah, and seventeen thousand dollars I paid to a school you got kicked out of."

"So, for that you're going to deny him being the first person in our family to go to college?" asked his mother.

"What the fuck is that supposed to mean?"

"He wants to get an education, and he's figured out on his own how to make it happen where we have to pay very little. Tell me you're not just a little proud."

"He doesn't want a fucking education. He wants to party for four years on my sweat and put off actually having adult responsibilities."

"If you think long term instead of what he did six years ago, it might actually be good for everyone. As you and I have learned the hard way, people who go to college make more money than people who don't."

"So, what, he's gonna get some fancy job—which, trust me, he won't—and cut us a check every month? Pay for the old folks home? Give me a fucking break."

"How about he doesn't need to ever borrow money from us? You know how many of my friends' kids are still living off their parents? When he leaves college, he's on his way to being independent, Tommy. And yes, maybe in our old age he takes care of us."

His mother sent weekly checks to Albany carved from her own earnings, though she rather too graciously pointed out that his father compensated elsewhere.

"Trust me, Paul, it all ends up coming from the same pot. I give money to you, he pays more of the groceries. The fact that I'm writing the checks is just symbolic. He's just never gotten over what you did."

"He never will."

What would my life be, he wondered, had I simply resisted the impulse to slug that spoiled fucking preppie? Why did I do it? To impress my friends? Live dangerously? What did it accomplish but confirm to my parents and to me that I was untrustworthy, ungrateful, out of control? I went from a haven for smart, privileged kids on their way to the best schools to a place that was pure mayhem. And Dad was right. The first year of college for me was just more of the same. I went so I wouldn't have to be an adult.

This changed sophomore year when he encountered Celeste, a freshman business major from Washington Heights on full scholarship. They met in the admissions office stuffing envelopes.

"Don't you give a shit?" she asked in slightly accented English after pulling headphones from over her ears. Fittingly, these were the first words she spoke to him. "You're stuffing those like it doesn't fucking matter, which, by the way, are early acceptance letters to students with good test scores."

"I know. I was one of those kids."

"So why no pride in what you're doing? The kids who get them are gonna see the crooked folds and feel like this place doesn't care about them. Do it straight. You gotta put in the time anyway. What does it cost you to do a good job? Lemme show you."

She took a fresh sheet, folded it deftly twice over, then tucked it into its corresponding envelope in half the time it had taken him to accomplish the same task sloppily.

"See?"

They went together to the dining hall that night and sat talking for three hours. She wasn't his type: a short, curvaceous body with large breasts and brown skin. Her family had moved to New York from the Dominican Republic when she was seven, and she'd graduated eleventh in a class of 112 from Gregorio Luperon High School, where she'd led the robotics team and was treasurer of the student council. In addition to sharing their biographies, they passed her headphones back and forth to sample her favorite music, all of it hip-hop.

When he tried to kiss her in front of her dorm, she presented her cheek but suggested they meet for breakfast the following morning. For two weeks they had at least one meal together daily, always at State Quad and, if possible, at the same table they'd first occupied, until finally she invited him to her room, where he spent the night. She would jerk him off, put her mouth on him, let him put his mouth on her, but allow no penetration. To spend time with her outside of her room or at meals meant sitting opposite her for hours at the library while she worked. Having no better way to occupy his time, he began to read the material he'd been assigned, and to complete problem sets without copying from others. He began to listen in classes, and he took notes she might espy during their sessions. He bought music she curated to play on his iPod when not with her, becoming more and more obsessed with both it and the woman whose tastes it revealed.

Physically he couldn't believe what he'd been missing out on with the pale, slender, small-breasted girls who'd previously comprised his sexual experiences. Celeste had a wondrous generosity embodied in physical proportions that seemed to envelop him. After two months she informed him she was ready to consummate. Afterward she wept.

"Celeste?"

"I gave myself to you."

"You mean ...?"

"Yes."

She asked that he join her in the city after Christmas for the remainder of the break. He walked from the subway at 168th Street south and west to the Riverside Apartments and beheld the red Johnson-era brick towers named on a stark utilitarian sign planted at the entrance to the complex. She'd instructed him to call when he'd arrived at Building 4.

"I'll need to bring you up."

She met him in front, where a security guard buzzed the two of them in through multiple doors, and immediately the smell of the place overwhelmed him: a stifling confluence of ammonia, takeout, and food being prepared, mostly in frying pans, on every floor. The halls were clean, the walls clad halfway up in green tile, with hard stone floors and white corkscrewed bulbs casting a cold glow every twelve or so feet.

"What's wrong?" she asked, taking his hand.

"I'm fine."

"I told you how I grew up."

"Yeah, I know," he responded curtly.

"Are you annoyed?"

"I'm fucking fine, Celeste. Just don't put me on the spot."

The apartment had two bedrooms shared by her mother, two brothers, a younger sister, and her younger sister's infant. While her mom, who worked the checkout counter at a Duane Reade a dozen blocks away, did her best to maintain a level of order and cleanliness, the sheer number of occupants, coupled with a sixty-hour workweek to feed her family, pay the rent, and send two hundred dollars to Celeste each month (in spite of Celeste's tearful protests) clearly stymied these intentions. The smell of baby shit and the faintly sweet deodorant that failed to suppress it only worsened the impact of clothes strewn everywhere and dishes piled in and around the sink.

"So, you're the famous Paul!" Celeste's mother announced. "It's a bit of a mess in here. I just got home, so in an hour you won't recognize the place, but welcome!" Her name was Soledad, and she stood just over five feet tall and was nearly half as wide, with Celeste's broad, smiling face under thick hair that bloomed off her head like an enormous plastered bouquet. She wore jeans and a black Sean John sweatshirt with gold lettering.

"Celeste sleeps in my room with me and Yoli and the baby. You can stay with the boys or on the sofa. It's up to you. We're kind of come-as-you-are here, but it's home."

"Sounds good to me," he offered weakly. "I really don't want to be any trouble. I can even—"

"Trouble? Stop it with that. I've been working all day on a double and didn't have time to do nothing but get in my comfy clothes, but the boys can go to Domino's and pick up some pizza and some beers while I clean up."

"Why don't I take Celeste, and we can get the food."

"You don't want to sit and relax?"

"No, it'll be great," he answered, visibly eager to flee. "Your daughter can show me the neighborhood."

"Yeah, Mom, Paul and I will go," said Celeste, glaring at him.

"Lemme give you some money, *mija*," she insisted, moving toward her purse.

"No, Ms. Reyes, I got it," he offered.

"Call me Sole, please."

He would always wonder why Celeste's work ethic and resolute decency, in contrast to his intolerance and lassitude, hadn't caused him to appreciate her all the more given the straits in which she'd been raised. Any shame should have been his as a white lower-middle-class kid with his own room in a three-bedroom house where a woman who could have been Celeste's mother came and cleaned twice a month.

"What is wrong with you?" Celeste demanded once they exited the building.

"I just ..."

"Look. Let's just both calm down, because I'm really pissed at you right now."

"I can't help my response."

"My mother works her ass off just to live like that. And raised all of us. We were here for all of six months when my dad split. Cleaned her out and disappeared."

"Why didn't she go back?"

"You think she didn't want to? We were already in school. She didn't know if he was really gone for good or not, and she had no money. She was fucking trapped."

"I can't stay in that apartment."

"Are you serious?"

"It's me. It's my own shit."

"You're damn right it is." She was crying now. "And how am I supposed to go back up there and say that the white boy I brought home and have been talking about all semester couldn't deal with how we live?"

"You tell them my mom called and I have to go home. I'll tell her."

"If you can't stay over, for just one night, we're done."

"Don't say that, Celeste," he protested meekly, but in truth he was grateful. Within just half an hour he'd lost all hope for a lasting relationship, a fact she clearly understood. The final interaction between them as a couple was her slapping him across the face. He turned and walked toward the subway to the sound of her heaving sobs. When in the apartment, he had never even put down his bag.

By the time he got to Cedarhurst, he regretted his actions and was as arrested by the terror of having lost her as he'd been by how her family lived. He called to say so, but she wouldn't pick up, and she certainly didn't call him. For the rest of the break he couldn't sleep without becoming so drunk he'd pass out. He thought of taking the train back to the city and presenting himself unannounced, but he dreaded seeing the apartment again. Theorizing it better to wait until they both returned to campus, he endured the remainder of the break with a twelve-pack each night.

Back in Albany she would neither look at him nor address him, and she avoided the spots where they'd once studied. He waited three hours at her door a week into the semester. She finally arrived at one in the morning still bundled up from the outside. At least she's alone, he thought.

"Paul, what are you doing here?"

"Could we please just—I'm sorry. I was wrong. I love you. I'm sorry."

"I've spent my life trying to be proud of who and what I am. Dealing with shame that I didn't put on myself but others did. I loved you, and you put that shame right back inside of me. You did that. I can't be with you. Not ever. It's done. Over. Go find a white girl, or a brown girl who's fancy. You and I aren't for each other, and we never will be. You proved it, and it's irrevocable."

He couldn't believe she'd used that word. It made him yearn for her all the more.

"Celeste, you're wrong. Please let me explain."

"If you care about me at all, just leave me the fuck alone so we can get over each other and move on."

"I thought you were in love with this girl," his father taunted, over spring break.

"Our worlds just didn't mix."

"Oh yeah, and what's your world? The realm of useless fuckups?"

He began to pursue women relentlessly, mostly at fraternity and sorority parties, and at the bar where he worked. He was angry and the sex was vindictive and had little meaning, but his increasing confidence made the game one he could win, especially if alcohol was involved. Always he hoped Celeste would see him with another and want him back. It never happened.

Eventually they became friends, though only when both were seniors. She had amassed enough credits with summer classes to graduate in three years and was engaged to a medical student at NYU who'd gotten his undergraduate biology degree from the University of Rochester. He too was from the DR; they'd met at Newark Airport, where she stood with a sign waiting to greet a cousin.

"Jesus, Celeste. I can't believe I fucked it up with you," Paul told her.

"That you did."

"How's your family?"

"My mom finally moved out of Riverside Apartments. She got promoted to assistant store manager, which didn't mean much of a raise, but my sister moved out and has a job now, plus my younger brother got into Seton Hall on a full ride, books included, so with all that savings and the raise she's renting half a floor in a row house in the Bronx. She cried when she moved in. Actually, so did I."

"That's amazing."

"In a weird way you being such a complete jerk probably helped inspire her all the more to want to move."

"You told her why I didn't stay over?"

"I didn't have to."

"What the fuck happened to me?"

"Let's not go into it, Paul."

As painful as their breakup had been—so much so that for all his angry promiscuity every woman seemed shallow in comparison—Celeste had changed him as a student. Above all, she demonstrated how a future could be eagerly planned for rather than staved off, and because of her he took pride not only in an improved GPA but in becoming truly conversant in the topics he chose to study. He also added classes with the goal of graduating a semester early.

"I saw your grades. Your father and I almost had seizures. Two As and three Bs? When the hell did that ever happen?"

"I guess I finally realized I'm there for a reason."

"I don't know what to say. It's like you're a different person, Paul."

Second semester junior year he took a film class on a lark with a friend, and the language of the star system struck him, particularly how movies seemed to lean on an audience's knowledge of what famous actors had appeared in before.

"Think of actors as adjectives in a sentence," explained the professor. "Who and what they are modify the story. This is true with every face and how they work on our psychology as we encounter them in a film narrative: the guy behind the ticket window when the star buys his seat on the train, the guy next to the star on the train, the voice of the conductor. It's all descriptive, and in a competent director's hands it inflects the story without you even knowing it's happening. Nowhere is this more true than with the stars, who also imbue each role with the history of preceding ones. In large part they are why people go to certain films, making the form viable as a mass cultural force. Movies as we know them can't happen without them. This is of course why studios pay the stars what they do. Stars are compensated not just for bringing people to the theater but for lending their very self, as a kind of metaphor, to the story. In our modern culture, with so much private information out there, even a star's personal life informs the narratives of the films they appear in. You don't want to see an actor known for drug use playing a squeaky-clean sitcom dad. Of course, that's always been true—you had gossip magazines—but now it's more powerful than ever with entire television shows devoted to the personal lives of people on TV and in movies."

He visited the professor during office hours.

"Why have I never seen you around the department before?"

"I'm a late arrival to the party," answered Paul. "I had a class available, and who doesn't like movies, so …"

"I'm glad to see you here. You don't exactly look the part."

"What does that mean?"

"That's the natural color of your hair. No piercings. Conservative clothing. It's not a bad thing. You're a business major it says here."

"Which actually has to do with why I came to see you. I need advice I guess, because I don't want to make movies or study movies, but maybe I do want to go into the business of movies."

"I'm not sure I'll be your best resource, but there are many ways to do that. Very few of them profitable, which if you want to know the truth of it is why I'm here and not out in Hollywood trying to produce and direct anymore. It's actually a terrible business, which can be extremely cruel to people. But you can start by reading these." He leaned back in his old, cracked leather Charles Pollock desk chair and reached for a foot-high stack of what looked to be periodicals.

"I've never thrown these away because I probably knew someone like you would come along. Frankly, I stopped reading them years ago because they just depress me."

He handed over about a year's worth of *Variety* weeklies.

"They're what's known as a trade paper. One of two, the other being the *Hollywood Reporter*. What both offer is 'journalism'"—he provided air quotes—"centered on the business of movies, television, music, and a bit of theater. You read all those editions I just handed you, and keep reading the new ones, you'll pick up far more than a schmuck like me can ever teach you about Hollywood right now. Come back every week, ask me questions about what you don't understand, I'll do my best to answer, and I'll give you that week's issue."

Paul devoured them, and rather than reviling the writing, as the professor had implied he might, he found himself enchanted: directors didn't direct, they "helmed." When an actor left a project, he "ankled" it. When a studio signed a star, it "inked" him. Movies didn't open, they "bowed." Commercials were known as "blurbs," sad movies "weepers," westerns "oaters," and songwriters "cleffers." He quickly noticed that in every article, almost without exception, whenever an artist or even producer was mentioned, so were their representatives, which included lawyers, managers, and agents. An entire culture seemed to exist around the promotion and representation of others, and in particular, stars. A performer decamping from one agency to another could garner front-page headlines.

"Of course!" exclaimed the professor. "It amounts to millions of dollars, plus a tremendous amount of access, and influence, because the agencies with the biggest stars and directors end up being the first to know when a movie's going to be green-lit, which means more stars and directors want to be with that agency, and then it just snowballs because that permeates to everyone represented by the agency, all the way down to the character actors and the craftspeople—DPs, production designers, everyone. I mean, can you fucking imagine? The power these people have—the reps I mean—without ever creating a damn thing, is tremendous, way out of whack. These agencies make a fucking killing. They're leeches."

Paul didn't perceive it quite the same way. After all, were artists supposed to represent themselves? Wouldn't that sully them somehow? And were they even equipped? In the winter of 2005, having graduated early with a GPA of 3.35, he drove a Toyota Corolla he bought from a classmate for eight hundred dollars down I-87 to the Palisades Parkway and across the George Washington Bridge, and moved into an apartment on the Lower East Side with two other graduates. The film professor had given him some parting advice: "Unless you're interested in becoming suicidal, or worse, homicidal, don't move to LA like every other poor soul thinking the industry is just waiting for you finally to arrive. Find a way in that gives you not only some life experience, but something of value. Go out to Hollywood empty-handed, and you'll regret it."

"I want to work at an agency."

"Oh my God. Well, at least do it in New York first. Much more forgiving."

In addition to talent agencies for actors, given a taste for hip-hop that Celeste had only deepened, he also sought work at every urban music management company and label he could find. Mostly his queries and follow-ups went unanswered, regardless of the target, until he was called in to interview at Brooklyn Boyz Peeps (BBP) by an HR representative who sounded decidedly white and suburban on the phone.

"A Massapequa boy!" said the beefy Caucasian who wore an Islanders jersey when they met up at a bar in Bed-Stuy.

"Yeah, I guess so. Then Cedarhurst."

"I grew up in Hempstead. Kick-ass. Just looking at you, I'm bringing you on, dude. And listen. It's really simple. Work your ass off, be where you're supposed to be before you're supposed to be there, don't piss anyone off, and mostly get out at night and meet people at every fuckin' club you can. You're white, I'm white. It doesn't fuckin' matter. Half the job—no, ninety percent of the job—is fuckin' hustle. And Italian, right? Aiello?"

"Yeah."

"Me too. And you know the music? Fuck, I didn't even ask. Who do you even like?"

Harkening back to his tutorials from Celeste, he spoke about the East Coast/West Coast schism, Dilla beats, the fast patter of Andre 3000, and his deep admiration for Rawkus Records, her favorite label.

"You're good! You're good! It ain't a fuckin' test, dude! It's just, you got to have the patter. And be fuckin' aggressive, which I can already tell ain't gonna be a problem with you. I know the killer instinct when I see it. It's mostly blacks and Jews—you've never seen so many fuckin' Jews. It's like a fuckin' plague. Kiss their asses, yes, but mostly just help them make money, because trust me, the rumors are true, there's nothing more important to a fuckin' Jew than money. Do everything I just said, and when it comes time for promotions, you'll end up getting on some teams, which is where you really earn your stripes, because until then, trust me, you're gonna be wiping a lot of the same asses you kiss! And finally, always be on the lookout for new clients!"

It astonished Paul that while the company paid lip service to the concept of female stars, it represented not a single one. He sought to change that. But instead of soliciting those already frontlining—for these invariably had representation of their own that a young white guy would never usurp— he concentrated on the dancers, which is how he met Selena Machado.

"Why me?" she asked over lunch at a diner near her apartment in Jackson Heights.

"Because I fuckin' couldn't take my eyes off you onstage. Plus, I could hear you singing backup on the hooks, and you were fuckin' outrageous."

"This ain't a come-on, is it? 'Cause we ain't gonna fuck."

"Furthest thing. I'm not an idiot."

"What's that supposed to mean?"

"That you're way out of my league in that way. And trust me, I do okay with women."

"Just checking."

"Do you write?"

"Of course I fuckin' write."

"So I bring you into the guys at Brooklyn Boyz, and we see about helping you develop a sound. That works, we get you with a label. People already know you from the club scene and videos. How many videos you been in?"

"Maybe fifty. It's like every fuckin' week."

From that afternoon on, for half a decade, not a day passed without a dozen or more communications between them, her ascent so brisk that within a year and a half her brand outearned every other Brooklyn Boyz Peeps artist combined, including the five other former dancers and backup vocalists he'd turned into headliners. Heeding his professor's advice, he could now move to Los Angeles with something the industry not only desired but desperately craved.

"What do you mean, you don't want to work on the music no more?" Selena demanded.

"I told you, I always wanted to get into movies. But more importantly, *you* want to get into movies. We've been fighting off the big agencies for years. I fucking negotiate your deals for you already anyway. This just puts us in the driver's seat. One of these places can get us the best directors, the best writers, the best producers, and fucking walk us into the studio head's office. It's the smart move. For you and for me. And Jesus, Selena, you've got four assistants. You don't need me as a manager anymore."

They chose UCM because theirs were the sleekest offices without seeming too self-importantly grandiose. They also stood next door to the promoters responsible for Selena's music tours.

"It's like we can sit at a table in the plaza between the two and have the fuckin' dirtbags come to us," she announced with the crass regality that had always slightly frightened him.

It was explained by the agency that actors compulsorily had "teams," with one in charge and others "doing the day-to-day." He chose his partner with an eye to who could teach him the most, spending a week with Selena meeting candidates, all of them women. They settled finally on a tough senior agent named Lizzie Gruber.

"Look at my list," she told Paul his first week. "Not a single one of them makes under five hundred K a year, and most of them a lot more than that. If I choose you as my client, if you're so lucky, then I make the offers happen and I make them very profitable. And with me, if the offers don't happen, it's the client's fault, not mine. If there's a room your client needs to be in, your client gets in that room. And it's a zero-sum game, because there are only so many rooms, and so many appointments in a day, only so many lunch meetings or drinks meetings a director or producer can have. You need your client in them instead of someone else's."

She only took straight men as assistants.

"Let HR come after me. I can't stand women out there answering my phone, and the fags drive me crazy."

He decided not to explore her issues with gay men.

"Why don't you want women working for you?"

"Too much shit to worry about that has nothing to do with the work: Am I setting a good example? Am I being too hard on them because they're attractive and I think they have it easy? Are they too feminine? A lot of it's my bullshit, but it still gets in the way, and—say it with me: *That's not good for the client.* With straight guys I can do and say anything. I don't need to set an example, and I don't give a shit if I hurt their feelings. I will never, and I mean not once *ever*, feel sorry for a straight white guy. The world's your fucking playpen. In this town especially. But take my advice on that score: don't shit where you eat."

When she signed Claire Fisher, she put Paul on the team.

"Are you serious?" he asked. "Aren't I a little green?"

"First of all, you're actually becoming a good agent. Selena is one thing, but those other rap artists you're getting jobs for, that shows drive. You'll also do what I ask."

In her teens Claire Fisher had appeared in a careful selection of highbrow movies she'd landed as a straight-A student at Spence, a tony girls' school on Manhattan's Upper East Side. By the time she was ready to graduate she'd worked with some of the top filmmakers in the world, but she surprised the industry by giving the years between eighteen and twenty-two to an art history major at Harvard, going so far as to drop her agent and manager to discourage any temptation to leave school. Upon graduation she started afresh, choosing Lizzie at UCM, not because she found meaningful kinship but because Lizzie's inelegance and aggression would allow Claire to remain aloof from the seamier aspects of negotiating deals, confirming Paul's earliest suspicions concerning the need for artists to have representation.

"You really represent Selena Machado?" the young actress asked Paul one afternoon early on.

"I sort of discovered her."

"You're like a young male version of Lizzie."

"Is that a compliment?"

"She's a bitch when she has to be, just like men have to be assholes or whatever the gender apposite would be. But like her, you always deal straight with me, and you never suck up. Plus, whenever I've asked you about a script, you've not only read it, you have smart comments without being pretentious. Did you ever take a film class?"

"At SUNY Albany if that counts."

"Obviously it sufficed," she responded with the benign condescension that would come to characterize too many of their interactions. When Lizzie left for a rival agency five months later everyone, especially Lizzie, assumed Claire would follow her, but the actress opted to remain, provided that Paul become her responsible agent.

"Are you fucking kidding me?" Lizzie yelled, storming into his office. "You're not even thirty! Why did I even put you on her team? Well, fuck her and fuck you. I was actually going to try to bring you both with me."

"I'm gonna take my chances at UCM, and I guess Claire will too."

"I'll actually miss you."

"I'll miss you too, Lizzie."

She closed his door.

"But Paul, I want you to listen to me."

"Yeah?"

"It's what I told you early on. Be careful with the women."

"What's that supposed to mean?"

"I've said enough."

"I can't have consensual sex?"

"Assistants? Potential clients? And showing pictures on your phone?"

"Who the fuck told you that?"

"Does it matter, if it's true?"

It didn't, because from the day Lizzie Gruber decamped, and he fully realized it *on* that day, his professional life was set. The responsible stewardship of the careers of both Selena Machado and Claire Fisher made signing any actress possible. While representing Selena inspired interest from a particular type, every serious young actress wanted to be Claire Fisher, or at least have access to the roles being offered Claire, not all of which she could do. By the time Selena finally left him, he had already aggregated a plurality of the actresses under forty considered the industry's best. There was even now talk of making him a partner.

Why then, just as on the seventh-grade trip, just as with Celeste now married to her thoracic surgeon and herself heading HR at one of the top investment banks in New York, had he again imperiled, in direct contravention of Lizzie Gruber's parting admonition, what he'd so carefully built? Why could he not master his ever more desperate need to control so utterly the women who attracted him? What prevented him from the basic decencies and discipline a productive life demanded, even as he had actually gained purchase on such a life? And why more and more did anger inspire so much of what he did?

Like his brother before him, Paul learned by his teens to manifest all the delinquency for which he was being punished by adults anyway. What difference, after all, did good behavior make if assumptions regarding his shortcomings were already being made and acted upon? He smoked, he stole, he drank, he lied, performing all with an indifference that represented its own sort of zeal, as if taking out a loan against retribution to come. And of course, such demonstrable confirmation only inspired paternal wrath more bitter, more focused, more severe. He came eventually to understand that his raging and the self-destruction it perpetuated came both through inheritance from his father and in response to his father, like a turbo engine boosting power from its own exhaust. Perhaps because of this, through all his doings, he simply could not escape an obsession with the man who had set the pattern in motion. In pursuing every success, from the relationship with Celeste, to his improving grades, to his move to New York City, then to Los Angeles and into agenting, to the purchase of his house, more satisfaction derived from vengeful ruminations about the envy they'd provoke in his progenitor than from any other feeling. And no matter the pleasures derived or in what stew of vindictiveness they were to marinate, he seemed inevitably to destroy the very accomplishments that had inspired them. As a result, regardless of the depth of his understanding or the acridity of the frustration that followed, Tommy Aiello seemed always to prevail. "You are what you are, and the world fuckin' knows it," his father seemed always to be saying, the belt of recrimination popping in Paul's ear.

Predictably, he had done it to himself again, and worst of all understanding that in the current environment, such behavior, once exposed, offered little opportunity for the accused to defend himself. Nuance had fled the scene, and simply sleeping with a woman in the context of a power imbalance wouldn't be tolerated. Both Janine and Susan had been at his house, had agreed to stay over. He could claim they had taken their drinks willingly. But none of the falsified details, no matter how exculpatory, would matter. He couldn't threaten or lie his way out of what now faced him.

PART THREE

CANNES

harlie Gold had changed everything.

Early on there was no film festival party or premiere to which he and his brother wouldn't scam an invite or crash outright. First ridiculed as boorish and uncouth, he found a niche in prestige films he then expanded into an industry. "Me and my brother grew up middle-class, so I don't try to impress people with a bunch of pretension. I just know movies. I also know what I like, and don't like, and I'm honest about it. I go in to watch a movie at a festival, and I look at it solely in terms of does it have an impact on me, and will it make money? If the answer to either of those questions is no, and I mean *either* of those questions, we don't buy it. If the answer is yes to both, meaning I love it and it'll make money, the movie becomes ours, no matter what we have to pay, because when I pay a lot, I figure out how to make a lot."

With women he was an unlikely suitor: not only married with three children but at a balding six feet he weighed just shy of 270 pounds. He rarely shaved his pocked face, and comported himself in a manner that could only be described as coarse. The more powerful he became, the more imperious, bullying his way to what he wanted—not just scripts, directors, writers, actors, Academy Awards, and Golden Globes, but lines of credit from banks, publicity in all media, political influence with those of his choosing.

This had a fortuitous impact, at least as Charlie experienced it.

"The best thing that ever happened to me," he said to his brother, "was all the hostility from girls early on. Not just being told no, but 'no fucking way.'"

"And why was that a good thing?" asked Rob.

"Because I could see them for what they were: just going for the guys who were popular or rich, which is what gave them status at the time, and mostly with other girls. So, I said fuck it: I'm gonna get so fucking powerful that none of that shit—looks and popularity—matters. And then guess what? I did, and now suddenly everyone wants to be around me, especially the women, because I have access to what they want. And now all those guys who used to get the girls are the fucking losers."

"I think you're a little full of yourself. And by the way, I still don't see all the women you keep talking about." He pantomimed a quick search. "Where are they?"

"I don't brag."

"What the fuck are you doing right now?"

"Do you hear any names?"

"All I have to do is see who's getting bit parts in our films."

"Not just the ones playing the small parts, asshole. I don't need to tell you one of 'em happens to have a statue."

"I'd worry more about statutes."

Rob never resisted the opportunity to belittle, though it had been Charlie who'd not only pushed them into the film business but had designed the evolving strategies for their continuing expansion. They spent relentlessly, buying real estate, television stations, a magazine. Charlie even insisted they take a stake in the restaurant that occupied the ground floor of their building in SoHo.

"What the fuck do we know about the food business?" asked Rob.

"It's called diversification," Charlie answered. "Besides, if we're owners, we'll always get the best tables. We can have meetings there. And parties at a cut rate but book them at a full rate. It's another way to increase marketing costs and lay them off to overhead. Everybody wins. And when we do that, what else are we doing?"

"What?"

"Keeping the restaurant in business with other people's money that goes into our pockets. Meanwhile, the asset's becoming more and more valuable."

"How's that?"

"We eat there. We get our stars and directors to eat there, it's the place to be. It's a gold mine six fucking ways to Sunday. We're doing this."

Not only did all transpire as he predicted, with the restaurant that served high-end bar food and craft beers becoming one of the most popular in lower Manhattan, but Charlie could meet aspiring actresses for dinner at the end of a day's work simply by stepping onto the elevator and traversing the building's lobby. The waitstaff grew accustomed to his brash ordering style in an inexorably developed routine. He designated a regular table toward the back and expected double vodka martinis for his female guest and him to be prepared before his ample posterior flattened the cushion of his chair.

"Whether she wants the drink or not, you give it to her. You leave it on the table," servers were instructed.

After appetizers and perhaps a second round, Charlie and his companion, typically not half his weight and at least twenty years his junior, would quit the table for his office upstairs, returning flush and disheveled after about half an hour to enjoy the rest of their meals.

"They always say yes eventually," he told Rob. "There's just too much upside. They want what I can give, and there's no better aphrodisiac. Because trust me, these women are not unwilling. They feel like they've plugged themselves into the socket of power. I tell them what I've done for other women, and they know. A lot of them even have boyfriends, but they're in my office or their apartments or a hotel room with me and they're fucking loving it. Look at me. Built like a goddamn bear, I'm balding, and I don't shave, and you know what they all say? That I'm sexy. Power is sexy."

Two types of women confounded him. First, those who wouldn't sleep with him a second time should he desire it. He would call them repeatedly, appear at their apartments unannounced, and ultimately force the issue, overpowering them if he had to. They could beg, weep, howl, but they would succumb. Should they threaten to reveal what he'd done, he would simply remind them of the predicament in which they'd put themselves.

"You fucked me once because you believed it could get you work, and now when we sleep together again—and by the way, let's not fool ourselves, it was consensual because you let me in here when we'd slept together before—"

"You forced yourself in!"

"Who opened the door?"

He would leave them in tears, sometimes raging, but so long as they didn't do as they'd threatened, he would continue offering parts. A deal was a deal, however tacit.

Others posed challenges from the outset, rebuffing overtures altogether, and with these he advanced more elaborate methods. Usually at film festivals or when traveling to Los Angeles, in the most capacious suites in the most opulent hotels, he would arrange a general meeting. Should the actress express anxiety, being met in the lobby and led upstairs by a female assistant who would then remain in the room for the first fifteen minutes or so helped reassure her. When finally left alone, they could settle into an easy dialogue, often abetted by alcohol.

A typical exchange occurred at the Hotel du Cap-Eden-Roc in Cannes with Chloe Paige, already somewhat established in her mid-twenties.

"Sorry about the champagne," he said. "I know this is technically a business meeting, but it's been a brutal day, so I opened it. People send this shit to me constantly. I could fill an Olympic pool. I don't know even where this caviar came from. I get sent everything. Chocolate, red wine, lately high-end vodka for some reason. I guess in an interview somewhere I said I liked vodka. I've probably got five thousand dollars of it in the New York office alone, all of it gifts. Two hours ago we signed a hundred-million-dollar infusion for the company that we didn't even need, but people want in. I shouldn't complain, but the terms were a fucking nightmare to get right—their lawyers just didn't get it—so suffice it to say, I need to wind down. You can help yourself to some. It's La Grande Dame, which if you've never tried, you don't want to pass up."

She took a glass and he poured.

"Pretty good, huh?"

"It is."

"I actually think it's better than Dom, but everybody gets obsessed with names. I just know what I like. Which, by the way, applies to you. You're a wonderful actress. That's why I wanted this meeting. We need to figure out what to do together."

"Sounds great."

"It's taken me, what, five months to get in a room with you?"

"It's been a tough year work-wise. I've barely been home."

"New York. I know. We live in the same damned city. It's like you didn't want to take a meeting with me. What the fuck is a studio head to do?"

"I'm here now."

"In the fucking South of France. Maybe it's better this way. We've got a picture we're going to make that I think would be perfect for you. As in you'll win every award you can name. That's what we do for artists like you. We get them what they deserve, which is the fucking hardware. Everybody wins."

"What's the film?"

"I like that. Just like your boyfriend—right to it," he said, referring to the actor James Pratt. "All right, but this doesn't go outside of this room be-cause we haven't announced it yet. It's a movie about Catherine the Great. You would be her."

"Are you serious? Didn't she die in her sixties?"

"I love it. Of course you'd know that. How about this: you age over thirty years during the course of the film. You act half in French. And the death scene is a fucking tour de force. We've got Georg Maerev to direct."

"*The Red Moon* Georg Maerev?"

"You think we were going to get him his Oscar and not do another film with him? Yeah, that fucking Georg Maerev, who's a prince, by the way."

"Holy shit."

"You think your boyfriend is going to be all right with this?"

"I don't understand the question."

"You suddenly becoming one of the biggest stars in the world?"

"I think he'll be happy for me."

"Because when we get behind someone, it's like nothing you've ever seen before."

"May I see a script?"

"Georg is still working on it, but trust me, it's fucking sensational. We're gonna shoot in Prague with three weeks in Saint Petersburg. They're going to let us film on the grounds of the Hermitage. I worked it out personally with the mayor. One of the most expensive movies we've ever made. I don't need your answer now, but tell me it interests you, and I'll see about an offer."

"Absolutely it interests me. Are you kidding?"

"Good. So there's that. But I also want to hear what you want to do. This goes both ways. It's not just me pitching you stuff."

"Well, James and I really want to work together."

"We can't afford James anymore. Besides, we're in the business of dis-covery. Not that if the role was right and James were willing to cut his fee I wouldn't hire him, but fuck James! What do *you* want."

"Well, okay, I love Emily Dickinson."

"You want to do a movie about her?"

"That would be fantastic."

"We could set you up as a producer, choose a writer and a director together, finance development. It could be your next film after *Catherine the Great*."

"None of this is what I expected."

"Look, Chloe. I don't pussyfoot around. I've looked at your career so far. You put it out there. Everything we're discussing right now becomes a reality with my say-so. That's how it works."

He poured more champagne.

"And I like what I do. No, I love what I do, because me and my brother operate on our own terms. We built our company from the fucking ground up by creating opportunities for artists and filmmakers all over the world who were being shut out by the studios. I'm in this for people like you. By the way, because I know you're socially conscious, I'm a powerful man, but you'll never meet a more generous fucking man. The money we make—I was with a filmmaker the other day, and he says, 'Spend another million dollars promoting my film.' His piece of shit about Renoir I made the mistake of financing where he plays Renoir. I asked him, 'What do you think I do with the money we make? You think it all goes to buy fucking dinners at Del Posto?'" He paused for a self-implicating smile. "Well, sometimes it does. I'd be happy to take you to Del Posto, but I didn't tell this asshole that. Instead I said, which is the truth, 'No, it doesn't go for fancy meals. We give.' Bet you didn't know that. We give to about a hundred organizations across the city, from the homeless, to the hungry, to after-school programs—Chess in the Schools, there's a Girls Club on the Lower East Side we practically float singlehandedly. We're huge in that way. That's who I am, which I look across at you and I know you're the same."

"I'd like to think I am, but obviously you and your brother are able to do that on a scale that makes an enormous difference."

"It's easy for us. But guess what? I'm gonna do everything in my power to make it so you can make that sort of difference too. How about that?"

He rose.

"Now, listen. Don't go anywhere. I don't want this to end, but I have a dinner tonight with the president of France, which you're welcome to join me at if you'd like. I was going to take one of our directors, but I'd have a better time with you. You want to hang with Nicolas Sarkozy? Carla's gonna be there. Amazing woman. Completely down-to-earth."

"I'm not really dressed for that kind of thing."

"I can call Sami, my assistant you just met. You give her your sizes, she goes downstairs to one of the boutiques and comes up with half a dozen options. Anyway, there's time. Think about it. In the meantime, I've got to take a shower. You sit there—"

"Oh. No, I really should go."

"You're not going to get weird on me now, are you?"

"I have people waiting for me."

"Please. This is no big thing. I go into the other room and shower, which is very quick. You get uncomfortable, you leave. Seriously, what's going to happen? Just enjoy your champagne. Don't make this uncomfortable. Why would you do that? Come on. Have another glass."

He poured more Grande Dame, then passed through French doors he left open to the bedroom. In the bathroom he turned on the shower before beginning to disrobe beyond the door.

"I'm gonna leave this partly open so we can continue to talk! It gets so crazy with my fucking schedule here. You wouldn't believe it. It literally takes three assistants to handle it all. One for the calendar, and two just to coordinate when I need to be where. I mean it's not so different in New

York, but there I could have blocked off more time. So, what do you know about Catherine the Great?"

"Um, not much actually."

"What's that?"

"Not much!"

His upper half, now dripping with water, leaned out across the threshold of the bathroom.

"Come into the bedroom so we can hear each other. Or fuck it, just come into the bathroom," he shouted. "The shower door is beveled and covered with steam anyway. You're not going to see anything you shouldn't. I really want to talk with you about this character, who, by the way, looked just like you. I mean how fucking lucky is Georg Maerev that one of the most talented young actresses around is basically a dead ringer, and that we're willing to fucking bank on that?"

No answer came. He stepped from the stall, dried himself, put on his robe, and returned to an empty suite.

He called her agent the following day.

"I don't know what the fuck your client thought she was doing, but we had pretty much one of the worst meetings I've ever taken with an actress. Ever."

"I've been trying to reach her. What happened?"

"Let's just say I pitched her probably the most important female role we have, with an Oscar-winning director, and she acted like she was too good for it. 'I'd have to read the script first. And I'm really busy.' Are you fucking kidding me? Like she was doing me some sort of favor. Well, what *do* you want to do? I finally asked her. And she says we should make a film with her and her fucking boyfriend, as if I'm in the business of making vanity projects for actresses and whoever they're screwing. She also drank three quarters of a bottle of champagne ... couldn't stop pouring for herself. I excuse myself to go to the bathroom, and she leaves without saying good-bye."

"That just doesn't sound like Chloe, Charlie."

"So now I'm a fucking liar? Do me a favor. Don't ever call me again. And that goes for your whole goddamn agency. Your clients are finished at Gold Films."

An hour later two senior partners called.

"Charlie, we're sorry about whatever happened with Chloe Paige."

"You fucking should be. What, she thinks because she's banging James Pratt I'm lucky to have a meeting with her? When she's half drunk walking in the door? And then her agent. What's her name, Sharon?"

"Cheryl Klosterman."

"Fucking Cheryl Klosterman tells me I must not be accurately describing what happened. Are you fucking kidding me?"

"Look, Charlie. Everybody's upset. You're upset, we're upset, Chloe is upset. Cheryl is upset. James Pratt's upset. What's the point? You don't want to hire Chloe, that's you're prerogative, but why take it out on the entire agency and all our clients? We've made a lot of money for each other."

"I have fucking saved this business. When the rest of you morons were following the studios down the drain making schlock movie after schlock movie, me and my brother actually were making films actors wanted to be in. And teaching America—that's right, teaching—how this was once actually a fucking art form. *Inventing* the term 'art film.' And hiring your shitty clients and turning them into bona fide stars, so that winning a fucking Oscar actually meant something again. And this little cunt and her bitch agent treat me like I'm lucky to be in a room with her?"

"Charlie, we're sorry."

"It also wouldn't hurt to know that this Cheryl woman—what's her name again?"

"Cheryl Klosterman."

"No longer had a job at your agency, but that's up to you."

"You'll never have to speak to her again."

The following night in the packed Hotel du Cap bar, where F. Scott Fitzgerald once held court, he was chatting with a young Russian actress when he felt a hard pull at his shoulder.

"What the fuck?" he blurted, rotating to discover James Pratt, several inches shorter at only five foot eight, his eyes quiet with anger.

"Charlie, you ever do something like that to Chloe again, I swear I will find you wherever you are and punch your fucking lights out."

Looking down at one of the most powerful stars in the industry, whose upward trajectory he'd abetted with several choice roles early on, Charlie wanted nothing more than to test the potency of a right hook he hadn't used since decking an anti-Semitic weight-shamer in high school. He'd broken the boy's jaw but received only two days suspension, as there'd been witnesses to the provocation, one of them a teacher with the last name of Cohen. In the case of James Pratt, however, a good twenty years his junior and the star recently of a film in which he'd played an Irish boxer, Charlie was uncertain he could land the punch without it being blocked or dodged. Moreover, should he connect, to what effect other than a surfeit of inimical press? Publication first in the trades and then in papers all over the world would be swift and damaging, without time to threaten them away.

"Hey, James, how you doing?" he asked as others in tight proximity turned to witness what might occur. "Let me buy you a drink."

"I can buy my own, and I'd just as soon not be seen talking to you."

"Yeah, well, I don't know what Chloe told you, but her misunderstanding of a situation, especially after half a bottle of champagne—did she mention that?—shouldn't get blown out of proportion. I offered her a part that could change her life. If you really love her, instead of trying to pick a fight with me, one of your biggest fans, you'd be thanking me and telling her to call us and say she'll play Catherine the Great."

"She's not calling you, Charlie. And stay the fuck away from her. You're looking at someone who's not scared of you. People don't go to see movies because of the head of the studio that makes them."

Before Charlie could respond, James was gone.

"Wow."

Charlie turned to a diminutive man in his fifties wearing white pants, a pastel blazer, and a crisp salmon shirt.

"What was that about, Charlie?"

"Do I know you?"

"We met at a party you guys held at SoHo Kitchen last year. I was invited by your brother." He stuck out a hand that Charlie didn't take. "Gabe Taub. From the Taub Agency. We've got two actors in films here. It's my first time at Cannes."

Charlie loathed supplicants. Everyone wanted to meet him, be seen with him, photographed with him. Once he rendered doing so easy, the value would diminish. He turned back to the Russian actress without responding.

"You didn't want to introduce me to James Pratt?" she asked.

"What, I'm not interesting enough for you?"

"I didn't mean that."

"He's been after us to put him in a film for about two years now. We make them stars and then they always want to come back. I basically had to tell him to get in line. Seriously, you can't name an actor who doesn't want to work with us. But I need to hear more about you." That she hadn't fled while facing his back for a good three minutes meant that as long as he kept her around for the rest of the night, he would have her in his suite.

"I'm from Tbilisi."

"Heard of it. Never been there."

"Then I moved to Moscow."

"Putin is a friend. Medvedev too."

"And now I live in Paris."

Try as he did to lose himself in their flirtation, the interaction with James Pratt gnawed at him. No one other than his brother had challenged him in this way, in private or in public, in at least five years. And what of Chloe Paige? Normally an actress would have remained to converse while he showered. They'd have a bit more champagne, perhaps he'd open another bottle, and then he'd ask, "This is going to sound weird, but do you have strong hands?"

"I guess I do."

"Would you mind rubbing my neck? It's been killing me all day."

"Um, sure."

"You seem hesitant. If it makes you uncomfortable ..."

"Oh no, it's fine."

"Well good, because the truth is, it's my whole fucking back. I'm a big guy. Most of it is muscle, which is murder on the spine."

In several instances he'd even have them apply his bacne cream; if a woman were willing to do that, she'd do anything. He'd lie facedown on the bed, and that would be that. He could overcome any resistance easily, sometimes by forcing oral sex.

"You're really not going to let me do this?" he would demand, incredulous, holding her down. "I'm a fucking master at it. You're not going to believe what I can do."

He would wound Chloe Paige, perhaps irreparably. He and his executives would whisper loudly that she had construed her affiliation with James Pratt to confer a kind of divinity. Charlie had offered a plum role and she'd shunned it, demanding instead that they develop only films of her choosing. She was difficult, unstable, erratic, pretentious, overemotional, entitled, not to mention reckless with alcohol. The publicity department would leak some of this to the *New York Post*, which would then alert other outlets, because the public loved to hate stars. He would cost her and her representatives millions. Above all, he couldn't allow her to do what too many had done in recent years: fleece him with legal action.

"What the fuck are you doing to us?" Rob asked more and more frequently in relation to such payouts.

"What I do in my private life is my fucking business."

"We hire actresses, Charlie. We give them work. How is that your private life?"

"First of all, I haven't sexually assaulted anyone. Ever."

"We've paid out over a million and a half dollars in the last year alone."

"To settle baseless suits and save money on the lawyers. And so I can get on with my work, which is to make the movies that keep us in business."

"My movies keep us in business."

"You go ahead and think that."

"I don't have to think it. I look at the grosses."

A six-figure sum meant a woman would drop her complaint and sign a nondisclosure agreement exposing her to ruinous damages should she ever break it. If any news organization learned of the accusations, Charlie would threaten a lawsuit, along with the choking off of advertising dollars.

"Remind the fucking *New York Times* again how many full-page ads we took out in the arts section last year alone. And if we stop buying ads, the studios stop buying ads. Everyone copies us. The papers need us more than we need them. I'm tired of reminding them to watch what they fucking write."

When the *Daily News* got wind of criminal charges being filed by a Slovenian actress claiming he'd groped her after hours in his Manhattan office, he dispatched investigators to Europe who discovered she'd filed rape charges there twice before, suggesting a pattern of entrapment whereby she'd seduce wealthy men for humiliation and extortion. The *New York Post* dutifully published this, along with a host of other smears that included quotes from jilted boyfriends, old roommates, and even an estranged sister living on the streets in Sacramento. His accuser dropped charges and fled the country.

But no one, and particularly not Charlie, anticipated the massive shifts in what consumers of filmed entertainment wanted and how they wished to view it. Especially with streaming services, the demographic interested in the art and genre films central to Charlie and Rob's model no longer needed movie theaters to experience erudite dramas and slasher movies—the unlikely twin pillars of Gold Films. In fact, it could be argued that the intimacy of living rooms made the experience preferable to the distraction of strangers masticating popcorn and blocking one's view. Moreover, subscription television, unencumbered by restrictions as to level of undress, coarse language, and depiction of sex and violence, could now create decidedly more sophisticated programming uninterrupted by commercials. With ten to twelve hours per season, exploration of story and character could occur more patiently than in two-hour dramas meant for movie screens. This in turn attracted writers, directors, and actors who'd worked previously only in film. Once television could be monetized in this novel, commercial-free form, new companies emerged with untold resources for creating content accessible via any device—from a home theater to a computer, even a smartphone.

"How are we supposed to compete with these assholes?" Charlie asked Rob and a roomful of executives. "They've got more fucking cash on hand than some countries do."

"We make content for them," offered their VP of production.

"What happens to our distribution arm? What, we're suddenly going to be freelance producers? You're lucky I don't fire you for that moronic shit you just said."

Promotion shifted as well, and away from print media. Those between the ages of fifteen and forty consumed advertising more frequently now on websites, less likely to read their news, eager instead to be told it by smart-mouthed pundits, comedians, and YouTubers. And as the Golds spent less on full-page newspaper ads, editors and publishers lost the impulse to restrain reporters.

The *New York Times* published first, drawing from a compendium of sources journalists had been aggregating for years. Eight women, four of whom allowed their names to be printed, told laceratingly consistent stories. Each had been offered a role or roles, each had been alone with Charlie in a hotel room, apartment, or office, each had been propositioned aggressively. Three had succumbed, the others had not. Two alleged to have been raped when they'd refused a second advance, both in Manhattan apartments.

An unbowed Chloe Paige recounted the entire encounter at Cannes. Charlie could not help but admire her persisting grasp of what had trans-pired, down to the brand of champagne and the color of the sofa on which he'd sat while panegyrizing it. Somehow she'd also been made aware that two months later when a young director had wanted her to play the title role in a modern adaptation of *Jane Eyre*, Charlie had squelched the idea by insisting, as he had in at least a half dozen other instances, that she was spoiled, difficult, a boozer, not to be trusted. When the director refused to relent, arguing that he'd handled nettlesome actresses in the past, Charlie had threatened to fire him off his own film. Somehow she even had the quote, which *New York* magazine published but the *New York Times* did not: "You've directed two films. I've produced over two hundred. You want to use Chloe Paige, go make another movie with another fucking studio. I say who plays Jane Eyre, and it sure as fuck won't be Chloe Paige."

Had it just been Chloe, he might have prevailed by discrediting her with information gathered swiftly by his detectives: her two stints in rehab for booze and painkillers, serial philandering, even having been paid to write papers for classmates in college (though he was warned this might actually endear her both to press and public, given her penurious upbringing). But the writers in both the *Times* and *New York* magazine had fortified their reporting with an uncontainable variety of named sources, scouring every nuance and habit of his life (even waiters at the restaurant downstairs), each corroborating the other.

More articles followed, amounting to a frenzy. Within six months, the number of female accusers topping eighty, Gold Films was no more, Charlie's wife had filed for divorce, and he and his brother were bankrupt and no longer speaking. His undoing catalyzed a movement that ramified into every corner of American culture, affixing itself to Charlie's name and legacy more than his transformative accomplishments in film. Chloe Paige too eclipsed her own artistic endeavors when she told a writer, "It's time people like Charlie Gold understand that 50.8 percent of the population in America isn't going to be relegated, demeaned, or ignored anymore," initiating what came to be known as the 50.8 movement, with Chloe its willing if unintended priestess.

BEVERLY HILLS

"I never liked Charlie Gold," Paul Aiello said to a colleague at the time of Charlie's undoing, "but now I fucking hate him. You can't have a dick in this town anymore without it being the mark of Cain. Now if I want to get laid, I practically have to get written permission. I'm not saying I've been innocent. Like any guy who's had too much to drink or God knows what else on a given night, I've blown through a stop sign or two. Fuck me if I know what's in my past that I don't even remember, and that some woman doesn't really remember either but thinks she does. Suddenly I could get fired over that? Are you fucking kidding me? I've done more for women in this business than anyone I can name."

"Paul," said the fellow agent, "what's done is done. All you can do is worry about the future, and over that you have some control. So yes, if you feel like you need written permission before you sleep with a woman, fucking get it, notarized and stamped if you have to. And if a woman says she's game but you still have doubts as to what she's about, drop her off at her house, say good night, and go home and jerk off till you're blue in the face, because trust me, a night of bliss isn't worth losing everything you've built for yourself. And especially you because, like you said, you're known as the guy who represents actresses. You fuck up with even one woman, and it's over, no matter how much you've made for all the others."

But Paul had been exploiting his industry power well before the pillorying of Charlie Gold. In fact the trajectory of his and Charlie's behavior somewhat mirrored each other's, intensifying over years as Paul couldn't escape the suspicion that women were amassing complete power over him, a feeling originating in middle school when puberty overtook him with such ferocity that he could think of nothing but girls day and night. Having a handsome brother two years his senior with an uninterrupted series of females he'd bed several afternoons a week only exacerbated this. By Paul's estimation Gus had screwed six of the fourteen-strong cheerleading squad during his junior year alone.

"The first thing to realize is that girls actually love to fuck," he instructed his younger brother. "Most guys, they think they need to beg—that girls don't want to give it over. But that's all just show. We're animals, and girls are on the fucking prowl just as much as we are. What do you think puberty is? So, once you know that, there's two issues. The first is, a girl does not want to get pregnant. You have a condom on you at all times so when the opportunity presents itself you show them you're ready and responsible and worldly. And second, confidence in who and what you are. Again, we're animals. A girl likes to know the guy she's with can fucking take care of business, protect her. It's instinct. We're out in the fucking wild, and you've got to be able to bash the lions away with a fucking tree limb, or worse, smash in the skull of the guy from the other tribe who wants to carry her off to his cave. It also doesn't hurt to be half good looking, which thanks to our asshole father, both of us are. Imagine if you looked like that friend of yours. The curly-haired blond kike with the acne from when you were at the private school."

"Brad Shlansky."

"Yeah. Then you're in trouble. That guy's never gonna get laid."

Perhaps because he actually wasn't as good looking as his brother, or father for that matter, Paul could only describe his infrequent exploits through middle adolescence as marginally better than adequate, a degree that hardly sated his obsessive needs. He bragged ceaselessly about girls to friends, but little of what he said was true. At night and each morning he went after it on his own relentlessly, loathing not only himself but his brother, his brother's myriad partners, and all the girls (save one blessed soul in middle school who'd let him feel her up) who dismissed him for older, more athletic boys. Even when he'd lost his virginity, an event that occurred uneventfully in a kitchen pantry at a tenth-grade house party with a girl named Mary, he couldn't shake the resentment. In fact, Mary only made matters worse because he didn't actually like her, her occasional willingness to have sex comprising the sole motivation to sustain a relationship.

"You're fucking breaking up with me?" he asked, incredulous, after he'd been on vacation with his parents in Fort Myers for two weeks.

"First of all, we hardly talk. Nothing I want to do interests you. All you want to do is like, have sex, which is fine, but I need more."

"More sex?"

"Fuck you."

"What, then?" He wanted to be in the backseat with her instead of autopsying their demise.

"You should also know that I've been talking about this with Mike Diaz. Him and me are gonna start going out."

Mike and Mary had been at it for his entire time in Florida. He knew Mike envied what he had with Mary, but the concept of romance between them had never crossed his mind.

"I bet the sex isn't better," Paul announced.

"No comment."

"You just answered my question. So obviously it isn't, you little whore."

"Since you put it that way, jerk, it's a lot better. He actually gives a shit whether I like it."

He begged Mary to take him back, but use of the epithet had destroyed what little chance he might have had. He rarely spoke to either of them after, though he did smash Mike's headlights with a golf club, and during his senior year he slashed Mary's tires late one night on his way home alone, so drunk he sliced his own hand in the act, leaving a permanent scar.

Other than Celeste, and perhaps Grace from Austin, he hadn't had a meaningful relationship with a woman in his life, and that included his ex-wife, an entertainment lawyer he never should have married, particularly considering he was cheating on her within a month after returning from their honeymoon.

"Somebody should have told me I was marrying a man," he explained to Brad Shlansky. "Seriously, as soon as we had rings on, and I mean from the minute it happened—we're talking the party after the wedding—she starts bossing me around. Get me this, get me that. Do this, don't do that.' Without so much as a please or thank-you. I said to myself, are you fucking kidding me? And then, no respect in public. Belittling me at parties like you couldn't believe, with the 'Oh, you'll have to forgive Paul, he only reads screenplays.' So, of course I fucked around on her. At least I married wealthy, so when she had to write me a check for two hundred grand, I didn't feel guilty. I got paid a hundred thousand a month, which was just about right for the three and a half weeks of misery that was being faithful to her."

As for work, initially his client list engendered a sense of pride, even virility. But one day near the end of his marriage, on a morning at home that had ended with his wife throwing a cup of coffee in his face, he sought solace on the drive in to UCM by rolling calls. His female assistant offered an accounting that included not a single male in need of his attention, and he realized in that moment that without actresses he was nothing. Moreover, because he worked for them all day each weekday, then read scripts for them on weekends, his entire life involved doing the bidding of a gender he'd long ago begun deeply to resent, the seeds of it in middle school, its first bloom Celeste's refusal to take him back and the vengeful promiscuity that had ensued.

"Do you have any idea what a relief it is just to talk to you every day?" he asked Brad Shlansky over drinks a month after Brad and his sisters had arrived in Los Angeles. "I can't say this during the day when we're on the phone because the assistant is listening, but finally a client who isn't complaining about the makeup artist or what the director said, or the size of her fucking trailer. I'm fucking drowning."

"Oh yeah, poor you," said Brad. "All day you've got to talk to Claire Fisher and all the other gorgeous actresses about their multimillion-dollar TV and movie offers with you skimming your ten percent."

"Fine, fine. Fair enough. I'll shut up," he said. But to depend on women, be beholden to women, and in his personal life to *need* women to the point of obsession had transformed him into a being he could no longer control. How, then, could he be expected to curtail the palliative need for more and more submissiveness from an increasing variety of partners, leading finally to the night with Susan and Janine? On a basic level this even exonerated him. He was who he was, so how could the two women not have known what would transpire? The whole episode constituted a lurid dance in which each played a part, the two actresses, whether they understood it or not, ultimately just as responsible for what had happened as he.

"I have the fucking photographs!" he kept reminding Martin.

"I don't want to hear about the photographs. Paul, you need to be doing what we're all doing right now—all the men in this industry. And trust me, I include myself."

"Oh yeah, what's that? Tell me what I need to be doing other than pay you eight hundred bucks an hour along with what amounts to, best-case scenario, a million and a quarter dollars to these two extortionists for a pretty unremarkable one-night stand."

"You need to look back over your entire past and think about any other incidents like this one—"

"You mean every time I had sex?"

"Be quiet and listen. I'm trying to help you. There's blood in the water here, and once one woman comes out publicly, if there are others—clients, I mean, or even potential clients—who might say you had sex with them nonconsensually, or that you had consensual sex that nevertheless was associated with a power imbalance, or even tried to have sex with, we need to develop a strategy for dealing with it, because regardless of these two now, you will be eviscerated. It's happening all over the place, and trust me, you will not be spared."

"Funny how this involves your helping me with this, meaning billable hours."

"You bet your ass it does. Or some other lawyer who's not as good as me. Go ahead, there are ten thousand of them in LA. Take your pick. And if you think I haven't hired counsel, think again. We're all in the same boat."

"You're sixty-five years old!"

"Exactly. And by today's standards vulnerable, and I've been smart enough to admit that to myself. Not guilty of anything, mind you, but legitimately vulnerable."

"What the fuck did you do?"

"That's between my lawyer and me, and so far as I know, you haven't passed the bar."

"Fucking Charlie Gold."

"This was going to happen regardless. Men in this business, all of us, are a bunch of assholes. And if you don't think we deserve what we're getting right now, then you're not being honest with yourself. Even now I wouldn't want to be a woman in this industry for a second."

"Oh Christ. Spare me the fucking righteousness. Or at least don't bill me to listen to it."

"I just deducted the last five minutes."

By the time he'd finished reporting the one-sided negotiation with Janet Liebowitz to Martin, Jen divulged a backlog of more than forty calls. Clients have no idea what we go through in a day, he thought. Were agents to answer every one of their queries, it would leave no time to pursue the very work about which they're pestering us. "The worst thing you can ever do is let an actor in on the secret that there are other people in the world," Lizzie Gruber told him early on. "You've been dealing with music stars. Actors are another breed. Movies and TV shows that don't have parts for the person you're on the phone with don't exist. And don't ever, and I mean *ever*, say to an actor, 'I've got to take this call' unless you say it's to talk about them."

"And I have Brad Shlansky," Jen alerted him.

"Call back."

"I already told him that. You were still on the cell call. He's been waiting on the line. He wouldn't hang up."

"Is that a joke?"

"Sorry to say ..."

"Christ on a fucking cracker. All right, put him through."

"I know you're supposedly very busy," Brad chirped maliciously, "so I won't take up any of your precious time."

"You're becoming my neediest client. Strike the word *becoming*."

"Uh-huh. Just reserve the conference room again for Friday morning."

"And why would I do that?"

"The meeting with David Levit and Jacob Rosenthal and Howard Garner is back on."

"You called me to talk about David Levit? My God, we haven't touched on that topic for a whole hour. David Levit is going home tonight, or did you forget? That's why you had me go embarrass myself by throwing a fit yesterday in Howard Garner's office."

"Just reserve the fucking room. All morning. Nine to noon."

"What about Jacob Rosenthal? Does he know about this supposed meeting?"

"He'll be there. Trust me. It's gonna happen."

CHATEAU MARMONT

"**D**avid, you're going to want to call me. I'm on cell."
Brad Shlansky's voice projected tacit regret, as if he possessed
a painful truth of which David wasn't aware but needed to be.
Then a text: "Did you get my message? Call me. You'll be glad you did."
David dialed Sammy's office in New York only to find him unavailable.
He began to pack, willing the phone to ring or not ring—hoping for Sammy,
dreading Brad. As he was about to zip closed his black American Traveler
bag, he heard the chirp.

"You didn't want to return my call?" Brad asked.

"I was on with my wife."

"I was thinking you might be talking with Iris."

"Excuse me?"

"Iris Wood."

David sat on the bed.

"David?"

"Who is Iris Wood?"

"You and a woman who calls herself Iris Wood weren't hanging out
together last night? She didn't leave your room early this morning? You
there?"

"Yeah, I'm here."

"Oh, good." Brad's voice remained malignantly casual. "I thought I'd
lost you for a second."

David wanted to murder himself: extinguish the person who had
succumbed so easily to the advances of a stranger. Had he simply pushed
his credulous ego aside, he would have understood something to have been
amiss. Even a cursory glance around the Chateau's patio would have
presented at least half a dozen men more intriguing than he: producers,
not one but two directors, a few A-list stars, each more appealing in looks,
artistic merit, and power than the next. Just after he'd agreed to show her
his room, several had even paused to say hello and then lingered once exposed to his unlikely companion. One even mentioned David's wife with
no absence of intent. How had he not understood her fawning presence to
have been anything other than a callous ruse?

"So, what do we do now?" he asked Brad.

"For starters, we meet at UCM on Friday like I've been asking. I'd heard you were going back to New York today. I don't think that's a good idea."

"I won't go back."

"Not just you. I want Jacob Rosenthal there too."

"How am I going to get Jacob Rosenthal there?"

"By telling him it's important."

"I'll back out of directing *Coal*, Brad."

"Who said I wanted you to do that?"

"It's what you've been saying the whole time. It's what this is all about."

"Now you're telling me what this is all about?"

"It's what you've been saying!"

"I want you and Jacob Rosenthal at UCM on Friday morning. Alice and Paul Aiello will be there too. And Howard Garner."

"So, you paid her?"

"Who?"

"You realize this is blackmail, Brad."

"You think I paid a woman who happens to teach a spin class to my sister Sarah? Who comes in this morning and brags to Sarah she was with the guy who directed the film *Revenge* last night? And didn't my sister produce that?"

"Okay, so what do you want? Money?"

"I know what you've made at UCM down to the fucking penny, and trust me, you can't afford to pay me off."

"So, what is it then, Brad?"

"Why don't we all think about it between now and Friday. How's that? And as for the girl you fucked last night, maybe I know about it not just because of my sister but also because who's to say I don't have friends who were at the Chateau and saw you sit with her at the bar and buy her drinks and dinner and then take her up to your room? But if you want to start claiming all sorts of other shit, you have your buddy from Brown call Alice and get into it. Then we can see where the shrapnel from the explosion goes."

"Jesus, Brad."

"That's exactly right." And the call was over.

Brad had hired the woman. Of this he had no doubt, but so what? No way could he call Sammy. No way could he call Charlotte. Not since Adam's passing had David felt so alone.

BEVERLY HILLS

Sometimes Jacob regretted not having come to Los Angeles sooner. He'd packed three lifetimes into more than thirty years there. So far as the quality of work was concerned, other than a few projects that had escaped more stringent oversight, he had few regrets. In fact, he could indulge a measure of pride in having followed his own instincts rather than insipid trends. He'd been true consistently, for better or worse, to what he wanted, not what others told him he should want. Even his love affair with Violet, in spite of the deception involved, evinced its own kind of purity. I'm not better than others, he often thought, I'm just unencumbered by self-doubt and self-delusion. I don't rely on anyone but myself for who and what I am.

Leaving aside his other reasons for wanting to do it, *Coal* would be the defining achievement of that ethos, at odds with so many of the self-serving pieties espoused of late by most of his industry cohort. Given his own past, he found it next to impossible to sit at dinner parties in Beverly Hills, Brentwood, and Bel Air hearing rooms full of all white guests discuss the "epidemic" of white privilege, and how "people of color," a term he loathed for its grammatical inaccuracy (was the hue of Caucasians not a color?), had every right to get their due. He and Larry had hired more Black directors, editors, cinematographers, and actors than any other company at his level he could name.

"I don't do this as a matter of restitution or to relieve guilt I don't have," he would announce almost reflexively. "I do it because I happen to have had a really good feeling about a lot of people wanting to be involved with shit I have control over who've been Black. This doesn't make me a goddamn hero. And guess what? When I've been wrong, a person's skin color hasn't gotten in the way of my firing them. You cross me or screw up, it doesn't matter whether you're brown, Black, yellow, white or purple, you're done. And not once have I been sued over this shit for improper dismissal." He could name at least four "people of color," two producers, one director, and one actor whom he'd helped make millionaires by giving them their first significant jobs. How many others could boast that degree of practical impact against inequities in the industry they so self-righteously decried?

Lately gender seemed to occupy as great a degree of morally charged space, as he watched grown men effectively castrate themselves to display their bona fides.

"Half of our projects in development have either a female writer or a female director. We make sure of it," said his friend Stan Karlan, who ran a foreign sales-based financing company. They stood poolside at a house designed by A. Quincy Jones in the Bird Streets neighborhood overlooking Sunset. Stan's fiancée, in her early forties, stroked Stan's arm as he expatiated. They each held a glass of Groth Cabernet. "Lila here is going to win an Oscar with one of them."

"As soon as we get the script right," she added. "No great script, no great movie."

"You don't know any really good female writers, do you, Jacob?" asked Stan.

"Can you even name a female writer, Jacob?" Lila wondered aloud.

"A few," he answered, not taking the bait.

"It's a mother-daughter story," she added, "so we need the right touch. Emotional, yes, but not sentimental. A writer who's young and badass and a maybe a bit mean."

"I'll have my assistant send over a list."

"Your female assistant?"

"That's right."

"How old is she?"

"Mid-fifties. Been with me since I started. She's from Chicago."

"Jacob has a thing about Chicago," said Stan.

"Good for Jacob. Nice to be the king, isn't it?"

"I don't complain," Jacob responded. "And I'd think you'd want me to hire a female assistant, Lila. We promote inside of my company."

"Then why's she still your assistant?"

"She headed marketing for six months ten years ago and hated it. I brought her back onto my desk without cutting the salary bump."

"It's just these men with their twenty-something hotties sitting in the meetings, and the executive stroking himself off while the poor girl sits typing everything he says into the two-thousand-dollar laptop he bought her. Hired because she looks good in a dress with her fucking legs showing."

"Does that really happen anymore?"

"Please. You're done, Jacob. I said the same thing to Stan. It's over for you old white guys. You walk onto a set today, and it's women, people of color, gender-neutral, trans, gays. Everyone but you. And it's so fucking refreshing."

"She's not wrong," added Stan. "We don't just do inclusion riders. We now do markups on our scripts that calculate percentages of how many lines white men have relative to women and people of color, so it's right there on paper for all of us to have to face up to. And the same with department heads and all crew positions."

"And how do you feel about that?" asked Jacob of his friend.

"What do you mean? I think it's fucking great."

"You don't agree, Jacob?" asked Lila.

"I honestly don't care one way or another. Just make the best movie. Give the people the jobs if they deserve them, and leave it at that."

"Yeah, that's exactly the kind of thinking that's used to keep people down."

"You're going to have to explain that."

"Come on, Jacob. The schools, the sets, the unions, the Academy, they've all been dominated for decades by white men who then keep choosing or hiring other white men because an exclusive system gives them their better resumes. So sure, you get to say 'I chose the best person. I never looked at color or gender.' But of course you fucking did, and you picked the white guy. The whole system did, and it just perpetuates itself, and meanwhile you get to call it a meritocracy when it isn't. It's a fucking aristocracy where instead of wealth it's having white skin and a dick that gets you access to the education and then the qualifications you need to get in the door. It's actually worse. It's a fucking kleptocracy. Which is why what's happening now is so fucking radical and people like you are scared shitless."

Jacob looked over at Stan, who like him had lived through the late sixties.

"What does that radicalism look like exactly?" Jacob asked.

"I just told you. You walk onto a set today—"

"So, what you were saying: you walk on and it's women, gays, people of all colors and ethnicities, tattoos, nose rings, hair dyed pink and blue, club feet, no feet."

"So now you're just being an asshole. But yes. That's exactly what I'm saying."

"I was at the stages today for the third movie in our *Exhumation* franchise—what keeps our lights on these days. The lead is an Australian actress—a woman. I don't much like her because she's awful to everyone, but she's great in front of the camera and carries the whole thing. She's also paid more than anyone else, including Larry and me. The director we hired is a white guy, don't know or care if he's straight or gay, the costume designer I know to be a lesbian, the AD is a woman, the production designer is a Korean woman, the DP is a white guy, his gaffer and first AC are women, the key grip is a Hispanic guy, as is most of his crew, one of the two producers is a woman, the script supervisor is an Israeli woman, the location manager is Black, and so is the woman running the makeup trailer. You think I even thought about any of their genders or races before right now?"

"Then how did you know them off the top of your head?"

"It's the kind of producer I am."

"But listen to yourself, Jacob. You and Larry have all the power. You call them *your* movies. *Your* hires."

"Because they are."

"And I'm talking about you guys no longer being in charge."

"Unless of course it's Stan writing the checks to make your big money-maker about the mother and daughter. Because I'm sure your estrogen-fueled masterpiece is getting made with its all-female cast and crew solely on the merits, not because you're fucking one of these evil men subjugating all the women and people of color."

He deserved to have the drink thrown in his face, he just wished it hadn't been red wine, because he was wearing the Italian suit his wife had coaxed him into buying in Venice the year before at the Biennale.

That night, as he readied himself for bed, his wife not speaking to him, he wondered if he was becoming the reactionary she accused him of being on their drive home. Surely he didn't feel threatened by the industry's current trends. After all, as he saw it, being untethered to the sorts of virtue signaling that now restrained others allowed him to make choices that remained entirely his. Moreover, wasn't he about to make *Coal*, a film based on perhaps the most incendiary and honest novel about race he'd read since *Beloved*? Was it that he felt old? Resolutely out of touch? Cast aside? Suddenly irrelevant, even despised?

He rebuffed Stan's offer to replace his suit when they spoke the next morning.

"I knew what I was doing when I said what I said. I just couldn't help myself. In fact, I was expecting she'd slug me, not throw the drink. I wouldn't have blamed her."

"Me neither. What gets into you?"

"These people have every right to be pissed right now, but it's turning into a land grab. At a certain point they're going to regret the overreach."

"It ruined my fucking night. She didn't put the engagement ring back on until six this morning, and for all I know she took it off when she got into her car."

"Same with Lila. She's still not speaking to me. Women and minorities have it better now in this country than ever."

"So, what, we're supposed to stop paying attention? I mean, listen to yourself, Jacob."

"I can't. I'm too busy listening to everyone else talk about how privileged I am."

"Because you are."

"Agreed. But do you know why I've been chasing that Rex Patterson novel all these years?"

"Why?"

"Because here was a Black guy with real credentials who dared to call bullshit on a lot of it. Yes, I'm lucky to be a white man in this day and age— I'm no idiot—but racism and sexism are a fucking sideshow, and Blacks and women right now are only proving that if they have the chance, they'll hold on to power just as strenuously as the white patriarchy."

"I don't know, Jacob. You're sounding pretty threatened."

"Of course I'm fucking threatened," he retorted, suddenly realizing the sad truth of it. "And I'm going to do something about it."

"And what's that?"

"Make *Coal*. It's honest. Not like these fucking Beverly Hills Marxists talking about privilege and pay equity so long as they themselves don't lose their jobs or take a salary reduction. Rex was the real deal."

"And look where that got him."

"Maybe he knew something we didn't, leaving the stage when he did."

"Drinking himself to death?"

"Soon enough we'll be gone like him, and Lila and her bunch will have the keys, which trust me, if they're not careful, they'll drive the car over the cliff with their percentages of hires and counting how many lines go to men and how many to women and all the rest of it that has nothing to do with just telling good stories. I can't believe you go for that shit."

"It keeps me on good terms."

"Look, Lila is a good director, so you're not a stooge for giving her a film. It's a smart business decision. I'd hire her based on merit."

"Then why haven't you?"

"Every time she's come into my office, she's had that chip on her shoulder I was trying to knock off last night."

"Once again, you didn't succeed."

Jacob and Larry had expected David Levit in Larry's office at 10 a.m. so they could finalize offers to their male and female leads. The director would leave that evening for New York on the redeye.

"He told Josh he was running late," said Larry.

"How late?" Jacob inquired of the doorway.

"He didn't say," answered Josh from his desk outside the office. "He sounded harried."

"Harried how?"

"I don't know."

"Well, you used the goddamn word," said Jacob. "Either you were trying to impress us with your vocabulary, which if it's true, don't, or you have some sense of what was going on with the man."

When David finally arrived, *harried* would have been the last word Jacob would use to describe what he saw.

"Jesus, David, you look like you've been sideswiped," said Larry, rising. "You want to take a seat?"

"Yeah, sure." He did so carefully, as if concerned he'd break a bone. "Sorry, I'm just ... give me a second."

"Why don't you tell us what's going on," said Jacob.

"I'm sorry, guys. I really am, but I'm in a situation I'd rather not go into. If I'm going to stay on this project, Jacob and I are going to have to meet at UCM with Brad Shlansky and his lawyer on Friday morning."

Jacob settled into his chair, opting not to respond impulsively.

"David, back in Chicago," he began eventually, "I had a couple of aldermen come into my office to try and shake me down. This was on a development downtown that was of particular importance to me because it involved a building that was one of the first pieces of commercial real estate my father bought back in the early fifties. And the more these two assholes carried on about their connections to the mayor's office and the chief of police and the national party, the more I knew they were lying."

"So, what happened?"

"My next two calls were to Mayor Daley and the DNC. Both aldermen lost their seats. They didn't know who they were dealing with, and neither do your friend and his lawyer."

"I've told you, Brad and Alice play by different rules, Jacob."

"How did this goofball and his crazy so-called attorney bully you into coming in here and asking this of me?"

"Again Jacob, I can't say."

"Well, I'm not going over to UCM to meet with them, so I guess you're not staying on the project."

"Please, Jacob."

"No one coerces me into doing anything I don't want. I've earned that over a lot of years. I'm sorry, but you're fired, David."

"Okay, I'm fired. I guess that should go without saying. But please, will you just come to this stupid meeting? Please? If you don't, it's going to mean some very bad things for me."

"Worse than your losing this job?"

"A lot worse."

"So, he's blackmailing you."

"That's essentially correct."

Jacob paused.

"Does it have to do with your wife?" David didn't answer. "Something she did, or that you did? Can you tell me that?"

"Does it matter?"

Jacob knew little of David's spouse other than a face on a phone. But the director's love for her, like Jacob's had been for Violet (no matter how short lived), seemed abiding and deep, no matter what had transpired.

"All right. Nothing about this is rational, but I'll go. And I'm not firing you either. Not yet anyway. But trust me, this is not going to be pretty, and I'm not talking just on Friday, but leading up to Friday as well, because I don't like being strong-armed, and I don't like my friends being strong-armed, and anyone who works for me, which for the moment you still do, is an ally. This little prick is going to wish he'd never left New York."

"Jacob, please don't do that."

"Don't do what?"

"Brad can become unhinged. And just for the record, he isn't little."

"You're saying what, he's going to come to my house and punch me?"

"Just that nothing about him is little. He and Alice have no scruples. A lot of bad shit has happened to him, so he just doesn't care. He can justify anything, and he puts people around him who are the same way."

"Look at this office, David. Look at Larry here, who is one of the most respected producers around. We have over forty people working in this building, three pictures going right now. Here's the deal: I'm going to UCM on Friday morning, but you're not going to fuck with what I do during that meeting or before it. That's what I want from you because, just so it's absolutely clear, I don't trust you to handle this. I don't even trust Larry, who'll be my partner to the grave."

"Okay."

"Now, if you don't mind, I'd like to get to the business at hand, which is deciding who's getting offers today, and how. Do you think you can pull yourself together so we can do that?"

"I need to call Brad and let him know."

"Text him. Do it right now."

David did, his phone dinging a response immediately.

"He always get back that quickly?"

"Unless he's avoiding you."

"Without lies and avoidance there would be mass murder out here."

"Jesus, Jacob," said Larry.

"There's too much at stake, and ultimately nothing at all. A very bad combination," Jacob said, looking at neither of the men in front of him.

The casting session, scheduled for two hours, took thirty minutes, with Jacob deciding it best for David to approach the two stars on the list he knew best directly before any contact was made with agents.

"Unless you're a major studio and they can push up the quote, or it's a film from one of their directors, these people don't want the client near you for movies like this anymore. We make offers on roles actors would kill to play, and the representatives are of absolutely no help. Then they hold on to your material so no one else gets a look at it. Artist to artist. That's the only way to go with a movie like this. But listen to me, David."

"Yeah?"

"You're going to be calling these actors—maybe even meeting with one or two of them since you're staying in town, and if you look and act as useless as you are right now, sitting there on that sofa like you've just gone six rounds with Tyson, they're not going to want to come near this. What they need from you is a clarity of vision like the one you've been projecting since we met you and before this jerk started fucking with you. Look at this like it's your last chance at making a real film, which it just might be. It's the end of a fucking era. The hills are on fire. Literally. I'm going to your goddamn meeting on Friday. I'm going to help handle this situation. Now it's time for you to help me and help yourself. Understand?"

"I do."

"Internalize it."

"I will."

"Now, what are you doing about your hotel? You said everyone's moving in because of the evacuations. Do you have a place to stay?"

"I was able to keep the room, but under my credit card."

"We'll cover it."

"Jacob, thank you."

"Stop it with the fragile tone. And get the fuck out of here before I change my mind."

"Should I start looking for another director?" asked Larry when David had left.

"Wait for his call when he's talked to the actors, and be ready to make offers. I'll be in my office. We're making this movie, and we're making it with David." He stopped at the door. "And get Nancy to call me."

"Our publicist Nancy? When do you ever want to talk to her?

CHATEAU MARMONT

O nce, in Santa Fe, David ended up at the home of a local makeup artist named Arlie. Older than him by just a few years, she was tall and slender with light blond hair. Her face at forty, unmolested by surgical work, had full red lips that only accentuated a beauty that seemed to be at its peak. David found himself sneaking glances on set, attention she reciprocated brazenly.

Before the proliferation of iPhones and digital cameras he carried an old Leica rangefinder to locations, shooting pushed Tri-X film and handing out three-by-five prints when he wrapped.

"You're like Alfred Stieglitz," she told him.

"Because I'm a Jew who takes pictures? I'm a complete hack, so I think that and the camera are where the comparison would end."

"I'm obsessed with Georgia O'Keeffe. It's why I moved here."

"You're not from New Mexico?"

"LA. I came here on a show and never forgot it. Then with the tax credit and all the movies shooting here, I was going through a really bad divorce and I wanted a new start. I took the money from my settlement and bought a house on a hill where I can see all of the city."

"Must have been a nice settlement."

"Not worth the pain. Have you been divorced?"

"Luckily, no."

"I don't recommend it, even though I'm a lot happier now. I guess what I don't recommend is marrying the wrong person."

Looking in the mirror at her reflection behind him, he now understood the melancholy in her eyes. She returned his gaze.

"You want to see my house this weekend?"

She knew him to be married; he'd in fact advertised it, as he did prophylactically at the start of any job, and particularly around women he suspected might interest him.

"As in come over?" he asked inanely.

"I could show you pictures, but I think that's a bit less interesting, don't you? You can come up and have dinner. Or pick me up and we can go out. Whatever you want."

"Sure," he said. "I'll come up, and then we can drive somewhere."

The invitation occurred on a Wednesday in the makeup chair before dawn, and for the remainder of the week he couldn't stop fantasizing about what might transpire. Each morning as she worked on him, he explored her lean face that pulled gently in around the mouth under cheekbones that fanned high and wide. While his wife's beauty astonished him still, he'd never had the opportunity with a lithe, athletic blonde the likes of whom seemed to be presenting herself. Was it fair that because he'd come into his own with women well into college that he be deprived for his entire life of the type of conventional beauty experienced only from afar by lanky, ill-proportioned types such as himself? Would it be so bad if he spent one or two nights with her, just for the experience? Would Charlotte even have to know?

That Saturday, as if on cue, a storm moved in over Santa Fe. He wound his way into the hills east of Paseo de Peralta, taking wrong turn after wrong turn, squinting past his wipers, calling her repeatedly as his frustration grew. When he finally arrived, she met him outside with an umbrella, encircling him with her arm as she led him to her door. She wore a tight floral dress, and he smelled perfume. Inside, after offering vodka, she took him on a tour of her home, starting in the living room, where they fetched up in front of what she informed him to be her prize possession: a small signed print of an orchid.

"I found it in a thrift shop when I was working in Dallas about two years ago. I paid fifteen dollars for it, and when I got home the first thing I did was to take it to the museum to get it authenticated. It's absolutely real." She pointed to looping letters in an almost schoolgirl cursive forming the name Georgia O'Keeffe. "She signed that."

"Wow."

"I'm going to make a movie about her. I've written the screenplay. You've got to play Alfred Stieglitz. You could direct it too. We could produce it together. Would you read it? I've been working on it for two years. I already have interest from this producing team—have you heard of Jane Lowenthal and Liz Wallace?"

"I haven't, but that doesn't mean anything."

"They're based in New York. I worked with them on a pilot that shot here last year, and they read it and gave some really good notes, and said they'd help me set it up if I could find the right cast." She looked down at his nearly empty glass. "You want another?"

He stared at the print while she freshened their drinks, losing himself in the recesses of the flower that went from pink to darkest pink to red and finally black.

She turned to face him in her bedroom at the foot of a bed laden with pillows sheathed in a paisley of green and yellow. Thunder shook the low-slung roof half a second after lightning flashed in every window. Both of them understood the moment to be as ludicrously propitious as any for what would transpire. But all he could think about was her Georgia O'Keeffe project. Should he actually like the script enough to give comments, direct the film, and maybe even play the role in the extremely unlikely event the movie got made, a precarious ambiguity would always mar their collaboration. Inevitably they would sleep together more than once, and any attempt to break it off would result in hurt and recrimination. And finally, he couldn't help but question her interest in him, and ascribe it to a naïve overestimation of the usefulness of his name for financing. While he couldn't argue against his suitability for the part—slap a moustache on him and you were halfway there—she could surely do better for raising money if the part were worth playing, she just didn't know enough to realize it. In fact, if he was right, she was downright squandering the role, and with sex thrown in needlessly, if that's indeed what was motivating the attraction.

"You're cute," she said, reaching to caress his cheek. "I loved you in the Noah Mendelson film. When I heard you were cast in this, I was so excited. I begged to have you in my chair."

"Thanks."

He hadn't kissed a woman other than Charlotte in over ten years. I just can't make the first move, he thought. I wouldn't be able to live with myself being that kind of guy—willfully cheating on Charlotte by initiating this. Moreover, what if I've completely misjudged the situation? She dropped her hand to her side, and they stood there, the moment in abeyance, until finally he presented his glass.

"If I'm going to drive us to dinner, I can't have any more of this, particularly since I want to have some wine later."

The two stared at each other, his clumsy non sequitur leaving little doubt he wished for nothing sexual to transpire.

"Yeah, we should go," she said, retreating toward the bedroom door. "And I can drive."

They ate just off the old square, and because of her offer, he had two glasses of wine with his chicken mole while listening to her full pitch on the film. The more passionately she described it, the more certain he became that anything physical between them would be a mistake. She's too dogged, too focused, too smart. Charlotte would find out, because this isn't the type of woman who has sex frivolously. And yet her fervency, down to the manner in which she gesticulated with the strong, elegant hands that massaged his face so expertly when applying moisturizer, to how her lips formed consonants with supple precision, had him wanting nothing more than to be up at her house with her supine on those paisley sheets, her blond hair falling to either side of her arched neck.

By the time he'd asked for the check he knew he'd be spending the night with her; the opportunity simply couldn't be shunned. Maybe her script was actually good. Yes, he loved his wife, but this had nothing to do with her; he simply had to sleep with this beautiful woman under the storm that hopefully still shook the roof of her adobe house on top of the hill.

Just as the check arrived, his phone rang. If it's Charlotte, he thought, it can't be good because it's nearly midnight there, and she'll have long gone to sleep with the girls, who at the time weren't yet one and three. He stared at the screen where "Blocked" appeared.

"Go ahead and take it," Arlie said.

"Hello?"

"Where the fuck are you right now?" asked Joe Dan Rawls, the lead actor in the film that had brought David to New Mexico.

"At dinner downtown."

"Well, I'm at Geronimo with Billy Gibbons, so pay your check and get your ass over here."

"As in ZZ Top Billy Gibbons?"

"He says he met you once in LA."

"I met him is how I'd put it."

"So, are you coming over here or not? I'll order whatever you want. My per diem is sick on this movie. I've taken to bathing in it at night." David stared across at Arlie, who looked back quizzically. "Yeah, I'll be there in about forty-five minutes."

"Who was that?" she asked as he punched off.

"Joe Dan. He wants me to meet him."

"Got it," she said flatly after a pause. "So I guess I'd better take you back up to my place so you can get your car."

"Yeah."

They scarcely spoke the entire drive up the hill. She certainly never asked why she couldn't join at Geronimo. Though David understood they'd just been out together in public, the message of arriving with her on his arm at eleven at night, and their leaving together hours later wasn't one he wished to promote, not even to the approving eyes of a thrice divorced louche movie star and his running buddy from ZZ Top.

At her house her umbrella shielded them once more from a steady rain that constituted what remained of the storm. She turned to say good night, and he leaned to kiss her.

"I don't think so, David."

"Oh, I was just ... sorry."

"Don't worry about it." With a faint smile she turned and closed the door behind her. He drove halfway down the hill to where he couldn't be seen and pulled over, suffused with guilt. I would have slept with her had Joe Dan not called. Yes, I'll be able to say I didn't cheat on Charlotte, but not because of any shred of virtue on my part. In fact, it could be argued that were I a more organized human being, uninhibited by a stupid need to hang with a movie star and a rock star, I would be in bed with her right now. And then I tried to kiss her! I'm both a deceiver and a star fucker—the worst of each.

At Geronimo he found Joe Dan and Billy, along with two unimaginably spent women in their thirties whom Joe Dan had brought along from the bar at the Cowgirl Hall of Fame. They sat at a booth along the wall to the right of the door.

"I figured you'd be out with that blond makeup chick," Joe Dan volunteered as David slid in beside him.

"What?" was all he could think to say.

"I've been seein' what's goin' on in the makeup trailer. You guys are all over each other."

"We did have dinner together tonight."

"Why didn't you bring her along, man?"

"It's not like that."

"Look at these two," he said, gesturing to the pair of women opposite. "If you want in, let me know."

"All yours. Besides, I don't think they'd be so interested in me."

"Why's that?"

"Let's just say I tend to be listed a little lower on the call sheet, not to mention you're over six feet tall and very good looking."

"You're in movies, man. It's all about your attitude. And I guarantee these two've seen you in shit. You gotta learn how to live."

"I'm married to a woman who wouldn't sympathize."

"Yeah ... and they do always find out. I always figure I'll deal with that later. And fuck, I'm what they call an artist. I've got to have experiences. Otherwise, I've got no reservoir, know what I'm saying?"

David imagined mooting this strategy for inspiration with Charlotte and the response it might garner, and suddenly relief overtook him. Regardless of the wending journey, he thought, I did not sleep with Arlie. Judged from a distance, my behavior was nothing short of exemplary.

Now he could no longer claim fidelity. All this Iris Wood had had to do was sit next to him for ten minutes, and he was buying her meal and lavishing her with libidinous attention. The lies to Charlotte had begun immediately, and would need to continue, become more elaborate, more vehement. He knew his wife too well. The suspicion she'd already demonstrated would only increase.

"Two more days, David? You, who say nothing's more important to you than the girls and me—a claim I've always disputed—won't tell two producers you don't even like, one of whom is actually suing you, to go fuck themselves, you're going home?"

"One and a half more days."

"It's the fucking principle. You have all the power here, yet for some strange reason I'm still not getting, you refuse to use it. Tell Jacob Rosenthal you're quitting the movie because you don't want to be his whipping boy. That calls Brad Shlansky's bluff: you're suddenly ready and available to direct the movie he supposedly has the money for, meaning he has no reason to sue you. You don't really want to direct *Coal* anymore anyway."

"Who said that?"

"You say it every time we get on the phone and report the latest tyrannical act of Jacob Rosenthal! Ever since he rejected your rewrite you've been saying it!"

"I'm actually growing to like Jacob, if you want to know the truth. He's become very protective of me, and that's worth something."

"Worth fucking over your wife and kids?"

"That's a bit strong, don't you think?"

"Is it? David, I don't know what it is, but there's something you're not telling me."

"I do want to direct *Coal*. And you think Brad Shlansky isn't going to try and shake me down the next time I have a job I want to take? It's spite at this point. Or worse. So long as he's idle, I'm idle. This will never end."

"No one can do that in America. Forgetting that it's simply outrageous by any standard, we're a capitalist society. The individual's right to get on with the lawful pursuit of gain is protected."

"Well, that may be how it works in the political science department at Sarah Lawrence, and thanks for reminding me why I married you. I hope the girls get your brain and not mine. But trust me, in Hollywood, whenever I get a job or even the whiff of a job, Brad Shlansky is going to interfere unless I deal with this."

"Then you sue him for harassment."

"I'm not suing anyone, Charlotte."

"Meaning you're just going to sit around while we blow through our practically nonexistent savings and this guy holds you and your family hostage? Are you going to fucking stay out in California forever? Move into his house and just be there waiting for whatever he wants whenever he wants it like his bitch? I mean, what does Sammy say?"

"This isn't about Sammy."

"He's your fucking lawyer!"

"I'm staying out here and having this meeting so that it can be done once and for all."

"Is Sammy even going to be there?"

He knew Sammy would fly out, but he simply couldn't ask. What would it say that he'd soiled not only his marriage but his own defense, for which Sammy had donated so much of his time?

"Sammy has to be in Delaware."

"Are you fucking kidding me? It's your perfect excuse! You say you'll only do it with your attorney present and he can't be there, so they have to postpone."

"I'm here, Charlotte, and it has to be Friday. I've got to stay."

"David! Please!"

Neither relented. Finally, she hung up in tears. When he called back, she wouldn't answer. He considered revealing what he'd done, adducing the hopefully mitigating circumstance of his professional unmooring. But given her father's infidelity, he wasn't interested in testing her capacity for revenge, particularly with him on the West Coast. She'd fuck her Edmund, her Kent, her Oswald, maybe even her Lear, who'd been propositioning her relentlessly since the second week of rehearsals, mentioning his shelf of awards whenever possible. He could of course leave that day, rush home before the meeting was to take place, and let Brad Shlansky do what he would. But doing so just as she began previews seemed as marriage-endingly insensitive as his deception, since he would have to reveal his infidelity before Brad exposed him. He needed to stay in California and see the situation through.

But should he succeed and free himself to direct *Coal*, or even relinquish *Coal* but pursue other work, would he ever really be liberated? Couldn't

Brad call him periodically to menace with the threat of a phone call to Charlotte, demanding whatever concession, monetary or otherwise, he wished? Given who Brad was, no matter the vehemence of his promises, the threat would always remain. At some point David would have to tell his wife what he had done, otherwise he'd face a lifetime of debilitating anxiety every time his phone chirped with a call, e-mail, or text.

He spent the remainder of the day at the Chateau, ringing Charlotte every quarter hour and sending her texts relentlessly. Eventually she turned off her phone. Though he'd promised to reach out to actors, such concerns felt nugatory, so his work on *Coal* amounted to a couple of outgoing texts in the late afternoon. Should Jacob inquire as to his progress, he could at least represent that he'd done as instructed.

By six thirty, when he descended the stairs for dinner, he had spoken with no one. I should go out, he thought—remove myself from the scene of my transgression—but I have neither the will nor the energy. At the hostess stand a tall Black woman with a French accent asked if he'd like to sit at the bar.

"No thanks," he answered. "In the dining room if I could, please."

"Of course, Monsieur Levit. Follow me."

As he turned above the sunken lobby, a waving hand caught his eye and he recognized Nigel Gleeson. As he beheld the older actor's strategically winsome smile, he wondered if he weren't encountering some sort of ghost of his own future, divorced with nothing but a career for company as he careened from job to job in avoidance of the wreck of his life.

"I'm just going to go and say hello to a friend," he told the hostess.

"Just let me know when you'd like to be ushered to your table."

"Hello, David," said Nigel, already halfway through a bottle of the same Cabernet he'd been drinking nights before in the very same chair, though it seemed to David a year had passed. "You don't look well at all. Everything all right?"

"Is it that obvious?" David responded.

"I'm a uniquely keen observer of the species. You eating? Care to join me? I was about to order some grub myself."

David hesitated.

"Come on, mate. Sit with me. Unburden yourself."

Not reluctantly, David did.

"So what is it? LA got you down?"

"LA has me down, Nigel."

"Well, have a sip of this diabolically mediocre red, and share with me your sad, sad fate."

LOS FELIZ

B efore Brad had descended into the basement for his workout Amanda was already up, the kitchen radio blaring. The wildfires seemed to have caused the evacuation of all of Brentwood north of Sunset. Let the houses burn. Let the pandemic even the score. Unlike my parents, I take care of myself, so even if I get it, my body will beat it back.

"I'm not going to go into the details right now," he told Alice an hour later as he entered the kitchen from downstairs. "It's better I tell you the story in person so you can really know what a scumbag David Levit is. But there's no way he's missing the meeting. He'll be regretting what he did to me for the rest of his life. And you know what? So will everybody else. Paul Aiello and UCM. And let's not forget those two douchebags in Texas who went behind my back with the studio. When I'm done with them, I will fucking own Lone Star Pulp."

"Let's focus on David Levit. You still haven't told me exactly what we're after."

"More later. I need to make breakfast."

He found Amanda spooning their twins bananas and muesli in high chairs designed with alloys of such sleek beauty, they almost justified the twelve hundred dollars she had paid for each. The more money she made, the more she spent.

He carried his granola to the computer she kept in the kitchen and saw a Google alert for David Levit. He clicked onto a *Variety* link with a headline: "David Levit to Helm Period Racial Drama for Chicago Films."

"Son of a bitch," he said aloud.

"What is it?" asked Amanda.

"Let me fucking read."

"I told you not to speak to me that way."

> Hyphenate David Levit has been tapped by Jacob Rosenthal's Chicago Films to helm a film adaptation of National Book Award winner Rex Patterson's controversial novel Coal, set in fifties Los Angeles. The screenplay, inked by Chicago Films scribe regular Carly Billings, centers on a young African American racetrack worker caught up in the nexus

*of gambling, a racist police department, and city govern-
ment after the Great Migration. Said Rosenthal, "This is an
actors' piece, and David Levit knows actors. He also knows
literature, and this is one of the most important books in
American fiction in the past twenty years. That's why we've
locked David in. He's our guy."*

The message was unmistakable. Brad grabbed the receiver next to the
computer and dialed.

"Get me Paul. I don't care who he's on the phone with."

"I'm sorry, Brad," said Jen, "he's in the indie staff meeting."

"He'll be happy for the excuse to leave. Text him. I'll wait."

Three minutes later Paul barked into the phone. "What the fuck is so
important?"

"Did you read *Variety* this morning?"

"This may surprise you, but I have other shit to deal with than fixating
on the trades like the rest of the morons in this town."

"Go to *Variety* and punch up David Levit."

Brad heard clicking.

"So the fuck what?" asked Paul. "It's somebody doing what everyone
does out here. I seem to remember you wanting announcements every time
Same Day Films got an incoming phone call, you were so obsessed with
having your name in print. These days you'd announce your morning shit
if you could."

"I'm calling Alice."

"Great idea."

"You don't think she might have something to say about it?"

"In spite of what you think, Alice just might—I'm just going to offer this
after ten years of watching her do her thing—just *might* not be the world's
expert on the entertainment industry, seeing as you're her only client west
of the Throgs Neck Bridge."

"My being her only client out here is why she isn't conflicted."

"In the movie business, being conflicted is a good thing."

"Then you're the fucking mayor of Los Angeles. Alice will say it's a way
of David Levit and Jacob fuckface Rosenthal presenting the Chicago Films
movie as a viable project so that I can be seen as interfering. You think they
aren't going to wave this around in court?"

"Did you not also do an announcement about *Appalachian Winter*?"

"We did."

"Over two years ago? So, does that not give you something of a jump on a trade announcement of *Coal* to present to a judge?"

"*Appalachian Winter* didn't happen."

"Exactly. You didn't get his piece-of-shit movie done, and you'll never get it done, which is why you actually have no case."

"What the fuck is wrong with you?"

"I have other problems in my life right now."

"What did you do? Break a kid's nose?"

Brad caught Alice in a cab on the way to the airport.

"I'm on the goddamn LIE getting clobbered in traffic!" she exclaimed. "And did you hear the fucking virus is here?"

"In Washington State."

"For now."

"Please turn around. I want you back in New York working on the complaint. I'm changing the terms."

"You're canceling the meeting?"

"No."

"If David Levit has a lawyer there, you need me there."

"He can have all the fucking frat buddies in the room he wants."

"His guy is a partner at a white-shoe firm, Brad. You don't get that without being very sharp."

"Let me ask you something, Alice. Do you think I got where I got by being impressed with people's titles or where the fuck they work?"

"Brad—"

"Let me finish, because you need to understand. *Everyone needs to fucking understand!*"

"The way you're talking right now, you need me in the room, and it's my job not to give you the choice."

"If you're in the room, I'm not going."

"Good. Listening to you right now, I'll represent your interests better than you will."

"How about this? I'm having Sarah cancel your ticket."

"I'll fly myself out. Which I would do for you, Brad. In spite of how you're acting right now, you're one of the best people I know."

"I'll tell Paul's assistant not to let you past the front desk at UCM, so you'll be flying out to sit in a lobby staring at bad art while the meeting goes on upstairs without you. And I swear to God I'll do it."

"You're fucking serious."

"Go home to your husband. Please."

"Driver," he heard her say. "Take me to Forest Hills. No, Forest Hills I said! I'll give you the address in a minute."

"Thank you," Brad told her.

"You're not going to be thanking me if you screw up and fly out of control tomorrow, or suddenly change your mind and try to negotiate terms and I'm not there. Which, by the way, if you no longer want to negotiate, why have the meeting in the first place? Cancel it. That's the strong play."

"I want their faces in front of me. All of them. Jacob Rosenthal, David Levit and his lawyer, Howard Garner, and Paul Aiello, who I'm firing as of this morning, by the way."

"Firing Paul? All right, you really need me at this meeting."

"You can be on speaker. How's that? You get to listen."

"Am I allowed to speak?"

"If you feel the urge, which trust me, you won't have the chance."

MALIBU

Paul closed the door to his office after instructing Jen to hold his calls. "Including Brad Shlansky?" she asked.

"Especially Brad Shlansky. What is wrong with you?"

"Let me start by asking you a question," Martin Lasher began as Paul put the cell phone to his ear. "Just how many women have you slept with associated with work? And it can be a ballpark number."

"This is Los Angeles. I'm a fucking agent. Every woman out here worth looking at wants to be an actress, so I don't even know what your question means."

"Leaving that matter of opinion aside—"

"You disagree?"

"Insofar as in Los Angeles there are attractive women who don't wish to appear in front cameras, yes, I disagree strenuously, but we're talking about your opinion, not mine, so what's important right now is your perspective. Let me narrow it down. How many women of the actress or in this case assistant variety have you slept with where there might have been some question as to consent?"

"Of the assistant variety? There was one early on, on a retreat, but UCM dealt with that. A slap on the wrist. Plus, it was consensual. One or two others, but trust me, not a problem."

"I'm speaking now of a woman named Angela Wilder."

"Who the fuck is Angela Wilder?"

"Worked for you in 2010 for two months, then abruptly quit. This would have been in February."

"Angie? Okay, yeah, I remember her."

"She alleges you raped her at a private home in Malibu in 2010 during a party. This would have been on a Sunday."

"She's calling that rape?"

"She is."

"Fucking hell, Marty. When is this going to end?"

"She has corroborating journal entries from the time, as well as the word of two female friends in whom she confided, also contemporaneously."

"Contemporaneously? What does that mean, while she was fucking me?"

"One by phone later in the evening, the other in person the following day."

"Okay, so if I'm remembering correctly, Sam Parker, one of my clients—"

"I know who he is."

"Sam and his wife had a party at their beach house in Malibu. Sam invited Angie too, and her and me ended up getting a bit drunk—she was frankly plastered—and we had sex, fucking consensual sex, like all the sex I've ever had, in a bedroom upstairs. To which she invited me, by the way. All her idea. I mean really, what the hell is this?"

"That's what I'm trying to determine. And she didn't show up to work the following day? A Monday?"

"How the fuck do I remember?"

"Well, let's just say that if we were to check with HR at UCM, do you think they would confirm she didn't show up for work?"

"Again, I have no idea. Do you know how many assistants I've had working for me over the years? It's the way the system works. I was an assistant back in New York at BBP. Just lay it on me, Martin. How much does she want?"

"She's not asking for anything."

"Everybody has a price."

"I don't think that's the case here."

"Then why are we even talking about it?"

"Because per Susan Painter's attorney, Angie Wilder has been engaged with LAPD. The same detective who first called you. They reached out to her. A case is being built against you, Paul, and I need to know, if the police are going down lists of clients and assistants who've worked with you or for you, just what we have in store."

Paul moved from his desk to his couch. He remembered Angie Wilder well. They had snuck upstairs to explore Sam Parker's house, which was designed by a famous architect in the sixties, the concept of which was that of a cave, with no more than one room visible from another but views of the ocean from each. He'd been representing Sam, one of his few male clients, for three years, and had put him on a television show that made him a household name in half that time. Two weeks later the actor would star during his hiatus in *The Recluse* for Same Day Films, for which he was to be paid a quarter of a million dollars for ten days' work.

Angie couldn't have been over twenty-three, fresh out of Occidental. She had long brown hair and dark skin that suggested Mediterranean roots. She stood five foot six, three inches shorter than Paul. As they entered a guest bedroom, she walked ahead of him and he saw from behind what he'd been staring at for the past three hours suddenly within reach. Just two years before, he'd been reprimanded for his behavior with an assistant on a company retreat, but surely this was different. Why had Angie suggested they explore the house, and with only a towel to cover what her thong had exposed poolside all afternoon? Moreover, this wasn't a UCM event.

"This is insane," she exclaimed as they trod the room's shag rug. "I've never seen a house like this. Cara has such incredible taste." Paul had to agree, though it didn't hurt that Sam Parker's wife had unlimited resources, having starred for ten years on one of the most successful television hospital dramas of all time, for which she and her cast mates were now being paid a million dollars per episode. She and Sam shared their good fortune generously, inviting as many as a dozen friends each Sunday for a catered meal, where they poured Silver Oak and Far Niente without restraint.

"This is fucking outrageous," Brad Shlansky had whispered to Paul an hour earlier. Sam had invited Brad and his siblings in anticipation of principal photography for *The Recluse*. "You realize those are hundred-dollar bottles?"

"Shut the fuck up and drink," answered Paul.

"Oh, I'm drinking. I'm just wondering why we spent a minute more on Long Island than we had to."

"Can you fucking imagine if our dads could see us now?"

"I guess I have mine to thank," said Brad.

"Why's that?"

"If he hadn't died, my mom wouldn't have, and me and my sisters would never have come out here. I probably would have gone to college and taken over the stores. What? I was going to become an actor?"

"That's pretty fucking morbid, Brad."

"You're the asshole who brought up our dads in the first place. You think my parents are going to come back to life or something? Me and Sarah and Emily are on our fucking own. But in answer to your question, I think my dad would fucking plotz."

"Mine, I'd like to grind his fucking face in it, but that would mean flying him out here and spending time with him."

Nearly an hour later his friend hadn't moved from his chair overlooking the pool and ocean. Why did I bring up our parents? Nearby, gawky David Levit, who'd appeared in Noah Mendelson's inexplicably successful film *Hillbilly Wedding* with Sam Parker's wife, chatted up Sam. Obviously David was a quick study of how the business worked, and had glommed on to his host—the most powerful young star at the party. Elsewhere guests chatted amiably in the perfect ocean air, easily two hundred million dollars of net worth in the dozen souls inhabiting the toned bodies of actors, producers, directors, and showrunners.

That's when Angie had approached him.

"What are you looking at?" she asked.

"You know me, always working. Seeing what my clients are up to."

"Is David Levit a client?"

"He wishes."

"I'm gonna go look at the house. Wanna come?"

"You're sure?"

"Cara told me I could."

In the bedroom upstairs he eased behind her, his pelvis in her rear, and cupped a breast in each hand.

"What are you doing, Paul?"

"Holding the most perfect breasts I've ever seen."

"That's not why I came up here."

"No?" he asked, moving fingers into each side of her bikini top. "Doesn't that feel nice?"

"I don't think it's appropriate."

"What's inappropriate?" he asked, nuzzling her neck.

"This." She disengaged and turned to face him. "You're my boss, and this is not our house, and I don't think Cara and Sam, who is your client, want people fooling around in a spare room upstairs while a party is going on."

"I invited you to this party."

"Sam did."

"You think Sam didn't ask me first?"

"But he still invited me."

"You don't think I'm attractive?"

"You're my boss, and I'm not interested. Sorry."

"Look, just let me kiss you." He placed his hands on her bare shoulders. "It's just too perfect. You're too perfect. I fucking look at you every day at that desk. I go home and fantasize about you. I mean, think about that, with all the actresses I represent, I think about you. Just kiss me. It's all we'll do. Nothing more. I promise. You really want to refuse me that, after all I've done for you?"

Without waiting for a response, he leaned in, and they began to kiss, her with the discernible reluctance of having been coerced.

"Oh my God," he murmured, loving her fresh young mouth. "You're so beautiful. You're unbelievable."

"Okay, Paul. We need to stop. If anyone comes up—" she said, trying to pull herself away.

"That's easy," he said, walking backwards, holding her to him as he reached behind to close and lock the door.

"Please Paul, no."

"Don't say that." He began kissing her again, reaching up to the middle of her back to pull the knot on her bikini top. Her breasts dropped free as he removed the tiny garment from her body. Now there could be no turning back. She'd allowed this, meaning nothing could be prohibited him.

"Oh my fucking God," he said.

"I don't want to do this, Paul!"

"What? What are we doing?"

She covered herself and made to shout. Instinctively he reached for her mouth to quiet her, covering her nose as well. She struggled against him with increasing strength.

"Angie, stop. If you make noise, it's going to freak people out and then they'll be up here and there'll be a scene. There are huge stars downstairs, and very powerful people who can have a hand in your future, which is going to be amazing or I wouldn't have chosen you for my desk. I know you're scared, but don't be."

He removed the towel and pushed her backwards onto the bed.

"Paul, please. Please don't do this," she whimpered through his hand, now choking back sobs, her body writhing to break free.

"No one's going to walk in, I promise. The door's locked."

"Paul, please, I don't want this! I don't want this!"

"Shhhh ... shhhhh ... It's going to be fine ..."

He'd never felt so hard in his life. Pulling her bikini bottom to the side, he spat on his hand then used it to help jam himself inside her, thrusting as she cried out.

"Oh my God, you're amazing," he said. "I can't fucking control myself."

"Please, Paul! It hurts! No, please!"

He no longer heard her, the orgasm coming in waves through his fingers and toes.

She sobbed beneath him freely now.

"That was fucking amazing, Angie. You are fucking amazing. I don't know what the fuck just happened. I just couldn't control myself. You're just so beautiful and perfect. You gotta believe me when I say I just couldn't not do that with you."

Paroxysms overtook her as he pulled himself out. She rose from the bed heaving now, pulling her bikini bottom back over herself, taking up her towel and disappearing into the bathroom with her top. He heard the door lock, and the water running along with the sounds of her gagging. The toilet flushed repeatedly.

"Angie?" he said to the door. "Angie? You gonna be all right?"

"Go away, Paul, please!" Her crying wouldn't stop.

"I know that got rough, but like I said, once we started ... that's truly never happened to me before. I've never had that experience. You're just so fucking attractive. And the way you kissed me back. It's almost not fair to a guy, you're so sexy. You know?"

The faucet ran and the toilet continued to flush as her sobbing continued. For the first time since having ascended he felt unsure what to do. Should he remain and try to comfort her, or give her the space she clearly needed? Suddenly he felt angry. They'd had sex. So what? Moreover, the sounds coming from the bathroom didn't exactly represent the sort of response one craved in a partner.

"Look, I'm gonna go downstairs so no one gets suspicious. That's to protect us both. I mean, I know when you invited me up here with you you said Cara said it was okay. Which you did. You invited me up here. But I wouldn't hang you out to dry. Take your time. If anyone asks, I'm just gonna say you weren't feeling well. You just come down whenever you want."

One seat remained empty an hour later when dinner was served.

"Who's not here?" asked Cara.

Sam scanned those present. "It's Angie, Paul's assistant."

"Did she leave, Paul?" asked Cara.

"I haven't seen her for at least an hour. I hope she didn't drive, 'cause she'd had a few. You want me to see if she's out on the beach?"

"I can send Maggie."

"No, she's busy serving. I'll handle it," said Paul, rising.

He lit a Marlboro while staring over the water as a low sun reflected slivers of orange and slate beyond the surf. When he told her he lost control, he'd meant it. Considering it honestly, had he raped the poor girl? He could say she'd gone into the room with him practically naked but for the towel. She had kissed him back, and even let him remove her top. Why was it some of the best sex he'd ever had, but seemingly the opposite for her? I'll talk to her in the morning, maybe even take her out. In fact, I can't not take her out. I've got to have more of her, and this time without all the drama. I'll treat her like a fucking princess. Maybe get her a job somewhere else so the agency isn't on my ass about it. Sam Parker needs an assistant. Do I feel guilty for what happened? Women know the score.

She didn't show up to work the following day, and he'd neither seen nor heard from her since, until Martin's call.

"If she wants to claim she didn't initiate what we did by inviting me into a room upstairs, she can be my guest."

"Did anyone see her do this?" Martin asked.

Brad Shlansky and David Levit came to mind, the very antagonists who would square off in the UCM conference room the following day, their faces, one anguished, the other lathered in ambition, the last he remembered before ascending the stairs behind Angie.

"You think I advertised that I was going off with a girl? That's not me."

"Did you tell anyone at the time that the two of you had sex?"

"The fuck do you take me for? No! I knew it was wrong from a professional standpoint, but she was twenty-three, twenty-four years old at the time, and I was, what? Twenty-eight maybe. So it's not like it was inappropriate age-wise. But I wasn't interested in being fired for fucking another assistant, even though, trust me, I was far from the only one. Back then everyone was fucking everybody. It's this goddamn business we're all in."

"Listen, Paul, I told you we might be headed here. I've been through enough of these now to warn you that I'm not sure you're going to be able to keep bailing water from this boat."

"Meaning what?"

"Based on what you've told me, and based on what's being alleged so far not by one but by at least three women, plus the one on the company retreat, there are going to be more. Once any of this gets out, every woman you've ever slept with is going to ask herself if it was consensual, and if there was any doubt—"

"So, what is this? You're abandoning me?"

"So long as you can pay me, I'm your lawyer."

"Can you contact Angie Wilder's lawyer? See if we can make a deal?"

"If she even has a lawyer. Like I said, this isn't about paying her off."

"I know that's what she's saying now."

"You're not hearing me, Paul. Criminal charges are becoming more and more likely."

He remained on his couch after hanging up. By a quick reckoning, around a dozen women would probably come forward, emboldened by one another. He could go to jail. His father would love it.

A knock at his closed door caused him to look up through the glass. Without rising, he motioned Howard Garner in.

"You okay, Paul?"

"I sometimes come over to the sofa to think. Different perspective somehow."

"I do the same thing. You mind if I sit?"

"My guess is you're here to talk about this David Levit and Brad Shlansky thing."

"Aspects of it concern me, yes. I get that Brad is upset—"

"I'd say it's beyond that now."

"But can we wrap this up tomorrow? What's it going to take? He's got Jacob Rosenthal coming in too. I thought it was just about a number, but I just got off the phone with him—"

"Jacob Rosenthal?"

"Brad. Shouting my ear off about this *Variety* announcement. He was completely out of control. Is that gonna be the tenor of the meeting? A bunch of unhinged screaming? Or is it all a show so he can get more money?"

"Honestly, I don't know anymore, Howard. And frankly I don't give a shit, other than the fact that if there is a settlement, the bigger it is, the more money we get."

"UCM is commissioning the settlement?"

"And it goes on my ledger, not yours."

"You think I want that on my ledger? It's fucking wrong. Both are represented here."

"You think Brad gives a shit where David is represented? In fact, it pisses him off even more."

"Whose idea was this? Yours or his?"

"Why does that even matter?" Paul felt his anger rise, happy to have an outlet for his unrelated frustrations. "Brad is my client, and I'm helping him get his pound of fucking flesh. He wants me and the agency compensated for the work we've put into protecting him against the bullshit and humiliation your client has put him through."

"Do you honestly believe any of that, Paul?"

"Brad extended himself, his money, and the reputation of his company for David Levit's pretentious fucking period drama because he thought he owed it to him for all the money we made off *Revenge*—money which, by the way, Brad made, not David Levit, because it was Brad who saw Charlie Gold for what he was before any of these lying bitches who piled on Charlie with their baseless allegations."

"Excuse me? You're going to have to unpack that one."

"Oh, fuck you, Howard. You notice that the only actresses who ever complained about Charlie Gold were the ones who needed an excuse for their failing careers? Nobody else is gonna say that. But I am."

"Paul, Charlie had over fifty accusers."

"Give me a fucking break. Half of them wouldn't have had careers without him."

"Not true, and what does any of that have to do with David Levit? This is nothing more than a shakedown. Brad doesn't have a fucking nickel to make David's film. If this weren't the movie business, where everyone is scared shitless, any concerned party would take one look at the claim and know it's frivolous."

"And that's just your problem. You and everyone else thinks Brad is frivolous. I guess now you're learning he isn't."

But Howard was right. Paul didn't believe a word he was saying, yet he refused to relent, animated, he now understood, by the fact that he despised Howard Garner and his ilk and always had. No matter how much Paul made for the agency, they condescended—dismissing his opinion in staff meetings, smirking when he didn't get their references, barely tolerating his jokes, not inviting him to dinner parties, ostracizing him in ways less and less frequently concealed.

"Here's what you've got to know, Howard. Sometimes people like Brad Shlansky get to win. And when they do, you have to play by their rules."

"What does that mean?"

"It's like the night Trump won. I was at Claire Fisher's with her husband and all her friends and her manager. It wasn't supposed to be a watch party but a fucking celebration. I walked in and the place was streaming with red, white, and blue crepe paper. And bunting. I'm not kidding you. Actual bunting around all the tables. Balloons everywhere. She had two cases of Dom in a goddamn ice chest. Three thousand dollars of champagne. I didn't dare tell a soul I hadn't voted for Hillary."

"You voted for Trump?"

"You bet your fucking ass I did. And so did Brad and both his sisters. In fact, I wish Brad had been with me there that night. By eight thirty it started to get real fucking gloomy." He raised his voice two octaves and feigned tears. "'What's happening? What's happening to our country?'"

He resumed his own voice. "'I'll tell you what the fuck is happening,' I wanted to say. 'Real people with real problems are taking it back.' You think the folks who voted for him didn't know Trump was an asshole? Of course they did. But the alternative was actually worse. And why? Because Hillary and Obama represented self-righteous hypocrites like you and everyone else out here. Seriously. The country knows how we look down on them, even while we're churning out shit product they go to to make all of us rich, and now our hedge fund overlords. The fucking hundred-million-dollar movies with explosions every five minutes and loss of life that's practically apocalyptic and women running around showing their tits and asses, made by condescending snobs who dole them out to the country and then look down on the people who go and see them. It's fucking disgusting. We sit in staff meetings down the hall, and I look around at all of you drooling over how to put your clients in these movies and take your commissions and go to the premieres to show off your new suit and your new wife and your new car at the valet stand. And then within the hour you're ridiculing the movie and talking about the spiritual downfall of our industry when you're gladly making money hand over fist. You think people out there don't see that? How movie stars literally go on talk shows and rant about violence or antigay bias or women's rights or racism, but meanwhile they just got paid ten million dollars to play some lone vigilante who destroys half a city with collateral damage chasing bad guys and fucking the babes whenever he can? And cue the rap music when the posse of Black guys shows up, and all the fag jokes. And don't get me started on the directors and screenwriters and studio heads. Every one of you out here in your echo chamber hating the rest of America for voting for Trump when your fucking dripping hypocritical superiority is what made them all say a big fuck-you by electing a reality TV star you all hate. I mean, a reality TV star! Think about it! The fucking enemy of everything we do! I wanted to stand up at that party and say, 'You know what? It serves you all fucking right. You deserve every bit of your pain.'"

"Wow, Paul," was all Howard could muster.

"Do I like Brad Shlansky? Do I respect him? Between you and me, I'm starting to hate his guts. But I hope he fucking rapes your client hard tomorrow, and you bet your ass I plan to commission what comes out of it at the full ten percent, and even that won't be enough. You and David Levit and all the rest can go fuck yourselves. Now, if you don't mind, get the hell out of my office."

Howard rose.

"Thanks for letting me check in."

"Shut the door behind you."

Paul sat in silence, blood throbbing in his face. He looked past his coffee table at all that had accumulated over the years: framed photographs of him with stars at premieres numbering in the dozens, movie posters, stacks of scripts from before the industry went digital, useless gewgaws from clients, the Mets memorabilia he'd been collecting since high school, much of which had accompanied him to Albany and then New York City before he moved west. Would it all fit in the trunk of his Audi? Should he wait to be fired, or simply leave? To quit deprived fellow agents—the Howard Garners and Janet Liebowitzes of the floor—their pious disavowals once news emerged of his transgressions. By removing himself he could at least snatch from them the self-serving theatrics of public expulsion.

But given the obligations contemplated in the two settlements, plus what a criminal defense might cost, he needed every cent he could eke, and leaving on his own would forestall any meaningful severance. To be fired before a trial would most certainly be actionable, worth easily half a million dollars for the agency to be rid of him without trial, of which he could see as much as $175,000 after taxes and contingency fees. That was it, then. He would remain and be fired, furnishing him the relief of not having to clear out his office for another few weeks. He rose and moved to his door.

"How many calls did I miss?"

"About thirty-five."

"How many from Brad Shlansky?"

"Three. Each increasingly angry."

"Yeah, well, for him I left the office on personal business and turned off my cell phone."

"Got it."

He picked up his katana and donned his headset.

"Get me Alan Berman first," he ordered, in reference to Claire Fisher's lawyer, who'd hopefully finished with Business Affairs at Universal on her contract for a romantic comedy Paul had persuaded her to do weeks before.

"If we can close Claire's deal, the day's going to take a good turn."

UCM LOBBY

J acob's trainer often extolled Jacob's fitness during their six-thirty sessions five mornings a week. Yes, this could be construed as empty flattery from a man paid handsomely enough by assorted clientele to be driving a Porsche 718 Boxster at the age of twenty-six, thought Jacob as he suffered through five supervised minutes on his erg. But Jacob felt more powerful physically, mentally, and spiritually approaching eighty than he ever had. Standing five foot eight in bare feet, he weighed 135 pounds, a number that hadn't deviated since his time in Mississippi when he ran four miles a day. In the mirror his cheeks hollowed in above the jaw, his skin rugged and taut, giving his face the ascetic severity he felt suited him. Contemporaries frequently asked who had worked on him.

"Nobody has fucking worked on me," he would answer sharply, though in truth he'd had blepharoplasty and ptosis repair simply because he was tired of the hoods of his eyes drooping into his line of sight and decided that so long as that was being addressed, he might as well treat the bags underneath as well. Otherwise, his visage remained unmolested by the scalpel and would stay so. He and his wife still had sex at least three times a week, and thanks to the Cialis he took (along with lycopene, multi-vitamins, omega-3, and Prevagen), he could once more perform with the proficiency of his thirties.

He stood on his back patio looking out over the swimming pool he'd not once used in the decade he and his wife owned the house. Smoke from the fires floated south from the hills as he considered what lay ahead of him several hours hence, starting with visiting UCM. When leaving any agency building, he always felt as though he'd been marinated. But at least he would demonstrate to David Levit how one took initiative. He'd begun the preceding day by advertising David's direction of *Coal* as industry fact.

"I thought you hated trade announcements," Larry said, entering his office after the release had come across on the *Variety* website.

"I don't hate them as much as assholes like this Brad Shlansky swear by them. Trust me, he's been on the phone with his representatives for the past half hour, and pretty soon he or his lawyer will be calling me. He should have stayed on Long Island and taken over his father's check-cashing business. Did you know that? That's what his father did? He was one of these assholes who charges larcenous fees to cash checks for poor people and illegals who don't have bank accounts. And meanwhile he thinks David Levit is swinging from movie to movie without a care."

"That's hardly how I would describe David Levit."

"I'm saying from this guy's perspective, at least if I'm to believe his insane lawyer. He's like every moron out here, perseverating on what's happening for other people and defining themselves by all they don't have or get. What they believe is real is more important than what actually is real."

"You think he's gonna leave us alone now that you've announced the movie?"

"No. He's going to destroy himself with his own rage."

As anticipated, Brad's lawyer had called and e-mailed throughout the preceding day, culminating in a hilariously overwrought desist letter construing the announcement as yet further actionable damage to Brad's ability to produce *Appalachian Winter*. The title alone had "squander your money" written all over it. *Coal* would prove itself to be the most fortuitous career opportunity in David Levit's life, if only because it would deliver him from such clear marginality as a director.

Jacob arrived at the UCM offices at a quarter to ten, leaving his car with the valet and stepping up two flights into the wide rectangular lobby where floor-to-ceiling glass faced Wilshire Boulevard. The shorter side walls were clad in matte black marble. Three women in their twenties sat at a long, slender desk, barren but for laptops. Each wore a headset. Behind them on the other side of a glass expanse matching that in front stretched a sculpture garden with immaculate teak tables and chairs that still held their original honeyed brown. To either side of the front-facing doors stood two security guards wearing earpieces common to network anchors and secret service agents.

"Good morning. Welcome to United Creative Management. How may I help you?" asked the receptionist in the middle, a tall Asian beauty. On either side of her the two equally stunning women, one Hispanic, the other white, answered calls one after another as if in meditative incantation: "Good morning, United Creative Management, how may I direct your call? Good morning, United Creative Management, how may I direct your call?" As was seemingly compulsory in reception areas all over Los Angeles, any of the three would have turned every head on Michigan Avenue.

"I'm here to see Howard Garner."

"And your name, please?"

"Jacob Rosenthal."

"Have a seat, Mr. Rosenthal. Help yourself to coffee, espresso, water, or a snack. I'll let them know you're here."

As he sat on one of six black leather Barcelona sofas, three facing three, the actor Adrian Deal stepped through the glass doors between the security guards, preceded by a young brunette assistant in a T-shirt and shorts holding two phones. She was followed by Adrian's manager, whose name Jacob had forgotten, though they'd survived a fierce negotiation between them many years before over Adrian's role in an inordinately successful thriller called *Original Sin*, which Jacob had produced.

"Hello, Adrian," he said, rising politely to shake the actor's hand.

"Hey, man," answered the actor, demonstrably uncurious as to how he might know Jacob. The assistant had peeled off to the reception desk while the manager asserted herself on Adrian's behalf.

"Hello, Jacob. Joan Little. I'm Adrian's manager."

"Of course."

"Adrian, you remember Jacob Rosenthal. He produced *Original Sin*."

"Oh yeah, man. Hey, Jacob. Sorry. In kind of a fog today. These morning meetings are a killer."

"Adrian's band played the Viper Room last night," Joan explained.

What was it with these male stars and their bands? Jacob wondered. One after another they pursued futile, often damaging recording careers for their barely listenable music. Months before, he'd watched Adrian, along with a drummer, bass player, and lead guitarist absolutely crucify a cover of "Mannish Boy" on one of the talk shows. Jacob had fled immediately to *Baseball Tonight* to learn how the Cubs had done.

He'd found Adrian mostly to have been professional during the filming of *Original Sin*, though the actor fought the creative team incessantly, questioning not only every page of the screenplay and ways to approach it but camera angles and staging. One week in, he began directing the other actors, including the film's star.

"It's gotten to the point where I look forward to the days without him," complained the director, a journeyman named Mark Hobson, who'd brought the project to Chicago Films.

"Yeah, well, he's gonna be more of the reason people come to see this film than you will, so just do your job, part of which is to deal with the actors and get the performances we need so this movie actually works."

When Adrian and the screenwriter received Oscar nominations, Jacob had to laugh, though the Academy campaign cost Chicago Films easily a million dollars in profits after the studio's accounting. And now Adrian didn't remember Jacob's name, or even show the decency to pursue a conversation, losing himself instead in the *Hollywood Reporter* that lay on the low table before them. Jacob couldn't remember when he'd last seen the print edition and felt vaguely reassured by its continued existence.

"We're here to see Janet," Joan offered buoyantly, referring to Janet Liebowitz, who'd represented Adrian since his television days. "Our twice yearly catch-up to set goals."

"Got it."

"I never imagined having too many opportunities for a client could be more difficult than not having enough. And all of them at or above his quote. And look at him. Still the same guy he was before we put him in *Original Sin* and everything changed."

"Today I couldn't get *Original Sin* made," said Jacob, ignoring that none of her bluster had any basis in truth, which was that she and Adrian were there to strategize against her client's seemingly inexorable demise. The star hadn't worked in over a year after succumbing to alcoholism and a gambling addiction. "Now *Original Sin* would be day-and-date," he continued, "which would make the negative cost prohibitive."

"You've been through it all, Jacob."

"I wasn't around for the first talkies."

"What's going to happen to our industry?" she asked, her winsome facade suddenly gone.

"If by our industry you mean the entertainment business, it's doing great. TV is better than ever. Opportunities for making content are democratized in ways they've never been because it's cheaper to film. There's soft money in states all over the country competing to get shows to shoot there. More stuff getting made than ever."

"But what about people like us?"

"Who gives a fuck about people like us, Joan? And who should? Besides, as you just said, you've got Adrian there with all the opportunities above his quote. Why are you complaining?" He immediately regretted his cruelty.

"Even for Adrian, things are changing so fast. Sure, there are all these cable channels and streaming outlets, but it's so much work to keep up, and no one gets their quotes anymore—except Adrian," she said, catching herself. "Of course, if you ever wanted him again, we'd do it for a price because he got his start with you, and you always have great material."

"I appreciate that, Joan."

"So, stuff is getting made, but look at how. Back thirty years ago when I was an agent, I sent a client in to meet Mike Nichols. I don't even remember the film. He sat in a waiting room with a dozen or so actors scheduled for ten minutes each with the director. Not just to read, but to talk and to work. He finally goes in, and Mike Nichols asks him a few polite questions—how's your day been, how long have you lived out here, are you married—that sort of thing, and time's going by and my client's wondering when's he going to read, and finally Mike Nichols says, 'I want you to play this part.' Not a known actor, mind you. But it happened because of the director meeting the actual person in a room and looking at a resume and seeing a body of work there and being able to pick up a certain level of ability to go along with the right qualities for the role. Can you imagine that happening today, with self-tape, and e-mailing it in, everything digital?"

"I'm not sure."

"I represent real actors. What's it say to you that you either make seven or eight figures a picture like Adrian here and a handful of others, which let's be honest, because I can be honest with you, Adrian isn't making close to that now. You read the trades. Adrian can't green-light a picture anymore. Can you imagine that?"

Jacob looked over at Adrian, choosing not to answer.

"For most it's scale or schedule F if they're lucky, and nothing in between. And what does it say that if you go to the movies in a theater now, you better want to see explosions or don't bother?"

"Please, Joan. I can't listen to this. The reason big action movies exist is because those are what people around the world pay to see. And by the way, you and I may hate that—though Larry and I have our own action franchise—but it's not necessarily bad for the industry. Have a look at the cast and crew size the next time you see one of those films. It's literally hundreds and hundreds, sometimes thousands of people being hired to make them."

"Listen to yourself, Jacob."

"Unfortunately, I'm stuck doing that."

"How many of those people are computer animators? What I see—when I stay for the credits anymore, which I don't because it's just gotten too depressing—is more people doing digital effects than the rest of the crew and the actors combined. And probably making more than most of the actors."

"For working a lot more hours, months and months on end, and good for them."

"My clients have devoted their lives to this craft!"

"Why are they making us wait, Joan?" Adrian asked, now staring languidly at his phone. "I've got shit to do."

"Jackie, go remind them we're still here."

"On it." Adrian's assistant rose and bounded away.

"I like her," said Joan.

"Yeah, she's cool," responded Adrian, not looking up from his screen. Jacob saw David Levit enter the lobby.

"I used to get up in the morning excited about what we do. It meant something," the manager continued.

"Joan, the minute we start getting precious is the minute we stop telling interesting stories. Your clients want to make a steady living playing challenging characters, put them on television where those stories still exist. If they don't want to be on television, they're going to have to do the action movies to get paid."

"Those roles aren't so easy to get."

"Hey, Jacob," said David.

"Hi, David," answered Jacob, not rising. "Have a seat." David did.

Joan began to fight tears. "I have bills to pay. I had to cut my assistant back to part-time. Do you have any idea how that feels?"

"We all made money way out of proportion in the nineties and early aughts," Jacob responded. "I was putting character actors like David here in single trailers, renting them cars, paying for assistants along with salaries into six figures for three weeks work when they had nothing to do with why the film was getting financed. You probably had a client list twice the size it is now, and you took your ten percent from all of them and everyone was happy. But I always knew there'd be some kind of shift. Movies we were overpaying to make just wouldn't continue to fetch the prices they did, because for one thing there were too many of them, and another, most just weren't that great. Oversupply with diminished quality. And capitalism is a nasty fucking ecosystem. Inside of it people are in an arms race against not only other industries but aspects of themselves—the industries inside of the industries. Television got smarter, and so movies got louder and stupider and more violent like theme park rides so that people would have to see them in 3D and IMAX.

"As for actors, everyone pays them less now because there are so many people calling themselves actors: every person who posts a video on Facebook or YouTube or wherever thinks he's got a unique talent that has to be shared with the world or we'll all destroy one another for want of their wisdom or comedy or goddamn pain. Agents and casting directors get on the phone with me and talk about a person's Twitter following. And don't even talk about the studios where we've got our output deals. They're obsessed with that shit. David, when did you get out of Juilliard? How old were you?"

"Twenty-six."

"Can you fucking imagine? In school till he was twenty-six. Who out here does that anymore? Who feels like they need to when the metrics, a word that never used to apply to talent, have no sensitivity to anything but clicks and followers?" He turned back to David. "How many kids from your time there are still making a living? From your class of—how many was it?"

"Twenty."

"From your class of twenty?"

"Four of us, maybe five."

"And now twice as many so-called actors out there. And maybe ten percent of what gets financed as movies—most of them never seeing the inside of a theater—you can watch more than fifteen minutes of. Very little of it advancing anyone's career, and rarely paying more than scale. Meantime, look at this ridiculous lobby."

At one end of the long stretch of glass in front of them a minimalist flight of cantilevered steps cut an angle against an unadorned black wall. On the other, a good twenty yards away, hung an enormous photograph. In it a famous actor stared gormlessly into the engine of an automobile in his garage, while his wife, another famous actress, stood lit in the doorway to their kitchen. She wore no clothing. Snow fell in the foreground. The entire scene was lit impeccably with sources just outside of frame.

To the left of the photograph, and set out into the room, stood an installation comprising a metal warehouse floor cart with a laddered push handle on one end. It was covered in chipped green primer flecked with rust and wear. Chained to its bed stood three letters, a good four feet high and riveted together from strips of metal painted yellow, to spell the word YES.

"That's new," Joan remarked as they all stared, including Adrian and his assistant.

"I love it," the assistant said. "It's like it's urging clients to embrace their art. Don't say no, say *yes*." A telling silence met her appraisal before Jacob continued.

"I'm told there's over fifty million dollars of art in this building. The big agencies figured out how to make money from all sides."

"Is there a point you want to make, Jacob?" asked Joan.

"We each have to evolve. I, who once insisted I would never make television, go to Netflix now and sit in the lobby like everyone else, begging for their money. A fucking streaming service that started out mailing DVDs to people but was smart enough to see into the future in a way Blockbuster didn't. You can get pissed about that and how all the other changes ramify all you want, cry foul, injustice, whatever. Nobody's making us do this. Be thankful you even get to sit in this lobby."

"And all the pain around you?"

"I avoid it."

A slender, handsome man in his twenties approached wearing a fitted Italian shirt with a nail-head pattern of white on navy.

"Adrian," he said, "Sorry to keep you waiting. Janet will see you now."

As the trio of star, manager, and assistant rose, a young woman, also in her twenties, with thickly framed glasses and a dress adorned with sunflowers, approached.

"Shira, this is Jacob Rosenthal," David said, introducing his agent's assistant once Joan had departed.

"Hi," said Shira. "We've spoken on the phone."

Jacob shook her hand. "I'm sure we have. Shall we go up?

HOWARD'S OFFICE

J acob insisted they take the stairs, for which David was grateful, as it would constitute his only exercise of the day other than walking with his carry-ons in both airports. He'd go straight from UCM to LAX and a 4 p.m. flight. Factoring in waiting for his luggage and the drive from Kennedy, that would have him at his apartment at around three thirty in the morning. He would devote himself to family: make dinner for the girls every night, wake with them each morning for breakfast and school drop-off, be wholly and deeply present in receipt of all his wife's anxieties through previews and opening. He would instill her with confidence, rub her hands and feet until she begged he desist.

"Right in here," said Shira, who was quickly becoming David's favorite among the dozen or so assistants who'd been on his agent's desk over more than a decade. Many times David had considered leaving UCM over certain lapses—unreturned phone calls, months without work, inadvertent slights that seemed to derogate his earning power—but he'd always concluded such affronts inevitable. The persistence with which clients fired agents attested more to the sensitivities and paranoia of artists than the larger agencies being measurably different from one another.

"Hey, guys," Howard said, standing as David and Jacob entered. "Can Shira get you anything? Water? Coffee? An early cocktail? You might need it to meet with these guys."

"I'll have a double espresso," David said.

"Just water for me," said Jacob. "No ice."

Shira turned to go.

"And shut the door please, Shira," Howard ordered congenially. "Okay, David, first things first, because we've only got about ten minutes. I talked with Paul Aiello, and you were right. UCM is getting a commission if there's a settlement."

"You're fucking kidding me," Jacob interjected.

"I'm not saying it's right—"

"UCM is commissioning what one of your clients is trying to extort off another?"

"Jacob, I don't like it any more than you do," said Howard.

"Then why are you letting it happen? David, this is dead wrong."

"Paul is letting it happen I guess," Howard answered, "because the fee is maybe part of his incentive to pursue the thing. I have no control over it."

"And the heads of this larcenous company you're working for? What do they say?"

"Brad Shlansky might be ridiculous, but he's helped bring in a lot of business."

"Not lately, from what I hear. And what about David here?"

"He remains a very important client."

"It doesn't seem like it. David, why are you still with these people?"

"We're not going to commission him when he gets *Appalachian Winter* made," said Howard before David could answer. "And we're not going to commission his fee on *Coal*. Plus, I think things are about to explode with Paul Aiello."

"What's that supposed to mean?" asked Jacob.

"There are rumors he's in some trouble."

"What does that mean, rumors? And what does that have to do with robbing David blind?"

"Could we just move on, please," said David, uninterested in further argument between two men he needed focused on his cause. "I don't care about Paul Aiello or who commissions what. All I want is for this to be behind me. Just tell us what to expect today, Howard."

"Brad Shlansky is not bringing his lawyer," the agent answered.

"That doesn't sound like a settlement meeting to me," said Jacob.

"I don't know," said Howard. "Maybe they agree on terms between them, Paul and I take notes, and the lawyers paper it. David didn't want his guy in the room either."

"Then why do I need to be here?" asked Jacob.

"Paul says Brad Shlansky thinks you've disrespected him."

"I don't respect him."

"So ... ," said Howard in a vaguely rhetorical way.

"And if he expects anything different from this waste of my morning, he shouldn't have demanded that I show up."

"Well, you're here," said Howard.

"I want this out of David's brain so he can direct my movie."

"Look," said Howard. "Brad is thrashing around, smacking at anything. David is the most vulnerable person. Along with the movie you guys are doing."

"My movie isn't vulnerable."

"So David's job directing it, then. I hate these kinds of people."

"And why's that?" asked Jacob.

"They're the type who used to bully me in school. I want them all throttled."

"Unless UCM is making money off them, in which case, call off the beating. This guy has David completely by the short hairs."

"He doesn't have David by the short hairs."

"He does actually," said David. "Among other things, I don't have any money to pay him. If he says a number that's beyond what I can afford—and trust me, that number doesn't have to be that high—I'm finished."

"You can do my movie for scale, and we pay him off out of the budget," said Jacob. "And it'll still be worth it for you for all the success we're going to have with it. But it's not going to come to that. Do you understand?"

Shira arrived with David's espresso and Jacob's water.

"David's just saying be careful," said Howard.

Jacob tilted the glass and took a long drink. "And I'm saying that's exactly the opposite of what I intend to be."

PAUL'S OFFICE

Sarah picked Brad up in the Yukon at eight thirty. She looks more and more like Mom by the day, he thought, seeing her softening features and hair blond like his. Their father had bought the vehicle the year of his passing, and it had aged well, not least because of the care Sarah and Emily gave it—yearly maintenance, high test gas, weekly washes. They'd even had it repainted during the year at Sony. The automobile tied them to their past in ways more nourishing than not. He relished any chance to drive it.

"Why can't you get yourself there?" she had asked the night before.

"My car's in the shop, and Amanda has a shoot up in Bakersfield."

"Does she ever stop working?"

"I guess not."

Speeding past the Celebrity Center toward Laurel, where he'd make a left down to Wilshire, he remained mostly silent, flipping to news about the fires on KCRW in hopes of distracting her from too many questions about what was to come. He didn't reveal that she wouldn't attend the meeting until they'd left the keys with the valet at UCM.

"So, I'm supposed to wait in the lobby like some pathetic loser?" she asked.

At the reception desk upstairs, he opened his wallet.

"There's a great coffee place around the corner on Little Santa Monica. It's expensive, but the almond croissant is insane. Like the ones Mom used to get us in the city."

"You're buying me coffee and a croissant? And they're expensive? What the fuck is this?"

"Look, Sarah, you drive me nuts half the time, but you're a loyal sister. Emily's loyal. We've only ever really had each other. You've been amazing, and I've never doubted you were out for what was best for the three of us."

"What's with the tone? I haven't heard you this way since Mom's funeral."

"You realize there's nothing other than a couple of measly gravestones at Mount Hebron Cemetery that would let anyone know Mom and Dad even existed? They fucking died and that was it. Everything liquidated, and their children gone. Even Uncle Julian moved to Florida."

"Of course he did. Woodmere is nothing but Orthodox now."

"This is a big moment."

"A meeting with that twerp David Levit at UCM?"

"I don't know how long I'll be. Thirty minutes, or it could drag on."

"You still haven't told me what—"

"If I hear what I need to hear, and get what I need to get, everything's going to be good. If not..." He shrugged.

"You're scaring me."

"What, you think I'm going to ruin us? I'm not letting that happen. That's what they want. But that's not what they're going to get."

"Let me go with you."

"I offer you the best almond croissant and macchiato in Los Angeles, and you want to sit in a conference room and listen to me scream at people? Get the fuck out of here and keep your phone on. I'll call you when I'm done."

Even the very name Shlansky's Same Day, he thought as he entered the elevator, once a fixture in Nassau County, had been erased, subsumed by the chain that had purchased all the locations, followed by the chain that purchased that chain.

Brad hadn't seen Paul Aiello in person since the last party at his house, which he and Amanda had left later than he'd wished to. Everywhere he looked people were lighting up, and the recycling bin outside overflowed with empty bottles. He'd detected cocaine residue beside the bathroom sink. As he made his way to the street, about a dozen others remained inside, including two of Paul's clients, one an olive-skinned brunette, the other a tanned, athletic blonde.

"I wonder which one of those two will end up staying over," he remarked as he opened the passenger door to Amanda's Mercedes.

"He sleeps with his clients?" she asked.

"Or his clients sleep with him. I've told you that. It goes both ways."

"That's disgusting."

"It's his business."

"It'll be your business if the agency finds out and fires him."

"Nobody's gonna fire him. He makes more money for UCM than ninety percent of the other reps. Trust me, I know. A lot of that money I brought in with Lone Star Pulp."

"Your agent shouldn't sleep with his clients."

Paul's behavior with women constituted the least of Brad's issues with him, but as usual Amanda was not wrong. They'd been to too many such bacchanals, all motivated by Paul's desire to aggregate power and influence, not to mention the young, attractive women vulnerable to both. At one the preceding fall, just after Lone Star Pulp had severed ties, Paul pulled him onto the patio, exuberantly content, flush with vitality.

"You see all these fucking people here, Brad?" he asked. "And not just the beautiful women. You've got everyone from Claire Fisher, to three VPs of development at major studios, a couple directors, and serious producers such as yourself."

"Yeah, right."

"You are. Fuck Lone Star Pulp. And everyone here because I invited them to my house in the Hollywood Hills where you can look down on the entire fucking city. Two weeks ago I got a letter from Woodmere Academy asking for money."

"Did you remind them they kicked you out?"

"Wanting me to give. I almost took a selfie on the deck out here and sent it with a note: Taken from the house I own in LA. Here's a list of the clients I represent. Here's what I make a year. And by the way, you don't get a fucking dime."

"You should have," Brad said weakly.

"Let them fucking stew in it, right? That fucking bitch Mrs. Powers."

"Paul Aiello doesn't exist," they said in unison, remembering what she'd proclaimed to their class after boarding the bus home from Philadelphia.

"I'd love for her to see me now. For all of them to see both of us now. What was that girl's name on that trip?"

"Laurie Dwyer." Brad felt the sudden urge to cry.

"Laurie fucking Dwyer, who had her friend come up and tell you she was breaking up with you. And now you live in fucking Los Angeles and you produce fucking movies."

"Don't shine me, Paul. I don't produce anything."

"One of these movies is gonna go."

"We're in bad shape, Paul."

"Would you stop it with that?"

"I would, but you don't seem to get it."

"You're a producer! *The Recluse*? *Revenge*? You've got your family out here, a beautiful, successful wife you adore, fucking twins."

"My beautiful wife isn't so nice to me these days."

"Laurie Dwyer is probably freezing her ass off right now in some suburb, in therapy five times a week, married to some douchebag investment banker who buys hookers and doesn't give her the time of day."

"I hope not, for her sake."

"Are you fucking kidding me?"

"She let me hold her hand at Melanie Blankman's skate party."

"Melanie Blankman. That's another one!" He raised his IPA. "Here's to everyone who wrote us off paying to watch the movies we make and seeing our names in fucking lights!"

Entering Paul's office, Brad wondered what had happened to his erstwhile friend. What had happened to them both? Brad now lived entirely off of Amanda's increasing earnings, stewing in a rage that fights with her and his sisters, or phone calls to Alice, could no longer suppress. Sarah spoke of taking a desk job at the gym where she worked out. Emily barely left the apartment, a drink in her hand by three each afternoon.

Paul rose from his sofa, his katana nowhere in sight. He looked to have lost not only all the color that normally animated his face but a good ten pounds as well.

"Are you sick?" Brad asked.

"Sick of waiting for you so we can get this meeting started."

"I've inconvenienced you?"

"I'm sorry, Brad. I'm on your side here."

"You've had a funny way of showing it lately. I can't even get you on the phone. My own fucking agent."

"I'm here, okay? Though you still haven't told me what it is exactly you plan to say or get."

"You'll know soon enough. Just understand it's gonna get ugly in there. As in shit your pants."

"I can handle ugly, particularly with assholes like David Levit and Howard Garner."

"Oh, come on, Paul." Brad couldn't help himself. "If either of those guys had a movie you wanted a client in, or if Howard Garner had a big earner he asked you to share, he'd be your fucking best friend. What did you tell me? 'Conflict of interest is good'? I get it. Just don't fucking lie to me. Not today."

"I just wanted you to know I have your back."

"We should just drop it, all right?" He moved to the door but simply couldn't allow himself to be conciliated with yet more dishonesty. There's time, he kept telling himself, and even then, you've got to remain focused. But as he reached the threshold, he turned. "Just tell me one thing, Paul. Do you still represent Lone Star Pulp? Does this agency still represent David Levit? Are you flush with money, and me and my sisters are fucking broke?"

"Brad, Jesus fucking Christ."

"The answer to my questions is yes on all four counts. You know it and I know it. So don't fucking act like you're loyal. When we were kids, and you got booted from Woodmere Academy, I kept calling your house. Your father threatened to drive over from Cedarhurst and break my arms, and I kept fucking calling."

"You think I wouldn't have done the same thing?"

"You know when the last time you called me was? I mean where it wasn't returning my call?"

"When?"

"It was to rub it in my face that David Levit was making a movie with someone else. Otherwise, I call you, and when I do, you're always fucking busy and mostly you don't bother to call back. So don't, please, act like you're any different than everyone else out here."

"Brad, I'm sorry. I know it's been hard for you."

"Hard for me? Me and my sisters are fucking tissue paper you blew your nose in and you're done. You're a fucking lying, ass-kissing prick with a short fucking memory for who his friends are and where he came from. Rotten to the fucking core like everyone else."

Paul gazed back, struck as much by the clarity of Brad's fury as by the delusion that lay behind it.

"Just look at where you actually are, Brad."

"Where's that exactly?"

"Here. In these offices. I gave you every opportunity. You. A guy who had nothing. No connections out here and no clue. I fucking admired and felt sorry for you because of what you'd been through. But now, I don't think I've ever met a person where the complete bullshit that comes out of his mouth and actual reality have more fucking space between them. You want to know the truth of it? The Lone Star guys couldn't fucking stand you. You're a joke, and everyone knows it, including at this agency, and I have stood up for you like you wouldn't believe. But if that's the way you feel about me, do the goddamn meeting on your own because I'm done."

"You're saying you're not going to go in there with me, and sit by my side to do the job I fucking pay you to do?"

"You can take the commission on what you fleece from that stuck-up prick David Levit and shove it up your ass. And trust me, I need every penny I can get right now, but at least I won't have to hear about it for the next ten fucking years."

"Again I'm going to ask. Are you saying you're not going in there with me?"

"Have a great fucking life."

The grip of the pistol pushed at the small of Brad's back, lodged in the belt he'd stretched to its second-to-last perforation that morning. He'd shot it only once in his life, when Carl Shlansky had taken Emily and him to a shooting range in Islip.

"My uncle has been after me for years to have one of these in each of the stores. He doesn't trust the neighborhoods we operate in because even though he sells to the Blacks, he's a racist idiot, so to get him to shut up I bought half a dozen. This one will go in the flagship," Carl had explained when, to their horror, he produced the weapon in the parking lot of the facility where he'd driven them.

Emily remained in the car, but Brad joined his father, who shot eleven of the twelve rounds, leaving the final one for his son. Brad was ten, Emily thirteen, and Sarah too young to have accompanied them. Though his father warned him about the recoil, the kick nearly toppled him, the bullet careening far to the right of its mark while Carl Shlansky doubled over with laughter.

So far as Brad knew, the weapon, a Smith & Wesson M&P 40, hadn't been shot since. With the memory of its near-deafening report and the jolting kick that numbed his entire right side down to the toes, he certainly contemplated visiting a gun range with it over the years, but the inertia of daily life intervened and he'd never done so. Telling no one, he'd spirited it west with his belongings on the drive from Long Island, having requested of Alice that she remove it from the list of assets to be sold from his parents' estate. It remained in the back of his closet in the apartment he shared with Sarah and Emily until he decamped to the home of his future wife. He bought a small lockbox for its concealment, which rested on the top shelf of their utility closet untroubled but never forgotten.

Over the months of ineluctable failures, as opportunities receded for him while seeming to abound for others, as debts and humiliations began to accrue, he contemplated the weapon more and more, summoning memories of its power: how it bucked in his hand, the cartridge's explosion erupting in his ear as the recoil threw him back and his father howled. On the day Eitan and Reggie sent their severance letter to Alice, he imagined driving to Texas, where he would step into the Lone Star offices and fire at everyone he saw, proclaiming this the result of disposing of a partner without the courtesy of a phone call. With David Levit he pictured doing the deed at the Chateau in what he hoped would be the director's regular room. But these were fantasies, nothing more.

Jacob Rosenthal had changed this. His callous arrogance, without any consideration for what Brad had suffered, or how hard he had strived to overcome tragedy unimaginable to most, seemed to represent the hostile indifference of Hollywood writ large. All of them, from Jacob to David Levit, to Paul Aiello, UCM, Lone Star Pulp, Charlie Gold, the studios who promised they'd make films of the properties Brad controlled then didn't, to the writers and directors and actors attached to them, denigrated him relentlessly, mercilessly, with their selfish indifference. The town seduced the naïvely aspirational, then devoured them. Jacob Rosenthal, together with the ungrateful David Levit, had left Brad no choice. He had tried to be patient, forgiving, generous, kind. But his overtures for compromise, his gentle (and then not so gentle) admonitions, had been derisively flouted by an entire system of pitiless exclusivity.

Fantasy turned to plotting, and to his surprise this brought comfort, not anxiety, his need for recompense from those who'd wronged him occluding all else. Not even his sisters or the certainty of a future with offspring and a spouse provided distraction. In fact, so far as it concerned Amanda, the greater his disappointments, the more insensitive she became.

"You could show a little sympathy. What? That's not a thing in Pittsburgh?"

"I listen to you day and night. When you're not yelling at me, I hear you shout on the phone."

"You don't know what it's fucking like."

"Here we go." She took a mocking tone. "I grew up with everything and you grew up with nothing. I got to say good-bye to my dad who left me money, and you had to raise your sisters and clean up everyone else's mess and not get to go to college and blah blah blah."

The marriage had begun to repeat the patterns of his earliest insecurities. He'd insult her, she him. They'd bicker, not speak, then he'd apologize for starting it, desperately proclaiming the love for her he indeed still felt.

"You're going to get out of this," she would insist.

"How? How the fuck am I going to get out of it?"

"We have kids now. You have no choice." Then her phone would ring. Another film desperate for her services and no one else's. Of all the women

I could have married, why a publicist? Every incoming call a reminder of films being made that aren't mine. What could be more cruel?

He took to visiting the gun nightly, locking the utility room door, climbing onto the counter below the cabinet, removing the weapon from its box, and standing there to test its weight and wonder how and why his father chose this model. He knew Carl Shlansky to have preferred buying American whenever possible. But why Smith & Wesson over Colt or Remington? Had the old man studied the specs? Handled rival models in the presence of an expert purveyor, no doubt in Valley Stream or Hempstead?

On a Post-it he carried for weeks in his wallet he wrote every letter and number engraved into the metal, including the serial number of eight digits. He presented this to the owner of a store in Oxnard where he hoped to purchase ammunition.

"You didn't want to bring in the gun itself?"

"No, I didn't," answered Brad.

"You have a permit? You gotta have a permit in the state of California."

"Of course I do," Brad said defensively. "If you don't mind, could I get a refresher on how to load it?"

"I'm not gonna do that in the store, but I can walk you through what you do when you get home. Yours is older obviously, but practically identical." He removed the magazine from a floor model and showed where Brad would insert the bullets. "Mash them in with your thumb. Any resistance is from the spring that pushes the next cartridge into the chamber after each firing. Then you turn it over and slide the magazine up into the grip. That's the only place it gets tricky with the M&P. Maybe it won't be with yours, depending on how much it was used, but there's some pushback with these at the seating. You've got to really press it hard before it locks in. It's only a problem for quick reload, which is why I prefer a Glock, but that's just me."

"This is the type of gun I have."

"Then you flip this down here and pull back the top to chamber the first round." He did so, then pulled the trigger while pointing toward the floor before handing it over. "You try it," he said, pointing. Brad complied, yanking the slide back and letting it snap into place. "Now if you'll let me, I'm gonna save you a little dough, because there's a lot of great companies out there now making really well-priced cartridges that meet the specs."

Late that night he bolted the utility room door and loaded the gun within minutes. He made the decision to fire it only when aimed at another. It's a pistol, he said to himself. I'll shoot from up close. If I miss, I miss. As for the recoil, this time I'll know it's coming, and I've got at least eighty more pounds on me to absorb the kick. I'm not doing this as a weekend warrior. I'll be focused.

"Sure, Marvin and the other guys want things to go great," his father once told him. "But Marvin has a small piece of the stores, and the workers have jobs and get bonuses and maybe a raise when we have a good year. Don't let anyone ever tell you they're in it for you, because it's a lie. And above all—are you listening to me?"

"Yes."

"Above all, don't let people ever forget you were there."

Brad held the pistol with both hands, pointed, and fired. The recoil, even with his memory of its power, still surprised him. The bullet struck Paul in the shoulder and spun the agent back against his desk. Brad righted himself, and as Paul turned questioningly to face him, he fired once more, this time striking his former best friend squarely in the belly.

"You fucking asshole," Paul said simply, falling back and slumping into a sitting position against the desk on the carpeted floor. His hands clutched at his powder-blue Ermenegildo Zegna shirt where it was now becoming soaked with blood.

"I can't … fucking believe this …" He tried to stand, but his legs failed. He remained unsteadily on his knees like an altar boy awaiting the wafer.

"I wasn't even going to shoot you," said Brad. "Just Jacob and David. Why did you have to say all that shit?"

"I should have broken your fucking nose …" Paul collapsed forward and began to clutch at the carpet as if testing its ply. Brad backed through the doorway. Outside, the sprawl of assistant stations had erupted in shrieks, with most fleeing for the elevators. Jen cowered behind her desk.

"Please, Brad …" She had been unfailingly nice, even when fibbing more frequently about Paul being unavailable as Brad called throughout each day. He'd marveled at how quickly she'd learned to dissemble. He'd once heard Paul explain that lying with a smile that could "be seen through the phone" was essential. Most assistants wished to become agents, a profession in which making the despised and unimportant seem loved and powerful was more necessary than the ability to type, dial numbers, or manage appointments.

Brad lowered the gun.

"I forgot which way the conference room was," he said.

"It's ... I ..."

He raised the weapon once more.

"Tell me where the fuck it is." She pointed. As he turned, she darted not toward the stairwell, where others had fled, but into Paul's office. "Trust me, Jen, he wouldn't check to see if you were okay," he offered more to himself than to her.

He strode calmly, wondering whether the two shots had been heard throughout the floor, and if so, whether David, Jacob Rosenthal, and Howard Garner would have remained waiting for him. All around him people screamed, footsteps pattered, and doors slammed. As he passed Janet Liebowitz's office, she stood behind her desk speaking insistently into the phone, most likely with building security. They locked eyes. She's the only one in this building who represents herself exactly as what she is, he thought, as he smiled and waved with his gun hand.

"What did you do, you fucking asshole?" he heard her scream, seemingly unafraid, from under her wig. He quickened his pace as others fled his path. Many he recognized but couldn't name. An alarm began to blare. Turning left and then right into the hallway leading to the conference room, he saw Howard Garner first, rushing toward him, David Levit close behind.

"Oh fuck," said Howard, clocking the gun.

"Hello, Howard," Brad said, relishing the weapon's power just as he imagined he would. "David. Where are you guys headed?"

"Out of the building," said Howard. "Are you going to let us leave?"

"Don't we have a meeting? Where's Jacob?"

"He never got here," Howard answered.

"That's not what Paul said. My guess is he's still in the conference room, so why don't we all go back in there and we can do what we came here for?"

"We don't want to do that, Brad," offered Howard, the calmly delivered words failing to conceal his abject fear.

"Well, how about you just stand there and I shoot you in the fucking mouth?"

"I have children, Brad. So does David. Please."

"I have kids too. Did you guys ever think about that?"

"All the more reason."

"Turn around and get back inside."

"You're not going to shoot anyone, Brad," Howard said, his tone pleading.

"Tell that to Paul Aiello."

Howard backed clumsily into David, who had not spoken, both of them retreating into the room. Jacob Rosenthal sat at the table end closest to the door, both hands resting on its surface as if waiting to be deposed by friendly counsel.

UCM CONFERENCE ROOM

When he first met Brad as the potential financier of *Revenge*, David Levit sensed a perilous combination of traits. He just couldn't name them, though over the years a few notions gained traction.

"He's got no conscience and a persecution complex," he described to Charlotte. "He's also at heart a misanthrope. That's all going on in this one very insecure person, who probably loathes himself when he looks in the mirror in spite of the fact he's likely overcome far more than ninety-five percent of the people he knows in his life. There's actually probably a good person in there, but life just kicked him in the teeth."

"And on the basis of that you're going to give him the best script you've ever written?" she responded. "Why would you do that?"

Facing Brad now, his back to the windows of the third-floor conference room, Howard Garner to the right, Jacob Rosenthal seated to his left, David remembered not having an answer that she or Sammy or Adam or anyone who'd never tried to get a movie financed could possibly have understood.

"Are you Jacob Rosenthal?" Brad asked.

"I am," Jacob responded with an oddly sympathetic ease. "Did you have us all here so you could shoot us?"

"We'll have to see," answered Brad.

"You seem to have left yourself little choice," Jacob said, staring curiously at the pistol. He hadn't taken his eyes from it since Brad had entered the room. "Your huckster agent isn't joining us?"

"I guess he isn't."

"Okay then," said Jacob, "let's figure out what happens now." It struck David that no matter the situation, Jacob could wrest control of any meeting.

But Brad had little interest in any transfer of power. "You two, sit down," he said to David and Howard.

"Brad, please ..."

"Shut up, Howard, and do what I said."

"What do we need to do to get you to put the gun down?" the agent asked.

"Security is going to be here in a minute with the alarm going off," said Jacob. "You should really just get this over with, whatever it is you want to do."

"Not before I say a few things."

"What if we don't want to listen to you?" asked Jacob.

"Are you just pretending I'm not pointing a gun at you?"

"I see the gun."

"I want to listen," said Howard Garner carefully. He still had not sat down as instructed, nor had David. "David wants to listen too. Say what you want to say, Brad."

"There was a time I was actually part of all this." Brad gestured to the long table with its two dozen chrome Knoll chairs upholstered in brown leather, then through floor-to-ceiling glass toward the art-covered walls that defined the floor's warren of offices. "But what I learned is that you guys need people like me to fail so your power has meaning. You need us always on the outside so you can feel how great it is to be on the inside. You never think how it feels to be shut out. That you're suddenly of no use to anyone."

"Oh God, please stop," said Jacob loudly.

"What is it you want, Brad?" Howard asked. "You want David to sever ties with Jacob and make *Appalachian Winter*? David will make *Appalachian Winter*. David wants to make *Appalachian Winter*. Tell him you want to make the film, David."

"Obviously I want to make it," David said, meaning it. "I've always wanted to make it."

"Yeah, you've really demonstrated that."

"Let's make his movie!" exclaimed Howard, his voice ascending a couple of octaves. "We'll work it out right now. Jacob will make it with you. Jacob can finance it."

"I'm not financing that movie with him," said Jacob. "Even if David changed its ridiculous title. I'd have to partner with this asshole and listen to him threaten to sue people every day." He hadn't taken his eyes from Brad, whom he now addressed. "Nobody, including you, seems to fucking understand that it's social out here, but it's not personal. People will even tolerate a moron like you if they can make a profit. No one was out to get you. You failed all on your own like almost everyone does. You're pissed about that, and your solution is you want to shoot us, so shoot us, but don't fucking lie to yourself."

David gaped. Surely Jacob didn't wish for them all to be killed. Was he challenging Brad to fire the gun because somehow he knew Brad wouldn't?

"Don't listen to Jacob, Brad!" Howard exclaimed. "If this agency didn't respect you, you wouldn't still be a client here. This whole situation is a ridiculous misunderstanding. All anyone wanted to do was get David here some work. We're in the business of making movies happen! That's all anyone was trying to do!"

"Oh, shut the fuck up, Howard," said Brad. "Did you listen to anything I just said? You're all fucking liars. So guess what? You're first."

David would say later that the weapon looked wrong from the moment he first saw it in the hallway. Something about its nose not being flush with itself. When Brad fired, it seemed to explode in his hand. Howard flinched at the report as the bullet flew wide, piercing the glass behind him, much the way it would in a movie, leaving a clean, spidered hole, the window otherwise intact. Jacob hadn't moved but simply gazed, oddly unsurprised, as Brad dropped the gun, wailing in pain, the index and pointer fingers of his right hand no longer there, the entire appendage covered in blood.

"What the fuck! What the fuck!" Tears streaked down Brad's face, whether from physical pain or some other kind of anguish, David couldn't tell.

Jacob began to chuckle, and Brad lunged. Voices could be heard in the hallway outside where two security guards appeared, pistols drawn. Brad seized Jacob by the throat with both his good and mangled hands, staining the older man's neck and shirt as they both fell to the floor. David leapt instinctively onto Brad's back, and Brad flailed with his elbow, catching David in the jaw. It felt as if the entire bottom of David's face had detached from bone to hang loose inside his skin, and he stumbled woozily, knocking the side of his head against the conference table. Blood curtained his forehead in a rush as the two guards tore past him. Wiping his eyes, he saw Brad's gun, which lay on the carpet, a rupture in its side.

It required all the guards' strength to subdue Brad. Finally, one sat on his back while the other pressed a knee into his blond curls above the ear. David recognized them both from the lobby. The larger of the two produced a plastic tie and secured Brad's wrists.

"Find his fingers," the larger guard said.

I've just been in a shooting, David thought. A shooting in Beverly Hills over a movie. I was about to be killed over a fucking movie.

"The gun was off battery," David heard Jacob say. "I could tell by looking at it. I didn't know it would explode in the asshole's hand, but I knew it wouldn't fire properly. I'm fine!" He gestured at Brad, now trussed a few feet away. "It's his blood, not mine. Go see to David, the one on the floor over there."

"Here they are," came a voice nearby, "but I can already tell you nobody's gonna be able to sew them on. There's nothin' left of 'em. It's a fucking horror show." The man stared at the floor, where presumably lay the obliterated remains of Brad Shlansky's sundered digits.

"Are you okay, David?" Howard loomed overhead. David responded with a series of guttural sounds that in any other circumstance would have seemed comical. "We're gonna get you help," Howard said. "Just hang tight. You're bleeding like a motherfucker, but that's what happens with cuts to the head. It looks like he got you in the jaw too." David nodded. "That was the craziest shit I've ever seen. I can't believe we're still fucking alive. But we are. We're still fucking alive."

Howard blurred to red as blood continued to pour from David's wound. Another attempt to wipe his eyes had his hand rowing the air. He felt himself recede, pulled into the floor as if in the center of a darkening vignette. He wondered if he were dying as his body then rose suddenly and came to rest on a wheeled stretcher, where straps then tightened over his body.

"I'm proud of you," his mother insisted as they stood in the front hall of their Charleston home.

"I'm gonna be back for Thanksgiving," he answered.

"I know you will, David."

"And I'm moving back here after college."

"If I thought that for a second, I wouldn't be crying."

In a few minutes a car would pull up, driven by a woman he'd never met. Because his mother couldn't get the days off from school for the drive east and back, and he didn't want to ship his stereo equipment and record collection, he couldn't fly and needed the ride. He'd called every one of the fifteen students from West Virginia headed to Providence and had finally found a sophomore from Huntington who agreed to carry him and his belongings so long as he shared time behind the wheel and paid for half the gas.

Indeed he would not return to live in Charleston. He wouldn't even spend summers there, beginning with working at the theater in Maine. After his second year he performed stand-up in Los Angeles, determining for himself such an assured future of mediocrity in the field that drama school seemed a far better destination for the life he'd begun to envision for himself. The next two summers he spent in Providence, one on his own trying to write and failing, and the next with the woman he thought he'd marry, before she departed for her dig in Pompeii and he to drama school.

As he moved in and out of consciousness on the ambulance gurney, the siren affixed to the vehicle's roof a fitting lullaby, he could not have felt further from home—either that of his birth or that in New York City, where he'd started his own family, was raising his own children, the city to which Adam had never returned.

It would be forty hours before he was released from Cedars Sinai, stabilized from a concussion, his head bandaged, his jaw set. The hospital was eager to clear beds. Charlotte had learned of the shooting at UCM from friends and had been in touch with Howard Garner when David didn't answer his phone. Howard's assistant extended his room at the Chateau and arranged her flight, neither of which was easy. Not only were hotel rooms scarce from the wildfire evacuations, airplanes were stuffed with those eager to finish business should predictions regarding the virus come true. She'd been back and forth between the hotel and the hospital, mostly sleeping beside David in the fold-out chair of the deluxe room paid for by the agency.

When the doctor spoke with her in the hallway, he wore a mask he didn't lower.

"Sorry," he said. "It's now protocol."

"I understand."

"You were Cordelia?" he asked, having learned of her hasty departure from New York.

"Yes."

"The dutiful one. Will the show go on?"

"There's an understudy."

"Well, I'm sure we can clear your husband to travel by the end of the week. He should wear one of these on the plane though. So should you."

On his way to the hotel in a car the agency had also arranged—no doubt already terrified of a lawsuit—David wondered how he could begin his life anew, if that were even possible. He contemplated giving up his career and returning to Charleston to teach high school as he imagined he would when first setting off for college. But even if Charlotte agreed to abandon her own burgeoning career in New York, which she certainly would not, he had no real desire to pursue any life other than the one in which he found himself so inescapably immersed.

In a moment of lucidity on the gurney as paramedics guided him away, he caught sight of Jacob Rosenthal between the backs of the two policemen. The producer of *Coal* had returned to the seat from which he'd so recklessly derided Brad Shlansky before the scion of Shlansky's Same Day fired his malfunctioning weapon. David had met him because of a story they each wanted passionately to tell. A controversial one, yes, but like most, even those that seemed so much of their moment, it would be forgotten within a couple of years of its telling, evanescent as any dream. As their eyes met, Jacob smiled quite sadly, then waved in a manner that struck David as perfect in its ambiguity.

EPILOGUE
(ORCAS ISLAND)

Their parents were still asleep in the living room when the two brothers left the house. They'd made it about a mile down the south shore along Doe Bay facing the strait. It had been a cold night on the island, and they walked lazily in a mist that had come with the dawn. The year 2018 was nine hours old. The older of the two, whose name was Danny, had managed to see the new year come in with his parents, who were both freelance writers, his father for various travel magazines, his mother a poet. The evening before had been an especially raucous iteration of the parents' annual New Year's party. Eight months before, another writer, who was Black, had moved onto the island, and the informal group of nine had invited him without reservation, especially given his level of notoriety from a novel he'd published some years prior that had put him on the cover of magazines.

No one even noticed the year had changed because of the escalating argument. From what Danny could remember, it had been provoked by another of the three Black men at the party. A woman was also involved. They were discussing a fire that happened in Philadelphia sometime in the 1980s.

"Fuck you, Rex," the other Black writer was saying. "You say that shit just to get attention."

"My uncle was one of the MOVE 9, motherfucker. Fuckin' died in prison."

"Bullshit."

"Now you're just pissing me off."

"If I wanted to piss you off, there's a lot of other shit I could say."

"Wilson Goode was a friend of my dad's. You think he was just wanting to bomb his own people? That's my fucking point. Y'all want to racialize everything."

"We all? What the fuck you been about your whole damn career, Rex?"

"Now it's an ad hominem attack?"

"The fuck does that even mean?"

"It's Latin, you idiot. Means against the person. Against the argument is how a man argues."

"You just go on with that, see where it gets you."

"Y'all want it to be so fuckin' simple," continued Rex. "And it breaks your heart when it ain't. Living in America has always been about one thing: who's got the money and who doesn't. And that includes slavery."

"What did you just say?"

"Slavery was about free fuckin' labor, and the slaves were Black, so it became about putting Black people down and it hasn't stopped. People want to be rich and protect the shit they have."

"That's just a straw man, Rex. What did I ever say about being rich or poor?"

"You want to know why I got my shit together early on enough to get my full ride at Howard and get my ass out there to make a fuckin' difference? The day after the MOVE bombing, my dad sat me down with the *Inquirer* and pointed to two pictures. One was of John Africa and one was of Wilson Goode. And he said, Rex, that's the man you want to be in this story, even on his worst day, and he pointed at Mayor Goode. You want to be him, not John Africa or your uncle rotting away in prison. All anyone, and I mean anyone, in this country wants is money and/or power. Usually both." Rex pointed to the woman standing with them, who was white. "Her people understood that a long time ago. Europe chased them out, tried to exterminate all of them, they came here and figured shit out just like they do wherever they go. My lawyer's a Jew, my publisher's a Jew, everyone I talk to in Hollywood is a goddamn Jew. People say to me, Rex, you can't say that. What? I can't tell the truth? Fuck all y'all." He reached for the whiskey bottle he'd commandeered from the bar for convenience.

"You've probably had enough of that, Rex."

"Fuck you, tellin' me I've had enough. This here helps me find the truth."

"Or it's why you haven't put out a book in seven years and came out here to hide."

"The fuck is that supposed to mean?"

"It means what are you doing, Rex?"

"You don't know what I'm up to all day, gonna say some shit like that."

"Everyone knows you burned through your advance, don't return the calls from Viking. Just waiting for the movie to get made? Is that it?"

"Stop this, you two," implored the woman as both men rose. Danny's father intervened before a blow was struck, and within minutes the men were laughing, drinking more whiskey, their arms around one another, and it was already the new year. Rex Patterson left alone, rebuking any suggestion that he relinquish his keys and stay the night.

At first it was hard to make out the car through the mist, but it faced the water, and beyond it the mainland at the edge of the promontory. The passenger door stood open, the engine running. Danny took a wide berth, but his younger brother walked straight for the vehicle.

"Hello? Hello? Sir? Mister?" he heard Jordan ask. "Danny, it's that man from the party. Mister? Is everything all right? Is everything all right?"

As Danny approached, before his eyes could confirm it, he knew it was the Black writer. His brother continued to await a response. Danny stared through the open door at the inert figure, knowing that response would never come, the silence as much an answer as any.

ACKNOWLEDGEMENTS

While the plot and every character in this novel are fictional, the book does draw on experiences gathered over years of working in theater, television, and film, and I'd like to acknowledge the representatives who've taught me how it all works, some of them deceased: Michael Braun, Philip Carlson, Ruthanne Secunda, Howard Cohen, Shani Rosenzweig, Sarah Clossey, Byrd Leavell, Marc Glick, Steve Breimer, Jeremy Barber and Amy Guenther, the last two of whom read early drafts. Other early readers to whom I'm grateful include Jodi Kahn, for her expertise on the Five Towns, David Aaron Baker, Will Bennet, Beth Colt, Ethan Coen, Debbie Liebling, Guillermo del Toro, Edward Norton, Silvana Tropea, Andy Davis, Keith Reddin, Regina Corrado, Matthew Specktor and John Turturro. On the legal side I express deep gratitude to my close friend of three decades Billy Savitt, who has always made me feel smarter and wiser for every minute I spend with him. He, along with Mathew Rosengart, Liz McNamara, Alison Schary, and Taylor Custer were essential in advising me throughout the publishing process, as was my editor Chris Heiser. Finally, I'd like to thank my wife, Lisa Benavides-Nelson, who has been there with me since my second year of drama school as we've pursued creative lives while raising our immensely tolerant children.